RUNES TO RAIN

THE BALANCING BRIGHTNESS TRILOGY
BOOK ONE

CHARLI NILE

NILE HOUSE

To all the people who read this book. Hopefully, you also like slow-burn romance with a side of mental and physical torture for your favorite characters.

Also, this book is dedicated to Fem. You play a mean fiddle, and I'm sure some of these characters wouldn't have survived without you. Thank you, buddy.

This book is a work of fiction and includes dark themes. I have attempted to portray this content respectfully and thoughtfully, but please check the detailed content information listed at the end of this book. This is content that may be triggering to some.
Please consider your mental health as you decide what to read.
It should go without saying that this is not intended to be a manual or self-help book.

INTRODUCING THE BAND

Members of The Boys
Open Role: *Lead Singer, recently departed*
Reem Fontaine: *Banjo, backup vocals, and band management*
Fem Grantham: *Fiddle and other miscellaneous instruments*
Lent Bietoletti: *Guitar and backup vocals*

Explanation: *In a world where technology and progress are worshiped, the arts and music have mainly died out. When people do hear music, especially at a concert, they lose their minds, much like an early Beatles concert. That's not to say The Boys aren't talented; it just gives some context to why the crowds are as insane as they are.*

Music I Imagine The Boys Playing
Wait So Long - Trampled by Turtles
Codeine - Trampled by Turtles
Victory - Trampled by Turtles
Burn for Free - Trampled by Turtles

CONTENTS

Pain Remembered   1

PART I
1. Of Beginnings   5
2. Let There Be Life   7

PART II
3. Life Begins   15
4. Emergence   22
5. Plans and Death   31
6. Escape   41
7. The Way of Things   46
8. Back at the Mansion   53
9. A Caged Bird?   60
10. The Calm Before the Storm   67
11. Dark Figures   80
12. Dark Figures and Rituals   88
13. Dio's Journal - Entry 148   95

PART III
14. Piquory Treatment Center   101
15. Dio's Journal - Entry 160   109
16. Bound   111
17. Dio's Journal - Entry 173   115
18. Awhile Later   117
19. Dio's Journal - Entry 190   119
20. Knight in Shadow Armor   122
21. The Real Recovery   128
22. Return and Retribution   135
23. Dio's Journal - Entry 191   141
24. Rabid Fans and Skeptics   144
25. Dio's Journal - Entry 193   159
26. Cracks Form   161
27. Dio's Journal - Entry 195   169

28. Memories of Trees   172
29. Dio's Journal - Entry 196   180
30. Shark Week   184
31. Dio's Journal - Entry 198   192
32. The One Where There Are More Friends   195
33. Dio's Journal - Entry 205   201

PART IV

34. A Caged Bird   207
35. Dio's Journal - Entry 208   210
36. Dio's Journal - Entry 209   213
37. Dio's Journal - Entry 210   214
38. Dio's Journal - Entry 211   221
39. Dio's Journal - Entry 271   223
40. Dio's Journal - Entry 290   225
41. Existence is Persistent   227
42. Dio's Journal - Entry 291   228
43. Dio's Journal - Entry 302   230
44. A Weapon Honed   233
45. Dio's Journal - Entry 336   237
46. Habeas Corpus   240
47. Something Unsaid   246
48. Dio's Journal - Entry 337   252
49. Excerpts From Malam   258
50. Thusly Armed   263
51. Dio's Journal - Entry 338   267
52. Excerpts From Malam   269
53. Frankly, a Surprising Request for Assistance   271
54. Dio's Journal - Entry 339   280
55. Dio's Journal - Entry 340   285
56. Excerpts From Malam   288
57. Dio's Journal - Entry 341   290
58. Well, That Changes Everything   293
59. Excerpts From Malam   299
60. Dio's Journal - Entry 342   301

PART V

61. Violence in the Streets   305
62. Dio's Journal - Entry 345   311

63. If Not Fans, Why Fan Shaped? 315
64. Dio's Journal - Entry 346 328
65. Dio's Journal - Entry 2 333
66. A Different Type of Lightning Strikes 336
67. Dio's Journal - Entry 15 340
68. Let's Start a Riot 342
69. Dio's Journal - Entry 16 350
70. Dio's Journal - Entry 17 356

PART VI

71. Love Is a Phoenix 363
72. Dio's Journal - Entry 37 380
73. Excerpts From Malam 384
74. What Happened to Dio? 391

Content Information 395
About the Author 397

PAIN REMEMBERED

PROLOGUE

To my dear and gentle readers,

In reading this account of my life, you will need to humor me for my memory is not what it was, and this story begins so far in the past, the distant beginnings of a full life, that I may not recount all the details with the level of accuracy I would wish.

What is true is that these events are my version of what happened and are what made me who I am today. Perhaps even as they changed me, they changed the world. As I sit in this quiet house with the scent of rain in the air and life going on around me, I slip into a remembrance that is both wonderful and sad. While I do not wish I could go back to that point in my life, I do wish I had the chance to see those people I loved once more.

You, my dear reader, will now have a chance to

meet, in a form, those I hold dear as well as my many enemies, and to examine the history of my life that made me what and who I am. In addition to my own version of the story, I have included, with their permission, some journal entries and notes from people in my life. Hopefully, these gifts will allow you to see another side to the story I tell, and hear another voice beyond my ramblings.

Sincerely,
Chaosta

PART I

OF BEGINNINGS

There once was a little boy whose life held no joy or point of light. His father is cruel to him, and his mother died some years prior. He has one thing he does for fun, and that is to create small working sculptures of clockwork. He creates these sculptures to bring himself happiness and to pass the time while he hides from his father.

One day, he begins his most ambitious project yet, a small working model of a human head, the size of a fist. As he works somehow without meaning to, "it" becomes "she."

The technology he builds for her is far more complex than one so young should be capable of. A technology capable of far more than what should be possible with clockwork gears. Such a striking intelligence that perhaps divine intervention from the little boy's chosen deity was involved.

As he builds the clockwork doll, "she" grows from the beginnings of a head to a head on a torso and from there to a nearly perfect model of a person. The working sculpture is nearly exact in every detail, but is small in scale and works only with help.

The boy dreams of more.

Then one night, a demon enters his dreams in the form of a darkly complexioned human. "My name is Malam," he says. "I see what you make and I see what you give her, that which is nearly life. I will make her what you believe her to be, and she will be the harbinger of balance to our unbalanced world."

With that, the demon disappears and the young boy, tossing in his sleep, moves on to another, less portentous dream.

The next morning, the boy wakes and dimly remembers the dream with the *man* and his promise. A dream far different than those which usually guide him.

He moves from his bed to the cabinet against the wall and takes a neatly wrapped bundle from beneath it. Carefully, he removes the wrapping and reveals the clockwork being. Seeing no new life yet, he begins to wrap her again. He pauses, takes a carved, wooden rose from beneath his bed, and wraps it in the cloth with her. Feeling more hopeful than he has in a while, he goes on with his day.

When he returns later that night, he finds her still inanimate, and with some disappointment, he removes the rose and places it beneath his bed again. This time, he leaves her form sitting out on the floor of his room, resting against a wall.

As the boy climbs into bed that night, he looks at her and thinks of how real her form looks there against the wall, as though she were already alive. In his mind, he can clearly picture how she would appear if actually given life. He pictures her with candy-pink hair, mismatched eyes, and a heart-shaped face with full lips. He imagines that she would be strong for her size, so she would be capable of defending those she cares for. He pictures her being tall, but since he is but a child, that still makes her short compared to most women. He also imagines her with a kind and loving heart.

Although he means to sit up and watch for a while, he is far too exhausted, and his eyes drift closed sooner than he intends.

LET THERE BE LIFE

Waking is pain.
Pain, and more pain.
Breathing hurts.

Air, is that what this is?

Whatever it is hurts, and continues to burn as breaths are taken.

A voice. Noise hurts.

The voice again.

Make it go away, please make it go away.

The voice continues, and words slowly begin to make sense. Words that sound like poetry grating over a rough surface.

"....pain will continue, you enter the world in pain, but it will leave you after a while. It is no great plan of mine. The act of living, particularly gaining life, is painful."

My eyes open, and I see a form that turns into a man.

No, not a man, a demon.

Dark shadows follow him in a nimbus as though he possessed wings in a different realm. Wings that didn't quite follow him to this world. His voice is guttural yet somehow melodic. That doesn't take away the pain at the sound. With my poor vision, I still note that he has dark hair, an olive complexion, and broad shoulders.

As I gaze at him in wonder, he continues, "I gave you life because I see in you a basic contradiction which suits my purpose. You have technology within you, thanks to the one who built you. You also have some of my life force, which will give you memories and skills far beyond your own. I believe you may be strong enough for the days ahead."

He lays a thin package on my lap, and the weight of it against my sensitive skin burns as though it is covered in acid.

"I sought to create you with the hope you might strike against the brightness which is currently too powerful in this world. I'm not one to set you against the other side, though, as both lightness and darkness are needed. Instead, I hope you might balance their power. Now, I suggest you leave this place before your creator wakes, so you do not terrify him."

He then bends close to me and says quietly, "Malam is my name, and saying it will summon me to you. However, I will not make the journey often. Now I must go."

He turns after a slight pause and says, "Be safe." Then he vanishes in a dark swirl that is less than black and more than white.

I feel as though I have been given a puzzle. I would like to follow his direction to leave, but pain and darkness pull at me too strongly. I weary quickly of fighting it. As I surrender, I'm dragged into unconsciousness.

When I wake again, I have little idea of where I am and even less, how long I dwelt in the blackness. The pain is still nearly unbearable but seems less than before. Without any conscious effort or knowledge of how it happens, I pull on the clothes that make up the bundle Malam gave me. Then, with a glance at the sleeping young boy, I leave.

. . .

*T*here is not much to say of those moments after leaving the room I first experience life in. Everything in this chaotic space hurts, my eyes blur unexpectedly, and my movements seem only partially under my own control.

What I do remember is stumbling in the middle of what seems to be a street and landing on my knees. There is dirt, and cold, and more pain. As I try to collect myself, I comprehend that I have come a distance from where I initially left the building because my hands are already covered in scrapes and other small wounds, my shirt is torn, and my hair is dirty and falling in my face. Still, I have no recollection of what passed between that moment and this.

Then, the sound of voices adds to the din in my head.

The dull light in this place still makes my head pound and my eyes tear.

One particular voice stands out. It is quiet, smooth.

Blinking, I see a hand in front of me. I take it.

I am lifted out of the grime of the street and half-carried to a carriage where I hear horses prancing and snorting. The door to the carriage is opened, and after some quiet conversation, hands emerge from the now open door. The hands help the boy holding me get his newfound and dirty package into the carriage, where I am wrapped in a blanket.

I regain consciousness in spurts as we travel, hearing words that make no sense as though lyrics spoken out of order. Even if I could remember those words, at this moment my mind is not up to the task of reconstructing the puzzle they create.

Finally, even as my eyes remain mostly blind, there are stairs under my feet, hands under my arms, voices in my ears. We enter a building and I am carried or dragged to something soft and covered with something warm.

Now, ironically perhaps, sleep will not come, not even the disconcerting blackness I have often sunk into until now.

The people who brought me here move around the room talking.

After some time passes, one of them approaches and asks me something. I try to respond, but only a quiet groan escapes. Without asking further, he puts something between my lips and against my teeth. I take it, chew at least partially, and swallow. Whatever enters my body is warming, numbing, and pulls me into a downward, dark spiral.

* * *

I open my eyes to a field of roses, the petals dripping with blood. The sky is white without any comforting hint of blue. There is no pain in my body, but the sadness in me is an almost palpable pain in my head. I see a figure moving and run to it, gasping for breath as I get there.

I have a second as it turns toward me, filled with relief at finding someone else in the empty space, before a scream fills me, tearing itself out of my throat. For the figure that stands before me is some version of the little boy.

His eyes drip with blood and are a blank space. His arms and part of one leg are missing, and there is a hole in his chest that frames several of the roses. Those blank eyes seem to search for something about me, some recognition, and then from the bloody lips a deep, masculine voice emerges.

The ancient voice tells me that a future without balance is death. Without action, the brightness will slowly take over the darkness. It will destroy those things we need for life, growing things, water, and clean air. Without those elements, humans and demons will cease to exist.

As I understand that my face is cold because of the tears

running down my cheeks, this dream leaves in a swirl of black, and I'm in another place.

*T*he demon called Malam is here, but his back is to me, and after the last dream, I hesitate. Before I can decide what to do, he turns to me. His eyes are bloodshot and dark, and his face is wet with tears. His arms are full of the body of a tall young woman.

She hangs limply, her only movement coming from him. Her light, curly hair hangs from her head, some of it sodden with blood that leaks from an open wound at the center of her face.

He looks straight at me and says, "You have failed."

The moment he finishes speaking, a crow flies directly at my face with a scream, before this dream too pulls away.

*T*here are many more, countless more, and although I seek to remember them and what they try to tell me, it is like trying to hold water.

* * *

PART II

LIFE BEGINS

I wake slowly, pulling myself from a heavy darkness. The air is thick and smells of smoke. Thankfully, there is no pain other than what I remember. My mouth is filled with the taste of blood, which seems to be from a bite on the inside of one cheek.

I rise slowly from a flower-print-covered couch. There is a boy lying on a couch across from me. I consider trying to wake him, but he sleeps the sleep of the dead, his mouth slightly open and his sides rising and falling slowly.

Looking around the room, I see two other boys deposited on a couch and an armchair, both deep in sleep. Deciding that even if I could wake them, I don't really want to. I examine the room instead.

The ceilings are high, and the entire room is painted in pastel shades that are highlighted by the dim light filtering in from the large window. My eye is caught by a painting on one wall of the room, and I walk closer to it. Examining the painting makes me feel unexpectedly sad. I don't know exactly why, but the trees, animals, and landscape depicted in the picture seem foreign and like a utopian idea in the middle of this garish room.

As I look at the painting, I find myself experiencing a very different type of pain than what plagued me the day before. I have lived for such a short time that I don't know where this feeling comes from, but it makes my chest hurt. My eyes sting with tears, and I try to understand the feeling.

Even as I look at the painting, I hear stirring behind me. Then I begin to hear voices.

"Where'd tha girl go?" asks one slurred voice.

"She's right here," says another clear, quiet voice.

I feel a hand on my shoulder, and he guides me to turn away from the wall. Seeing my tears, he directs me to one of the couches, sitting me down upon one of the other boy's legs. As my eyes meet the bright blue of his, he says kindly, "Are you ok? Why are you crying?"

All I can respond with is a slight shake of my head.

His expression as he looks at me is soft and slightly concerned. "I'll leave you here to talk with Fem; this is more his area of expertise than mine," he says kindly. Then the blue-eyed boy rises and roughly punches the shoulder of the boy beneath me.

To the side of the room, I hear the third boy rising. He was sleeping sitting up in a large brown armchair. His face is narrow with high cheekbones and a dark complexion. Long black hair sticks to one cheek. His eyes are still squeezed shut as he runs a hand over his face. Then, groaning, he pulls himself to his feet and stumbles from the room.

I turn to look at the boy underneath me, and he looks at me through half-closed eyes. His hair is brown and cropped short to his head. He turns his head away from me, but I can see that he wants to say something.

Suddenly, I believe I understand what it is, and I pull myself up off the couch, freeing his legs as I walk to the window.

As the boys rise, I keep my back to them and look out at what I can see of the city through the thick smoke in the air. I again wonder how I know what any of this is, but that knowledge seems unimportant, and so I decide to ignore the thought for not the first nor last time.

After a few moments pass, a hand touches my shoulder again, and the boy who led me from the painting is at my side. He offers me a cup of something, and after a moment of hesitation, I take it.

"Did you talk to Fem?" he asks.

I shake my head, not sure what or who that might be.

As he sees me looking at the cup in my hand, he says, "I brought you coffee. Good, strong coffee."

I examine the liquid in the cup. It is dark and looks like mud. As I try to decide what to do with it, he touches my arm, and without consciously meaning to, I look back up at him.

"You don't need to worry," he says quietly. "We know what you are, and there is no need to be ashamed. One of my friends was addicted for a time and was without money or a place to stay. We have found those without support in the past, and now that our circumstances allow, we try to help." He nods slightly, still holding my eyes, and then, dropping his own, walks back toward the couches.

As I hear him speaking to the others behind me, I try to decide how to tell him I don't know what he means. Deciding that now is not the time or place, I look worriedly again at the cup in my hands and then, not knowing what to expect, take a small drink. My concerns, it would seem, were entirely granted. Coughing and spluttering against the taste of whatever poison this is, I badly wish I hadn't tried it.

Hearing surprised exclamations behind me, I turn and see three faces looking at me. The tall one looks at the blue-eyed one and, laughing, says, "We always told you that you make awful coffee! Are you trying to poison her?"

He comes to my aid, taking the cup from me and rubbing my back. With a stunning smile on his face, he says, "My name is Lent. That's Fem," pointing to the one I sat on, "and Reem is the dashing fellow who tried to kill you with his coffee."

Reem frowns and, grumbling quietly, begins to leave for the other room.

"No, no old son," Lent says, rising from beside me. "Let me make the coffee, and you stay here to play host to our guest and get Fem off his ass."

Blushing slightly, I look down at my hands.

Reem says something to Fem about making himself useful. Then he turns to me and asks, "Would you like me to show you to your room so you can freshen up?"

Looking up at him, I nod again, unable to keep the enthusiasm from it.

He grins, awful coffee apparently forgotten, and then I follow him out of the room. He leads me past the painting, which I brush lightly with my fingertips as I pass. I walk out into a wide entry space and then follow him along a narrow hallway. From there, he directs us down another hallway and to a closed door.

"This will be your room," he says, looking at the door instead of me while he thrusts his hands deep into his pockets. "There are towels in there, and I will have one of the house employees bring in a change of clothes."

As I reach for the knob, he turns on his heel and makes his way back in the direction we came from without looking at me.

I open the door and step into the room. It is dressed in black and white with traces of red as though two crows quarreled in the depths of snowy woods. The bed, which is large and more than dwarfs me, is flanked by two large cupboards, and there is an enormous black rug on the white marble floor.

It would feel cold and clinical except that it is a bit worn around the edges with bare wood showing where paint has rubbed off. The linens are threadbare, and there are small stains on the cupboards. There is also a connected bathroom with a clawfoot tub.

Going to the bath, I turn both knobs on the faucet and undress. As I remove my clothes, I see just how dirty they are, and register that I have not changed since falling in the street.

No wonder the boys looked at me oddly.

As I climb into the tub, I catch a glimpse of my reflection in the mirror and freeze. I guess I didn't know what to expect. I had no idea what I looked like, and up until now, it didn't seem to matter.

Mismatched eyes stare back at me, one blue, the other yellow. They are set in, what I take to be, a plain face, but it is framed by waves of pale pink hair that is currently tangled and wind-knotted. I reach my hand up to it, running my fingers along the length of it, but it doesn't magically turn brown or black as I have seen on others.

Still staring, I drop my hands to my sides and examine the rest of my new body. Still unsure how I come by this knowledge, I feel that I am pretty but certainly no beauty.

Even as the importance of being different fades, I settle into the hot bath. The hot water slowly sinks into muscles that, without my realizing it, were tense and sore. I slowly relax, pain draining into the hot water even as the dirt and grime do.

I nearly fall asleep, my tongue playing with the cut inside my cheek, before a knock on the door pulls me back to the present. I jump slightly at the sound and quickly sit straight while calling out to ask what they want.

"Lady, I've brought the clothing that was requested for you. May I bring it in?"

I call out for her to enter and watch as she walks into the bedroom. She is dressed in a neat grey outfit and walks with a quick confidence. She sets a folded pile of clothing on a chair beside the bed. Then, without saying or doing anything else, she turns and leaves, closing the bedroom door again.

As the door closes, I begin to wash myself, quickly scrubbing the last of the dirt from my skin. Freshly washed and slightly pink from the scrubbing, I open the drain and step from the tub onto a fluffy towel. Finding another towel hanging nearby, I wrap myself in it. Then I find a brush and slowly begin to pull it through my hair, pulling apart the knots and wincing as it tears at my scalp.

Finally feeling better, I move back to the bedroom and examine the clothing left by the woman. The pile on the bed contains a short and silky skirt that, when pulled on, falls to only my knees in loose waves. There is also a tailored shirt with short sleeves and a standing collar, as well as long socks that cover each of my legs entirely. There are shoes, but some part of me refuses to put them on while in the house. I tie my hair up loosely with a ribbon and pick up the shoes before leaving the room.

I slowly find my way back to the room with the floral couches, only to find it empty. After wandering for a bit, I find Fem and Reem arguing quietly in a nearby room with a single large table. I turn at a motion at the edge of my vision and see that Lent has joined us.

"Hey ho you two," he calls to the two arguing. He is carrying a tray of food and drink.

Fem and Reem go quiet, but then slowly begin back up with their argument in hushed tones as Lent carries the tray to a short table near the wall.

"Here, eat," he says to me while grinning. He begins to serve himself.

I drop the shoes on the floor and walk to the side table.

"Take this," he says while setting a plate in front of me, "and help yourself. That is the syrup, and this pitcher here is juice. If you don't like that, there is water in this glass bottle."

I pick up a fork, spear a couple of pieces of bread, place them on my plate, and dump the syrup on them. Then I carry my plate to the large table. I'm already tearing off pieces of bread and putting them into my mouth as I drop onto a chair.

As I eat, the other two stop their argument, and Reem leaves. Fem takes a plate and, after heaping it with food much as I have done, he drops onto a chair across from me. Lent finishes first, after stuffing his face too quickly for manners. I eat nearly two full plates and sense a quiet shock from Fem, but ignore it.

Finally full, I rise from the table and make to leave in the same direction as the others, but Lent stops me. "I need to go out on an errand," he says. "Would you like to stretch your legs and accompany me?"

"I would like that."

"What do we call you?"

For a moment, I'm not sure what I might be named, but then it comes to me and I say, "Chaosta."

He grins at me and says, "Welcome to the mansion, Chaosta." Gesturing to me to follow, he leaves the room. I trail behind him from the room, through the entry hall, and out the front door.

EMERGENCE

Stepping out onto the street after Lent, I have to fight to hide my emotions as intense sounds and smells crash over me. The street is narrow and carriages rush down it in careening paths as though in the middle of some race. There is a thick and smoky fog in the air that immediately burns my lungs.

Just down the street, several people seem to be fixing a building, and the tools they are using send sharp, explosive sounds through the air and directly into my skull.

Carriage drivers yell and scream at each other as they speed past, and the sound of wheels driven fast over cobbles on the street adds to the din.

"It's too early to be very busy," says Lent, speaking over the wild noise, "but all the same, stay close so you don't get lost."

Then, without looking at me, he steps off along a narrow path running along the building, which seems to be the only safe place from the speeding carriages.

I follow close behind him and try to keep up and not trip over my own feet. As I do, I crane my head up, looking at buildings so tall they disappear into the smoggy sky.

"Magnificent, huh?" calls Lent, turning to face me for a second with a grin. He then continues on rapidly, leaving me to think that this is not the word I would use to describe this place.

His long legs attempt to outpace me, so I break into a jog. Suddenly, as though realizing I'm not easily able to catch up, he slows down, walking beside instead of ahead of me.

"I'm a bit of a researcher for the other work the band does," he says. "I have a book I must pick up for that work. Do you like books?"

An answer rises unbidden from my lips, and I'm likely as surprised as Lent as I say the words, "I love books."

Lent flashes me a grin. "You'll fit right in then," he says enthusiastically.

Soon, we arrive at a crossroads. Catching the fabric of my hood in his fist, Lent looks across the street and then, pulling me, darts across. We only narrowly avoid being run down. I hear curses hurled from the carriage behind me as Lent continues on, apparently accustomed enough to this to be unflustered by the near-death experience.

We continue for a while at a fast clip down the same street, and then he turns off to the left and almost immediately steps into a small door at the front of one of the tall buildings.

I follow him into near silence, especially relative to the noise outside. In this small shop, the smell of musky books mixes with the acrid scent of smoke from outside. Books line the walls from floor to ceiling, and we have to walk through a maze of shelves before we get to a small counter.

Lent clears his throat, and the tiniest man I have ever seen, not that it means much at this point, appears from somewhere behind us. Taking a pull on his pipe, he walks around to the opposite side of the counter. He peers through narrowed eyes at Lent, who waits as though for the man to recognize him.

Finally, Lent grumbles, "You were holding a book for me on

hag stones. You told me to come back today and you would have it."

"Ah, though I don't remember you, I remember the book," says the little man. "It is over here, no wait, wait, I'll fetch it." Grumbling quietly to himself, he disappears into the maze of bookshelves that are behind and to both sides of the counter.

While this happens, I wait, standing slightly behind Lent. Catching my attention, he crosses his eyes as though telling me something about the little man I didn't already realize. I smile, looking down to hide behind my hair, and while I look at the floorboards, the little man returns.

He takes the pipe from his mouth and sets a small book on the counter as he says, "That'll be forty coppers."

"No way," says Lent, "you told me you could get it for cheap. That price is not what we agreed on."

"Hmm, well, I'm certain I don't remember that. This book will cost you no less than forty, and look here, son, I've got plenty of customers who will take it for that, so no bargaining."

I can only see Lent's back, but he seems upset. Finally, he digs something out of his pocket and sets it with too much force on the counter.

The little man slowly counts it as though expressing boredom at Lent's outrage and then nods and, wrapping the book in brown paper, hands it over.

Once again smoking his pipe, he grins at Lent and says, "Enjoy it there, young man, great book that." With that, he turns and disappears again into the maze of books.

Lent stomps out of the shop, and I can tell that I've been forgotten. I pause when I get outside and, looking down a small alley, see something that brings a smile to my face.

I turn down the alley as Lent continues down the street, heedless of my change of direction. Soon, I am at the side of a harnessed horse. He is mainly white with some strange mark-ings. He arches his neck to blow at me, his nostrils standing square. Unsure from what part of myself I draw the knowledge, I know that he is a young stallion and full of himself, but well-behaved. He is also well-loved, and his shining coat shows it.

I run a hand over his shoulder and blow into his nostrils, getting to know him. Suddenly, I hear a loud shout from behind me, and the horse and I shy apart.

"Hey!" Lent yells as he walks swiftly towards me. "Those horses are dangerous, you will get kicked or worse! I don't know what I'll do if I have to explain to the others that you ended up as sausage in the street."

I glare at him from under the fringe of hair that fell into my eyes and then step forward to the horse as it snorts. His ears are pinned at Lent, but I return to our previous silent conversation and begin to stroke his shoulder again. Calmed after a moment, the horse leans his head against me, his ears forward, and with a snort expresses his disgust at stupid boys. I laugh and then turn and walk to Lent, brushing the hair out of my face.

"Don't stray, you don't know this city yet," Lent says before he starts off again. Thankfully, it seems his mood has improved, and he leads me more calmly on the rest of his errands as I trail in his wake.

Next, we stop at a small shop that seems to sell random items. I'm not sure what he buys. They look like strings made of metal and some type of writing instruments. Finally, with his shopping done, he turns us toward home.

When we arrive back at the mansion, Reem meets us in the entry hall. Glancing at me, he then looks at Lent and asks, "Did you get the banjo strings I asked for?"

Lent nods and hands him one of the packages.

Reem frowns as though unsure whether Lent would have correctly fulfilled his task. After checking the contents of one of the small packages, however, he mumbles a thanks.

Then he looks at me and back at Lent before saying, "The others are waiting in the floral room, let's go talk."

I feel as though there is something he isn't saying.

Lent says, "Lead the way, fearless leader."

The corner of Reem's mouth quirks up, but he shakes his head at Lent. Then he leads us into a room I haven't been in yet. Painted flowers cover the walls. In the center are a couple of leather couches sitting facing each other. A few other chairs are set across the open spaces. The ceilings are high with white designs painted on them, and there's a large chandelier in the center of the ceiling.

Fem is already here, standing along a wall with a book in his hands. When we arrive, he takes a seat on a couch, watching me closely. I stand awkwardly as Lent and Reem each sit, and then, realizing they intend for me to as well, I sit at the end of the couch Fem is on.

As I wait for them to speak, I look at each of them again. Some awareness, I've been gifted with, tells me they are in their mid-twenties. That same awareness tells me that I appear to be about the same age despite my rather recent gift of life. That same awareness also tells me that they are young for them to have experienced the success they have.

Studying them, I note that Lent fiddles with the package he brought with him, seeming to have rather too much energy to sit still. Reem sits with his arms crossed, looking at all of us as though wondering who is going to start this conversation. Fem sits quietly, still studying me.

Finally, as though he's grown tired of waiting, Reem begins, "You have been dragged into our life with almost no explanation. You should know that we are a group of musicians, a rather talented group, and we live here in relative decadence. Right now, it is the three of us, as our fourth bandmate recently left us for love." Reem scoffs, as though leaving this band for love is a ridiculous practice, one that he doesn't endorse. "Lent is our guitarist, and he also does some work for our other project." He gestures vaguely in Lent's direction.

When I glance at Lent, he grins at me and gives me an awkward wave that makes me laugh.

Then Reem continues, "Fem is our fiddle player. He also has some experience as a healer from his work prior to joining the band."

Fem just nods at me, eyes still searching as though he might find the answer to a puzzle. Unsure what is expected, I avoid his eyes.

"I play Banjo," Reem says simply.

As I wait for him to say something else, Lent chimes in, "Reem is also our fearless leader. This band is his passion, and he has led our group to much success."

Reem makes a noise as though he might disagree, but there is a smile on his face. Then he continues, "We have a performance soon, and tonight we are setting up to rehearse and prepare for that concert. I fear it will be terribly boring for you here, and if you would like me to arrange some other mode of board for you I would be happy to."

I consider, looking at the floor and thinking about what he has said. Finally, I look up, meeting his blue eyes for a flash and then quickly looking away. "I would like to stay here," I say. "It is nice enough, and you three are the only people I know."

"Truly?" Fem asks, looking worried. "You really know no one else? Where did you live before?" Because I can respond, he says with a slight shake of his head, "No, do not answer that. I really don't mean to pry. Only I fear you will be bored with no entertainment. Is there anything we could get for you?"

"Truly, I'll just explore for now and try to figure that out," I say quietly and note that my voice shakes slightly.

Reem is quiet for a moment. I feel his eyes on me. He has a serious look on his face as he says, "We are quite busy and have important work to do. I expect that you won't become a bother. If you do, we will need to find you another place to stay. Otherwise, you are welcome to live here with us for the time being."

I nod at him, understanding that his work is important. Reem considers and, perhaps finding my assurance acceptable, rises and leaves the room.

Lent is silent for a time, as though wanting to say something but not knowing what it is. Then he rises slowly and walks towards the door. As he leaves the room, I hear him saying something to Reem about being rude.

Fem looks over at me and says, "We will be downstairs in the ballroom if you wish to find us." His tone is quiet and kind. When I look at him and nod, he rises as well and leaves.

I sit for several moments and have to admit that I shed a few tears, not hopeless tears, nor angry nor from pain. They seem to be from some emotion that I don't quite know yet in my short life. Finally tiring of them, I wipe them from my face and explore, first this room, and then out into the rest of the house.

As I begin my exploration, I hear a sound rising through the floor. At first, it is noise only, and quiet at that, but slowly it turns into music. I begin to hear a voice singing, although it is too muted to make out the words. With curiosity building, I eventually find my way to the stairs down to the lower level. As I descend, the music grows louder and the words slowly become clear.

"I hear the knife pierce flesh and bone
And gasp as though it were my own"

The stairs continue into the darkness, and I travel down them slowly, lost in the music floating up from where the band plays without knowledge of their audience.

"The pain of flesh doesn't bother me
It's the pain of heart that's broken free"

The music is fast-moving and rough. I don't have names for

the instruments, even when I finally see them. Focusing on the sounds they make, I settle myself against the doorframe at the base of the stairs, unnoticed in the shadows.

> "The cry that bursts out from my lips
> Can any sound compare to this"

I rest there with eyes closed and lose myself in the threads of sound that, when mixed together, create this thing which is more than noise.

> "A mix of horror and of pain
> The worry that my love is slain"

Finally opening my eyes, I watch the band. Fem and Lent have their eyes closed, faces blank with concentration. Reem, who is singing, is looking at a scrap of paper pinned on one wall, while he plays one of the instruments, which is swung over his shoulder.

> "I'm at her side fast as sunlight shaft
> I wish I knew the healing craft"

For the first time since I arrived here, I think of the demon Malam. He gave me this life, and I feel I have much of his knowledge. I have memories that I know are not mine, of killing, fighting, and the use of weapons. I know proper courtesies and dancing and how to ride a fine horse fast through clogged streets. These aren't just memories either. Somehow, I feel as though my body might know these things as well, and it feels as though I have a physical strength that isn't entirely mine.

I also have an awareness within me of things I'm sure Malam wouldn't know. There is some intelligence in me that is not my own nor the demon's. There are also instincts that seem like a map in my head, and while it's spread out in front of me, the paths are as of yet not clearly marked.

> "I press my hands to where blood rushes forth
> Her body lying pointing north"

I wonder at my knowledge of angels and demons. I remember darkness and flight without wings. I'm aware of a great conflict between light and dark, and of the danger of the poisonous smog in the air. I feel the danger of the lack of green things as though it is a weapon poised over me. However, most of that knowledge seems useless to me as of yet.

> "The sirens wail and scream in the night
> An echo of my silent plight"

The Boys play their music, investing themselves in it, and I sit here at the foot of the stairs without anything clear to invest myself in.

PLANS AND DEATH

I wake slowly from a deep sleep in the center of a strange bed. Slowly fighting my way out, I touch my feet to a cold floor and, gasping, dress myself quickly as the memory of how I arrived here returns to me.

Recollection of leaning against the wall, trying to figure out my place, and of music that slowly lulled me to sleep returns bit by bit. Finally, I vaguely remember that one of the boys, having discovered me asleep leaning against the wall on the stairs, carried me to my bed.

My stomach growls, and I think suddenly and unexpectedly of food. I stand to leave with the dining room clearly marked in my head. As I go to the door, though, I grasp how rumpled my appearance is, so I pause and turn back to the cupboards. I pull open the door, the clothing inside interests me not at all. Other than, as a way to be an appropriate guest who would certainly be welcomed to eat a grand, enormous meal.

I pull out a combination of an uneven short skirt, jacket, and another pair of long socks. As I dress, I eventually notice that the colors of the clothing seem to match those of this violent room. Finally dressed, I leave thinking only of breakfast.

When I arrive, the boys look up quickly as I enter. Feeling their eyes on me, I drop onto the nearest chair and begin to serve myself food that I don't recognize.

"You found it," exclaims Lent. He seems cheerful this morning.

I nod, my mouth full of mystery food which is actually quite tasty. As I eat, I look around the room.

Lent is shoveling food into his mouth, standing near the window, talking to Reem. They seem to be arguing good-naturedly about some of the words in the song I heard last night.

Fem is sitting across from me, completely silent, eating his food and drinking massive amounts of the coffee in front of him, which must not have been made by Reem. With that assurance, I pour myself a large cup and slowly sip at the hot liquid, still unsure whether I like it or not.

Fem finally leaves the room with a mention of getting a bath, and Lent joins me, sitting in Fem's vacated place at the table. "We have a concert later and I wondered if you would like to come?" he asks.

I hesitate for a moment and then nod at him with a smile.

"Alright then, I will arrange it," he says cheerfully. "We will leave at about thirty past noon. I will ensure a house employee leaves appropriate clothes in your room. Until then, we have to get ready, so hopefully you don't mind entertaining yourself for a short while?"

I shake my head, and he rises and leaves. Then I stuff the last bite of food in my mouth and finish the coffee.

For the rest of the morning, I busy myself in my room, looking through the clothing in the cupboard and pots of various cleaning supplies in the bathroom. Sometime later, I hear strands of music floating up through the floor, but there is mostly silence. By eleven, I am beginning to be twitchy with the wait, and I pace for a while before slouching onto my bed. Without meaning to, I fall into a restless sleep.

I am woken later by someone who must be one of the house employees. The time must be just a bit before "thirty past noon" because she seems harried and stressed.

Once she sees my eyes open, she turns in a quick movement and throws open the doors of the cupboard that I have not yet explored. I watch as she pulls forth some combination of cream, gray, black, and red clothing, which she arranges in the shape of a person on the untouched end of the bed.

As she does this, I slouch up and rub at the grit filling my eyes. The house employee finally looks at me, clothing now arranged to her satisfaction, and points me to the floor.

I climb off the bed, and pull on the clothing, slowly making sense of the tangle. I must pass the test, though, because upon leaving the room, she looks me up and down and gives a firm nod. Then, with me caught in her wake, she turns and makes her way through the winding hallways. We walk down the grand staircase and into an entry hall that is full of strangely shaped boxes. This place seems to be caught in some combination of panic, confusion, and a military procession.

The boys and several house employees are carrying the strange-shaped boxes out the large, open front doors and packing them with much precision, and some cursing, into a waiting carriage.

Suddenly, the horses catch my attention, and I am out the door, caught in the river of servants and boxes like a piece of well-dressed jetsam with at least one of the boys calling at me from behind.

The horses are a neatly matched pair of black mares with high, arched necks and long curly manes. They stand not moving upon the rock of the street, but from the first hair above their hoof, they look as though they want to take flight and are completely capable of that action.

They twitch as I run to them, but as the nearest cranes her head to me in order to see past the blinkers, I see her relax. She blows at the other to do the same. I move to the front of them where they can see me more comfortably, mostly oblivious to the shouts from their driver. Then I reach up my hand to them so they can catch my scent, feeling very small in front of their large, black forms.

Suddenly, two carriages race past only inches from their side, and the energy within the horses explodes. They grow taller even and toss their heads as though cursing those who can run. Their manes seem to turn to flame at their necks, and their nostrils flare, but their well-trained feet remain upon the stone without movement. I whisper to them and they focus back upon me, slowly becoming horses again.

Suddenly, there is a hand gripping my arm, and I am pulled to the side of the carriage roughly and without warning. I look up, feeling angry for the first time, and meet the eyes of Fem. He looks so worried that my anger leaves me in a rush, and I follow him meekly away from the horses.

We wait quietly together near the entrance to the mansion while the other boys seem to attempt to direct the flow and ebb of the rapids of boxes and packages. I allow Fem to keep watch over me like a troublesome shadow until the carriage is fully packed. Reem then directs us to the carriage and packs us in, not so differently than the strangely shaped boxes.

The carriage starts off and, without a window seat, I have nothing to do but sit quietly. The boys are all quiet and tight-lipped to various degrees. They seem to be lost in thoughts of the concert and not fully in the present, so I feel as though I am alone. It is easy in the relative quiet to lose myself in thought, and as the carriage sways quickly along its route, I daydream of strange things that I don't have names for but seem to remember clearly.

Finally, the carriage stops and we all step out onto the street.

I follow meekly behind the others to a door at the side of a building. The room inside is large and dark. There are people everywhere, and I am lost in the sheer number of them and their sounds.

Then I feel a hand on my arm, and I look up into Reem's face. He leans close to me, his body along mine, and speaks into my ear. Reem tells me that the boys have gone through a different door and are preparing to perform. "You are welcome to follow me backstage," he says, "or you can find a place here to watch the excitement."

I nod to him, still looking at the front of the room where, through a gap in the crowd, I can see the stage. There is an excitement in the air that I cannot understand, and yet it is infectious. I look back at him and, meeting his eyes, I call out over the crowd, "I will find a place here."

He pauses a moment, his expression doubtful, as though he would like to try to change my mind, but then nods and turns to make his way through the ever more excited crowd in the direction of the rest of the band.

I push my way slowly through the room. I'm shorter than everyone, so it's difficult to see where I'm going. I use my elbows to my advantage. At the other wall is a gap, and I make it mine, settling against the support of the wall and closing my mind to the quiet roar all around me. As I do so, I look around, as though looking for someone that I recognize in this world where I have only spent a handful of days.

As we wait and watch, suddenly the stage lights up and the band, The Boys, walk out onto the stage.

It is both as I expect and not.

The crowd roars so loud that I am in the present again, pulled along with them to a place that they recognize, and I am lost.

Then the band starts playing. At the first notes, the crowd becomes insane. I am caught, somewhere between a celebration and a feeding frenzy. At every moment, I am at risk of being crushed against their flow, and yet I am lost in the beauty of the sound that is being created. The crowd worships every minute.

After some time has passed, The Boys go silent, the music pausing, and the madness increases until they start again. This time, as the crowd surges forward, I fall as someone behind me runs into my back. On my knees, I scramble for safety, but the people around me are simply too frenzied to care.

A foot comes down suddenly on my back, and it knocks the wind from my lungs. I'm gasping, crushed against the dirty floor. At that moment, everything slows down. I notice every tiny detail from the size of the foot on my back to the groupings of dirt, dust, and old food on the floor in front of me.

As I'm beginning to panic, there is suddenly a hand on my shoulder pulling me back to my feet and through the crowd to another empty pocket of space against the wall.

Gasping and still feeling lost, I pull air into my bruised lungs, trying to find the breath to thank my savior. I finally look up and see Malam.

With my vision working better than last time, I get a closer look at him. Light green eyes sit within a face that is chiseled with high cheekbones and an olive complexion. A mop of textured black hair sits on his head. As he brushes his hand through it, pushing it out of his eyes, I note how predatory his movement is.

His shoulders are broad, straining against the black, long-sleeved linen shirt he wears. Tailored black pants sit low on his hips.

For a moment, as I look into the green eyes of my creator, I am lost. Everything that is me evaporates, and as the sound plays over us, I am frozen, unable to feel anything except the music pounding through me. It feels as though I'm looking at a part of myself, an oddness that makes the breath freeze in my lungs.

Vaguely, I am aware that The Boys have moved on to their next song and the crowd, their next frenzy, but I remain lost from myself, still unable to react.

Malam grins, a look that is both terrifying and comforting. "Interesting crowd you fell in with," he says dryly.

Somehow, despite the noise, I am able to hear him clearly as though we are standing in a quiet room together.

"They are kind and the only people I know," I say. Even I am aware of the irritation in my voice.

He frowns and examines me carefully, and then looks away, seeming satisfied that he found the answer to his question. As he looks up at the band, he says, "I was admiring your choice, or rather chance, more than questioning it."

He looks back at me again and grins.

A chill runs down my spine. Something about the grin screams of violence despite the clear lack of that emotion on his face.

I begin to watch the band again, my mind trying to find the path back to my tongue. Triumphantly, it succeeds, and I turn back to Malam only to find his lips moving, following the words that Reem sings. He looks as lost in the music as I feel, but he also fits into this crowd, this place, in a way I do not.

Finding me watching him, he becomes still and then more quietly says, "They have been my favorite since before any of these people knew them. None of their success was a surprise to me. You being taken in by them, on the other hand, is a wonderful and bittersweet twist to the story."

After a few moments pass, he continues, "I rarely attend their concerts, but I am often around to support them in their work to learn dark magic, so I will be seeing more of you than I expected. Perhaps the deities above us are laughing about it even as we speak."

As I consider his words, and try to make some unconscious decision myself about this being who seems to feel he knows me, he suddenly looks behind me. I watch as his eyes grow hard, and I turn to see what he is looking at.

Whatever it was is hidden from me at the moment, and I turn back to him to ask what is wrong, but Malam is gone, missing from the spot he occupied just moments before.

I turn back to the crowd and try to find something out of place, something that would make a demon mad, and this time I see him. A man stands quietly in the middle of the crowd, but perhaps I shouldn't call him a man.

Bright shadow wings, the opposite of Malam's, jut from his back. Although it should be hard for him to stand in the middle of that wild crowd, he is poised and standing with an unnatural stillness. There is a peace to him standing there in the middle of the frenzy that is wildly wrong. Thanks to Malam's memories, I know he is an angel. Thanks to Malam's memories, I also feel rage as I look at him.

Then he focuses on me and opens his mouth. A hush falls on the crowd. I note that they don't seem to see him and continue their celebration, but their sound is now lost to me completely.

In my awareness, there is only me and him.

I turn and walk, or weave, or dance more calmly than should be possible through a crowd that doesn't seem to see me. I know he is at my back and narrowing the space between us. However, some part of my mind has calculated the equation between the danger behind me and the door well enough to be content in my seemingly slow progress.

Reaching the door, I pull it open and am on the street before I am consciously aware. I am acutely aware, however, of the landscape in all of its detail, and which of those details will help me in my plight and which will hurt me.

An unbidden thought comes to my mind of a weapon, a form of safety, on the back of one of the haphazardly parked carriages. I turn, trying to find that which some instinct has already located. I move left, down a long row of carriages of all types, colors, and sizes.

Some part of me can feel him behind me, but even as my ears strain to catch the sound of him, I am moving along the street.

The horses' focus is on me, and with ears tipped to the danger behind me, they watch my progress like spectators at a bullfight. Trapped, fastened to their carriages, they have no ability to run or to help.

I see it then.

A sword handle reveals itself to me where it juts from the foot space beneath a coachman's seat. In a smooth, slow movement like a sort of dance, I pull it out and remove it from the sheath. Then, subconsciously, I turn my whole body to meet his sudden charge.

His face is so near me as I turn. The beautiful stillness of it is far more dangerous, far more deadly than any expression of rage. My body is stiff and still unfamiliar to me, but there is that gifted strength that I suspected might exist within me.

He pulls back and strikes at me suddenly, and somehow my body moves the sword to block it.

The sword in my numb hands, the ground beneath my numb feet, the fight before my blind eyes progresses both slowly and too fast.

The world spins around us while the sights and sounds pass us by, and there is only us, only survival, and this awful, beautiful, wonderful dance. Still, even blind, the landscape somehow changes as time moves.

For a moment, I feel as though this is all I've ever known.

Then instinct moves me quickly to the left, and I strike out strongly to the right and front, still unseeing in this subconscious space.

There is a gasp, and slowly vision returns to me, and I see him, there in front of me. His face is still soft and glaringly beautiful. Then I see the trail of dark red, so dark it is nearly black, running down his chest. He falls, slowly, crumpling onto the middle of the open street.

There is a silence that seems almost to be its own sound. It is a roar in my ears, and then I hear them. There is a crowd around us.

There are people of all types standing in the street with smoke and fog surrounding them, watching me, where I stand frozen in the middle of a spreading sea of blood with a naked sword in my hand.

There is a sense of peace in finding your place.

ESCAPE

The silence is loud.

Then there is a quiet rustling that grows into a hum. The crowd is waking up, and even as I stand there looking at the sword in my hand, and the angel and the blood, I feel the tension increase and know it's time to run.

I look around with desperation, but I'm unsure what I'm seeking. Hoping the same instincts that provided guidance with finding the sword and helped me with the fight will assist, I search faces within the crowd. It is, as a whole, angry like a large beast that has been awoken too soon from a quiet slumber. Then, my search ends as I see a small boy watching me from within the crowd. That subconscious feeling guides me. As I look at him, I see no anger, no fear, only sadness and curiosity.

I take the chance and step towards him, wiping the sword idly on my skirt, scrubbing at the dark blood. Perhaps not the best idea to leave a blood stain on the white cloth, but a piece of me knows the rules of weaponry too well to break them with a dirty sword. A tattoo I bear on my soul without knowing the artist.

The boy looks up as I stand in front of him, and with the

wisdom that only a young child can possess, he takes my hand. He pulls me through the crowd so quickly that they part, separating, clearing the way for us to run. We take off down the street in the momentary lull before outrage hits, and they turn fully into a mob.

The boy leads me to a carriage, but not into the conveyance; instead, he moves around it to where a horse stands. As it has in the past, my sense of horses identifies this one as a mare, and it also shows me that she feels protective of the young boy who still has my hand.

Her ears are pinned, perhaps against the angry emotions of the crowd. As I watch, she drops her large, Roman-nosed head into his arms. He wraps his arms around her muzzle for a moment, and I see his lips moving at her ear.

As she listens to his quiet plea, she rolls an eye up to look at me, and I see something shift. She lifts her head to me and blows at my face. As this happens, the boy does something with the leather that connects her to the carriage.

I must pass her test. The mare lowers herself to kneel and the boy clambers inelegantly onto her back, and even as he gestures to me to do the same, I am swinging myself up behind him.

The hairs on the back of my neck are standing on end, telling me the crowd has continued to rouse and is advancing on us and our location. We don't have long before a fully formed mob will be upon us.

Even as I open my mouth to ask the boy to please hurry, the mare stands and, in a powerful leap that knocks the air from me, she is making progress fast down the street. Her feet strike sparks from the stone, and I feel as though we've grown wings. We move so quickly through the smoke and fog that I blink rapidly, trying to clear my vision without result. Thankfully, either the horse can see better than I or she has some way of sensing without sight.

There are still narrow misses with a carriage and a young man riding at a gallop down the street, but the mare seems to command the others, and they move from our way. I cannot say for sure how far we travel, but the speed of our flight is enough to drive tears from my eyes.

Soon, we come to an equally fast stop at the base of a building not so different from those that we were just flying past. The boy slides, with very little grace, down her side and waves a hand at me in a way that clearly says to follow. I dismount similarly and land on wobbly legs that scarcely hold me. I force their movement, a strict taskmaster, and follow the boy into the depths of this building.

As we go through the door, I see the mare toss her head and trot off to an unknown stable.

This building may appear similar to the others from the outside, but inside it is different. Something about it feels familiar and comfortable. Smoke, which smells sweet and heavy, is so thick in the air here that I feel as though I could climb it like stairs to the top of the building.

I follow the boy closely, nearly treading upon his heels, knowing that if I am separated, I will be well and truly lost in this maze of smoke. Thankfully, he leads me straight to a hidden flight of stairs and we begin to climb. I put one foot in front of the other and wish that I had wings, although a lift would be nearly as welcome.

I have not had rest since I climbed from my bed, and an unknown and yet lengthy amount of time has passed.

Suddenly, the little boy stops, and I run into his back. With the shock of it, I drop the sword. It rattles down the steps, and I spin and chase it, scooping it up by the handle and then turning to make sure the boy is alright.

Thankfully, he is standing unscathed, but there are two men, no, not men, two demons standing behind him. The little boy looks surprisingly calm despite standing near two beings who are surrounded by swirling shadow. The demon's eyes seem to look into my soul, and I lower the sword unconsciously to my side and climb back up the steps to stand directly in front of them.

One of them gestures to me and says something to the boy, who responds, "She needs help, she just killed a guard."

I see the eyes of the demons widen. One looks unsure, the other looks down at my skirt and nudges his companion, pointing to the bloodstain from cleaning the sword.

I realize belatedly that the little boy is walking past me, back down the stairs. As he gets to me, he asks for the sword, and I hand it to him. I've formed no great attachment to it, but it still takes an extra moment to release it to him. As he takes the sword, he turns and begins the downward journey.

I again climb the few remaining steps to where the demons stand. As I get closer, one of them says something in a guttural language that makes the hair raise at the nape of my neck. The other reaches down to my skirt, and I stop and stand still, only trembling slightly, as he touches the dark blood there. Then, in a quick and pain-driven movement, he yanks his hand away with something that sounds like a curse.

Looking at each other, the first demon says, "It's the blood of an angel," and the other's eyes widen in shock.

The demons then look at me, scanning me as though looking for something. Their faces are similar masks of surprise, and I feel uncomfortable in the quiet as they look at me.

Then their eyes stop, looking at my leg near the floor, and they say something to each other in that same guttural language. When I look where they are, I see a small pool of black near the outside of my right foot. I begin to step forward, but it's as though the pool and the rivulet of it that runs down my leg have roped me to the ground. My leg feels too heavy and doesn't fully listen to the order I've given it, and I tip forward, gracelessly.

One of the demons catches me roughly by the arm, and then, in a swift and inhuman movement, he picks me up.

In that moment, the same instinctual part of me that fought the angel rebels. In a smooth, quick twisting movement, I end up crouching in front of him, having escaped his hands like a small silver fish. I hear them swear and am vaguely aware of them moving to restrain me, but then the world begins to grey out, and I pass out.

THE WAY OF THINGS

I wake with half-remembered dreams in my head and a strange taste in my mouth. My head feels like it's full of the smoke that seems to be ever-present here. As I return to awareness, I feel my body resting against a firm surface. I try to move, but can't yet make my body obey.

The room I'm in is filled with darkness and smoke. The walls are painted black, and cupboards line one of the walls. There is a cot set along another. The bed I'm in protrudes from the middle of the wall into the room.

The space seems as though it could be hiding beasts or spirits in the dark, shadowed corners. I can see a door along the final wall; it is also dark with a brass knob. There is a tray resting on one of the cupboards. The tray seems to contain several items, including a pitcher and a cup.

Suddenly overwhelmed with thirst, I struggle with the blanket, which seems to be trying to chain me to the bed. I work myself free and manage to push myself more upright, the wall at my back. My vision tries to fade, but I ignore it and push myself forward.

The moment I put a foot on the floor, the pain is back,

thrashing in my head. However, the chance for something to drink pulls me to the table more strongly than the pain pulls me back.

I lean against the bed, then the wall, and then the cupboard, and I make it to the tray. When I look into the pitcher, though, it contains nothing but a thin layer of slime at the bottom, which can only be from whatever drugs they've been giving me.

I slide down the cupboard to sit on the floor. Whatever tenuous control I've had over my body is gone. The pain in my leg is no longer something I can ignore, and I fold myself so that I can see what they've done. What I find is a neatly wrapped bandage that nearly covers my leg below my knee. A quickly spreading black stain shows through the white cloth.

I lie on my side and rest my cheek against the floor. It's cool. The part of my memory that isn't my own tells me it feels almost like earth.

I'm not aware of losing consciousness, but when I wake, I'm back on the same bed.

This time, there are no dreams, and the pain is less. Enough that I am able to push myself up and stand on both legs without other support. I take a couple of shaky steps to the door. Nearly there, I hesitate a moment. Part of me knows if I try the knob and it doesn't open, like a caged animal, my instincts will take over. I fear what might happen if they do. I shut my eyes for a breath, put my hand on the handle, and push.

The door opens into a wide space, filled with the trunks of trees which seem to rise through the ceiling.

Everywhere I look, I see green. I have never seen anything like this in my short life besides in paintings. The small forest created by the trees in this massive room is filled with underbrush. There are small openings that seem to lead into clearings. As I look at the plants with wonder, a demon emerges from one of the openings in the trees. I don't recognize him, but he seems to recognize me as he walks toward me with an urgency to his gait.

He looks young and is not overly tall. He is more slender than Malam. He has the same dark hair and olive complexion, but with blue eyes instead of green. His hair is black and horrendously curly. It looks as though he gave up taming it a long time ago, as it flops into his face, attempting to crawl into his eyes. Of course, as is the case with demons, wings of shadow emerge from his shoulders.

As I look at him, I try to release the frame of the doorway I am clutching, but I can't seem to make my fingers work. I hear him say something to me, but can't quite make out the words. However, as I look up at him again, it is as though he's released me from some sort of spell, and I can suddenly open my fingers.

I move to walk, or limp, to him, but I stumble.

His longer legs close the space between us, and he reaches out and takes my arm, stabilizing me. "You're not meant to be out of bed yet," he growls, his voice twisting the words until they are nearly unrecognizable.

Then he directs me by the arm back into the room I just left with a strength I have no chance of resisting. I allow him to help me back onto the bed and watch as he draws some shape in the air above me.

Seeing me watching, he says, "I'm called Chiron." His voice is rough, and it is clear that he's not used to speaking in this language.

After a few moments of whatever it is he's doing in the air above me, his expression grows more worried. He turns to the cupboard and removes a small wooden box. Taking something from it, he walks back to the bed and hands me a small tablet. "Take this," he says quietly, "the poison still has hold of you."

Fear strikes me at the thought, and the significance of the pain in my leg begins to make more sense in the memories that

Subconsciously, my body changes the steps of the dance suddenly and twists away.

I move, as of yet unaware of my body's plans, towards the clearing. I hear Elling call behind me, but it is not of importance to me at this moment.

I make my way through the undergrowth, navigating this as I navigated the fight with the angel. Suddenly, I break through into the clearing I somehow recognize. As I look around, a few demons step through the trees in front of me, and as one, they turn and focus upon me. One of them has a large black crow perched on his shoulder. I recognize another as the demon who introduced himself as Chiron.

As I stare at them, Elling, who is now behind me, grabs my shoulder and begins to direct me back in the direction we just came from.

Chiron is looking at me, at my bandaged leg specifically, and he opens his mouth as though to say something.

Before anyone can do anything else, Malam himself emerges from the middle of the group and says something to Elling in their guttural language. My legs shake while the conversation happens above my head.

Eventually, although still speaking, Elling releases his hold on my arm, and I am left to stand unaided. Finally, the conversation ceases, and he leaves. Malam holds out a hand. I take it and allow myself to be pulled behind him through the center of the group, which parts for us.

He brings me to a different clearing with a bench. We are alone here. Pressing me to sit, he then settles himself on the bench next to me. Kindly, but with the sound of violence behind the words he says, "Why did you have angel blood on your skirt, and why is there a wound from an Angelforged blade on your leg?"

Unsure what exactly his meaning is, somehow, the memories he placed in my head have a response. "An angel attacked me and I killed him," I say even as my vision starts to grey out at the edges. "I must not have fought as well as I should."

"You fought with swords?" he asks, his guttural voice sounding tight.

"Yes, I found one on the back of a carriage."

Malam hesitates. Glancing briefly at me and seeing something that worries him, he stands. Drawing me up with him by my hand, he begins to lead me somewhere. I'm aware of being pulled after him for a couple of steps, and then I feel my knees hit a firm surface. Moments later, the blackness pulls me toward unconsciousness. Even as it overtakes me, I have the sudden feeling of shadowed flight before I'm pulled completely under.

BACK AT THE MANSION

I open my eyes to find all three of the boys looking at me with tight expressions. I try to rise to reassure them, and myself, that I am alright, but am pressed down by a hand on my shoulder.

I trace my gaze to follow the arm and see that the hand belongs to Fem, whose face is full of concern as he looks at me.

"Just lie still," he says quietly. "It seems you were injured at our concert, and we all take that upon our shoulders."

Before I understand it, consciously, I'm shaking my head at him, but even as I deny it, I see him opening his mouth to protest.

Before he can express what he's feeling, I hear one of the other boys say, "We should have had you backstage. If we'd realized the crowd would be like that, we would have."

As the sound moves, I try to track it, but my vision is still grey at the edges, and I have to blink a few times. When my eyes can focus, I see Reem there, alongside Fem. They look at each other, their expressions saying something in a language I don't understand.

Still unable to focus, I hear Fem say, "One of our acquaintances found you, got you bandaged up, and brought you back here. I think you might know him? His name is Malam."

I nod weakly, which Fem seems to note.

"I tried to take the bandage off to tend to you, but it doesn't look right. I should have been able to help, but it seems the wound was infected somehow. We are having a healer stop by to check your injury, as this is beyond my abilities," Fem says quietly.

"For now, just rest," one of them says.

It doesn't matter who, as unconsciousness pulls me into blackness even as the last word is spoken.

* * *

*A*s I descend into blackness, more dreams greet me. There are people and shapes and sounds, but no map to follow to understand what is happening. Small things stand out to me.

Shapes written in ash on a table top that some part of me recognizes as runes. There are many runes on the table top. It is in a place I don't recognize, and there seems to be the ghost of a woman standing behind it. Even as I try to see her more clearly, the dream pulls away.

*T*hen I watch as blood from a cut on someone's hand is traced into a shape. The hand that contains the cut is masculine, with long, blunt fingers. Tattoos peek out, just showing at the wrist from beneath long sleeves.

*T*hen there is a dream of a young woman who is looking at me with wonder in her gaze. It makes me uncomfortable until I register that she's looking not at me but through me. I turn to see an angel standing behind me, and even as I finish turning, the angel throws a knife.

As I brace for the painful impact, the knife passes through me. I whirl just quickly enough to see it strike the young woman in the middle of her forehead before she drops to the ground bonelessly. I rush to her, feeling desperately that this is something which should not come to pass. Tears wet my cheeks as I crouch over her body, somehow loving her even while I don't know who she is. Then, out of sudden darkness, a crow flies directly at my face with a scream, and I'm removed from the dream.

* * *

My eyes open as I return to consciousness, and, blinking, I see the black ceiling above the four-poster bed in my room at the boys' house. There are voices, and I turn to see Fem standing at the side of the bed, Reem again behind him.

"Lay still," he says quietly, "we have the healer."

Even as I find the meaning of his words and begin to understand, I find that some of the pain and most of the dizziness are gone. The clouds have also cleared from my vision. I feel well enough that I wonder if I even need a healer.

The look I see on Fem's face, even in the dim candlelit room, tells me he doesn't share that thought. Since Fem is more experienced with this, I remain quiet as another form enters this space.

The form moves to the side of the bed. Something in me screams silently, the hair on the back of my neck standing up. They wear a cloak with the hood upon their head in a way that hides their face. They look at me, but I cannot see them through the shadows, and then they turn to Fem and Reem.

"Leave us," they say, and the two boys comply without another word.

The door closes, and the form lowers the hood. As I behold their face, a hiss slips unbidden from my lips. I push myself to stand, stepping back to lean against the wall at the head of the bed.

In the same way, I knew the sword would be found upon the carriage, I know this time that the only weapons in this house do not reside in this room. I am cornered away from the only exit, so I crouch, trapped and injured, while the angel regards me.

They are neither clearly girl nor boy. They are pale with light blue eyes and dark brown hair that just caresses their jawline, the strands curling gently. A scar streaks across one cheek from their chin to their lower eyelid. Under the cloak, they look to be slender and fit, and that same innate sense tells me they are skilled with a blade. That sense also tells me they don't carry one at this moment.

What has made me move away so quickly, however, is not the bright wings that appeared at their back but instead some sense of them that came to me when they entered the room. As with the other angel, the wings are not corporeal and instead seem to be made of light. The opposite of the wings of shadow that Malam possesses, a nimbus of light, instead of a nimbus of dark.

Unbidden, the memory of the angel I killed as he slumped to the ground plays in my mind's eye.

They tilt their head as they regard me. "You are so small and meek to have killed one of us," they say in a raspy voice that doesn't feel as though it fits them.

I stay still and hope I can find a way out of this.

They must see me looking at their wings because I hear them rasp, "Yes, they can be hidden by some of us who know the trick of it. We had realized you were able to see us for what we are, and thought it would be prudent to see if you were able to identify us solely through our wings. Apparently, that is not the trick, based on your reaction when I walked into this room."

I'm beginning to think about shouting with the hope that the boys may create a distraction. Perhaps that might allow me time to find a weapon.

As I consider it, the angel straightens and looks forward, across the room from me. They make a summoning motion with their hand in my direction. "Sit and let me look at your leg," they say, the raspy sound pulling goosebumps from my skin up and down my spine.

I hesitate, but some part of me bids me to obey, so I step forward even as my heart pounds. Shakily, I lower myself to sit upon the bed.

"I cannot tend to it all the way over there. Come closer," they rasp. Then, with a grin that doesn't touch their eyes, they look straight through me and rasp, "I don't bite."

Even as my teeth grind and a chill joins the goosebumps along my spine, I push myself closer. The smile drops from their face, and they look down at my leg.

I follow their gaze and see the familiar neat white bandage wrapped around the lower part of my leg.

They neatly unwind it with fingers both warmer and more gentle than I expected. They then poke and prod delicately around the bloody gash. "Who's seen to this already?" they ask, slowly looking back up towards my face. They still look through me, and I pause.

"I'm not sure who has seen to it." I carefully put the demons from my mind for reasons not fully known to me. I avoid looking at their light blue eyes as I say, "I remember little after receiving this injury."

They roll their shoulders in an unsettling way that does nothing to reassure me.

I fight back a shudder.

They then pull a small tin and a handful of bandages out of a large pocket on their cloak.

I consider whether I should resist, but, despite how unsettled I feel, they haven't done anything to hurt me. Also, that strange intelligence says I should trust them.

They apply the ointment to the gash, and I confess that while I would enjoy telling you it stings or burns, instead, it removes the remainder of the pain in my leg and further clears my head. They then wrap my leg neatly in a fresh bandage. Finishing that task, they step away from the bed and hold out a hand toward me. "Take my hand and follow," they rasp.

I note the long, delicate fingers and short, clean nails as I hesitate, but something moves me to obey, that intelligence again prompting me to trust them. At last, I take their hand.

I'm dressed only in a simple, white shift with bare feet, but they don't seem to care. They lead through the door into the rest of the house. Again, I consider calling the boys or pulling free and running to find a weapon. I feel my muscles tense slightly as I consider.

Their hand around mine tightens, iron strength around my fingers. "Don't flee, little bird," they say without looking back at me. The sound of their voice is filtered through a smile, and chills run down my spine yet again. "While you hold my hand, no one will see or hear us," they say as though this thought might bring me comfort.

It does not.

They lead through the apartment and out to the street. In my experience so far in this world, limited though it may be, the smoke is usually thick enough to bring shadows to most places. At this moment, however, it is darker than I have yet seen, and again I hesitate.

This time, instead of speaking, they just further firm their grip on my hand, nearly crushing my fingers, and pull me forward in their wake.

A small squeak escapes from my lips, and I struggle to breathe as their longer legs drive us forward at a pace more swift than I can easily match. Thankfully, we don't have far to travel on our feet, and even as I feel a bead of sweat rise upon my hairline, we arrive at the side of a carriage.

I look to the front to see the horses, but they are mostly covered by the dark, and the steel grip of the angel doesn't hesitate to pull me into the carriage door. I'm deposited on a bench, and the best I can do is fall gracefully onto my seat as they release me. They close the door firmly and then sit opposite me. Offset from me, they lift their hood to cover their head and stare out of the depths straight through the back of the seat behind me.

As the carriage moves us swiftly toward whatever fate, I focus on breathing and trying to calm my racing heart.

A CAGED BIRD?

Eventually, the carriage comes to a stop. The angel rises from their seat and, taking my arm in their strangely strong hand, they pull me from the carriage.

Somehow, I manage to remain upright as they tug me after them. I look up to see a building in front of me, indistinguishable from the others on the outside except for a large double door that looks strangely out of place. As we get near, the doors open as if of their own accord, and I'm pulled through by the angel without pause.

The inside of the building looks like nothing I've seen in my short life, nor does it seem to exist in Malam's memories. Everything is white, and the lights in the place burn with an unnerving stillness reflecting off the floor and sending daggers into my eyes. The wide hallway eventually opens into a cavernous room.

There are many angels and some humans in this space, and some of them pause, looking at the angel who leads me as our movement carries us through that room and into the next. I note that, true to their word, none of the others seems to notice me, whether human or angel. I look around with curiosity as they drag me forward, but I can't take the time to discover anything beyond brief glimpses as our rapid pace continues.

We move through two more rooms, each smaller than the initial cavernous space but still larger than anything I've seen before. We eventually stop in front of a partially clear door that seems to be made of glass.

Finally, they release my hand and I hear them say, "Stay with me, little bird."

They move quickly forward, and without their hand on mine, I'm left standing behind for half a breath. As soon as I realize, I rush after them, trying to stay close to the only being in this space that I know. As I'm concentrating on keeping pace with them and their cursedly long legs, I don't notice my environment, so when they stop, I pitch forward into them. I catch myself and then peer around them curiously.

We stand, it seems, in front of a dais with an angel sitting upon it. He has a long, narrow face and curly hair that nearly brushes his broad shoulders. His nose is hawkish and curves at the bottom, and he clasps long, narrow fingers in front of his chest.

Unlike the other angel, he is not looking through me. Instead, his gaze is so pointed I feel like a small animal in the gaze of a hawk. It makes goosebumps stand along my back for an entirely different reason than with the other.

Without moving, he says, "You brought her, thank you, Bonum. With that, you are released."

Bonum steps off a few paces to my left and turns to face me, but doesn't go further. With a suddenly stiff posture, the angel on the dais turns to them and glares for a moment. Then he looks back at me without saying anything. His expression unreadable, he takes a few moments, still studying me, before he speaks again.

"So, you're supposed to embody balance? Or is it that you're supposed to bring balance?" he asks in a voice that hides a laugh behind it, as though this is all funny to him.

Without conscious thought, I lift my shoulders in a shrug while still meeting his gaze. "Is that for me to know or to figure out?" I ask. The words are unknown to me until they leave my lips.

All humor is suddenly gone from his face as he drives himself forward off his seat and wraps his long fingers around my neck.

"Who do you speak for?" he growls, his face close to mine.

I fight to breathe past the strength of his grip but manage to gasp, "Who but myself would I speak for?"

As he continues to regard me without moving, I feel a bit of sweat slowly run down my spine, dodging the still present goosebumps. Still silently fighting for breath, I follow it with my attention while watching his face.

In a similarly sudden movement, he removes his hand from my neck and returns to his seat on the dais. Once seated, he snarls, "I've heard that you killed one of our kind. For that, I should end your life. However, our laws are unclear since you should not exist. Instead of death, I offer you one more chance to go free from this place and choose our side over theirs."

For the first time in my short life, I feel vulnerable. Standing here small, unarmed, in just a shift with bare feet.

He stares at me, clearly reading my discomfort as he says, "My recommendation, *little one*, would be that you figure out which side you are on without the *help of others*. The shadows have given you life only so that you may serve their own dark purpose."

"While we significantly outnumber the *dark forces* in this world, we are all that is progress, all that is peace for the humans. It would do you well to consider what it is you seek, what consequences your actions will have, and who you attempt to bestow hope upon. It is not as simple as it may seem in your very limited view of the world."

"While I have nothing but mistrust and distaste for the *artificial* life you were given, it has been done, hastily though it were, and to remove it would cause fallout. The consequences would destabilize that which I want stable."

As he speaks these words, his eyes drill into mine, and I fight to keep my chin raised and not look away.

"As you will soon see, the life you were given was given selfishly. This is not, and never will be, about you."

I place his words among the other memories in my head and nod deeply to him. Even as I dislike him, that strange intelligence in me tells me this, too, is accurate.

"I will take that advice in the spirit it was given," I say. The response once again falls from my tongue without conscious thought.

I watch his jaw slacken for half a breath before it then tightens enough that I wonder how he doesn't break a tooth. He growls out, "In that same spirit, I offer you a *gift* so you may not be unwillingly or unevenly *burdened* by one side in this."

As he states this, he places his left hand, palm up, on his knee. "Give me your hand," he orders.

Despite my misgivings, my instincts drive me, so with only a moment of hesitation, I place my hand in his.

He closes his eyes, and a sudden slash of pain radiates from both of my shoulder blades. My vision darkens for a moment, and when it clears, I understand I must have fallen to my knees. My hand is no longer in his.

As the pain courses through my upper back with willpower alone, I stand again. As I do so, blackness briefly tries to fill my vision, but I don't need to be able to see to hear him as he says, "Bring her to a mirror, Bonum, so she may see the beauty of this gift *I* have bestowed upon her. Then take her home so she can begin to figure out her role in this world."

Rex's voice is as strong as ever. However, as I blink the darkness from my eyes, I see that he looks pale, and there is sweat upon his brow. I turn to Bonum, only wobbling slightly as the pain continues to recede, and they lead at that same quick pace out of the room.

I can't help but mouth, "ass," under my breath as I follow.

Bonum leads me back through the same path, but after a bit turns, down a different hallway. We walk through a doorway into a much less bright room. There are benches and mirrors arranged around the edges.

I move forward without bidding to catch sight of myself in the reflective surface and can't withhold a gasp. Protruding from behind my shoulders are wings just like the angels have.

I twist my body side to side, admiring them despite myself as Bonum stares blankly, straight ahead.

As I regard them in the mirror behind me, their eyes move up towards, but still through, where my face is, and they rasp, "The nickname has become more fitting."

I feel another chill run down my spine as their mouth smiles without their eyes changing.

"Come," they order as they turn and walk away, and again I rush after them.

Moving along more quickly than is comfortable for my injured leg, we soon stand in front of a carriage. This time I climb in of my own accord and settle on the seat. I lean back before thinking and feel a modicum of surprise as the pressure of the seat does nothing to change the pain in my back.

As we travel, I find myself replaying the conversation with the other angel. I look at Bonum, who is once again sitting with a hood over their head, their face hidden in shadow. "Was that your leader?" I ask, my voice higher than I'd like it to be.

Without moving anything else, they nod their head once.

I hesitate, unsure if even talking to them carries a risk of some sort that I can't yet see or understand.

As I'm grappling with those thoughts, they rasp out, "That was Rex, the High Leader. As the leader of this world, he is also your leader, little bird." I can feel their eyes on me despite not being able to see their features beneath the shadows of the hood.

Even as I file that away, I find my mouth betraying me. "Rex is kind of an ass," I say. As the words leave my lips, I wish I could take them back.

I wait for some blow to fall, but instead a single snort sounds from beneath the hood. Thankful I'm still alive, I pinch my mouth shut and look at the wall of the carriage opposite me until its movement grows still.

Once the carriage stops, Bonum moves smoothly out the door and, without turning in my direction, holds out a hand. I exit the carriage without taking it, but my injured leg doesn't move as smoothly as I'd like. Stumbling forward, I roughly grasp their hand as I descend. I expect some admonishment, but they say nothing; instead, they continue forward towards the mansion. I follow once again as they stride up to the doors. There they pause and, reaching out, grasp my arm as they open the door.

As they bring me into my room and press me back towards my bed, I, for the first time, ignore their orders and remain standing.

They snarl at me, a raspy, dry sound like dead leaves skating over the pavement of the street. Then they press on my chest again. "I won't have us discovered this way," they rasp.

As I consider whether to obey, I reflect on the strange feeling, as though I'm playing some part in a large theater production without understanding the plot or my role. While I stand frozen, still not wanting to follow the orders of someone I don't trust, a knock sounds on the door. They press more firmly, and despite myself, I relent, climbing into bed. I settle back, mostly under the sheets, dirtying the bed with feet that have tread bare over city streets.

Bonum turns to the door and, in a voice that is not their own and far too pleasant for my liking, calls, "Please come in."

As the door opens, they are already re-bandaging my leg, which I notice has bled through its prior wrapping. The blood is thankfully a bright crimson now instead of black.

I note that Fem is in the room with us before I close my eyes and lay my head back on the pillow. I'm not tired, but the room is spinning slightly. I hear Fem talking quietly with Bonum, but can't, or don't care to, make out the words they are speaking.

THE CALM BEFORE THE STORM

I wake and feel a sudden sense of relief as I realize I'm looking at the ceiling of my own room. I'm thrown for a minute, not remembering why I should be relieved to be in my own space. Then I remember the events of the day before.

I push myself up and pull back the blankets to inspect my injured leg. It is again wrapped in a fresh bandage, and there is no trace of blood. Something tells me to remain in bed, but I am quickly becoming restless with the recent lack of free will, so I push myself out from under the covers and onto the floor.

My face contorts with pain as I put weight on my leg. However, after a moment and a breath, I'm capable of moving to the small attached bathroom. I tend to my needs, remove the silky shift I am wearing, and clean myself as well as I can with a cloth and the sink. I pay particular attention to cleaning the dirt from the prior day's adventures off my feet.

On a small shelf, I find a few nondescript bottles and a brush. I pull the brush through my hair, flinching as I catch on the multitude of tangles in the waves of pink. Once my hair is untangled, I reach up and somehow twist it against the nape of my neck. My hands act without conscious thought, which is something I'm beginning to become uncomfortably familiar with. I find a couple of silver pins, which I knew were on the shelf from my previous exploration, and pin my hair.

Still looking in the mirror, I sigh at my mismatched eyes and the bright shadow wings now protruding from behind my shoulders. However, there is nothing to be done about either, so I turn back towards the bedroom.

Walking to the closet, I sort through and find a pair of leggings that I pull on. They're mostly black with a few white and red swirls in a strange pattern down the side of the left leg from hip to knee. I also pull on a loose tunic that is a smoky grey. The back is lower than the front, and the sleeves are long enough to hang over my hands. My body thus hidden, I head towards the door.

As I get there, the knob moves as though of its own accord, and I brace myself, those thoughts of where to find a weapon renewing themselves feverishly in my head.

As I instinctively ready myself to disable whoever walks through the door, instead, I catch sight of Fem. He seems both surprised to see me outside of the bed and surprised to see whatever expression must be on my face. I pull myself back from whatever ledge I was about to leap from and walk forward and past him into the rest of the house.

He's surprised enough that I get nearly past him before he reaches out to take my arm.

I pull it roughly from his grasp as I say, "What?" in a voice that sounds strangely like a blade being removed from a sheath.

His eyes widen further as he says, "I was just coming to check on you. You shouldn't be up yet." His voice is steady, but I can see how off balance he is.

That strange intelligence in me seems to be running figures instead of emotions, and it causes me to hesitate. My voice is softer as I respond, "I just don't know why you would send an angel healer to me after what happened."

Fem is frozen for a few breaths, looking at me strangely. "What?" he finally asks, looking surprised.

"Why would you send an angel to care for me after I had just killed one of their kind?" I hear the steel sound back in my voice.

Both of us stand frozen, neither moving nor likely breathing. The room feels strangely still, like there is an energy that is hesitant to break us free from this spell. Unsure what else to do, I begin to look for answers amongst all the chaotic memories in my head. Suddenly, a door opposite my room opens roughly, running into the wall behind it, and Reem and Lent enter this space, caught in some argument.

They don't seem to see us and continue to argue, their voices loud in the space, blind to all else but their disagreement.

Looking at them with narrowed eyes, Fem hesitates. Then he looks back at me as he says, "We'll talk about this later."

What I see on his face as he speaks to me isn't apology, shock, or horror. Instead, his expression is more akin to sadness, and I pause, again wondering what great plot line to my own life I'm not understanding.

Fem moves towards the others and says wearily, "What now?"

Reem and Lent are pulled from their blindness back into the world as they notice Fem and me.

"Should she be up yet?" Reem asks, looking at me.

Fem half shakes his head, "We'll talk about it later, but what are you arguing about now?" he repeats himself.

I'm desperately clutching at plot threads for what my next action should be. *Is it so normal to be provided with a healer who was on the side so recently involved in violence? Do they wonder why I have wings of light protruding from my back? Can they even see them? Are these things so normal to those who live in this world, and is it just me that is off balance?*

My attention is then pulled back to the boys' conversation as

Reem says, "That's it, we're holding an audition for a singer. I know you can sing Lent, as can I, but that doesn't mean we *should*. Nor does it mean any of us has the talent to be lead."

As Reem speaks, Lent holds his hands up as though surrendering.

I note that Fem smirks slightly at both of them.

"Next thing we know, Fem will want to audition for the part," Lent says with a laugh.

At that, Fem's face goes red, but he doesn't say anything.

"Alright, old boy, as you say, it shall be so," Lent says to Reem as though he didn't notice Fem's reaction. "If I may ask, though, are we to get on the road to complete our errands, or may I take a nap?"

"*Gods* Lent," Fem says, "I'm the one who's supposed to always be sleeping. What's with you?"

"It's all these late-night *sessions*," Lent says with a yawn.

With his mouth still open, Reem punches him hard in the shoulder and shakes his head slightly. Lent snaps his jaw shut and looks at me. With that motion, I note that there is something they don't want me to find out about the "late night sessions." As with many things, I note it for later.

"What errands?" I ask, irritation filling my voice. Luckily, more than thinking me an ungrateful guest, they seem relieved that my question is about errands and nothing else.

"We will be having the auditions in the basement of a small shop a short distance away," Reem says. "We need to bring some of our things from here to that shop and get set up. Since the band is well known, we expect many people will want to audition. We'll need some basic refreshments and seating for ourselves and those auditioning."

"I'll help," I offer quietly. Anything to get out of this house and relieve my boredom.

Even as I say it, Fem is shaking his head. "You're not yet

healed enough to help with this. You'll stay here with our employed help after I re-bandage your leg."

"My leg feels fine," I say.

"It's not only your leg that I'm worried about," Fem says.

"Then what?" I ask, and I hear the steel back in my voice

"Your recovery seems to be impacted, perhaps by the pain meds," Fem says. His voice is now soft. An attempt, however late, at kindness.

As I glare at him, Reem puts his hand on Fem's arm and pulls him aside. While they talk, I muse about what he might mean. Do the pain meds slow healing? Even as I consider, they turn back towards me. It's clear that whatever Fem was feeling about my recovery, he has shared it.

Reem stands, arms crossed against his chest, looking irritated.

Without further explanation of what's happening, Fem says, "I'll re-bandage your leg. If the wound is healing well, you may accompany us tonight. If your leg doesn't look healed enough, you will agree to stay here."

The order is clear in his voice, and without hesitating, I agree.

Fem nods and says, "Come with me," as he walks out of the room.

I follow him to a room I haven't been in yet that resembles some sort of office. There is a large desk along one wall, and bookshelves line that wall and two others from floor to ceiling. Along the fourth wall, there's a large couch.

"Sit," he says, nodding to the couch.

I sit myself at the edge of the large piece of furniture and watch as he pulls a small, structured bag out of the desk. He carries it over to the table in front of the couch and sets it down. He then turns on a lamp near the center of the room and brings it close to us.

"Sit back and set your leg here," he says as he gestures towards the edge of the couch near him.

I oblige and watch as he gently unwinds the bandage.

He works in silence for a few minutes and then, glancing briefly up at me through his eyelashes, says, "I can tell you still think the healer was an angel."

"I don't *think* anything," I say with a tight voice. "The healer was an angel."

Fem shakes his head slightly.

"Even if the healer wasn't human, which he was, angels don't work as healers," he says.

"I know what I saw," I say, and he's quiet again.

I focus back on the work he's doing, careful to keep myself from showing the pain on my face as he inspects the gash on my leg.

"While it would be fun to think so," he says, his voice lilting in a way that makes my jaw clench, "no one has *actually* seen an angel in centuries. It is much more likely that the pain meds are messing with your head."

"What do they work as?" I ask.

He lifts his head, clearly surprised by my question.

He pauses for long enough that I'm caught off guard when he responds.

"According to the histories that Lent is always talking about, if there were to be a non-human healer, it would be a demon. We suspect there may still be angels placed in high-level government positions. However, we have no proof of that."

After a few more minutes, Fem says evenly, "Your leg seems to be healing well." He looks up then, meeting my eyes again. "You will accompany us, but if you attempt any physical activity or don't obey orders, we will have someone bring you back here."

He pats my knee gently as he pushes himself to his feet, turns off the light, and returns the medical kit to its place.

"Come on," he says as he leaves the room, and I push myself up and follow him.

As we return to the main living space, I see that the others have gathered their things, and the house staff are again helping to pack the carriage.

"Get your shoes on and meet us out front," Reem says in passing, his voice still rough with frustration. Whether at me or Fem, I can't quite tell.

I go to my room, careful to disguise my remaining limp, and pull on a short pair of boots that won't press on my wound. I also gather a cloak, remembering the chill in the air from the day before. As I leave my room, instincts pull at me to bring a weapon, but because I don't have access to one, there's nothing for it at this moment.

I leave my room and catch sight of Lent standing near the front door. He gestures for me to hurry. I follow him through the door and to a large carriage.

I settle myself onto the seat as the boys continue to discuss plans, such as what type of voice or person they think will fit into the band. Thankfully, I have a window, and as we rush past buildings and other carriages, I note that it seems to be early evening. The smoke is as thick in the air as it's been, and an occasional raindrop falls, painting across the windows of the carriage.

I note Lent looking out the window, and he catches my attention and gestures with his head to the scene outside the carriage. "Lucky," he says, looking back at the occasional raindrops.

"What is?" I ask.

"The rain," he says as he looks at me. "Even those few drops are so rare it's a lucky thing on a day where we could really use the luck."

Before much time has passed, the carriage stops. Lent leaves to run an errand at a small shop while the rest of us remain behind. After that, there is one more shopping errand that Fem takes, and then we arrive at our final location.

When we come to a stop, I follow the boys out onto the street. I hear the horses snorting behind me, jumpy with the occasional raindrops hitting them. I want to go to them, but I've promised to obey, so instead I meekly follow the others.

Reem leads us around the front of the building into an alley and down some steps through a small side door. The space inside is dark with a few guttering sconces along the walls. The floor and lower part of the walls are a dark color, with the upper walls a lighter grey that seems to almost disappear behind the smoke that gathers at the edges of the room.

As I look around, I hear someone descending some stairs from behind me and turn to see an older, pot-bellied man emerge from a door. He looks around and, catching sight of Reem, holds out his hand, a smile on his face that I read to be fake.

"You've found the space, huh?" he says, his voice overly loud as they shake hands. "Make yourselves at home." He falters suddenly as he catches sight of me. "Who's this?" he asks as he focuses his attention on me in a way that makes me wish to reach for the weapon I don't have.

Instead, I carefully keep my face blank and not just of pain this time.

As I wonder what to say, Fem steps forward alongside me and says, "She's just a friend. I think we have everything we need here. We will fetch you if that changes."

Then, without saying anything further to the man, he turns to Lent and they begin to discuss details such as where people will sit and where we should set the refreshments. The man is undeterred for a moment by the dismissal, but then Reem begins to move towards the door. As he walks away from me, the man slowly follows, and I hear Reem say something about getting the place paid for. I can't hear what he says when the man responds.

Shortly thereafter, when Fem moves to bring some things from the carriage, I see that it is just the four of us again. I release a breath I hadn't realized I was holding and then look around for something I can be useful with.

As though he can read my mind, Reem says, "Could you please set out the refreshments?"

I agree and begin organizing the pastries and small glass bottles of drinks along with piles of cups, plates, and cloth napkins.

The next hour flies by, and suddenly, people begin to arrive in the space. I move to the back of the room, sitting in a place where the shadows and smoke seem to dance between the scones of light. The crowd arranges itself in the main part of the room. Eventually, the boys get things organized, telling those who showed up to audition to take turns singing what they have prepared.

I watch as person after person goes to the platform at the front of the room and sings. They all seem to know the music, but I do not, at least not until today. Some of the music pulls at my emotions. Some of it does not.

There must have been over sixty people who showed up, and as about half remain, I locate a piece of paper and a charcoal pen and begin to sketch something to pass the time.

I'm midway through my sketch, which has slowly taken the shape of a horse, its mane caught in an active wind, when I hear something familiar.

> "I hear the knife pierce flesh and bone
> And gasp as though it were my own"

The sound of these familiar lyrics in a new voice pulls at me in a way that none of the others yet have. I look up and see a man with broad shoulders who is of average height. He has dark brown hair that is slightly wavy and falls just past his ears, kissing his wide cheekbones. His lips are full, and his face is broad and neatly shaven. His hair is neatly combed and contained somehow, but looks as though it would like to be messy. I would guess him to be a little older than the boys, maybe thirty.

He wears a button-up shirt with a tailored vest over it, his sleeves long and buttoned at his wrists. Even as I watch him, he tugs at a sleeve, as though attempting to further organize something which is already neat. He wears grey pants which are also impeccably tailored and fall to neat, shined shoes. A tattoo crawls up his neck on the right side, just revealing itself above his collar.

> "The pain of flesh doesn't bother me
> It's the pain of heart that's broken free"

I'm captured by this moment, his voice seeming to add some magic to this music, these words that I know. Even as I'm caught up listening and watching him, his focus seems to be caught fully within the music he sings. He arrives at the end of the song far too soon. Everything is silent for a few moments.

"Bold of you to sing that particular song," says Reem, but he's grinning as he says it. He gestures at the singer to sit in one of the chairs they've placed off to the side of the room.

There are only two others there, clearly those select few who will proceed. As the remaining ten or so singers complete the process, I go back to finishing my drawing, occasionally glancing up at the small group of those selected, my attention drawn to the neatly dressed man as he waits and watches the others perform.

In the end, only four singers remain. As I wonder what might happen next, the boys stand up and proceed to the platform, where they begin to set up instruments and other band clutter. While I may be naive to this process, the band and the singers seem familiar with it.

As they finish setting up, the boys point to one of the four singers who moves to the platform with them. They begin to play another song, this time accompanying the singer who is auditioning.

That singer does a good job, and now that the full band is playing, I find myself swept up with the music again, my drawing forgotten. They choose another singer at random and go back through the same song. It's both the same and different, and as I tease apart the small differences, I understand how difficult it would be to choose. That singer finishes and leaves the platform, and they choose another, this one the singer who caught my attention earlier.

I attempt to begin a new drawing so as not to be tempted to stare, but fail as soon as he stands. I watch him as he moves to the stage. His movements are controlled in a way that tells me he knows how to fight. As he stands in front of the band, they start up again, and when he opens his mouth, my drawing is quickly forgotten.

My attention narrows to only the music, truly only the singer. His voice is something entirely different than the others, and even though they didn't sound bad, they didn't sound like this. Again, before I'm ready, the music ends, and everything is silent for a few moments before Lent calls out something which must be the name of a different song.

The band launches into another set of words and music, and again, I'm captured and pulled out of this world that we live in.

As this song finishes and the silence fades, the boys step forward, surrounding the singer. Their excitement is infectious, and as they celebrate and embrace him, the remaining three singers read the room and leave out the side door without comment.

Suddenly unwilling to remain where I am, I move forward towards the stage. Standing closer, I hear him introduce himself as Dio. They're asking him questions about who he's sung with, where he's from, and so on.

One question seems out of place, and that is, "What industry do you work in?" Or perhaps the question doesn't seem out of place, but the answer does, as I hear him say, "Oh, I don't work in industry, I adore the trees."

Even more out of place, the boys move on as though he hadn't said something that sounded suspiciously like code.

"Have a seat for a minute," says Reem.

Dio leaves the stage and walks to the chairs at the side of the room, not seeming to notice me.

"Can we help you, Chaosta?" Fem asks, and they all look at me, where I'm standing nearly directly in front of them now.

I freeze under the sudden attention and just shake my head.

"Please go clean up the food and drinks, and we'll be done here soon," Reem says to me.

I go to do so and momentarily make eye contact with Dio. I can't read the emotion on his face, but his expression is hard, and I feel him staring at me as I go to begin cleaning up the remaining refreshments.

Once or twice, as I work at my assigned task, I catch sight of him and note that he continues to stare at me. His expression seems to judge me without yet knowing anything about me.

As I clean up, helping myself to a pastry that tastes like heaven itself, I continue to feel his eyes on me. The hair on the back of my neck raises under his scrutiny. What began as admiration for his voice quickly turns into annoyance at being caught in his scornful gaze.

As I'm nearly done with my task, I hear the boys welcome Dio to the band.

I gather up my drawing and remain at the back of the room again as they, all four of them now, clear the rest of the room.

Once everything else is gathered, Fem fetches me and leads me out to the carriage. As I dutifully follow him, we pass the others who are finalizing plans for Dio to move into the mansion. My chest grows tight for a moment as I imagine this judgmental stranger moving into the place that is slowly beginning to become my home.

On the trip back, just the four of us in the carriage, the boys are fairly quiet. Occasionally, interrupting the silence, they discuss rehearsal plans and tease Fem about when he's going to write more songs. I sit silently watching out the windows into the near black, still reeling from the feeling of Dio's eyes on my back.

DARK FIGURES

The following day, when I arrive in the dining room for breakfast, I belatedly realize it's actually lunch and I must have slept in.

Only Lent and Reem are here. Lent has his nose buried in a book, and Reem offers me a plate of food and a cup of coffee. I start to decline before he says, "Lent made it," his voice thick with a grumble.

I take the cup and swallow a sip before smothering my bread in gravy. I eat slowly, still thinking through the events of the day before. Dio's voice and the cryptic sentence, along with the feeling of his pointed glare, run on repeat in my head.

After a bit, Fem joins us, filling his plate at the sideboard. We all eat without speaking in a silence that is still companionable.

Eventually, Fem stands and says, "Let's get your bandage changed."

I rise and follow him to the office. As he gathers the healing kit from the desk, I settle on the couch, the same as the night before. He makes quick work of it in silence this time.

I remain quiet until he moves to put the healing kit away,

and then finally ask the question that's been pressing at me for the past several days. "Where can I get a sword?"

His shoulders tighten. "Why would you want one?" he asks as he turns back to me.

"So that I can defend myself if I'm attacked again."

His face gets stormy as he says, "The crowd didn't attack you; they got rough and you were injured. It's on our shoulders that you were where you shouldn't be. It would be irresponsible of us to allow you to have a weapon at all, much less around a crowd at one of our concerts like that."

The breath freezes in my lungs as I realize the boys believe I was hurt by the crowd and not in a sword fight with an angel. An angel whom I ended up killing. Now that I think of it, the death of which should have been shouted across the city.

I suddenly remember Fem telling me that no one has seen an angel in years, and I feel as though puzzle pieces are falling into place in my head. I have questions, but I can tell this isn't the place or time to ask them. Instead, I focus on the reason for the other spike of irritation in me and ask, "Do you really think I would hurt someone in a crowd like that? Someone who doesn't intend to hurt me?" The steel sound is back in my voice.

"I doubt you've ever *intended* to hurt anyone," he says. His voice is soft, but there is an element of coldness to the words.

I'm filled with so much anger suddenly that I can't speak, the strength of the emotion freezing me so completely that I can't seem to locate any of the knowledge available to me in my compendium of a brain.

As though belatedly realizing that perhaps he took this too far, Fem sighs and bites his lip. "If we bring you to a concert again, we'll bring one of the house staff to stay with you," he says as though that solves everything. He certainly seems to consider it solved as he turns and leaves.

I'm left standing in the office by myself, my rage swirling around me not unlike the constant clouds of smoke. As I try to gain some control over my anger, the only thing I can think to do is leave this house and the stifling behavior of the only people I know.

I stride to my room, thankful the boys don't seem to be around. I grab a cloak and stuff my feet in some boots and make my way back to the front door. I truly expect to run into one of them at some point. If I do, I'm sure they'll try to stop me, but none of them show themselves, and soon I'm outside.

As I approach the street, I pause as two carriages rush past, the wind of their movement toying with tendrils of my hair and tossing them into my face. I pause for a moment. Now that I'm outside, I can think more clearly, but without anger driving me, I'm suddenly stuck in indecision.

Finally, I decide to go to the only place I know how to get to on foot and head towards the small book shop I visited with Lent. I retrace my steps carefully. Unfortunately, a map of the city doesn't roll itself out for me in my head.

"Of all the things that would be useful," I grumble out loud to myself.

I stick carefully to the walking path on the side of the streets so I don't get flattened by one of the fast-moving carriages. Thankfully, before much time has passed, I arrive at the front of the bookshop.

As I enter the small shop, a bell chimes above my head. The musty smell of books surrounds me, and I enter the maze of bookshelves, looking for the counter and shop owner. I wind through the books, titles, and spines catching my attention as I walk. Without thinking, I pull a couple off the shelf and, tucking them under my arm, bring them with me.

Eventually, I locate the shopkeeper at the center of the store and lay my books down on the counter.

He looks at the books. Idly, I notice that he doesn't seem to see the wings of light. "Interesting choices there, young one," he says. "Do I remember you?"

"I was here a few days ago," I say. Then, without a pause, I listen to the strange instinct driving me and ask, "Where do you keep the books on angels?"

I catch his eyes widening momentarily before his face resumes its impassivity. Then, without further comment, he gestures at me to follow as he heads into the maze behind the counter. I stay close behind him, careful not to trip on the piles of books on the floor. It seems to be overflow storage for the countless books in this place. Eventually, the narrow pathways open up into a small room with walls lined with bookshelves.

"This is the section you're looking for," the little man gestures. I see that above the shelf is a sign that identifies this as the *History* section.

"Anything in particular I can help you find?"

I decline his help, again driven by something I don't quite understand. He leaves with a slight shake of his head.

Left to locate something I don't know how to look for, I begin at the bottom shelf on the left. I scan the spines of the books, reading titles in languages that mostly seem to be familiar. There are many books on historical events and the government. It's not until I get to the middle of the sixth or seventh bookshelf that I find something.

This book is unassuming, grey, and small with black letters on the spine that spell *Ali D'Angelo*. I remove the book and flip through the pages. There are many drawings and illustrations, most of which make little to no sense to me. However, toward the back of the book, I see drawings of the wings I'm familiar with. Those same wings that emerge from my shoulders when I look at myself in a mirror.

There are words beneath the drawings, but I don't understand their meaning. The strange instincts and map in my brain don't seem to understand either at this moment. Despite that, I know I need it, so I close the book and take it back to the counter along with one other history book that stood out.

Without looking at me, the tiny shopkeeper pulls out the other books I left, and I add these two books to the top of the pile. He takes them and tucks the books into a small canvas bag.

Turning to me, he says, "That will be twenty-three coppers."

"Please put it on The Boys' tab," I say with a confidence I do not feel.

His eyes widen further and stay that way. "This is highly unusual. I really need their approval, miss."

"You're welcome to get it."

He stares at me and then, as though realizing that I mean he can go check with them himself, he says, "Ok, alright, I mean if they have an issue with it they can take it up with you?"

"That will suffice," I say firmly.

He goes to a drawer in the back to make a note. With that recorded, he asks, "Anything else?"

I shake my head, and he wishes me a good day. Thus dismissed, I leave the shop and head back to the mansion.

When I get back, I kick off my boots and head straight to the office for the other book that my instincts are suddenly drawing me to. I find it easily on the same shelf where I'd subconsciously seen it previously. I tuck it into the canvas bag with the others and head back to my room.

As I leave the office, I catch something at the edge of my vision. Turning towards the front door I see movement through the window set in the door. As I go to investigate, my hand wrapped around the handle of the bag, ready to use it as a weapon if needed, the door opens, and Malam steps through it.

We freeze simultaneously, eyeing each other. I see him note the bag in my hand and relax it to my side.

"What are you doing, Chaosta?" he asks. His voice is guttural and dangerous, but no more than usual.

Those black shadow wings stand out from his shoulders. As I see them, I think of my own wings of light. At that moment, he tenses as he looks past my face to either side of my shoulders.

Then, with a growl, he grabs my arm and pulls me into the office. He drags me into the middle of the room roughly, towering over me, his grip bruising on my arm.

"What happened?" he asks, and his voice is now surprisingly gentle, at odds with his behavior.

I attempt to shake him off and, despite my small size and lack of weapons, he releases me and stands back. "You can see them?" I ask, slightly breathless.

He stares at me for a moment and then nods, his face still a mask of some strong emotion.

Is it rage?

"The boys don't seem to be able to see them," I finally say.

"Humans aren't observant enough to see angels or demons unless we specifically allow them to, as I have," he growls. "I will ask again, what happened to you?"

"The healer the boys brought me was an angel, and that angel brought me to talk to one of their kind named Rex."

"And?" he asks, his voice more of a snarl at this point.

"Rex gave me the wings as a gift to ensure I wasn't burdened by the darkness," I respond.

"And are you *burdened* by the darkness?" he asks, his voice far too quiet.

"I'm not sure yet." I stare back at him.

I watch as his shoulders tense at the words and then, closing his eyes, he reaches up and pinches his nose between his thumb and forefinger. I hear him muttering something, the words of which are mostly lost to me. The only thing I hear is, "...measuring contest will get us nowhere," and then he drops his hand to his side and looks at me again.

"Did you get the name of the *healer*?"

"They were called Bonum."

He flinches slightly and then nods. "I see," he says and then grows quiet for a moment.

"Why are you here?"

"I was summoned," he says.

"By me?"

He shakes his head and says, "The band. For them, it's a ritual that takes at least six hours; they can't bring me instantly like you can." Then, as he takes a breath, I see a shudder run through him, and he says, "I am compelled again to join their company." With that, he turns and walks towards the back of the mansion.

I follow, but as he arrives at a door I don't recognize, he turns to me suddenly, so I stop too close. Rather than step back, I hold my ground, looking up at his face and meeting his light green eyes.

He peers down at me, unreadable emotions burning across his face. "It is up to you to determine what must be done, as that is the contract I created when I gave you life. I know one of my people spoke with you about what we stand for when you were at our stronghold. Just know that I feel my kind are more in need of help, and quickly. I only ask that you review all before you act."

With that, he turns and, opening the door, steps through and closes it before I can follow.

As some strong emotion runs through me, I look down and see my fists clenched, the bag hanging from my left, the books momentarily forgotten.

A map, although not the useful one I looked for earlier, reveals itself in my head with two paths extending. One path leads me into my room for an afternoon of research and reading, the images from the book playing in my memory.

The other...

Even as I think of it, I decide.

I quickly go to my room, set the bag of books beneath my bed where the house employees won't quickly find it, and go to the wardrobe. I choose a skirt and leggings in black and dark grey, and pull on black socks. I slip a dark, hooded, long-sleeved shirt over my head, pull the hood up to cover my hair, and then examine myself in the mirror.

Only a glimmer from my eyes looks back at me from beneath the hood. Everything else is cloaked in shades of darkness. Thus attired, I return to the door to the lower level and follow Malam's footsteps into the dark.

DARK FIGURES AND RITUALS

As I delicately push the door open, I see the familiar set of stairs leading down. The same stairs where I fell asleep listening to the band rehearse. With only a brief hesitation, I proceed down the steps into the pitch black. As I continue, I begin to hear the low hum of voices and pause for a moment. Focusing on where the sound is coming from, I see a line of light near the floor, rising up in a thin L shape. I step closer, careful to move slowly and purposefully so as not to give myself away.

As I get nearer, I can pick out specific voices. Malam's guttural, deep tones, Fem's voice a rich, dark sound, Lent soft and mid, Reem's throaty and light, and finally the most unfamiliar, which must be Dio. His voice is a low, rich tone, at odds with the way he sang.

As I hear him speaking, I feel my shoulders tighten at the memory of the way he looked at me after he auditioned. I pull myself away from that feeling and focus on the words they are speaking.

Malam's voice says, "You will tell me why there is a fourth." His voice is a low hiss.

Reem says, "Dio auditioned and is part of the band."

"Yes, but that doesn't explain why he's here."

Fem begins to say, "He—"

Malam cuts him off. "He'll speak for himself."

There is silence for a moment, and then Dio says, "I've been against the government and all their policies since I was—"

"With who your parents are, I find that highly unlikely." Malam's voice is stony, and as I risk a glance through the crack in the door, I see his back. The boys stand beyond him, facing him and the door I stand behind. His whole body is tense as though he's nearly ready to turn and leave the room.

I prepare to hide, noting a small cubby alongside the stairs.

As I risk another glance, I see Dio move closer to Malam, his eyes on Malam's face. Even from here, I can almost feel the clash of their gazes like blades in a silent swordfight.

"You don't need to believe me for it to be true, *demon*," Dio says.

I step back, careful to be quiet, ready for Malam to come through the door at any moment. There is a lengthy pause in the room, and I stay still, my heart pounding, listening for movement.

Then Dio's voice, a deep growl, says, "Who my parents are is immaterial to this discussion. Just because they were aligned with our political leaders doesn't mean I follow in their footsteps. Early on, I was able to think for myself and felt strongly that what they were doing wasn't right. All that money doesn't come from something good. When they died and deeded me their estate, I accepted it and began investing and involving myself in anti-government actions."

Dio pauses, and there is silence in the room. After a few minutes, he continues. "Starting many years ago, I learned about dark magic from a friend, and since then, I've been a solo practitioner. I was introduced to your ethos several years ago by those I met in my practice of magic. The guys from the band saw my tattoos and thought to ask. When I explained my background, they invited me here."

Another pause, then Dio says, "I'll learn from you if you'll allow it, but if not, I'll continue as I have."

Silence falls over the room again.

Finally, I hear Malam's voice say, "Let's see them then."

I hear a quiet rustle and again peer through the crack in the door in time to see Dio finish unbuttoning his shirt. He removes it carefully, folding it over one arm.

Tattoos twist around his torso, arms, and up his neck in shapes I can't untangle. Every part of his abdomen and upper arms is covered in ink. It's not just tattoos, though. From what I can see, there are also multiple scars cutting across skin that covers corded muscles. By his build and neat, controlled movements, I am again confident he's either skilled at fighting or dancing, perhaps both.

Malam steps forward and runs his fingers over the twisted shape of a tattoo that travels from Dio's collarbone to the bottom of his ribs on his left side. I wouldn't have noticed that shape amongst the other twisting lines. Malam, though, has clearly identified it as something specific. As his fingers near Dio's last rib, he pauses. From his body language, I can tell he looks back up, meeting Dio's eyes.

They both remain there, still for a moment, and then Malam steps back and, in a quieter voice, says, "Put your shirt back on. We will begin."

With that, Malam moves deeper into the room beyond what I can see from the door, and the boys follow him. Dio pulls his shirt back on and begins to button it as he joins the others.

I step back from the door, trying to process what I just watched. When I close my eyes, the shape that Malam traced on Dio's chest is visible as though it's been burnt into my memory.

As I think through everything I just saw, breathing as quietly as I can, something catches my attention. A low murmur increases in sound until I can hear chanting. I clench my hands in fists, unable to see what's going on because of the placement of the narrow crack in the door.

Finally, unable to remain patient any longer, I push at the door trying to widen the crack so I can see more of the room. For a moment, I think I might succeed at my goal. Then the traitorous hinges let out the slightest, high creak of the ungreased. I freeze in the darkness, holding my breath. Moments pass, and the chanting continues, low and guttural from the other room, and I let out my breath.

I am not unwise, however, and having already nearly given away my presence, I know better than to tempt fate again. Instead, I turn and head back up the stairs, moving carefully to avoid any further incident. I pass through the door at the top of the stairs and push it closed.

My heart rate is returning to normal, and the door is nearly latched when resistance meets my palm. I'm pushed back roughly into the room as Dio steps out from behind it. There is a wild storm of emotion across his face. I smell a coppery tang clinging to him.

He looks at me as he gets through the door, and his expression darkens. "I knew I heard something," he grinds out through a clenched jaw.

I'm trembling slightly, my hands in fists and chest heaving.

He shoves his hands into his pockets and regards me with a sneer. "Why are you spying?" he snarls.

I remain frozen, and after a few breaths, he steps forward with another snarl. "You will tell me."

"I don't know why you are so angry. I was just curious what you were doing," I grit out. Anger is crashing through me at the way he is treating me.

"I'm angry because I recognize what you are, and this behavior is unacceptable."

That strange intelligence must have understood something

that my own mind has not yet because, before I recognize them, words emerge from my lips. "And you want to control me? You want me to just go away? What is it you see in me that is making you so angry?"

He takes another step towards me, his whole body shaking. He pulls his hands out of his pockets and clenches them into fists at his sides as he snarls at me, louder this time. "I see a spoiled brat with an addiction who, through her actions, is endangering the people who are trying to help."

My chest heaves, "Addiction?" I splutter out, "What does that even mean?"

Dio throws his hands in the air in a wild gesture as a mirthless laugh leaves his chest. "What a surprise. She denies it," he says as he takes another step towards me.

I remain in place as he closes the distance between us. My feet are still, but my brain is running, trying desperately to understand the meaning of the words he is throwing at me. They feel like knives despite my lack of understanding. I know it's important for me to figure it out if I have any chance of survival in this sudden and unexpected battle.

Of course, my brain chooses this particular, clearly important detail to not understand. The strange intelligence granted to me by the little boy, which has led me through so many important and mundane interactions in this world so far, doesn't help with this.

"Look, just like a good addict when confronted, she doesn't have anything to say," Dio spits at me.

My body does what I tell it, which is nothing, and stands still in the same spot as he closes in and stands directly in front of me. My chest is tight, breathing is difficult, and despite the absence of physical pain, my eyes begin to water.

Suddenly unable to deal with the feelings in my body, I spin and walk quickly, nearly run, away from Dio. I go to my room, the only sanctuary I can think of at the moment.

"I'd recommend you stay in there until we decide what to do with you," says Dio, darkly from behind me.

I break into a real run until I crash through the door to my room and slam it closed.

I don't understand Dio's anger. He caught me watching something private, but his emotion seems too violent for that alone. Tears slide down my cheeks from the brutal interaction.

After a few moments, I give up trying to understand and decide to ask one of the much more reasonable boys about what "addict" means when I see them. With that decided, I scrub the tears from my face. I grab the bag with the books out from beneath my bed and settle myself across the covers. Then I spread the books around me and begin looking through them, still battling tears as I attempt to read.

*H*ours pass as I work to gather more knowledge of angels to fill in the continued gaps in my understanding.

As I read the history book I purchased, I discover that angels ruled openly in the past. The writer credits them for developing an effective and successful system of government that has led to many decades of prosperity. I read that the population increased to such an extent that, as of the publication of this book, one large city covers the entire world. My stomach twists, a sick feeling filling me as I think of it; however, the author seems to feel this is an acceptable cost of progress and prosperity.

The book also postulates that there may still be some angels in high levels of government. However, it seems that no one has proven the theory. As I consider, I picture Rex sitting on the dais. In my mind's eye, I can also see all of the angels that were in that space when Bonum brought me before the High Leader.

Eventually, though, I can remain awake no longer and sleep claims me.

* * *

I dream of dark figures chanting in a guttural language. There is a spark of something directly in front of me, and the outline of a face is revealed behind it in the momentary light. The light flashes again, and I feel as though I recognize the face, but I don't know from where. As I try in vain to search for the memory, the chanting increases in volume.

I hear an intake of breath and then someone says, "You didn't need to cut that deep, fuck that hurt."

The light flashes again, and this time catches. In the light, I see I'm standing behind a torch outside a circle of men. In the center, one of the figures moves, drawing a shape in blood on the ground in the center of a circle of arranged plant stems.

As I watch, the figure completes the shape, stands, and returns to the other shadowed men. As they all clasp hands and step backwards to the edge of their reach, a heavy, soaking rain begins to fall. In that moment, the dream changes, showing me a street littered with the bodies of angels, and heavy rain falling around me.

In my ear, Lent's voice says, "Even those few drops are so rare it's a lucky thing."

* * *

DIO'S JOURNAL - ENTRY 148

The following is an entry from one of many journals Dio shared with me. It is transcribed without any of my own edits and is a direct recounting of Dio's thoughts and feelings at the time he wrote it. I have notated this and other select entries to fill in gaps and provide another voice to the narrative I share with you, dear reader.

Annum:5614
Entry 148 - fiat

What a fucking mess. I finally find a group where I can perhaps be of some use. Maybe even fulfill some purpose, and their little charity case just has to meddle.

I recognized her for what she was at the audition. Her behavior was far too odd for her not to be a drug user. She kept standing and staring at the band, at me. Her face was nearly blank. She's this little waif-like thing, and her hair is fucking pink. I couldn't help but stare at her. Everything about her was screaming addict at me.

Then, to add to the dysfunction of it, I caught her spying on us. Of course, I lost my temper, wouldn't anyone if they caught some nosey girl spying on something so fucking important. We can't risk having her impact our livelihood or our work to fight back against our out-of-control government.

Anyway, I shouldn't even feel bad. Of course, she tried to manipulate me with her tears. What is an addict without their denial when confronted with the cold, hard truth. If not me, someone else would have called her out like this. She's lucky it was me because I know what I'm doing, and this is for her own good.

When I talked with the guys, I discovered that she's been a mess since they took her in. Even though the band was kind enough to give her a clean, warm place to stay, she's been difficult from the beginning. When I talked with them as I was moving in, they admitted they'd even bought her clothes, and they've been feeding her and providing medical care for her. Clearly, they're all too soft.

After I learned all that and caught her spying, I knew something needed to change. They just shouldn't be taking the risk. Still, it took me putting my foot down too damn firmly for them to see sense and agree to send her to a treatment center where she can actually get help. At least it took a lot of convincing with Lent and Fem. They both tried their best to defend her. Reem seemed to see the sense in this. I think he was already worried about the risk to the band.

In the end, though, reason won out with all of them as it always does. Really, it's the best thing for all of us. It's not like the other guys are truly experienced in helping someone recover from addiction.

I need to let that go, I guess, but it's tough when people I'm starting to let in made such a poor choice. Hopefully, those won't continue, or I might need to move on. It's so hard for me to trust others, especially in this particular area. I did set a clear boundary that I wouldn't be able to stay if we didn't send her somewhere that she could get help.

Also, I decided to pay for the treatment. It's not like the others are poor, but I have ample resources for something like this. If I'm going to align my actions with what I say is important to me, it's right for me to pay for her treatment. Call it a gift, a gift which is more than she deserves.

Of course, we're not sending her somewhere fancy, just clean and serviceable. I guess I knew something like this might happen when she caught my attention at my audition. In fact, after that night, when they told me how they'd found her and taken her in, I did some research and found a place with a good reputation that is nearby. It's not like I'm going to visit, but I guess the others can if they want.

We just put her in a carriage that will take her to Piquory Treatment Center. When we told her this morning, she cried and acted as though she didn't know what we were talking about. Just more manipulation, clearly. Fuck. I hate cleaning up other people's messes.

Thankfully, with that dealt with, we can get back to the important work of trying to even the stakes and give this world a fighting chance. I hadn't thought I was cut out for coven work, but it will be good to learn a new skill, and I'm happy to help however I can.

Our shit government isn't doing anything about any of the issues we currently face. Thankfully, this demon the other guys have been working with has a plan to fight back against our government. If we're going to see it through, we really need to make as much progress with our coven work and group magic as quickly as possible.

PART III

PIQUORY TREATMENT CENTER

T he carriage ride is a blur. Hours ago, when I arrived at
the breakfast table, it was clear something was wrong.
There wasn't any food set out, and yet all three of the
boys and Dio were standing in the back corner of the room.
Their words were too quiet for me to make them out. They
were so distracted they didn't seem to notice I was there until I
said something. When I asked about breakfast, they all turned to
me, their faces like different pieces in the same puzzle. In this
case, one that pictured dismay.

Well, that is, other than Dio, who just had a self-satisfied
expression on his face.

I froze for a moment, but then offered to get myself something to eat and began to make my way to the kitchen, carefully
ignoring the feelings in my stomach that were clearly not
hunger.

As I turned to leave, however, Fem told me to stop and sit. I
hesitated, partway out of the room, before I was able to make
my feet listen to orders and take me back to a chair at the table.

When I sat down and the boys began talking, though, I

hoped I was still in some dream. Although this dream was clearly a nightmare.

Dio and Fem led the conversation and shared with me that they had located a place for me to move to that would "help [me] recover from [my] addiction."

Even as I tried to ask what that meant, Dio became visibly frustrated and interrupted me.

I finally stopped trying. Clearly, whatever this thing is, it's common enough that everyone but me knows what it is.

Then they told me that the carriage was waiting outside and they would go with me to gather my things before I left.

While I put on my shoes, they were already packing clothes and things in a bag. I was too numb by that point to say anything else.

*P*ulling myself out of the memory of this morning, I turn and rest my forehead against the cool glass of the window in the carriage. There are two people with me. One who introduced herself as Ethel. Another man whose name I don't remember shared that he is a healer at the "Piquory Treatment Center."

Ethel has acted with kindness, but her words of comfort don't reach her eyes, and other than occasionally glancing at me and looking up and down my body, the healer doesn't say anything. He also regularly stares at my pink hair until I want to scream at him that I also don't know what to do about it.

I have just one bag with some clothes and one book I had previously left on the table beside my bed. I think Lent packed it for me because the clothes are thrown together chaotically, but the book speaks of someone kind who loves to read.

At this moment, it feels as though the only hope I possess is that the other books remain hidden in my room. Something in my head still urges me to review the knowledge in those books, and right now it feels like the only thing I have to hold onto.

Eventually, the carriage comes to a stop in front of one of the generic-looking buildings. The healer exits, and then Ethel ushers me out while the healer watches. I hear him speaking quietly with Ethel behind me before they both catch up.

Ethel and the healer guide me through an entrance area where a woman sits at a desk. After telling her my name, she does something with a terminal in front of her. Eventually, she hands the healer some paperwork.

"Already an order, is this right?" the healer asks as he reads over the piece of paperwork.

"That's what's documented," the woman behind the desk says with a shrug.

"Then I guess that's what we do," the healer says hesitantly as he takes the paperwork back. He glances at me briefly and then walks forward past the desk. Ethel presses on my shoulder to get me to follow.

The two of them guide me through a couple of hallways into a small room. There is a cot along the back and a small table with some drawers in the front corner. Ethel is holding my bag of items, and I note that she doesn't offer it to me.

The healer hands me a folded pile of clothing and says, "Change into this. I'll be back shortly."

They leave before I can ask for my things.

I close my eyes and try to stop the tears that still fall, but it's a useless endeavor. Instead, I do the only thing I can think of and follow the healer's orders, stripping out of my clothes and changing into the items he gave me. It turns out to be a shapeless, grey, short-sleeved top and loose pants with a tie at the waist in the same color. In the absence of anything else to do, I fold my clothes neatly and then sit back on the cot with my hands folded in my lap.

When I look at my hands, I can't help but remember

wielding the sword and the angel's blood dripping onto the street in front of me.

Then the door opens, pulling me from the memory as the healer walks into the room. He sets something down on the small table. As he does so, he says, "Good, at least you follow orders."

I look up at him, still trying to understand the circumstances I find myself in. He collects my items of clothing and puts them into a small bag.

"If you work hard, you will get these back at the end," he says.

Then he sets the bag on the ground and picks up the items he set on the table and holds them out to me. They turn out to be a cup of water and a small, shallow dish with several pills on it. The pills are different shapes and colors, and I find myself staring at them without moving. Belatedly, I realize he's speaking to me.

"Take the pills and swallow them," he says.

The silence presses on as I continue to stare at the pills in the dish.

"Are you able to understand me?" He looks at me harder and takes a step closer to me.

I halt him by finally making myself take the pills, deposit them in my mouth, and swallow them with the cup of water. One pill sticks in my throat, and I swallow harder. He remains where he is, watching me until I manage to swallow it. Then he turns and walks through the door. When it closes behind him, I lie back on the bed, my knees bent and feet resting on the mattress. With nothing else to do, I look at the ceiling.

Slowly, the room begins to spin, and I feel as though there is movement at the edges of my vision. I eventually comprehend that it must be the pills. At least the tears stop, and the ugly feeling in my stomach goes away. As the room spins, I find it's easier with my eyes closed, and with my body now relaxed, I fall into a restless but dreamless sleep.

*W*hen I wake, I'm not sure if I'm in a dream or not, as everything has a dreamlike quality. My ears ring, my vision is cloudy, and everything seems to move on its own.

The door opens, and I clench my eyes shut to keep from getting dizzy. I hear a voice but can't understand what they're saying. The noise of the voice stops, but there's a hand wrapped around my arm pulling me up and dragging me out of the room.

It's purely instinct that allows me to remain on my feet as the hand pulls me down a narrow space and into a larger open area. The larger room spinning undoes whatever control I have over my stomach, and I fall to my knees and vomit. The hand releases me, and I somehow identify disgust coming from whoever it belonged to.

I'm pulled up by my arm as soon as I stop vomiting and dragged to a soft surface, a couch, I think. I curl up on it, making myself as small as possible. I cling to the fabric covering it as I try not to get flung off the piece of furniture with the spinning of the room.

As time passes, the room continues to spin, but I begin to grow accustomed to it. I still curl in upon myself on the couch, but at times I'm able to open my eyes. The only thing that helps the nausea is keeping my eyes closed.

I note, fuzzily, that there must be others in this space. Sometimes voices are audible. Sometimes the voices are soft, sometimes loud, but I can rarely understand what they're saying. I'm not sure if I'm imagining them or if they are coming from the other figures moving around in the room. Then again, I'm pretty sure the table in front of the couch moves regularly of its own accord, so anything could be true.

. . .

*A*fter some additional time passes, more pills are given to me. I try to resist swallowing them this time. I'm not sure how I'll survive if the room continues spinning and the furniture keeps moving.

Instead of going away, though, two people roughly pin my arms to my sides and shove the pills in my mouth. They pour water down my throat while pinching my nose shut until I swallow. Tears slide down my cheeks.

A body leans against me, a mouth close to my ear. "Keep that up, and we'll just inject it into you," the voice says, and I choke down a sob.

More time passes, and I'm led, *dragged*, to a restroom. I relieve myself, clinging to the toilet to keep from falling. Then I'm brought to a room with a man in it who might be the healer who traveled here with me. He examines my leg and rewraps it in a fresh bandage. Then I'm taken to a small room that I vaguely recognize. I'm pushed flat onto a small, fairly soft surface. The lights go out, and I eventually lapse into a deep and yet restless sleep.

*T*hen it all repeats.
  The passage of time ceases to matter.

*A*fter some time passes, days, perhaps, or weeks, or even months, the spinning of the room becomes normal. So normal that I can walk on my own without being dragged by the people who work in this place.

After some time, the voices start to make some sense again, or at least I start to understand them.

After some time, they begin leading me to an office with a

person behind a desk before I go to my room for the night. The person behind the desk asks me questions while I sit in silence. Each time I see them, their questions get louder. Some part of me that's buried deep screams at me to keep my mouth shut and not respond. With nothing else to believe in, I listen to that voice.

*M*ore time passes, and I'm sitting on one of the couches in the big room. Two women whose voices I recognize are sitting at the other end of the couch and talking about a ghost they're acquainted with.

Another voice that doesn't have a body tries to tell me ghosts don't exist, but that's ridiculous, so I tell them to be quiet.

Then the women tell me to be quiet or I'll scare the ghost. I sit on my hands so I'm not tempted to speak again. I certainly don't want to scare the ghost. I learn from listening to the women that the poor ghost lost its hat, and I get up to help look for it.

My chest hurts as I worry that we might never find the hat, and I rub at the pain with one hand as I look around the room for where it might have been lost. I hear a voice with a body say something to me, but I don't listen. The hat is more important.

I blink, and then I'm on my knees on the ground near a couch that's not my couch. I reach under it with my left hand as my right hand tries to rub away the pain in my chest.

Poor ghost, there's no hat here.

I push myself to my feet and nearly run into a male body ahead of me. I'm looking around still, trying to figure out where the hat might be hiding.

The body moves away from me, the voice attached muttering an apology.

Remember not to speak and scare the ghost, I think to myself.

I look in the other direction, but as I turn my head, my

attention is caught by the body I nearly ran into. As it moves away. I see bright wings protruding from its back.

I blink.

I know it means something, but I'm not sure what that could be. Maybe that's what's making my chest hurt. Actually, maybe that's what scared the ghost away.

Poor ghost, I think as I launch myself at the body in front of me.

I collide hard against whoever it is, and we both fall, crashing through a table in the middle of the space. Purely by instinct, I have a piece of the table in my hand, and I stab at the body. It tries to roll me over, and I use all my strength and a nimbleness I shouldn't have in this fuzzy state to keep myself on top. I stab at the face as it watches me.

That will teach him to scare ghosts away.

I feel a sudden pain, and my body freezes up. I look down and think I see a blade in my stomach. I look back towards the face as I attempt to figure out what happened. As the face swims in my vision, I look down again, and there's no blade.

I blink.

The body forces me onto my back, pins my arms above my head, and the voice attached yells loudly.

"Help me! She's trying to hurt herself! Maybe trying to kill herself! Help me restrain her!"

Something about the words feels wrong, but maybe it's just because I'm worried about the ghost.

More bodies surround me, pinning me to the ground. There's pressure on my stomach and so much pain. I hear a voice screaming that sounds a lot like my own, and then blessedly everything goes dark.

DIO'S JOURNAL - ENTRY 160

Annum:5614
Entry 160 - serenus

Everything has been smoother since that girl left.
I'm getting to know the guys, and they've been great.
Other than being a little distracted about the girl, that
is. Actually, it's just Lent and Fem who seem distracted.
Reem has really thrown himself into the band now that
I've joined.

We have a concert scheduled soon, so we've been
rehearsing at all hours. I may be good at what I do, but
there is always an adjustment period when getting used
to a new band. The others are still figuring out how to
best accompany me, and that will take them some
time yet.

We've also been practicing our group magic work. At
some point, we will need to summon that demon again,

but for now, there is plenty the other guys can teach me about working as part of a coven. I'm also teaching them more about some of the rare runes I know. Even without the demon, we've been able to produce rain a couple of times. Not much rain, just a few drops, but weather work is challenging. It is an esoteric practice, and knowledge of magic is already rare enough. Of course, it is also the ultimate goal, the tool to achieve our cause.

Next time we summon that demon, it will be helpful not to worry about being interrupted. That way, we can spend the entire time focused on this critical work. Despite myself, I can't help but feel honored by the way he reacted to my tattoos. Even though he was kind of an ass. Of course, it's not like I've met many demons, so maybe they're all like that?

I'll talk with the guys about summoning him again after the concert and see what they think. The passage of time hangs over us like a blade poised at our throats. We need to make progress on our magic quickly if we're to be ready on time.

BOUND

I return to consciousness with a cry.

Every part of me is in pain.

Breathing is painful, the bright light is painful, and the sound of voices is painful.

My head hurts, but that pain pales in comparison to the pain in my stomach.

I whimper, but it turns into a scream as someone jostles me. I feel a sharp sensation in my arm, pressure there, and then everything blurs and darkens into unconsciousness again.

When I return to consciousness and my eyes scrape open, I see a ceiling above me and feel a bed beneath me. There are others in the room moving around. The room doesn't spin, but my vision is clouded.

One of the people, a healer, moves to the side of the bed. As they get close, I feel my instincts rebel. I struggle only to find myself bound to the table.

For a moment, the breath freezes in my throat, and my

instincts desire to fight. In that frozen breath, I see the healer look at me. He has his hand on my shoulder, and there is something there. Not in his eyes perhaps, but behind them, or maybe something I can't even see. That strange intelligence tells me there's no use trying to fight, and I close my eyes again as the breath whimpers out of me.

As I'm resigning myself to being trapped here, the other healer does something to my abdomen. With the increased pain, the same instinct as before threatens again to turn my body against these two, even if, consciously, I won't. As I win the internal fight again, the breath emerges from my lips as a sound even I don't recognize.

The healer who was working on my abdomen stops, and as the waves of pain she inflicted wash over me, she moves into the cloudiness at the edge of my vision. I turn my head and try to focus on her, but whether it's the drugs or the pain, I can't make her out as she moves away from me. I close my eyes to clear them, and when I open them, she's back at my side, this time with a cup in her hand.

She pushes the cup towards me, and even as I try to understand her intent, she is pouring the liquid into my mouth. I gasp, choke, and swallow a great amount, too much.

With that, the instinct I was fighting gets past my defense and makes its grand escape. Unable to stop myself, I fight my bindings despite the futility of it. Even as increased pain crashes through me, the room spins in a motion I'm too familiar with, and the two healers seem to twist sickeningly to the side.

All of the strength has gone from my body, and pain is crashing through me, tearing at my self-control. Just before the cloudiness thickens to pure black, I see the healers quickly continuing their care of my wound.

· · ·

*T*he next time I wake, the pain is less. With the decrease in pain and, what must be a change in the other drugs I've been given, I can understand words that are passing between others in the room.

I keep my eyes closed and listen as a voice I recognize, the one with the angry questions, says, "Self-harm is serious. If the mess of drugs we had her on before didn't halt those urges, we'll need to keep her bound or fully sedated."

A different voice, maybe the healer says, "Last time she woke up, she fought the bindings so hard she tore her stitches and started bleeding internally again. We can't risk a repeat of that."

"So then we keep her sedated."

"We told the person who committed her, Dio, I think his name is, that we would help her recover. There are others who have reached out to ask about her. I think Fem and Lent. How long do you think it will be before they follow through on their words and actually visit her? If they see her like this when she walked in here on her own two feet, do you think they'll feel like we've actually made progress?"

"No one knows how an addict will act when they're confronted with healing. Self-harm is one potential outcome."

"We both know the drug cocktail she's on isn't helping with her *healing*, sir."

"What are you saying? Hmm? That I don't know my own job? That the degree on the wall in my office doesn't mean anything? That you, a *general healer*, know better than me?"

"Nothing, I'm saying nothing," the voice is quieter, breathy, and overwhelmed. "I just hate it when they hurt themselves."

"I know. I'm sorry I snapped. The orders come from above me. We just do as we're told, whether we like it or not." The voice is gentler but still commanding. "How about you see to getting that wound healed, and we'll keep her sedated until she's ready to be back on her feet."

I hear the person whose voice I recognize turn to leave, but before the door closes, he says, "Like we talked about before, we can't take any risks with this one."

Then the door closes. A moment later, I feel a sharp prick in my arm, and then whatever drugs they're giving me pull me back into unconsciousness.

DIO'S JOURNAL - ENTRY 173

Annum:5614

Entry 173 - concentus

Finally, things are going my way.

Practice has been going well. The guys are figuring out how to accompany my voice, and I've memorized all the lyrics. Thankfully, I've always been good at memorization, so it didn't take me long. We've even started to work on some new material. It has been helpful to focus on the upcoming concert. Focusing on our music has allowed me to put my energy into something new, something creative and far less serious than our magic work.

The guys continue to grow on me. Despite their continued lack of ownership in the situation they created by welcoming that girl into their mansion, their decision-making as a whole is tough to question.

They've sure made a name for themselves as musi-

cians. Reem is an excellent leader and has a good sense of what the fans will enjoy. Fem is excellent at songwriting. Lent is solid in his role of researching magic for our other purpose, and he is quite talented on the guitar. Plus, they've really buckled down to learn what I can teach them when it comes to magic.

I'll even admit I've learned a bit from them as well.

They eventually stopped talking about visiting the girl. I think it's partially because they were turned down last time. I did try to tell them that people with addictions usually do better if they aren't confronted by elements of their past lives while they're in early recovery. They did listen when the professionals agreed with me, so I can't be that mad about it.

Hopefully, she recovers quickly and can get an apartment somewhere. I was happy to pay to get everything on the right track and get her out of our hair, but my generosity is not boundless.

I keep forgetting to ask the other guys about summoning that demon again. We need to do that soon. We haven't been making much more progress on creating rain. I know weather magic is difficult, but I'm sure we should be further along by now. We must be missing something, and I'm sure the demon would be able to help.

Actually, I'll go talk to the guys about it now.

AWHILE LATER

I move gingerly as I walk to the tables on schedule for our midday meal. My abdomen still aches under the bandage. The healer tells me that it will take a while to feel better. He hasn't been wrong about anything so far, so I believe him. Sometimes the voices tell me otherwise, but I'm learning to ignore them. Last time the healer checked the wound, he said the stitches should come out soon. Hopefully that helps.

The mental work has been difficult, and it's taken me a while, but I'm beginning to be able to shut out the voices in my head. The healer, whom I see twice daily, tells me I need to allow them to talk but turn the volume down so I can't hear them. It's not easy when they seem to make so much sense, but he says that's because of my addiction, whatever that is. All that really matters is that I'm making progress, and they tell me if I make progress, I'll be able to leave someday.

I try not to think of the boys and Malam. That life feels like it barely happened, like it only exists in my deepest memories. I protect it from everyone here and am careful not to share details, just small, unimportant things here and there. Dresses I liked, listening to the boys' music, and how much I liked good coffee. Maybe if I were sharing more, I'd heal quicker, but it's the one thing I have left that means something to me. The thing that feels like it makes up the core of me, and I haven't been able to give it up just yet.

For the meal, I sit at the table and eat what I'm given. One of the other patients starts screaming, and the healers and other attendants rush to him. I'm so used to outbursts at this point that I continue on, eating the food in front of me, wondering how much more healing I'll need to do before I can leave.

I truly miss coffee.

DIO'S JOURNAL - ENTRY 190

Annum:5614

Entry 190 - periculum

I'm beginning to worry we might have made an error. I kept forgetting about summoning that demon. Malam is his name, I guess. When I finally remembered and asked the guys about it, they agreed it was a good idea. We decided to wait until after the concert since we had so much going on leading up to it.

I wrote about the concert in my last entry, so I won't dwell on it here, but being in front of that crowd, gah. Seeing the crowd lose themselves in our music, the moment we started playing for them. The noise of all those people as they screamed for us. Something to hold onto while I deal with this mess.

After the concert, it took a few days before we remembered and had time, but then we completed the summoning ritual for ~~the demon~~ Malam in the morning. It's always a weird feeling waiting around after that ritual. When he did show up, the conversation started off well. He watched our process and had some feedback for the other guys that I agreed with. We finally made some progress.

It all started to go wrong as we wrapped up and invited him to have dinner with us. When he sat down at the table, I was shocked when the first thing he asked about was how Chaosta was doing. I shared that we'd finally gotten her into a facility to help with her recovery. Before I could share more about why, or tell him that she was spying on us that night and putting everything at risk with her addiction, he fucking freaked out. He stood up so quickly that his chair tipped over. Then he came at me like he was going to kill me. I can still feel his hand around my throat and have bruises where he slammed me against the wall.

He was snarling about who did this and why we'd think she was an addict, and it all got to be a lot. If he'd been anything other than a fucking demon, I would have put him in his place. Thankfully, I have excellent self-control, or he might even be dead.

I couldn't even speak for myself with his hand around my throat. The guys were talking, but they were all going at it at once, and I couldn't understand anything they said. I'd have thought Reem would be able to get control of the situation, but I think Lent was leading the chaos as always.

Then, just as suddenly as he freaked out, he was striding out the door without another word. I'm still not sure exactly what set him off or where he went, but I'm reluctant to summon that particular demon again. He was clearly enraged about something with that girl. Until today, I didn't even know that he was aware of her existence.

The guys were upset after he left. I think they've trusted him as an expert in teaching them magic and are worried he won't return after how he reacted. I've tried to reassure them that once we can actually talk with him and explain how Chaosta was spying, he'll understand why she's better in the facility for now. I'm even willing to consider having her live here again once she's recovered if that's enough to mend things because fuck, the guys are angry at me.

It's not as though I haven't endured far worse. It's just unfortunate timing after the high of the concert. We really need to make progress with our magic, and now having him around to teach us would be difficult, I think. That's if he's even willing, with how enraged he was. I'll figure it out, I always do. There's so much more at stake that we can't risk.

KNIGHT IN SHADOW ARMOR

Breakfast the next day is again bland porridge. I'm yet again wishing for coffee. It's a mark of how desperate I am that I'd probably even drink the stuff Reem makes at this point.

I concentrate on the food to keep myself from itching at the stitches on my abdomen. The other scratches and bruises have faded, and the pain meds keep the healing wound comfortable enough for me to make it through most of the day now without needing to go back to my room to rest.

My schedule is the same as it's been since the beginning. A fact I didn't realize until they changed the pills after I hurt myself. Now that I can think more clearly and the room isn't constantly spinning, it's easier to remember the routine.

I also feel as though it's easier to keep the voices at bay. A fact that the mind healer I'm working with has been praising me for. Just yesterday, he said again how proud he was of me and all the progress I've made.

I wanted to ask him when I might be healed enough to leave. However, terror filled me at the thought that his response might destroy the hope that has been building recently, so I kept the question to myself. I'll ask eventually, but I need to hold onto this hope for a little longer.

If I can just keep from hurting myself again, maybe it won't be that long before I can go back to the mansion and the boys.

*T*he day passes, the routine familiar. Lunch is my least favorite because there is almost always at least one outburst from the other patients, but there isn't today. Everything is quiet. It's going to be a good day.

After lunch, I see the mind healer, and we work on quieting the voices in my head again. He challenges me this time, making me upset as he asks me questions about why I hurt myself. I get upset because I can't remember. After, he shares that he felt I had good control over the volume of the voices. He tells me again how proud he is.

Next is my free period, and I find the book I started reading last time. It's a story about two people in love. Somehow, it doesn't seem like something I would read, but the new, healing version of me is enjoying it. The two people are idiots because they're fighting, and I can't figure out why they haven't talked to each other and worked it out yet. By the end of free time, I want to throw the book at one of the other patients, but I resist the impulse.

The mind healer would be proud. I'll make sure to tell him.

After that, I see the healer who has been caring for the wound on my abdomen. The wound from when I hurt myself. The small room smells strongly of some cleaning agent. He has me remove my shirt and then lie back on the bed like usual while he checks my progress.

This time, he tells me the stitches can be removed, and hope fills me. I'm healing and getting better. He prepares some things and then starts removing the stitches, which is agonizing, but I lie as still as I can. Once he's done, he wraps a bandage around my abdomen again and tells me to keep the bandage on and see him for two more days.

As I sit up and then stand, the room wobbles and my vision darkens.

*W*hen I wake, I'm in my room. I lay quietly with my eyes closed for a while. There are no windows in this room, so while it is dark, that doesn't mean it's late. Lying still like this keeps the pain at bay as well as the voices.

Suddenly, I remember losing consciousness after having my stitches removed and realize they must have brought me here. It's been a while since I needed to rest during the day.

Does that mean my healing isn't going as well as I thought?

As I lay quietly resting, the door to my room opens and someone steps through it. My heart races; this isn't the routine. No one is supposed to be in my room right now.

Maybe a healer has come to check on me? The voices get loud, trying to tell me how to defend myself.

The pain is making the voices worse, and I press my hands to either side of my head, "Please stop, please. Stop talking to me," I whimper as I squeeze my eyes tightly closed.

"Chaosta?" This voice comes from the person in my room. The voice is male and sounds entreating as it says, "What medication are they giving you? Wait, never mind. Just put this on."

I feel him set something on the bed near me. I open my eyes and see a small cloth bag that looks vaguely familiar. Before I can look up and see who is in the room with me, the door opens and shuts, and he's gone.

I push myself up and open the bag. When I see its contents, I freeze. As I sit looking at clothes that were familiar to me at some point, I feel damp trails on my cheeks.

Why are they testing me?

What happens if I put these clothes on?

What if I do, and I'm not healed enough to leave?

My heart pounds as I sit locked in indecision with my eyes shut. Maybe if I just leave the clothes in the bag, I won't need to make this decision. If I don't take any action, then I can't fail this test.

After some time, the door to my room opens again, and I hear someone enter the room. As this happens, my body seems to take on a life of its own. I sense the person move toward me, my eyes still gritted shut, and push myself up in a quick movement. My back is now against the wall as I crouch on the surface of my bed.

Damn the voices, I think to myself. I struggle with the volume, trying to turn it down.

I hunch against the wall, my legs shaking, trying to gain control again. As I finally manage it, I open my eyes and see a large man standing in front of me. He's wearing the familiar clothes of the center, but he doesn't belong here.

There are shadows protruding from his back in a way that is somehow both menacing and yet strangely comforting. The voices scream at me to go to him, but I manage to turn down the volume and shut them up again.

Damn, they're persistent. Good thing I didn't put the clothes on. I'll be here for a while. At that thought, a sob escapes from my throat.

He's looking at me the way one looks at a wounded bird, as though if he stays very still, I will remain here and not take flight.

He holds a hand towards me. "Chaosta," he says gently, his voice guttural and low.

The voices try again to tell me something. *Why does he know my name?*

"Do you not recognize me?" he asks, and something about his voice makes it sound like he's in pain.

I reach my hands up to my ears and press them to keep the sound of his voice out. The sound of it makes the voices in my head even worse. I concentrate on not hurting myself. The voices are louder than they have been in a long time, and I'm quickly losing control of them. They're whispering the words *Malam* and *demon* to me on repeat.

Something about those words feels comforting, even hopeful.

I stop fighting and listen.

I look at him standing across the room. Something has cracked open in his expression, and pain is clearly visible on his face. I forget for a moment why I was afraid and remove my hands from my ears.

"Did I hurt you?" I whisper.

He closes his eyes, and I see his hands are clenched in fists at his sides. Something tells me that he's terrifying, but I don't feel it.

I take a step forward, then sit and push myself off the bed. I'm worried about him rather than myself, suddenly. "If I hurt you, we should go to the healer. It's ok if I need to stay here longer to keep healing. We should make sure you're ok," I tell him.

He doesn't move, his eyes remain closed, but he says, "Chaosta, you didn't hurt me." He opens his eyes, looking at me now, and while his face is still pained, his expression is angry.

"They made a mistake sending you here, and I'll never forgive myself for not checking on you sooner. If I'd known…" He heaves a deep breath, and I watch his body relax, his hands no longer in fists. He takes another step toward me, moving hesitantly as though I might still try to take flight.

"I came to get you out of here and fix the mistake. Let me get you out of here?" he says gently, although I still hear the pain and anger in his voice.

For some reason, I'm still not scared.

"Are you taking me home?" I ask. The amount of hope I feel is painful. I don't know what I'll do if he says no. I wrap my arms around myself, tucking my hands in.

I can't hurt myself even if the answer is no, repeats in my head.

"Yes, although not to your home. I'm taking you to my home," he says, "When I bring you to your home, I need to have a conversation I'm not ready for at the moment." His voice turns to a growl at the end, but for some reason, I'm still not afraid.

"Ok," I say softly, and I see him relax further. I turn to the bed and the bag of clothes, but he stops me.

"We have limited time, and it has run out. You can change once you get there."

As he says that, he steps past me and grabs the bag of clothes. Before I can do anything else, he wraps his arms around me snuggly. Then we are surrounded in shadow. Blackness crosses my vision, and I lose consciousness.

THE REAL RECOVERY

I wake up in a bed that is unfamiliar to me. I try to open my eyes, but the spinning of the room quickly makes me dizzy, so I close them again. My whole body is shaking and stiff, my brow damp with sweat. I want to cry, but tears won't come. I try to push myself up off the bed, but my body won't obey. The voices scream and cackle loudly in my head. I sob quietly without tears until my exhausted body can no longer fight off the shadowy blackness, and it takes me, pulling me into darkness.

When I next open my eyes, there is a female face above me. "It's ok, Chaosta," she says quietly. "My name is Lily. Malam asked me to help you."

I squeeze my eyes shut against the pain. When I open them again, her face is still above me.

"What hurts?"

"Everything," I whimper.

She leaves the room and comes back a short while later. I

feel her hand go around the back of my head, and she lifts it gently, holding a cup to my lips. "It's just water," she says quietly. "Try to drink a little, please."

I manage a few sips, and she gently lowers my head to the pillow. Then I feel her lay a damp cloth over my forehead. It feels lovely against my hot skin. It's soothing enough that I'm able to sleep again.

*W*hen I wake up next, my muscles feel stiff and my throat is thick, making it tough to swallow. The pain is less, and I don't feel like my body is on fire anymore. The door opens, and the woman who introduced herself as Lily steps into the room.

When she sees my open eyes, a smile draws across her face, lighting it up. Light hair curls to her shoulders. She's tall for a woman. She moves across the room to the side of the bed, and I see that her eyes are green as she bends over me.

"Glad to see you awake, Chaosta. I think your fever broke. If you're up to it, let's get you changed out of those clothes."

I nod at her shakily, and she pulls the covers back. It takes a lot of help from her to get my stiff body sitting at the edge of the bed, but we somehow manage it. My body still feels out of my control, and now that I'm sitting, I feel dizzy. I'm also still struggling to swallow.

"If you can just stay there, I can help with the clothes," she says quietly. When I look at her, I can see her gaze assessing me.

I nod, closing my eyes again as the room spins.

Her cool, gentle fingers undo the buttons at the collar of the shirt I'm wearing. Then she gently pulls it over my head, helping me get my arms through the sleeves. I open my eyes and watch as she drops the shirt into a hamper in a corner of the room.

She turns around and heads back to the bed, but as I watch,

she freezes, her gaze on my abdomen. She blinks a couple of times, and I squeeze my eyes shut again against another round of dizziness.

"Are you hurt?" she asks softly.

"I was, but it's mostly healed," I say quietly, my voice hoarse as it's forced past my tight throat.

"May I?" she asks.

I nod.

Her cool fingers gently unwrap the bandage. She's quiet for a bit, but I'm thankful she doesn't prod at the wound. After a few minutes, I look up at her again, and it's as though nothing is different as she helps me into a clean shirt. I'm guessing it's one of hers. The shirt is cool, the fabric smooth against my sensitive skin. After the rough fabric of the uniform from Piquory Center, it is particularly welcome.

My pants are tougher to change. She eventually has me lie on my back as she helps me into loose, flowing pants in the same silky fabric. "They're a little long," she says as she smiles at me, "but hopefully more comfortable?"

"Much more comfortable," I manage past my tight throat.

She helps me lie down and arrange myself again on the bed. She removes the blanket that was covering me, adds it to the hamper, and brings me a fresh cover. After she helps me drink a little more water, she leaves the room, and I sleep again.

I wake later, feeling better than I have in a long time. It's still difficult to swallow, and my body is stiff and achy, but it feels like it's under my control again. Some voices still whisper to me, but they're so quiet I can barely hear them. As I wonder whether I should ask for some food and water, my stomach growling, I hear voices outside the door.

A male voice I recognize says, "Lilith, my love, how is our patient?"

Lily's voice is slightly muffled as though her face is pressed against something, but I hear her say, "Improving, her fever finally broke. She's still really sick, though, Malam. I'm worried."

"They had her on powerful drugs, love. It will just take time, and with you caring for her, I'm sure she'll make a quick recovery."

"I thought she was recovering from addiction?" says Lily's voice, quiet and curious and no longer muffled.

"That's why Dio sent her there, but she's not an addict." Malam's voice has an edge to it.

There's a pause, then Lily says, "How did she get injured?"

"What? Injured?"

"She has a wound in her abdomen that's not fully healed. It's recent." Lily's voice sounds hesitant. Then I hear her say, "Malam, don't upset her," and there's an edge to her voice as well.

At that moment, the door to my room opens roughly, hitting the wall behind it as Malam strides into the room.

I startle at the crack of the door and then look up at him as he stands next to the bed, his shoulders tense. He's glaring at my stomach as though he wants to tear the blanket off me, but he doesn't move. He looks up at the wall behind the bed, closes his eyes, and takes a deep breath.

"How did you get hurt, Chaosta?" he asks as he looks at me again. Though his voice is calm and composed, whatever is swirling in his expression screams of unleashed violence.

"I hurt myself," I respond quietly. "Please don't send me back," I say as I close my eyes.

"*Malam*," I hear Lily say from the doorway. It's a warning of some sort. I hear footsteps, and when I look again, it's Lily standing over the bed, and Malam is gone.

Lily smiles at me, but it doesn't reach her eyes. "It's ok," she says softly. "This is hard for him because he feels responsible. He just needs a little time."

"So he won't send me back?" I ask quietly.

"No," she says, "you won't ever go back there."

I relax, and finally, tears begin to flow. Lily sits with me for a while, wiping the tears from my cheeks and holding my hand until I fall asleep again.

*T*he next time I wake, I feel nearly like myself again. The voices are completely gone. I push myself up, feeling a little weak, but other than some pain in my abdomen, my body feels better.

I notice that the door is cracked open. I also see a cup of water on the table by the bed and my clothes laid out on a chair in the corner of the room. I pull off the soft shirt and pants and fold them neatly before dressing in some of my own things.

Strong emotions bubble up in my throat, but I don't have time for them right now. There have been far too many emotions to deal with recently, and I'm tired. I'll deal with it later.

I wander out the door and follow the smells of breakfast and glorious coffee into a small dining room with a table set under a window. Malam sits at the table and looks up as I enter. I freeze under his gaze, and the voices suddenly start up in my head. This time, without the drugs confusing things, I recognize them as the intelligence and instincts that have helped me in every action until I went to the center. With that, I relax, walk to the table, and drop into a chair.

Without meeting Malam's gaze, I ask, "Can I have some coffee?"

He pushes an empty cup and a carafe of coffee to me without speaking. I pour myself a cup and sip it gratefully. The first joy I've felt in a long while perfuses my body.

I hear Lily walk in the door behind me. "Chaosta," she says cheerfully, "you're awake! Do you want breakfast?"

I nod, still focused only on the coffee in the cup in front of me. However, she must understand because moments later, she sets a plate full of bread, syrup, and some kind of meat in front of me.

As she takes a seat at the table, I hear her say, *"Malam,"* with a soft growl in her voice.

Another warning, although again I don't understand why. This time, though, the intelligence in my head tells me I don't care, so I dig into my breakfast without thinking further about it. However, the pressure in the room lets up, so that's nice.

I finish clearing my plate, my stomach happily full and my heart filled with joy from the good food and coffee. Lily sets her hand gently on my arm, and I look up at her.

"Now that you're feeling better, Malam is going to take you back to your home." I watch as she looks across the table at Malam, her expression strangely annoyed. "Isn't that right, Malam?" she prompts, her voice overly bright.

She stares across the table for a minute, and the energy in the room shifts again, the tension increasing. Then she looks back at my face, her eyes bright with joy. "It's been lovely to meet you, even with the less-than-happy circumstances," she says to me quietly. "You are welcome here anytime."

"Thank you, Lily," I mumble. As I glance at her, I note that her eyes are a little too bright.

"One minute," she says with a forced cheerfulness. "I made you a small traveling bag with your things and some food for the road." She leaves the room and comes back with a small linen bag that has a shoulder strap.

I take it from her with shaking hands and hang it over my shoulder. Belatedly, I realize Malam is no longer here. Lily directs me to the front door, where I see him pulling on his shoes. As I pull my shoes on, he turns and leaves without a word. Lily silently squeezes my arm, but her attention is on Malam as he walks out the door.

"Don't worry," she says quietly, "this too will blow over."
While she says it to me, I have the feeling she might actually be
speaking to herself.

I thank her again, and with that, I walk out the door
behind him.

RETURN AND RETRIBUTION

I follow Malam down the stairs. After I make it down several flights, I pause, my legs shaking and the wound pounding with my heartbeat. Malam continues without me. After a few moments he must realize I'm not following anymore because he turns and comes back.

"Do you need me to carry you?" he asks, his voice soft. His face is still frozen in a mask. Strong feelings flit across it, and he's focusing on something over my head, against the wall.

"I don't need to be carried, I just need to rest for a minute," I say, and the annoyance is clear in my voice.

He nods, still staring at the wall.

A few moments later, my legs have stopped threatening to give out, and the pain in my side has receded. I move forward again, and Malam turns, walking in the lead. This time, though, he walks more slowly and stays closer to me.

After several more sets of stairs, we arrive at the ground level. After taking a few more moments for me to rest, we leave through the front door of the building, and Malam hails a carriage. As it comes to a complete stop, the horses snort, trying to crane their necks to look at me around the blinders. I huff at them as I move to the carriage, agreeing with them somehow about the irritation of emotional males.

The ride is quiet. Malam continues to stare at something above my head, his face still a mask. In the silence, I lean my head back against the carriage and take the opportunity to rest.

Eventually, the carriage slows, and I hear him shift and feel him staring at me. I open my eyes and see him glance away momentarily. His shoulders are tense, and his throat bobs as he swallows. "I would be thankful if you don't tell anyone about the apartment or Lily," he says, and I hear vulnerability in his voice.

I meet his eyes and nod. "I won't tell anyone," I say, my voice still slightly raspy with disuse from the past couple of days.

"Are you going to tell them about your injury?" He asks quietly.

I shake my head.

"Can I at least tell Fem so he can help?" He asks, his voice pleading.

"That's alright, I guess," I say tightly.

I don't quite know why I don't want the others to know. Well, other Dio of course. He's given me plenty of reasons to not want to confide in him.

When I risk a glance at Malam, I see a muscle in his jaw tick as his eyes search my face. Then he departs the carriage, and I follow him.

When I look up and see the steps to the familiar front door, though, my feet freeze for a moment. As I look at the door to my home, I'm not quite able to move towards it. It feels like a lifetime ago I was last here, and while I knew this was our destination, seeing it feels different.

Malam stops and turns to face me. Then, to my surprise, he steps close and wraps his arms around me, holding me gently for a breath. After a few moments, he steps back and offers me his hand, "Come with me," he says.

I take his hand, and he draws me gently but firmly up the

steps and through the front door and into the entry hall, where Fem and Lent close in around me. Arms embrace me and voices welcome me home.

"Gentle," Malam growls quietly.

Suddenly, I feel the energy in the room shift. I detangle myself from the embrace of the boys and glance up just in time to see Malam point at Dio.

"You!" Malam snarls and, grabbing Dio by the upper arm, shoves him through the door into the office.

Stalking after him, he slams the door behind them, and we can hear raised voices.

"Fuck," Fem says, gnawing on his lip. "I'd better go keep an eye on that and make sure the mansion doesn't turn into a crime scene."

I feel a spark of something in my chest, not worry for Dio, of course, maybe concern for Fem? Malam can handle himself, and there is something gratifying about imagining Dio facing an angry demon.

As I consider, Lent says, "Come on." He takes my arm and then directs me gently from the room. "Let's give them some space to work that out." His voice is calm, but his face is full of worry as he looks back over his shoulder at the closed door.

He leads me to the room with the floral wall and settles me on a couch. Reem joins us, walking through the door behind Lent. As I sit, carefully masking my face against the twinges from the stab wound, Lent takes the linen bag from my shoulder.

"I'll put this in your room," he says quietly.

"There's some food in there," I say, and have to smile as his face lights up.

"*Her* food is in there," Reem admonishes.

Lent's face falls.

"I'll share," I say to him, "I just ate a massive breakfast."

Lent brightens up again and pulls the food out carefully,

setting the neatly wrapped packages on the table in front of the couch.

Reem ignores him and asks, "Is there anything I can get you?"

"Some water would be nice," I say quietly. "Oh, and my books, they're under the bed."

"I'll get the books for you, and *Lent* will get you some water," Reem says. Irritation creeps into his voice as he glares at Lent, who has already begun rifling through the packages of food.

Undeterred, Lent pushes himself up and heads out the door just in front of Reem.

I close my eyes and lean my head back against the couch, more than a little glad to be home.

Reem and Lent soon return, and we fall into a companionable quiet with Lent occasionally offering me bits of the food Lily packed. When he asks where I got it, I tell him that Malam gave it to me for the carriage ride in case I was hungry.

I'm happily focused on my book, munching on some small pieces of strongly spiced, crisp bread, when the door behind me opens.

The boys look up, and I turn around to see Fem walking into the room. His shoulders are drawn up and tight, and his face is blank. He looks at me momentarily, and I see strong emotions quarreling on his face. Then he pushes his hands into his pockets and turns sideways, looking away from me. He's clearly uncomfortable about something, and I look back at my book, giving him space.

Unbidden, Lent and Reem rise and move to stand near him. They begin talking, and I hear the words, "still alive," before deciding that whatever they're talking about doesn't concern me. Still, I can't help but hear Fem say, "I need to speak with Chaosta privately."

"What's going on?" Lent whispers just a little too loudly.

"I just need to speak with her for a moment," Fem says.

I can't hear any further responses. A few moments later, the door opens and then shuts, and everything is quiet except the sound of footsteps. Then one of the boys moves around the couch to sit, facing me, on the table.

I glance up, away from my book, and see Fem looking at me. He still looks uncomfortable, and he swallows as he searches my face. "Hey," he says simply, but his voice is tight.

"Hi," I say as I try to determine why he's so uncomfortable.

I sense him fiddling with something and see that he has his medical kit on his lap.

"Can I look at the wound on your stomach?" he says, his voice soft.

"That's fine, I guess," I say quietly.

He gently moves the blanket on my lap and then unbuttons the lower part of my shirt and pulls it aside. I watch his face as he focuses on his task, and I can tell when he sees the wound. His whole body freezes, and he stops breathing for a moment. He licks his lips, and then he masks his expression as he says, "Hold this."

I take the bottom of my shirt and hold it open so that he can get to the wound. I wince as he pokes at it gently.

"How long ago did the stitches come out?" he asks matter-of-factly.

"I'm not quite sure. I was sick for a while and lost track of the days," I say.

I note that he hesitates again, but his expression is still masked, and after a moment, he begins to breathe again. "It seems to be healing well," he says softly.

He digs in his medical kit and pulls out a small container. I expect he's going to apply something to the wound, but instead, he hands it to me.

"This can help with the pain if it still hurts. Otherwise, it should be good as long as you take it easy for another fortnight," he says as he looks searchingly at my face.

He then closes up his kit and stands. "You can close your shirt."

As I'm fastening the buttons, looking for where I put my book, I notice he's frozen in place.

He says softly, "Do you still want to hurt yourself?"

I pause for a moment, searching my thoughts.

"No, not at the moment," I say.

He turns and leaves the room as I return to my reading.

DIO'S JOURNAL - ENTRY 191

Annum: 5614
Entry 191 - livor

If my handwriting suffers in this entry, it is only
because my hands are shaking. Neatness is paramount
in such an important written account, so it bothers me
that this is not up to my usual standards. However, this
is an important entry, and I need to write it down
before any details fade.

Fuck

I'm surprised I just survived that. I'm glad I was
able to control myself under such duress. The anger of a
demon is not a small thing, and of the few demons I've
met, this one clearly carries a much more immense
power. A far more immense power, in fact, than I realized until today. I'm annoyed at myself for underestimating him. It's not a mistake I'll make again. Not that

I tried to make him angry, of course. Nor do I have any reason to want to make him angry in the future.

Fuck, am I even making sense? Pull yourself together, Diogenes!

Normally, my actions, which are always taken with careful thought, are calculated to move me towards my goal. Yet somehow I erred this time. Clearly, there is some understanding I lack, something I'm blind to. That much anger over an action I took to try to get that girl some help isn't right.

Between all the snarling and a damn solid right hook to the side of my head (that I was too shocked to defend myself against), my thoughts were and are scrambled. I think the gist of what he told me is that Chaosta isn't an addict. What the fuck she is if not an addict? I don't know. I should recognize these things after all. Also, if she's not an addict, why did that center not just immediately send her home? I feel like I have to trust the professionals over an angry demon on this one. It worries me that he might have had her discharged without their approval.

Other pieces I managed to understand from the tirade are that Chaosta is "HIS", whatever that means, and I'm not to make any decisions about her without talking with her. If she's unable to make a decision about something, I must consult with Malam. I guess if he feels like marking his territory like that, I can comply. It is not as though I have any real interest in her other than as a risk to the band. Or as a risk to my continued sobriety, I guess.

He did agree with me that she shouldn't be listening in on our magic practice, so at least he's not completely without sense. Although if he'd just given me a chance to explain that last time, maybe his anger could have been reduced.

After the tirade eventually ended, he dismissed me and stayed in the office with Fem. I didn't much care what he wanted to talk about at that moment. I just wanted to get out of there and get some ice on my face. We have a fucking band event coming up. What will people think as I'm signing records, that I scrap like an immature, emotional boy? That I'm not a skilled enough fighter to protect my face?

Now I wish I had maintained the presence of mind to listen at the door and understand what he wanted to talk to Fem about. Of course, if my head hadn't still been spinning, I would have thought to do so. Messiness such as this isn't like me.

RABID FANS AND SKEPTICS

Life settles into a mostly comfortable pattern for the next few days. The boys hover, but after so long without them, I don't even care. They seem to be focused on feeding me and making sure I rest. Both things are welcome, so I allow it.

I'm particularly happy to have time to finally read the books I've collected. I pore over them for hours every day, making notes in the margins that probably make sense only to myself. Honestly, sometimes the notes don't really even make sense to me. The map in my brain seems to be turning into a being. That cartographer is charting a route to something my consciousness is oblivious to, but I hardly care. Without the medications I was being given at Piquory Center, there is a soothing element to it.

It is clear, however, that the purpose set by Malam upon my creation aligns me with the demons. Elling's words about the angels seeking to eliminate the threat of my existence echo in my memory. Those words, along with Rex's thinly veiled threats about the danger I would be in if I didn't choose their side, are a constant drone in my head. I don't know what to do about it yet, but it is clear that further violence from the angels is inevitable. It is uncomfortable to feel as though I am waiting around for the angels to take that action. Yet, some part of me also knows that I am doing what I need to. This time to learn and fill in gaps in my knowledge is imperative.

On the morning of my fourth day back at home, when I show up for breakfast, it's clear something is up. The house employees are swarming, carrying items to the front door. Reem, arms crossed against his chest, is again directing the flow. I see him snapping at a man who is moving too quickly.

As I watch, the man runs into a pile of boxes set near the door and knocks them over. I hear something inside the boxes break, and Reem curses.

He seems to feel my eyes on him, and he looks up, meeting my gaze as he says, "Sorry about this, Chaosta. We had this record signing scheduled before we knew you'd be back with us. We plan for you to stay here at the mansion with one of the house employees."

"Can I please go with you?" I ask.

Reem looks harried, his conversation with me causing him to lose ground in the battle to maintain organization. One that he's waging against complete chaos.

"Ok, sure," he says, clearly distracted. He's already turning away from me, but he calls out, "Be quick to eat, we're leaving in twenty."

I walk to the dining room, load up a plate at the sideboard, and drop inelegantly onto a chair at the table. Dio is sitting across from me, the only band member here. I glare at him, but he doesn't look up from his plate. He's neatly cutting his bread into small pieces and dipping the pieces daintily in syrup with his fork.

He has a cloth napkin tucked into his collar. There's a bruise on his left cheek. It is especially colorful against his pale complexion and dark brown hair. He's dressed in the band's uniform, a white pressed button-up shirt and a grey vest under a black suit jacket. His hair is neatly combed.

As I note that it's the first time I've seen him in band attire, the door opens, and Lent joins us. Like Dio, he's wearing the band outfit. Unlike Dio, his hair is mussed, his collar standing up in places, and his shirt buttons are mismatched. He's also smiling at me, the most stark difference. "Hey Chaosta, how's breakfast today?" he asks cheerily.

"Good," I say with my mouth full.

I feel Dio looking at me, but as I look at him, he concentrates on his plate again.

Lent piles food on his plate and sits next to me. Even before he's fully seated, he's shoveling food into his mouth, and I note that Dio is glaring at him. At least now that we've both captured his attention, the daggers from his stare are diffused.

"I heard from Reem you're coming with us," Lent says to me excitedly.

I grin at him, and I'm about to respond when Dio says, "There must be some mistake, Chaosta is remaining here with the house staff."

I glare at Dio, but his attention is on Lent, who glances at him idly before looking back at the food on his plate.

I see a momentary look of disgust on Dio's face as he watches Lent eat.

Through a mouth full of food, Lent mumbles, "Reem says she's coming and he's in charge. You don't like it, talk with him."

I look back at Dio as he pulls the napkin from his collar. He sets it firmly on the table and pushes the chair back roughly as he stands and strides out of the room.

"Someone's grumbly this morning," Lent says as he wiggles his eyebrows at me.

I laugh and go back to my food. Thankful as ever for Lent's relaxed attitude.

"What books are you bringing with you today?" he asks me.

"Am I so transparent?" I ask, laughter clear in my voice.

"Just one book lover acknowledging another," he says with a grin.

I reach out and wipe a drop of syrup off his chin.

He laughs, "No wonder that neat-freak doesn't like me."

"You do eat kind of like a starved animal," I say with a grin.

He laughs again, then locates a napkin and cleans his face. "You done?" he asks.

I look over with shock at his empty plate. I can't hold back giggles as I respond, "Done enough. I'm full."

I rise from the table, a smile still covering my face and my heart lighter than it's been in a while. I follow him out the door, back into the ocean of chaos. I note that Dio and Reem are standing just outside the front door, engaged in a hushed but tense conversation.

When I get to my room, I pick two books and put them in the linen bag Lily gave me before swinging it over my shoulder. I turn to leave, but at the last minute, I pause, return to the stack of books, and add one more for good measure.

There's no telling how long we'll be gone, I remind myself as I walk back towards the front door.

I'm just finishing with fastening up my short, ankle-high boots when Reem calls to me, "Nearly ready? We need to set off."

"Just making my way to the carriage now," I call back.

I finish fastening my boots quickly and head to the carriage. Dio, Lent, and Reem are already inside, and I squeeze in next to Lent. Anything to avoid sitting near Dio, who stares at me, his whole body tense. His stare feels like shards of glass against my skin, and I curl into myself in the small space.

Fem joins us in short order, and the carriage starts off. At least with all three of the other boys now in the carriage and in high spirits about the event, the tension is diffused. Realizing I no longer feel the sting of Dio's stare against my skin, I note that he's not looking at me. I uncurl myself a little and look out the window.

When the carriage eventually stops, Dio brushes past us, and Lent and Fem file out behind him. Reem asks me to wait. His face is serious, and he looks irritated. Somehow, I'm fairly sure it's not with me.

When it's just the two of us, he sighs and crosses his arms as he says, "In retrospect, it probably would have been better for you to stay behind."

I open my mouth to say something, but he cuts in.

"However," he says, meeting my eyes, "we're not disappointed you're here, we just need to make sure you're safe."

I again open my mouth to correct him that Dio doesn't seem to feel that way, but once again, he cuts me off, his expression stern.

"Do you promise to do as you're told?"

I glare back, annoyed at being interrupted and spoken to like a child. However, I'm unwilling to have an argument when I know this is important to him. "I will listen to direction," I grit out.

I see his shoulders relax infinitesimally. "I need you to stay to the edges of the crowd, along the wall, or behind the table where we'll be signing records, alright? We just don't want you getting trampled and hurt like last time."

I open my mouth to remind him, yet again, that it was a sword fight with an angel, not being trampled by a crowd, which caused my injury last time. Then I stop myself. There is really no reason to continue to bring up this clearly futile argument. Instead, I meet his eyes and promise to follow his directions.

He relaxes further before turning and leaving the carriage with me at his heels.

Unlike the relatively intimate basement event space of the concert I attended, where I saw Malam, this is a massive venue. I barely have time to wonder at the difference, though, as our group rushes around to get set up. The others organize photos of The Boys on stands, lay cloth over tables, and set up a signing station. I set my bag of books down on one of the chairs at the signing table and help set up refreshments again.

By the time everything is set up, my body is sore. The wound in my abdomen sends angry stabs of pain. I ignore it long enough to go back to the table to gather my book bag. When I get to the table, though, I don't see the bag. Finally, I see it, lying on the ground to one side of the table where Dio must have tossed it as though it were some sort of trash. I snatch it up, wrapping my arms around my precious books and apologizing to them wordlessly.

I find a spot along the wall behind the table and sit on the floor. At least back here, Dio has to turn around if he wants to glare at me, so I feel buffered from his anger for the time being.

I settle against the wall, pull the books out of the bag, and check for damage. One book has some pages that are slightly bent at the corner. Another has a small tear along the top of the spine; otherwise, they're intact. Anger fills me, and I realize I need to have a conversation with Dio. I need to speak with him about how he's treating me, but this isn't the time or place. I push the anger down, smothering it for now.

Choosing the book I found in the office, I pull my pen out of a pocket in the bag. Then I find the place I marked and begin reading. I've made it to a section on the use of runes and how they can impact the weather. Something about it sounds vaguely familiar, and suddenly I remember one of the dreams I've had. I close my eyes and rest my head back against the wall as I try to remember the shape of the rune in that dream.

Just as I feel as though I'm close to remembering it, the energy in the room shifts. The sound of voices is suddenly drowned out as a humming sound fills my ears. I slowly realize that my chest has been aching, and I rub at it. A sense of deja vu surrounds me, and I open my eyes.

There are people everywhere. While I've been reading, a massive line has formed leading up to the table where the members of The Boys are sitting. A record player in the corner adds noise to the room as it plays the band's music against the din of the crowd. I look around, trying to understand what my instincts are pulling me towards. As I glance across the sea of people, something screams at me, and I pause and turn back, scanning across the crowd where I looked a moment before.

There, standing amongst the others, but yet somehow separate from them, I see a face I recognize. The ache in my chest increases, and I take a sharp breath, rubbing harder at my chest and trying to center myself. Then I remember the owner of the face and push myself to my feet as I move into the crowd. Reem's instructions and the promise I made are forgotten at this moment.

Pushing through the press of this many people is tough work, and they seem upset that I'm trying to wind my way through them. I get shoved and pushed, and I struggle to maintain my footing.

Pausing, still in the chaos for a moment, I look out through the crowd again. I try to find the face I recognized as Bonum's, but I've lost them.

The ache shoots through my chest again, and in that momentary distraction as I'm shoved, I miss my footing and land on the ground. I whimper as someone steps on my hand. Then a heel collides with the wound in my abdomen, and I cry out. I attempt to push myself up, but there are too many people moving over and around me, and I can't manage to regain my feet.

Suddenly, there's a break in the crowd, people swearing as someone pushes between them. In the chaos, I feel an arm wrap around me and drag me up, carrying me roughly to the edge of the room. I'm dropped to my feet with no ceremony.

I turn to thank my savior, only to see Dio's angry face glaring at me. We're pressed together between the wall and the ocean of people. He turns us, putting himself between me and the crowd. His arms create a cage as he leans against the wall, closing the space between us.

"Why the fuck can you not follow simple directions, you godsdamned idiot girl?" he asks tightly.

My eyes fill with tears, prompted by his anger but also the pain of my old and new injuries. I'm unable to speak, mute with pain and emotions churning through me in this moment. For some reason, in the absence of words, my mind focuses on the specks of gold that I can see in his irises as he glares at me.

When I don't respond, his eyes narrow. "Are you hurt?" He asks tightly.

Still mute, I look down at the floor as another tear drips down my cheek. I can't share without divulging more about my injury, and I have no interest in being vulnerable with him about the cause of it.

"I asked you a question," he says, his voice slightly quieter.

Focused on his first question, I finally manage to mumble, "I thought I saw someone I knew."

"Great, now you're seeing things *and* not following directions," he sighs. He looks briefly toward the ceiling as though he's praying for patience.

I'm frozen where I stand against the wall, trapped here by a man who again seems angrier than the situation calls for. A knot of emotions begins to form in my chest.

After another moment, when it's clear I'm not going to respond, he runs his hand through his hair. Then he grabs my arm and drags me forward. The crowd doesn't seem to recognize him in the tumult. People growl and shove as he pushes past them along the edge of the room. His grip on my arm is bruising, and he seems to have no mind for my comfort as he drags me forward. Somehow, he navigates through the press of the crowd as though it is easy, following the wall until we reach the space behind the table.

I'm thankful to be back in this sanctuary even as I'm annoyed at the circumstances I find myself in.

He leads me back to my space along the wall before releasing my arm. Glaring at the wall behind me, he says, "This time, stay put." His voice is harsh.

Then he turns on his heel and strides back to the table. He pulls his suit jacket straight and runs a hand through his now rumpled hair, organizing himself for his fans again.

Gods, he's vain, I think shakily to myself.

Lent catches my eye as I look toward the table, his expression tight. "Are you ok?" he mouths.

Without knowing what else to do, I nod.

He turns to Reem and says something, then they return to signing records as though nothing happened.

I want to check my injury, but I don't want to remove my shirt in front of this crowd of people. I settle for leaning against the wall and breathing shallowly through the pain until it starts to ease again. Then I check on my books. The pages of a couple of the books are wrinkled, and one is torn nearly off. There's a shoe print on one page that's clearly the size of Dio's foot rather than mine. I tend to them carefully. Their injuries are easier for me to focus on than mine at this moment.

Once they're as mended as I can make them without tape, I close the books and put them back neatly in the bag. Then, clutching them to my chest, I huddle against the wall with my chin on the bag on top of my drawn-up knees and my eyes closed.

I am so lost in my thoughts that a while later, I'm jarred by a touch on my shoulder. I jolt upright, still sitting against the wall, afraid of another confrontation with Dio, but it's Lent who's leaning over me, and I feel my eyes fill with tears.

"Easy Chaosta," he says quietly.

I feel tears prick at my eyes because of his kindness and the pain.

"Were you hurt?" he asks.

I shake my head, closing my eyes to try to fight back the tears. At this moment, I'm not sure what to say without revealing my self-inflicted injury.

"You sure?" he asks, his voice gentle.

"I think someone accidentally kicked me, and I guess someone sort of stepped on my hand," I mumble.

"Well, that sounds kind of like you were hurt," he says. I look at his face, expecting condemnation, but his eyes are twinkling at me, and unexpectedly, I feel a smile tug at my lips. "We'll have Fem check you when we get home," he says. Then he steps back, offering me a hand.

I take it, and he pulls me gently to my feet.

"Let me take those," he says as he gestures to the book bag. I gladly hand them over. "Come on," he says, and then heads towards the door.

I follow Lent to the carriage. For a moment before I climb through the open door, I hope that maybe he is taking me home by himself. Unfortunately, my luck isn't nearly good enough for that. Instead, I'm faced with Dio staring at me as I sit on the seat across from him next to Reem.

Dio opens his mouth to say something, but Lent cuts him off. "Pretty sure she's been sufficiently scolded, old chap," he says, and while the words are friendly, his tone isn't.

Dio shuts his mouth and looks out the window. I relax a little.

"Are you ok?" Reem asks.

Instead of responding, I look at Lent and he says, "She'll live."

Reem grumbles quietly but doesn't ask again.

Lent meets Fem's eyes across the carriage. Something unspoken seems to pass between them before he looks back at me and winks. Glad he isn't sharing with Dio that I got hurt, I can't help but smile at him, thanking him silently for keeping the secret. I close my eyes and lean my head against Reem's shoulder and the back of the seat as the carriage starts out on the journey home.

*B*efore I know it, the journey is over, the movement of the carriage slowing and then finally coming to a stop. Lent climbs out first, offering me his hand as I step down. I'm careful not to whimper.

As we all get through the door, Fem says, "Let's go get you checked out just to be safe."

As I wait for him, I hear Dio begin to say something, but I notice movement out of my peripheral vision. Reem and Lent are moving to stand in front of him, placing themselves between us.

Reem says, "We need to talk." His voice is harsher than I've heard it.

Before I can pay attention to what's going on with them, Fem rests his hand gently on my shoulder. When I look at him, he points towards the office. I follow him through the door, and he closes it behind us as I settle on the couch.

I unbutton my shirt without being asked as he grabs his medical kit. I brace myself, waiting for a lecture, but it doesn't materialize. Instead, I see concern on his face.

"What exactly happened?" he asks.

I had the whole carriage ride to think about what I would say if I were asked more questions, so I have a response prepared. "I thought I saw someone I recognized and went to find them. I know it was idiotic, and I wasn't following Reem's orders. I broke a promise to him, and I'm sorry." My voice shakes, and I can't make myself meet Fem's eyes.

"Who did you think it was?" he asks, seemingly ignoring the rest of my statement.

I begin to say Bonum's name, but catch myself and instead say, "The healer you brought here to tend to the injury on my leg."

When I catch his eyes, I see that he's noticed the omission, but when I don't say anything further, he sighs and reaches out to pull back my shirt. His fingers prod at my side, pulling a whimper from me at the increased pain.

"Speaking of healers..." he mutters. After a moment or two, though, he sighs again and says, "Let's see your hand."

I hold it out and get a look at it for the first time, noticing the angry bruising that covers it. He pokes and prods and has me make a fist. It hurts, but in the end, he determines it's just bruising.

"Put that ointment on both and get some rest," he says. "I want you in bed for the next two days. If anything changes for the worse, we'll be getting a healer."

I nod, still waiting for a lecture, but again it doesn't materialize. I start to button my shirt, but wince as I struggle to do so with my injured hand.

He sighs and does the buttons for me. Then he opens the office door and begins to follow me to my room. The other boys are nowhere to be seen. I'm midway across the entrance hall when I hear Dio's voice and freeze. Fem moves closer to me, but he remains quiet as I turn to Dio.

Dio is still wearing his band outfit, but he's removed the

jacket and vest and unbuttoned the top of the crisp white shirt beneath. Because of the open collar, I can see more of the tattoos that crawl up his collarbone to the base of his neck. He's rolled up the sleeves as well, his tattooed forearms on display. I note that small, straight scars and partially healed cuts cover his forearms. Something, likely one of Malam's memories, tells me that it is the cost of using blood for magic. His hair is also mussed as though he's continued to run his hand through it.

It's the most rumpled I've seen him, and something about his appearance makes me want to lash out at him even more. As I glare at him, standing with one hip cocked, he stares back. I turn to walk to my room, not interested in engaging in a staring competition, but I hear him begin to speak and pause.

"I hope you understand why I'm angry," he says. His voice is a quiet growl.

I remain where I am, still facing away from him as waves of hurt and anger crash over me. The knot of emotion in my chest tightens. I hesitate to speak because I don't know what I'll say if I open my mouth. Whatever words might escape, I'm confident they won't be kind.

"Look at me when I'm talking to you," he finally growls, and my last shred of control snaps.

I round on him. My voice is low, quiet, and sounds like steel. A tone that sounds dangerous to me, at least. "Of course I don't fucking understand why you're angry."

I somehow keep my tone steady as I continue, "I don't understand anything about you, and your behavior toward me certainly isn't making me want to get to know you. Furthermore, none of your anger at me is logical unless somehow you see something in me that you relate to and that makes you angry at yourself."

My chest heaves as I glare at him. He begins to open his mouth, but before he can say anything, the instincts cause me to interrupt. "Taking out your self-loathing on me is the only thing that makes any sense."

He snaps his mouth shut and glares back at me, neither of us breaking. "You didn't need to make this personal," he finally says, his voice quiet.

"You're the one who made this personal," I say. My tone is still quietly dangerous.

I see his jaw tick; he's so still, he seems to be barely breathing. He finally looks over my shoulder at Fem and asks, "Is she alright?"

"You'll need to ask her," Fem says quietly.

Dio focuses back on me and heaves in a breath. "I came out here to offer to teach you self-defense," he finally says.

I reel at the change in topic. The ground feels unsteady under my feet. "Why would I want you, a massive prick, to teach me anything, especially when you clearly couldn't defend yourself?" I ask, gesturing weakly at the bruise on his face.

His expression darkens, and he tenses. Then, suddenly, he turns on his heel and leaves the room.

"Well, that was unexpected," Fem says quietly behind me.

He says it softly enough that I don't know if he intended for me to hear him. A part of me wants to ask him what part of the argument was unexpected, but instead, I heave in a breath, count to some undefined number, and then proceed to my room.

Once we get through the door, Fem asks me quietly if I'll be ok, and I nod without looking at him. After reminding me again that I'm to remain in bed and get some rest for the next two days, he leaves, shutting the door gently behind him.

I undress awkwardly, undoing as few buttons as possible and pulling the shirt over my head carefully. Every part of my body hurts. Now that I have a chance to see myself in the mirror, I note the deep bruising already showing on my abdomen around the healing wound. My hand is slightly swollen and stiff with dark red bruising showing.

I lie down on my bed, close my eyes, and try to rest despite my inner turmoil. Now that I'm lying in bed, I have nothing to distract me from my anger at Dio and how he's treating me. I also don't like who I just became when I responded to him.

As I lie in bed, trying not to think about the golden specks in his eyes, I'm confident it's going to be a long two days.

DIO'S JOURNAL - ENTRY 193

Annum:5614

Entry 193 - vera colora

Fuck. Yet again, I lost my temper with her. I need to get control of myself. I'm surprised at the fear I felt when I saw her get knocked down in the crowd like that. I suppose the fear is related to the fact that she could have been injured. Still, that amount of fear for some girl I barely know doesn't feel right.

The plan was that she'd stay behind when we held our record signing. It was for HER OWN SAFETY and because we couldn't be distracted by protecting her. Instead, she went to Reem and must have begged him to let her go with us. How she managed to convince him doesn't matter; he caved. I really need to remember to talk to him about it. This giving in and changing the plan is just making things worse for all of us.

We were all distracted by her being there, or at least I know I was. It turns out I had a right to be. I don't know what what have happened if I hadn't been there to rescue her. I'm still not convinced that she didn't get hurt, but she wouldn't tell me, and I wasn't going to force her. This just shows that Malam should have left her at that treatment center longer. At least there she would have been safe.

To add insult to injury, after we got back to the mansion, Reem and Lent cornered me before I could talk with her and scolded me for how I'd "treated her" when I rescued her. I honestly couldn't believe they scolded me instead of her. She's the one who didn't follow directions.

After that, I went out of my way to try to be nice to her, so as to mend things with the other guys. I even offered to teach her some self-defense. I'm quite proficient at boxing and thought maybe teaching her some of those skills could help prevent this sort of situation in the future. I also thought it might be good for me to get to know her a little.

It doesn't matter, though; she turned me down. Instead of taking it as the peace offering it was intended to be, she pushed me away. She even made it personal. She is observant, I will give her that.

CRACKS FORM

Early the next morning, there's a knock on my door. When I call out to let them know they are welcome, Lent and Fem let themselves in. Lent brings my books in their linen bag and his own breakfast. Fem brings food for me and reminds me to take it easy while the bruising heals before leaving. Lent, however, sits down, cross-legged on my bed, and begins to shovel food into his mouth.

Lent dives right into talking about what he's been researching, and we fall into an easy, companionable discussion about books. After he's finished eating, I ask if he has any experience repairing books. When he says he does, I pull mine out of their bag and show him the damage.

"Oof," he winces, "that's pretty bad. Good thing you're looking at the wizard of book repair!" He speaks grandly, which is quickly ruined by getting hit by the pillow I throw at him and nearly falling off the bed as he tries to avoid it.

Once the giggles recede, he leaves to get his repair kit, and I pull a different book off the stack, looking for something I was just reminded of as Lent spoke about what he was reading. I find the passage as Lent comes back into the room.

As he sets up his repair kit on top of my dresser, I call out to him to get his attention. "Hey, something you were talking about reading in one of your books reminded me of a passage I read, and I just found it."

He moves to the side of the bed, standing close to me so our heads are both leaning companionably over the book. I point out the passage to him, and he reads it out loud.

As is known, rain always falls down and not up. This action shows the cleaning and renewal of darkness, but not in the traditional sense. Because darkness and shadow brings the rain, it instead enforces balance. Light and the sun on one side, shadows and rain on the other. In Nuton's research of magical effects, he has found that when looking for change, a good rain is nearly always the best approach.

Runes connected to this particular magical phenomenon are Ehwaz and Laguz. If combined, these will bring not only renewal to the rain but also help to usher in the change you are seeking.

Excitement is clear on Lent's face as he gets through the passage. "Nice find, shorty," he says, punching me lightly on the shoulder. "Mind if I borrow this book for a bit? I'll return it, of course."

I nod, the smile spreading across my face is a lovely feeling, a beautiful contrast to the emotions of the day before. I give him the book, and he tucks it carefully into a back pocket before returning to his task of mending my books. When he gives them back to me, I have to look carefully to see the prior damage.

$\mathcal{T}$he rest of that day and the next pass in a similar fashion. Fem stops by more often than is needed or expected, but it's nice to have him checking on me. I closely follow his orders, applying the salve and resting. Slowly, my body heals and begins to feel stronger, and the pain continues to recede.

Lent spends a considerable amount of time in my room as we compare notes on books or read in companionable silence.

I spend most of my time reading the history book and continue to fill in gaps in my knowledge. Lent reads books on weather magic and shares small bits and pieces on different weather effects, such as rain, that the boys are trying to recreate. He asks me to keep this a secret, and I happily oblige. Honestly, it's not as though I have anyone else I could share this information with, even if I wanted to.

On the morning of the third day, Fem shows up at my room alone and checks my injuries. I barely dare to breathe as he gnaws on his lip while examining my abdomen and the remaining bruising on my hand.

After it feels like too much time has passed, he declares them "healed enough," but warns that I need to take things easy for at least the next several days.

When he leaves, I quickly leave my bed as though, if I wait too long, he might change his mind. Pulling on black layers of clothing without really looking, I stack my books neatly on the table beside my bed and then head to the door of my room.

As I put my hand on the knob, though, I hesitate. The realization that outside of this safe space, there will be more interactions with Dio crashes over me. I close my eyes and rest my forehead against the door for a moment as I compose myself. The image of him trapping me against the wall at the concert plays on repeat behind my eyelids. Emotions knot in my chest. Eventually, though, I can delay no longer and open the door.

The full group is sitting at the table when I arrive in the dining hall, and my stomach churns.

Thankfully, Lent grins at me as I walk in and says, "There she is."

I can't help but smile back as I fill my plate at the sideboard and then settle into the chair next to him. As I begin eating, I notice that Dio's glare doesn't seem to have the same hold on me as it did before. Instead of glass, it feels like sand kicked up in the wind and is easier to ignore.

As I'm beginning to relax, Lent turns to me and says, almost conspiratorially, "You know, I was thinking, you seem to have a talent for finding books that could be helpful to our work. How would you feel about an excursion to the bookshop?"

Before I can help myself, I gasp back, "Yes!"

Dio grumbles from the other side of the table, but I ignore it.

"Which shop?" I ask as I think of the crabby little old man and all the piles of books.

"How about we start with the one that's close but extend our errands and go further afield if we don't find anything interesting?" Lent asks.

I could kiss him. Instead, I settle for leaning across the space between us and throwing an arm around his neck in a warm, one-armed hug.

He stops shoveling food into his mouth for a minute, his cheeks pink. "If you respond like this to an invitation to run errands at the bookstore, I'm going to offer to bring you with me on research trips more often," he says, happiness clear in his voice.

I can't wipe the grin off my face. At least, that is, not until we finish eating and are readying ourselves to go. I realize Dio is walking toward us, and my stomach knots again. I grimace and turn away as I fasten my boots. However, even his presence can't destroy the joy I'm feeling at the prospect of a book-related mission.

However, the joy does crack when I hear him say to Lent, "I think I'll come with you."

Even Lent seems surprised. He pauses in lacing his boots and peers at Dio.

I can't bring myself to look at him, but I watch Lent, who glances over at me hesitantly.

I realize belatedly that he's waiting for something from me, and despite myself, I say, "It's a free world, not like we can stop you," while carefully concentrating on my boots.

My shoulders tighten as Dio grinds out simply, "Right."

An awkward silence descends over the room, the simple joy from before gone.

The joy reemerges, though, as we leave the mansion and walk down the side of the street. Lent and I walk shoulder to shoulder, and Dio trails behind. I can feel his gaze against the back of my neck, but it's easier to ignore him when I can't see him, so my mood immediately improves.

As we walk, I ask Lent what we're looking for.

"Hmm," he says and looks around the street before leaning towards me and conspiratorially saying, "I'm hoping maybe your luck will help because it's pretty broad. Anything weather magic related, specifically rain, but we need more. Maybe wind, lightning, thunder," he says. His already quiet words trail off as he says "lightning" and "thunder," so I need to strain to hear them.

The words are unfamiliar to me, but so much of this world is that it doesn't really matter.

"Not here," Dio says from behind us. His tone sounds annoyed.

When I hear his voice, I realize he's closer than I thought. Goosebumps travel up my spine at how near he is. I walk faster for a moment, trying to put more space between us.

Meanwhile, Lent is looking back at him, and out of my peripheral vision, I see him roll his eyes. "Where am I supposed to tell her then, wise guy, huh?"

Dio doesn't respond, or if he does, I don't hear him, and Lent speeds up to stay beside me.

Suddenly, I feel a different type of attention on me. I try to figure out why, only to see a pair of horses. They're fastened to the side of an ornate carriage, but they're being fed and watered, so their bridles are off. Since they're off work, I don't hesitate to go to them.

As I approach the horse nearer to me, he lowers his head, wuffling his breath against my hair as he examines me with his nose. He's telling me about how the hay isn't to their liking, and do I maybe have a carrot or two? I let him down softly that I don't have any carrots. Then I remember I grabbed an extra biscuit from breakfast and reach into my pocket.

Pulling it out, I break it in half and give some to each of the two horses. The one who is further from me butts her head ever so gently against my torso in thanks. She seems to sense that I have an injury and is trying to avoid causing me additional pain.

I wrap my arms around her massive head and breathe in the calming, musky scent. Suddenly remembering our mission and Dio's impatience, I thank both of them for their time and comfort and then walk back to Lent.

Lent is looking at me with a grin on his face. "You really have a way with them," he says.

From the glance I catch of Dio, he's staring down the street away from me, looking uncomfortable even for him. Surprised and slightly emboldened that he's not scolding me, I link my arm through Lent's, which is a stretch since he's so much taller, and lead him down the street towards our destination.

"I nearly forgot that you know where you're going for this one," he says.

"After being here twice, I'm pretty sure I can find my way back," I respond with a grin.

"Wait," Lent says, pausing and turning toward me, "twice?"

I flinch, remembering suddenly that I hadn't asked permission for the second time.

"Yes," I say hesitantly, "I went once on my own."

Then I remember how I paid for the books and feel my

cheeks flush. Looking down at the cobblestones beneath my feet, I say, "I may have put the books on your tab." I look hesitantly up at Lent, but his face is split with a grin.

He chuckles and shakes his head slightly, "Well, that explains some things. Reem wondered how I'd run up a tab I didn't remember." He meets my eyes and must see my hesitation because he just grins at me as he says, "You're a clever one, Shorty."

I can't help but laugh at that, and my chest feels light again until I hear Dio speaking behind us. "Wait, what? You find out she left the mansion without your knowledge or permission, bought books, and ran up your tab, and you call her clever?"

I hesitate, but Lent pulls me forward as he looks over his shoulder at Dio and sticks his tongue out at him.

"Real mature," Dio growls behind us as we keep walking.

Lent leans toward me, conspiratorial again, like we have a secret, and says quietly, "I feel like we have an angry guard dog following us."

Both of us suddenly have a fit of the giggles, and that's how we arrive outside the door of the small bookshop.

Somehow, we get control of ourselves before we walk through the door, but the little old man still glares at us as though he recognizes trouble as we enter his shop. A giggle tries to break loose from my chest, but I push it down, burying it before I get in further trouble.

Before the shop owner can kick us out proactively based on his suspicions, Lent pulls me further into the library. I follow him for a bit before I remove my arm from his hold and begin wandering on my own, getting lost among the stacks.

As I walk, I occasionally pull a book off the shelf, the cartographer in my head somehow pointing them out as landmarks. As I choose them, Lent takes them from me, following and carrying the ever-growing pile. After he's amassed quite a large stack, we return to the shopkeeper and pay for our treasures.

As we leave the shop, I wonder if we'll go home based on how many books we found. However, Lent doesn't seem to feel we have enough books yet and says, "On to the next shop, Shorty!" as he hails a carriage.

Dio is clearly annoyed that we're not done, but doesn't say anything and climbs into the carriage with us without further complaint.

The trip to the second bookstore doesn't take much time, so I don't need to deal with the awkward tension caused by Dio's moodiness for long. It also helps that Lent and I are already digging through our purchases. As we talk animatedly about the books we found, Dio sits silently, staring out the window and only occasionally glancing at us.

Shopping at the second bookstore is much like the first. The only real difference is that the books are organized differently, there is a pet cat with fluffy orange fur, and the shopkeeper is a little old lady.

Finally, with another armful of books purchased, we load ourselves back into the carriage for the drive home. This trip is quieter because I'm exhausted, and even Lent must be a little tired because he's unusually silent.

When we arrive outside the mansion, we discern that we may have purchased too many books for the two of us to carry, at least with my still unhealed wound. Dio surprises both of us and offers to Lent that he'll carry half the books. After the brief moment of shock passes, Lent accepts.

I follow the two of them as they carry our prizes inside. Even after a long day, Lent clearly can't help himself as he turns to me and wiggles his eyebrows while gesturing at Dio. When I get close, he whispers, "I think he might be in love with me."

I punch him in the shoulder.

Laughter follows us into the house, and that night I have the best sleep I can remember.

DIO'S JOURNAL - ENTRY 195

Annum:5614

Entry 195 - agnosco

After the "conversation" I had with Lent and Reem, where they warned me to "play nice" with the girl and told me again not to piss off Malam, I decided that some things had to change. I'll repeat again, I'm not without reason.

I also have an excellent grasp on my self-control.

With the aforementioned "conversation" freshly in my mind, I offered my services for the errands that Lent was kind enough to allow Chaosta to tag along on. She was still behaving rudely towards me, but I did my best to ignore it. I thought it would be good to ensure Lent wasn't hassled as he went about his errand, especially since the books he is after are imperative to our cause.

The side effect of being able to keep an eye on her didn't hurt.

If I hadn't realized it before, it was clear on this trip that Lent is smitten with her. He follows her like a love-sick puppy and takes every opportunity to make her laugh, even at the expense of his fellows. I don't know why, but his behavior rubbed me the wrong way. He's always seemed like a decent sort, but seeing him making up to her like that made me angry.

I was impressed at how she handled herself around those carriage horses. They're massive, aggressive, and have a history of being dangerous to humans. When she approached them, I initially stepped forward to intervene, but wasn't quick enough to stop her. I was worried that one of those massive hooves would crush her. Instead, she managed famously, even feeding them something from her pocket. Why she had food in her pocket, I didn't ask, but that doesn't really matter.

The rest of the trip went as smoothly as it could. Lent irresponsibly allowed her to randomly pick books from each shop. I have no idea what he was doing other than wasting money. I was watching closely, and she didn't read the titles or look closely at the books. Neither did he.

I almost said something to him because now they're going to waste a bunch of time reading through trash. They'll be spending time we don't have reading random books instead of making progress on our understanding of weather magic. In the end, though, I decided I needed to keep my mouth shut rather than risk further confrontations with the others.

There has already been enough strife with my bandmates and the girl. I'm not quite ready to try to mend things with her again after the way she spoke with me after the record signing. However, for some reason, I can't seem to rouse the same level of anger at her that I was feeling. I'm beginning to worry that she is going to be bad for my recovery despite my efforts to keep my distance.

MEMORIES OF TREES

The next few days pass calmly. I continue to heal, and it becomes easier for me to make it through a whole day without needing to return to my room to lie flat and rest.

The Band has a concert schedule soon where they plan to play some of their new music, so most of their time has been spent rehearsing. When he isn't rehearsing, I manage to fit in some reading time with Lent, but even he is tight-lipped and tense. They're all clearly feeling the pressure, and tempers are short, so other than breakfast and my occasional "reading dates," with Lent, I tend to avoid them. Instead, I read in my room, sketch on the blank pages of books, or explore the mansion.

In my exploration, I find that the mansion is larger than I first thought, although many rooms are uninhabited and filled with dust. Some have old furniture covered with heavy sheets to keep the dust off, and others are empty. Seeing the large, open spaces of the empty rooms pulls at feelings buried inside me. As I consider, I realize the feeling is drawing me toward discovering, or rediscovering, skills with a weapon. The threat from the angels hangs over my head, and the idea of being able to defend myself with more skill than in my last fight presses at me.

With that thought, in a sudden rush of inspiration, I locate the broken broom I found previously during my exploration. After that, I spend some of my time cleaning and dusting one of the empty rooms until it's fit for my use. Once the room is clean enough, I begin practicing with the handle of the broom as a makeshift sword. Because I'm confident the boys wouldn't approve, I sneak away while they rehearse or practice magic.

Fluid, dancelike patterns emerge from my subconscious as though they've been there for decades instead of moments. The magic of Malam's memories is helping me once again. Even in the short bursts of practice I carve out from my day, I feel myself improving and getting stronger. Since I'm not prepared to broach the topic of a weapon, it will have to do for now.

A few more days pass, and we're eating dinner in the dining room.

Fem and Reem are deep in discussion about what key one of their songs is, or should be, in.

Lent sits quietly, eating with his eyes closed as though he can't keep them open any longer. Since they have been rehearsing late into the evening, it doesn't surprise me that he's tired.

Before I can encourage him to go to bed, Dio leans over and engages him in conversation. I absentmindedly pick at the food on my plate, trying to decide if I should risk a third practice session after my meal if they continue rehearsing tonight.

My attention is grabbed by something I must have subconsciously overheard in Dio and Lent's conversation. I focus on what they are talking about and hear them disagreeing about how tall something was, "back in the day."

I'm losing focus again, unsure why I suddenly thought I

cared. I'm concentrating on how I might make the broom handle more like a sword when my focus again pulls me back to the conversation as I realize they are talking about trees.

In my memory, I can see the trees surrounding Malam, where the young boy brought me after I killed the angel. I remember not being able to see the top of the trees where they rose through the ceiling. The heavy smoke in that place nearly concealed the trunks and plants surrounding them.

Suddenly, I register that everyone in the room is staring at me, and I have the uncomfortable feeling I may have said some part of my memories out loud.

"What did you just say?" Fem asks quietly.

"I'm not sure, I was just distracted and then I heard Lent and Dio's conversation and remembered the trees I saw after I ki— got hurt at the concert," I say quickly. The words tumbling over themselves.

I simultaneously feel the intensity of Dio staring at me and hear him ask, "What were you going to say before you caught yourself?"

At the same time, Reem says, "What do you mean you saw trees?"

I ignore Dio and respond to Reem. Carefully, I stick to information that they won't refute as I say, "When I left that concert, the one where my leg was injured, a small boy helped me and brought me to a place with trees where someone wrapped up my leg."

Dio is staring at me, his eyes slightly narrowed. As I stare back, he shakes his head slightly and then stands and leaves the room.

Lent glares at his retreating back as he says, "Trees don't exist anymore, not for centuries now. Everywhere they would have grown is either covered in paved streets or buildings. It was probably a dream you had from the pain medication, right?"

Suddenly remembering what I learned in the history book about how the city covers all of the land now, I wish even more that I'd kept quiet. "Yeah," I say quietly to Lent, "that must have been it."

I go back to my meal, eating woodenly with less of an appetite than I had just moments ago. I can't help but glance at the door, unable to keep myself from puzzling over Dio's sudden absence.

As I do so, I notice Fem looking at me thoughtfully, unmoving in his chair. He's focused on me as the others return to whatever conversation they were having.

After clearing my plate, I return to my room but leave my door open. When I hear the boys tramp back downstairs to rehearse, I escape to the empty room for more sword practice.

The focus of putting my body through the movements helps me drive the uncomfortable interaction at dinner from my mind. It's gratifying to feel my strength, flexibility, and coordination improving.

* * *

That night, my dreams again show me the memory I saw at dinner. Although in the dream, the trees rise above my head without the ceiling to conceal them. I stare up at the leaves, the green completely concealing the blue sky that I somehow know is above.

I hear something and glance around, only to see Malam standing beneath them with a crow on his shoulder.

"You can stay awhile, but this is not your place," he says knowingly. I can't recall him saying that when I was here last. I walk among the trees and breathe in the smell of earth. Even though it is a dream, it feels like a balm for lungs that normally breathe poisoned air.

* * *

*T*he next day, I eat breakfast by myself. It would appear the boys have slept in, or perhaps gone back to bed. After I eat, I manage to escape to practice with my sword for a while. I eventually hear them stirring and quickly return to my room. As I busy myself with reading, there's a knock on the door that I recognize as Lent's.

"Come in," I call with a smile.

Lent opens the door and sticks his head in.

My smile falls as I realize he's not joining me to read.

"How's the reading going, fellow knowledge seeker?" He asks with a grin.

His joy is infectious, so the smile returns as I respond that I'm enjoying my book.

"I'd love to join you," he says, "but we've decided to take a quick break from rehearsing to meet with Malam since it's been a while."He grimaces and then laughingly says, "I think Dio will desert us if we don't *work towards the cause*." Grinning at me while rolling his eyes, he says, "His words."

I can't help but laugh at how uptight and accurate his impression of Dio is.

Eyes twinkling, he says, "Malam will want to see you while he's here." Then, with another grimace, he says, "I've also been asked to remind you not to try to listen in on our meeting with him."

"Of course not, I really am sorry about that."

He nods seriously, but then he's already smiling at me again. "I promise after the concert we'll dig into all those books we made Dio carry."

I laugh with him for a moment before he needs to leave.

After the door closes behind him, I go to the bathroom to freshen up and pull on less rumpled clothing. I have limited outfits that allow for the movement I need. Because of that, I've been wearing the same few things to make sure there's no delay when I can sneak away. They are getting fairly rumpled and grungy, even with the house employees washing them for me. That won't do for a meeting with such an important demon.

Just as I'm finished dressing and cleaning up, there is a knock on the door. When I open it this time, it's Fem standing outside. He looks slightly surprised to see me at the door, but recovers quickly and tells me to follow him. He leads us to the office.

Malam is already here, and he's clearly been pacing. His eyes trail over me briefly, and he relaxes. He steps forward and sinks onto one of the overstuffed chairs, leaning forward with one elbow resting on his knee. I sit on the chair across from him, and Fem remains where he is, behind me, near the door.

"You look good, Chaosta," Malam says, his voice composed this time.

I note the lack of anger on his face and relax a bit.

"You're actually looking surprisingly well," he says thoughtfully.

I bite my lip, hoping that if he notices, as I have, that there are muscles beginning to show on my arms, he'll keep it to himself. I'm confident the boys wouldn't support my sword practice, so I'd rather Fem not find out yet.

"I've been resting and reading a lot. Fem has been making sure I rest," I say quietly.

"That's good," he says. Then I see him tense slightly as he asks, "Have you had any thoughts about hurting yourself?"

I glance briefly over my shoulder at Fem, wondering what he's told Malam before saying, "No, I haven't. There was an incident at the record signing, though."

Anger crosses Malam's face.

I hear Fem shift slightly behind me.

"An incident?" he growls, glaring briefly over my head at Fem before looking back at me.

"I thought I saw Bonum in the crowd, and I went after them. I lost my footing and got stepped on. Fem checked me out after, though, and it was just some bruising. I'm fine now," I rattle out quickly before taking a breath.

Behind me, I hear Fem shift again.

Malam glares up at him over my head for a long moment. "Fem didn't mention anything to me," he growls, his eyes flashing.

"It really wasn't that big of a deal. Like I said, I'm feeling good now," I say, suddenly worried about Fem's safety.

Malam pinches the bridge of his nose. Eyes closed for a moment, he sighs. When he opens his eyes, he fixes them on me. "Why was Bonum there?"

"I don't know, that's what I was trying to find out."

"What were they doing?" Malam asks, a dangerous note in his voice.

"Just standing in the crowd and watching me."

"Watching you, or watching the band?"

"Watching me."

Malam opens his mouth to say something, but then pinches the bridge of his nose again. "Actually, never mind."

There's a long pause, and the energy in the room feels tense.

"Glad to see you're feeling better," Malam finally says. He moves to stand, but I interrupt him, asking my question with a slightly shaking voice.

"Can I have a sword?"

"You don't have one?" he asks, sounding horrified.

I shake my head.

"I'll see to it," he says firmly. Then he ruins the scary persona slightly by reaching out and patting my knee comfortingly.

Suddenly realizing I have one more question, I blurt out, "Can you tell me what an addict is?"

Malam's expression turns to stone, and he glares at Fem

behind me as he says, "An addict is someone who doesn't have any control over taking drugs or drinking alcohol."

"I've never taken drugs or drunk any alcohol."

"I know," he says, his gaze not moving from Fem.

I have many unanswered questions, but before I can ask them, Fem jumps in.

"Wait," he says. "Why would you trust her with a sword, and who's Bonum? Also, what do you mean she hasn't ever had drugs or alcohol? The way we found her in the street—"

I'm again worried for Fem's safety as Malam stands suddenly and strides over to stand inches in front of him, shoulders tense. "Make note, Fem, the only reason you're here is because I told you about her injury so you could help keep an eye on things. You don't need the answers to these questions. I expect you to keep all of this knowledge to yourself."

There is a pause, tense silence swirling between them, and Malam's anger perfusing the room. Then he turns and leaves. As he walks through the door, he calls back, "Come along, Fem, we have work to do."

I hear Fem turn and leave the room, and I'm left sitting in the office by myself. All I can think of is my new sword and when I might next see Malam so that I can have it.

With those hopeful thoughts, I leave the room and escape again to practice with my current, makeshift sword.

DIO'S JOURNAL - ENTRY 196

Annum:5614

Entry 196 - turbatio

Apparently, it's been a while since I wrote. This written account is greatly important, as is our work toward the cause, and I've been distracted from both, clearly. I realized a couple of days ago that we hadn't made any progress on our REAL work in a while. I told the others that we needed to make time to summon the demon again. As much as I'd like to avoid him, for now, his help is necessary. Perhaps once this concert is over, I can talk to the guys about finding a different demon to summon. For now, the most important thing is making some progress toward the cause again.

I think it's easy for all of us to want to delay that work for so many reasons, and yet the rationale behind taking on this distasteful and monumental task is sound. This morning, I saw in the newspaper that food shortages are affecting even bread now. Yet, when I brought it up, the guys were reluctant to summon the demon again. I know they didn't want to take time away from rehearsing. I know how important this concert is to them, and we are playing a lot of new material. I know we all still feel unprepared, but if we aren't able to figure out the weather magic we need for the cause soon, all of this might cease to exist. Our work on magic needs to come first. They did finally see reason, and the day was determined, which was today.

It might be the lack of sleep from all the hours spent rehearsing, but the energy felt weird leading up to Malam's arrival.

We successfully completed the ritual the night before, early in the morning, actually, since we were up late rehearsing. When Malam showed up around midday, he asked to see Chaosta first. I thought he'd just want to check on her in passing and then move on, but instead, he cloistered himself in the office with her. He included Fem for some reason. They weren't in there for long, but it still took more time than I expected. While they were otherwise occupied, Lent, Reem, and I set up our space in the basement ballroom. When they joined us (without Chaosta, of course), Fem had a weird expression on his face. I think frustration, but maybe also confusion? I need to remember to ask him what happened.

At the time, that's not what I was focused on. We were just about to begin our magic work when Lent grabbed a book out of somewhere and brought it over to Malam. When Lent asked him if it might help, the demon paused and read through a passage. Malam looked surprised, which is not an expression I've ever seen on his smug face. He said it would help and asked where Lent had found the book. I was surprised when Lent said Chaosta had found it AND pointed out the passage to him. I couldn't help but consider if I've underestimated the girl again.

We spent the rest of our time working through that passage, and it actually helped. We produced real, soaking rain for the first time. We were all elated.

As we wrapped up our practice and began to pack up, things took another turn. I was focused on cleaning the runes off the floor with Reem while Lent and Fem packed up the items we used. Malam was just leaving when Fem asked him about something Chaosta said. Last night, when she said she'd seen trees, I thought it was a drug-induced hallucination and had immediately dismissed it. At the time she said it, I was more focused on the fact that she was beginning to say something else and then changed it. I tried to get her to admit to what she was starting to say. However, Reem interrupted me, and she, of course, responded to him. I had to leave. The suspicion that it was a hallucination, and her reluctance to accept that she is recovering from an addiction hit too close to home.

I'm fairly certain that before she caught herself, she was going to say she kissed someone in the crowd at

that concert before she got hurt. She's not unattrac-
tive. I guess I could see that happening. If it did, I don't
know what to think. I guess it makes me angry. Fucking
emotions. It's not as though they'd be easy to deal with
anyway, but in my situation, they're just extra volatile.

Let me get back on topic, fuck the lack of sleep is
clearly showing. When Fem asked Malam about Chaosta
saying she'd seen trees, I was sure he was going to laugh
it off. Instead, he got tense and balled up. Then he
shared that she had been taken to the demon stronghold for healing, and there are trees there. I didn't
know what to say or think. Lent, of course, chimed in
asking more questions, but Malam refused to answer
and left shortly after. I can't speak for all of us, but I
was shocked. I'm still guessing that it was just halluci-
nations. I can't imagine why she would have been
allowed in the demon stronghold.

I need to figure out what's going on with her before
it negatively impacts all of us. Either that or I should
likely move out. I don't like feeling this confusion and
doubt. My emotions have been particularly volatile
recently, and even when I've had a chance to sleep,
insomnia has been kicking my ass. It certainly doesn't
help that when I do sleep, I've been having this odd
nightmare. Every time it's the same. In the dream, I
don't get to Chaosta in time when she's knocked down in
the crowd.

Fuck, I need some sleep.

SHARK WEEK

The day of The Boys' concert is suddenly upon us, and we're eating breakfast together in the dining room. They ended rehearsal early the day prior so they could get enough sleep, which cut into my sword practice.

Because the concert is tonight, there won't be any rehearsing, so they can "rest and recover before the big night," as Reem said yesterday. That means no sword practice today either, so I'm in a foul mood as we eat breakfast.

Reem already pulled me aside this morning. He told me that the house employees are nearly all taking a holiday to thank them for their work, so I'll be going to the concert. He emphasized to me, firmly but not unkindly, that I needed to promise to listen to orders and act thoughtfully. Despite the fact that I'm sure Dio put him up to it, I agreed. I've continued to feel irritated at being treated like a child, but I certainly never intend to cause a disruption to their work, and today is no different.

The boys are quiet as they eat, the room buzzing with tension. Everyone seems to be trying to focus on their breakfast except Lent, who's reading a paper as he shovels food into his mouth.

As he reads, he suddenly stops eating, and his expression goes tight. "Look at this," he says. "There are more food shortages. Even bread is getting tougher to come by."

"Yeah," Dio says darkly, "that's been reported for a while now. On the next page, there's an article about the new air pollution numbers. They're also grim. This is why our work is so important. After this damned concert, we need to get our focus back."

Lent's face goes pale, and Reem looks angry. Dio seems oblivious as he stares at his plate, cutting his food into neat pieces. The room is quiet, other than the swishing of paper as Lent folds the newspaper and pushes it into the middle of the table, clearly done reading this morning. The tense quiet continues until everyone leaves to do whatever needs to be done before the concert.

I spend the rest of the day in my room, first picking out my outfit for the concert and then reading one of the books on weather magic. Finally, with hours still to wait, I sketch a bit more on some of the blank pages in the books I keep in my room. At some point, I must fall asleep because I'm woken to a knock on my door.

"Twenty minutes and we're in the carriage," Reem says through the door. He sounds frazzled.

I jump out of bed, cursing that I fell asleep, and quickly get ready. I freshen up in my small bathroom and dress myself as fast as I can, but I know I'm still taking too long. I leave my room, still fastening my corset top as I head to the front door. I shove my feet into my boots and run to the carriage with them still unfastened. I drop breathlessly onto a seat next to Lent as the carriage begins moving.

The trip passes in a blur, the energy in the carriage even more tense than it was at breakfast.

When we arrive at the venue, I follow the boys through the front door and, as is typical, down to the basement. This place is certainly not typical, though, and all the worry and tension from the boys over the past few days begins to make sense.

The space we walk into is enormous. In addition to the massive open room with only stone pillars dividing it, there are passageways leading out at multiple points to fit additional spectators.

Unlike other venues, this place is also mostly set up. The only thing the staff are doing is setting up the instruments on the wide stage. As I look around, I note that Lent, Reem, and Fem are heading to the stage, and I begin to follow them.

However, I suddenly run into a solid form.

Blinking up at whoever or whatever it is, I realize it's Dio. I step back as he grumbles about his suit being rumpled, but I don't know what he's talking about. There isn't a single wrinkle to be seen. In his neatly pressed concert outfit, he looks even more like the prick he is, every bit the spoiled rich boy.

His concerns about his outfit apparently resolved, he points behind me. "I have a spot for you back there," he says. His voice is carefully controlled.

I stand unmoving, glaring at him, and feel my fingers curling into fists.

"The only reason you were allowed to accompany us this time is that you promised, yet again, to listen to orders," he reminds me. He's staring over the top of my head and not meeting my eyes. The fact that he can't see me glaring at him just increases my anger.

"After what happened at the concert and signing, I took it upon myself to ensure there was a safe place for you this time."

I continue to glare at him, my control over my emotions close to snapping.

He glances at me, and I see his throat bob as he swallows.

"Are you going to accompany me of your own accord?" he asks more quietly.

My control finally snaps, and my instincts take over. As I glare at him, without thinking, I lean close and snarl, "I'm not a fucking child, and if you try to drag me again, I'll fight back this time." Then I turn on my heel and walk towards the back of the room where he pointed.

As soon as I turn, I see what his plan is. There's an alcove that is free of people, thanks to a satin rope surrounding it. There are two muscular security guards present.

I hesitate as I get to the velvet cord at the entrance, but Dio steps alongside me and says to the guards, "You will guard her and won't leave her alone for the duration of the concert. Do I make myself clear?"

"Yes, sir," they both respond confidently, glancing from him to me.

I watch as one blushes as she looks at him. I'm instantly concerned about her taste in men.

The other pulls the rope aside, and I walk into the alcove and deposit myself on one of the tall chairs that look towards the stage. I'm careful not to look toward Dio, but I might as well have not bothered because, with his task complete, he turns and heads to the stage without another word.

I'm immediately bored and wish I had brought some books.

With nothing else to do, I watch as fans start to mill into the space, rather quickly filling the massive open room and beginning to overflow into the tunnels at the back. The security guards move around me, watching to make sure no one encroaches on the alcove, and occasionally glancing in my direction.

Then, finally, the concert starts. The band runs onto the stage, and they each begin to grab their instruments as they welcome the crowd. I can barely hear what they're saying with all the screams, shouts, and whistles, but I have to admit I have the best seat in the place. The alcove is raised slightly, so while I'm a significant distance from the stage, I can clearly see over the crowd.

When The Boys begin to play, I can't help but get caught up in the performance. The crowd is wild. I have no idea how we can still hear the music. There must be some magic to it because the crowd roars so loudly that it sounds like a massive, angry beast. They're swirling and moving to the music. I can't imagine how people aren't being trampled; maybe they are.

As the set continues, I find myself watching the band. Their focus and joy as they play to the crowd is clear.

Watching Reem play the banjo and occasionally provide vocal accompaniment while blending in with the group is lovely after seeing him assume the role of leader all the time.

Lent's serious side comes through as he focuses on his guitar and backup vocals. He is clearly a talented musician.

Fem looks more joyful than I've ever seen him as he throws himself into playing the fiddle that is tucked under his chin.

Despite my best intentions, though, it's Dio who most captures my attention.

By the time they're three songs into the set, his hair is tousled and he's removed his suit jacket. By the fifth song, he's rolled up his sleeves slightly and unbuttoned his collar. He's completely immersed in the music and the crowd. His passion for singing shows clearly across his face.

I feel disgusted with myself for not being able to look away from him.

Then, suddenly, I'm scrubbing at my chest, which I belatedly realize has been aching for a while.

Distracted from the band, I look for my guards and see them resting near the entrance to the alcove, their focus trained on the performance. One guard is mouthing the words to the song the band is playing. As I glance back up, I catch a spot of brightness at the edge of my vision. My fingers tighten into a fist involuntarily as though grasping a sword hilt I don't have.

The angel stands in the crowd, but instead of facing the stage like everyone else, he's facing me. He stares directly at me even as I stare back, his gaze predatory. The stillness of him as he stands among the moving crowd is familiar. Like a monster in the water.

As I watch him, my chest continues to ache more strongly, and I scrub at it again, trying to make the pain go away. My gaze moves for a moment, and I catch another spot of brightness. There is a second angel, also standing in the opposite direction of the crowd. This angel is also staring at me.

The hairs on the back of my neck stand up, and the ache in my chest continues to increase despite my efforts. I'm suddenly brought back to a different time, a different crowd, and then a fight in the street.

The cartographer in my head directs me to the guards.

I move closer to one of them and, even leaning toward her, have to shout, "I need a restroom."

She looks uncertainly at the other guard, who moves closer, and I hear her repeat my request.

The other guard looks at me and shakes her head as she yells back, "It's risky to try to leave this space, miss. The band was very clear about us ensuring your safety."

The ache in my chest increases, and I can see the angels still standing unmoving in the swirling crowd, still staring at me.

I wince at the increased pain in my chest and shout, "Please, I REALLY need the restroom."

"Oh!" the guard closer to me says and nods as though she's just understood some big secret. She leans even closer to me and, directly into my ear, says, "I'm sure those men wouldn't think to expect a woman's issues, right?" She nudges me gently with her elbow, a friendly smile on her face.

I have no idea what she means, but since she seems willing to take me, I just grin back at her and nod.

She turns back to the other guard and they confer for a moment before she gestures to me with her head to follow. With that, she leads me along the back of the massive room, through the crowd, and to a small, crowded restroom.

She cuts the line with me and claims one of the small rooms as another woman leaves. The next person in line begins to yell at us, but I leave the guard to deal with that mess and escape into the bathroom.

Still allowing my instincts to direct me, I think of Malam and speak his name clearly and as quietly as I can in the small space. Almost instantly, there is a swirl of black, and then he's standing in front of me. He smells of earth, and his short-sleeved, black, linen shirt is rumpled. He doesn't have shoes on.

I grimace, thinking of his bare feet on the dirty bathroom floor.

He stares at me, and we both freeze for a moment. Then his face goes hard as he says, "Are you ok?"

"I'm not sure," I say as I rub again at the ache in my chest. I see him note it, as I say, "There are two angels in the crowd watching me."

"You or the band?"

"Me."

"Fuck," he says harshly. Then, after a brief pause, he says, "Give me a moment," and disappears in a swirl of shadow.

There's a knock on the door. "What's going on in there?" asks the guard outside.

"Sorry," I yell back, "just talking to myself." I wince as I register how that sounds.

Just as I'm preparing myself for her to break down the door, there's another swirl of darkness, and Malam materializes in front of me again.

"Take this," he says, holding out a sword in a sheath with

straps hanging from it. "As you know, this isn't my fight, and I can't stay. I can't be involved directly in violence against them, or I will break the tenuous truce, and we aren't ready for that," his eyes flash as he speaks, and I can see by the set of his shoulders that he is worried.

"Be safe, please?" he says after another moment, and his voice breaks slightly at the end.

Then, without another word, the shadow swirls around him, the sound of wings in the air, and then he's gone.

Another knock resounds in the small room, which snaps me out of whatever thoughts I was lost in. I quickly strap the sword to my back. With that done, I go to the door and open it to see the guard raising her hand to knock again.

As I'm trying to figure out my story for the sword, I look at her face and see how harried she looks, the crowd pressing against her trying to get to the open door. Because of the chaos, I'm saved from needing to answer. She leads me back through the crowd to the alcove.

Thankfully, neither guard seems to notice my new weapon. As we arrive back at the alcove, I look out to the crowd, searching for the two angels, but I don't see either of them.

I'm distracted through the rest of the concert, constantly scanning for them in the crowd, even as I enjoy the feel of the sword against my back.

DIO'S JOURNAL - ENTRY 198

Annum:5614

Entry 198 - colligere fragmenta

Gods be damned, that concert was amazing. We all put on a good show, but I, in particular, was at the top of my game. The crowd was massive, and we were all so immersed in the music that hours passed in what felt like moments. I don't think I've ever experienced such a natural high. This is becoming my new favorite drug.

Thanks to all our hard work, the new material went off without a hitch, and the crowd went crazy for it. It's been nice to be able to add my stamp to things and not just parrot the previous lead singer. It's nice to have some of my own stuff out there for our fans now.

Thankfully, my plan to keep the girl, all of us, and our fans safe at this concert worked. Of course, it took hiring two extra security guards and roping off a clear section to "contain" her, but it was worth it. I was actually able to concentrate on performing instead of trying to keep an eye on her. She was clearly angry at me when I told her about my plan with the guards. I guess I can't blame her; I sort of had her well cornered. I guess it's not a shock that she lashed out.

Despite that, there was still some oddness. She somehow found a fucking sword. She, I'm still laughing at this one, said Malam gave it to her. Not only is that ridiculous on its own, because why would a demon ever give anyone a sword, much less a mere girl, but she claimed she'd summoned him.

When she initially mentioned Malam, I gave her the benefit of the doubt. I asked if he was there to watch the concert because that would honestly make sense. He's sort of an acquaintance, and our music is top-notch. I don't know what he does with his free time, but he could do worse than attending one of our concerts. When she said she'd summoned him, though all I could imagine was that she's using again.

Fuck, I don't need this right now.

Of course, she can't have summoned a demon. The ritual takes a group of dark magic users and at least six hours. She obviously doesn't know magic. Even if she did, she isn't part of a coven, so it's impossible. My guess is she took the sword from someone in the crowd. If I were a betting man, I'd put money on one of our fans reaching out about a stolen sword.

I have been thinking a lot about the conversation the other day, and I must admit, even though I continue to doubt Malam's story about her seeing trees and believe he's covering for her, if it's true, I'm envious. She kisses someone in a crowd, starts a riot, and gets taken to the demon stronghold. What do I need to do to go there myself? Seeing trees in person would be such an honor. As much as I hope that the work we're doing with the cause begins to reverse all the damage to our environment, it is unlikely I'll live to see trees growing on this world.

THE ONE WHERE THERE ARE
MORE FRIENDS

After the concert, the boys sleep for nearly a full day. I take advantage of their absence and spend as much time as I can practicing with my new sword. The rest of the time, when I'm not eating meals, I admire it while trying to read in my room.

The sword is a saber, slender, curved, and well-balanced. It's not overly long, but it is long for my short frame. Longer than my broken piece of broom handle, at least. The handle is also a little too big for my hand, but I know it won't take me long to get used to it, especially if I can continue to find time to practice.

By the end of the day, my whole body aches from the time spent practicing. That night, I'm exhausted enough that I fall into a deep, dreamless sleep.

The next morning, I wake up later than normal with my body punishing me for the sudden increase in activity. I can't help but groan as I sit down at the breakfast table. Only Lent and Fem are left at the table by the time I get there, and I feel their eyes on me as I start to eat.

"Everything ok?" Fem asks, his voice worried.

"Fine," I grumble back, "I must have just overdone it yesterday."

I look up to see a look of confusion on Fem's face, but Lent jumps in, saying, "Maybe it was summoning a demon by yourself?"

I glare at him and wonder if he's going to make a big deal about it. I couldn't believe they all laughed at me after the concert during the carriage ride home. Yet again, I clearly did or said something wrong. When I see Lent's face, though his brows are raised and one side of his mouth is tilted up in an uneven grin.

I make a growling sound at him, and he laughs.

Relieved I'm not being scolded, I return to my breakfast. The room is quiet while I finish my meal, and I enjoy the companionable silence.

As I finish eating, Fem says, "I thought maybe the three of us could spend some time with those new books you found?"

Feeling hopeful, I glance up and see Lent looking at Fem with his brows raised in surprise while Fem continues to look at me appraisingly.

"I'd love to," I say breathlessly. I quickly stand and scrape off my plate before he can change his mind.

We move to the floral room and spend some time gathering the books we brought. We stack them in neat piles on the central table between the couches.

After a short silence as we each take a book and begin scanning through them, Fem says, "How did you even choose this one?" There is a presumptuous tone to his voice.

Before I can respond, Lent cuts in, "Hey now, Fem, we had our own method, didn't we, Chaosta?" As he says it, he winks at me.

I laugh and say, "I mean, honestly, I just followed my instincts."

Fem glances at me thoughtfully and then looks at Lent as he says, "Did you choose these or did she?"

Lent pauses and glances at me, his cheeks going pink. "She did," he finally says.

"Hmm," Fem says and continues to page through the book, which seems to be called *Weather It Will*.

After a few minutes, Fem looks as though he is about to put it down, but then he freezes. I see him lean closer to the book and stare at the page. Then he reads a passage about how we draw power from and give power to the weather. Lent listens thoughtfully.

None of it makes sense to me, but as he finishes reading, he looks up at us, his eyes slightly wide. "There are notes in the margin," he says, "including a rune I don't recognize."

He turns the book toward us so we can see. Sure enough, in small, dainty, faded handwriting in the margin, there are a couple of notes and an odd, twisting shape. He pages through the rest of the book, but there aren't any others.

The thoughtful, appraising look is back on his face as he looks at me. "Good find," he says. "We'll show this to Malam when he's here later."

"Malam will be here today?" I ask. I want to thank him for my sword. Of course, I don't plan to mention that to the boys since they clearly think it couldn't have been him who gave it to me.

"Yeah," Fem says, "we started the summoning ritual this morning. We need to make up for the time that we lost to our concert preparations." As he speaks, he marks the page and continues to look through the rest of the book.

The rest of the day passes in a similar fashion. The boys find passages to mark, and I find a couple more margin notes, but only one more that includes a rune.

By the end of the day, the three of us have several passages we've marked, and yet we have barely begun on the massive pile of books we bought. Fem and Lent stand and stretch. I join them, groaning as I stretch my tight, tired muscles.

Fem looks as though he's about to ask me again why I am stiff. Thankfully, though, Reem interrupts by coming to the door and reminding them that they have preparations to make before Malam arrives. They follow Reem out of the room.

I want to disappear to practice with my sword and work out the stiffness, but I linger in the entry hall for a few minutes, waiting for Malam.

Finally, I hear him walk through the front door. When he sees me, he relaxes as he says quietly, "Thank the dark gods."

Before I can overthink it, I go to him and wrap my arms around him, mumbling, "thank you for the sword," against his torso.

He stands stiffly, but then I feel his arms wrap around me in a brief and still rather stiff hug. After a moment, he takes my shoulders and gently pushes me back, scanning my face.

"Will it do for now?" he asks. "It isn't what I wanted to give you, but I knew time was short, and it was a spare I had on hand."

I can feel a massive smile splitting my face. "It's perfect," I say.

He actually smiles at that, and then, with an awkward squeeze of my shoulders, he looks behind me to the basement door and says, "I must go." With that, he steps around me and heads through the door, closing it firmly behind him.

Not wanting to waste any time, I disappear to my bedroom to collect the borrowed sword. Then I go to the large empty room and practice until my muscles cramp. I sleep well that night, the physical exhaustion keeping the worst of the dreams at bay.

· · ·

*T*he next few days pass in much the same way. Most of the time, I don't see Malam since I escape to the upstairs room with my sword immediately after the boys head downstairs.

I know somehow that I need to take advantage of every moment.

Something is driving me beyond my general interest in being stronger, and while I don't understand what or who it might be, it is a vicious taskmaster. I fall into bed every night, exhausted and sore. My hands split open before calluses can form. I cover them in bandages and pretend I'm covering paper cuts.

Fem looks doubtful but doesn't pry beyond the occasional, thoughtful question.

Meanwhile, Fem and Lent continue to review the massive pile of books with me, but also begin to show me bits of dark magic.

I learn from them that anyone can be educated on runes and how to use them to create magical effects. However, there is danger in practicing incorrectly or making errors, so they warn me against trying without formal instruction.

I realize, as the days pass, how much I enjoy both of their company. Lent's humor and irreverence make everything fun. The caring I feel from Fem leads me to enjoy his company just as much, even though he is always serious. The two of them provide a sense of support I wouldn't have realized I was missing if it weren't for the slow recognition of how much better I feel in their company.

For the most part, I don't see much of Reem or Dio. I sleep in, and they wake early, so they've already eaten when I get to the dining room in the morning. Then the rest of the day, while

Lent, Fem and I look over our pile of books, the two of them are off doing whatever it is they do.

After a few days, when I see Dio at breakfast, he almost seems happy. Not to see me, of course. He avoids meeting my eyes, but I can feel him looking at me occasionally as we eat. When I glare at him between bites, for some reason, I can't help but notice how long his eyelashes are.

Why the fuck must the prick be attractive?

As he leaves the room, talking with Reem about how much progress they're making, "toward the cause," his voice is less snarly than it has been.

The knot of emotions in my chest tightens. All I can hope is that the research I am doing isn't the reason things have turned around for him. He certainly doesn't deserve that.

DIO'S JOURNAL - ENTRY 205

Annum:5614

Entry 205 - profectum

Finally, we're making progress again. I've been consistent with my entries in this journal, and we've been meeting with Malam every evening to practice magic. Even better, we're making significant progress on the weather work, which will eventually support our cause and create the storm we need.

I've also started taking Reem out boxing during the day while the others are locked in that room with their books. In doing so, we've been getting to know each other better.

When I first asked him, he declined, but the next day he asked about it, and I made the offer again. This time, he took me up on it. He hasn't done anything like this before. His hands are too important to risk since he plays the banjo and other instruments. However, he seems to be enjoying learning the basics, including the footwork, and is clearly more confident as he's gotten stronger. It's also been good to get to know him better.

He even shared a bit about why he got into magic and met Malam. It turns out that one of his siblings was mistreated by the government and ended up taking her own life. He went through a dark period and then threw himself into music while he dug into the information behind her death. As he did so, he met the previous lead singer, who was involved with an anti-government group. The rest, as they say, is history.

In spending all this time with Reem boxing, I've also been able to avoid the girl. At least it's easier not to worry about whether she's using again when I'm not around her. I think it's better for both of us if I keep my distance.

Truly, though, much of our progress is thanks to Lent and Fem. While Lent was already good at researching, together they've made exponential progress. They're also managing to distract Chaosta and have her locked up with them all day, every day, so it's doing double duty. Hopefully, Fem isn't also falling for her. I don't know what I'll do if he does. They've been trying to give her some credit for their findings, but I can see through it. At some point, I'll put my foot down and call them out. However, it does seem to be soothing Malam to think that she might be helping, so I'm not in a hurry to do that right now.

I also haven't seen any sign of that sword. At this point, I'm guessing Malam may have taken it from her, which is for the best. If I hadn't seen it myself, I'd think she hallucinated the whole thing. Trying to keep her from getting trampled at events is bad enough. I don't know what I'll do if she starts carrying a weapon around.

Of course, there is always a dark side, and currently, that is the news. It makes me that much more thankful we're making so much progress because things continue to get worse. On top of all the other ongoing shit, the illness that's caused by the pollution is continuing to claim more lives. Plus, we also have some sort of toxic creature in the storm grates that's attacking carriage horses.

At first, the creatures were only attacking horses at rest, but there have been two carriage accidents this week where they've attacked while moving. It's only a matter of time before the beasts start attacking humans. The government officials, who are complete scum, have decided to put additional armed guards on the streets. Of course, that's only a temporary solution. The real answer is figuring out the weather and getting the storm drains serving their purpose again so they're less friendly to these beasts.

I could go on about politics and the evil in this world all day. At any rate, it's a good thing we're making more progress with our weather work.

PART IV

A CAGED BIRD

A few more days have passed, and Lent, Fem, and I are again sitting in the flower room doing research. Lent and I just pulled ourselves back from a giggle attack after sharing a particularly funny passage about the wind.

Through the partially open door, as I get the giggles under control, I hear a house employee calling for Reem to come deal with something. It's likely some package full of band equipment, so I focus back on the book I'm reading.

I'm just about to get into an interesting passage when the door to our room opens fully, and I see Reem standing in the doorway. I begin to glance away, but register suddenly how pale and miserable he looks.

As I scan his expression, trying to understand what might be happening, Fem asks, "What's wrong, Reem?"

"There are city officials out front asking for Chaosta," Reem says. His voice is wooden, but I can hear a note of fear.

My stomach flips, and as I watch the two of them, I realize that my chest has begun to ache.

I rub at it as Fem says, "They need paperwork for us to produce her."

"They have it," Reem says, and the room falls completely silent.

It's so quiet I can hear the pounding of my heart as I try to rub away the ache.

Lent walks over and crouches in front of me, laying his hand gently on my leg. "It's probably nothing," he says quietly as he meets my eyes. Even his face is unusually pale. "Let's just go talk to them and we'll sort this out." He stands and holds his hand out to me.

I take it and let him help me up. Then I follow as he leads to the front door. There is a harried-looking house employee standing there with the door open, wringing his hands as he looks at me. My stomach flips again, and the ache in my chest increases.

Then the entry hall spins because, as I look out through the door, I see Bonum in front of two other angels. All three wear official-looking white uniforms, and Bonum has a stack of papers in their hand.

"Come here, Chaosta," Bonum says as they see me in the doorway. Their voice is the pleasant mask they used around the boys last time, rather than the raspy sound I know belongs to them. Still, shivers travel up my spine.

I hesitate. They watch me silently, rolling their shoulders in the unsettling way I remember.

I finally manage to force myself to move forward, the fingers on my left hand cramping as I fight not to reach for a sword that isn't there. I continue to rub my strongly aching chest.

As I get closer, the two angels behind Bonum step forward around them, take my arms, and press my front against the stone railing of the stairs.

As they do this, Bonum, in their pleasant voice, says, "Chaosta, you are under arrest for the murder of a city offi-cial..." They continue to speak, but my ears are ringing too loudly for me to hear anything else.

The angels bind my hands. Somehow, I manage to control my instincts and not struggle or fight back. The cartographer in my head gives unhelpful directions about sweeping their legs out from under them. I think we both know it's futile. His voice is a quiet mumble in my head.

I barely register Bonum handing Reem the pile of papers and Dio's face at the door, asking the others something. I feel him staring at me.

Then the angels direct me to a waiting carriage, load me roughly onto a seat, and sit pressing against either side of me. Bonum sits across from me, and their face is a blank mask.

My chest aches badly, and my heart pounds too fast as I'm carried toward whatever fate has hold of me now.

DIO'S JOURNAL - ENTRY 208

Annum:5614

Entry 208 - profunde in merda

A lot has already happened today, and it's still only morning. Everything was going normally, and then, apparently, some city officials knocked on our door. I got there in time to see a group of them arresting Chaosta on murder charges.

I've made my feelings about those government positions known previously, but I just need to say what scum I feel they are. I know the angels are out there somewhere pulling their strings, and they just go along with it. Just because they've made life easy for people, too easy if you ask me, and protect us well, doesn't mean that they're in the right. Much of what they are doing is ruining this world.

Despite knowing that what we're doing is dark and

twisted, I'm confident that the cause is our best bet for a workable solution. I'm also confident that we're doing all this for the right reasons. If only more people felt the way I do.

Anyway, let me get back on track. Not only is Chaosta charged with murder, but the supposed murder victim was a city official. The officials who showed up this morning didn't provide any additional information because an investigation is still occurring.

I'm certainly not crying over a dead official. Fuck the scum enforcers, is all I can say; anyone under our "overlord's" thumb can rot. But Chaosta? Killing some-one? I mean, her behavior is all over the place, classic addict behavior, really. I wouldn't be shocked if she hurt someone, but killed? And a city official at that? Normally, they're armed.

I'm not making the same mistake again, though, and with my encouragement, we moved up the summoning ritual. Fuck the damnably long time for this ritual. I think I'll see if Reem wants to go boxing with me, take our minds off it for a while.

I'm having a strong reaction to Chaosta's arrest. If she did hurt someone, or I guess if she did actually kill someone, she should face consequences. Something about this just doesn't feel right.

Also, it doesn't help that I'm worried about this going public. If The Boys' charity case ends up in the midst of a scandal, there will be an impact on all of us.

For so many reasons, it wouldn't be good for us to be in the spotlight.

DIO'S JOURNAL - ENTRY 209

Annum:5614

Entry 209 - maleficium

Damn. I don't even know how to begin this journal entry. I believe I have significantly underestimated Chaosta.

No, that's not right. I've been fucking blind.

Normally, my single-mindedness is an asset. Sometimes it bites me in the ass, and this is the latter.

Fuck, I can't get the words out. I'll try later.

DIO'S JOURNAL - ENTRY 210

Annum:5614

Entry 210 - acedia

Everything is still swirling, but I need to try to get this written down while I remember. This is important.

After Chaosta was taken, we moved up the ritual to summon Malam. Six hours is a long time to wait (trust me, it feels even longer now that I know more), so I asked Reem if he wanted to go with me to the boxing gym. He declined. I could tell he was struggling. Chaosta's arrest puts all of us at risk. Reem likes Chaosta well enough, but I think mostly he's worried about the impact on the band and the cause if this goes sideways. I could tell that Lent and Fem were having a tougher time since they've been getting close to her.

I decided to go to the boxing gym by myself to kill some time, and I had some good matches. The physical exertion was grounding, and the new bruises were a good distraction.

When I got back to the mansion, there were still multiple hours to wait. The house employees made us lunch, but some of us couldn't eat. I don't think I've ever seen Lent not eat what's put in front of him, so that really showed how miserable he felt. I was surprised at my lack of appetite. The limited discussion we had was tense, and arguments kept springing up about what to do. I wisely kept my mouth shut, even though at the time I was still under the assumption that she'd made an error while she was high. I was worried about the potential threat to the four of us and the cause. It's not exactly a good idea to be in the spotlight when you're part of a group that is taking anti-government action.

Eventually, the time came, and Malam walked through the front door. I may still not like him, but that demon can read a room. He took one look at all of us standing in the entry hall and asked in his guttural, angry voice what happened to Chaosta. We all hesitated. It was Fem who found the words first and explained about her arrest.

That was the first moment I realized there was more coming because Malam was amazingly calm and composed. He asked a couple of questions about paperwork, which we answered, and asked us to describe the officials, which we did. Finally, he asked if she had her sword on her when she was arrested, and we told him she didn't.

I was surprised, of course, to hear about the sword. When he heard she didn't have it on her, he asked calmly to be brought to her room. Fem led us there, and we watched as Malam crouched and pulled a sword from beneath the bed as though he knew it would be there. Then I got a better look at it, saw the blade, and realized that indeed he did know it would be there.

The reality of the truth that Chaosta had been telling us crashed down on me as I saw the fucking Demonforged blade she'd had under her bed. Not some steel sword she found. This was a sword that was crafted by demon magic. A sword that belongs to Malam. Still, I had to ask. He confirmed she had summoned him at the concert, that she's able to summon him instantly. He told us that he was collecting the sword so it didn't fall into the wrong hands in her absence.

In that moment, I was pulled back to memories of comedown and withdrawal symptoms when I first spent time at a recovery center. The room was spinning, and there was sweat on my forehead. I escaped outside to get some space and a little fresh air. Those were not pleasant memories, and certainly not things I wanted to share with the other guys. Once outside, I managed to get everything to stop spinning and settle myself a bit.

When I got back into the entry hall, Reem had Lent pulled off to the side, seemingly comforting him while Malam spoke quietly with Fem in the corner of the room.

I joined Fem and Malam, and finally spoke the words I've been wanting to say for a while. I was angry and didn't know what else to do. I'll admit I raised my voice. I'll admit it was unfair of me at that moment to direct my anger and other strong emotions at him and the other guys. I just had to share my frustration about why she has to be living with us, how she's bringing government attention and therefore danger to our door when our work is so important.

All I wanted to do was try to convince Malam that she's still struggling and not getting the help she needs. As I explained the concerning behavior, I finally saw the side of him I recognize. He came right back at me. It was somehow worse than the last time we clashed. He didn't concede anything. Specifically, he said, "Her creation was mine, but her destiny isn't mine to own. You think there is a problem, talk to her about it, not me."

At the time, I found it confusing since there's no way he could have literally "created" her. There is no way demons have that power. It felt more like posturing than anything else.

There's also the small fact that none of us seems to want to talk about. She may not even return.

Eventually, Lent pulled me away, and somehow in that infuriatingly charming way he has, he got me calmed down. I'm surprised he was able to do that. He must be struggling more than any of us with her absence. He's so clearly infatuated with her.

Lent and I eventually went back to the conversation, and if I thought I couldn't be more shocked, I was wrong. As we returned to the group, Fem, Reem, and Malam were discussing the murder charges and what truth there might be to them. I waited for Malam to profess her innocence. Instead, he pulled the rug out from under all of us when he confirmed he not only believed she had, in fact, killed someone, but that she had killed an angel.

I've had a day to process this, or I wouldn't be able to write this calmly. This one took a while. At the time, I reacted strongly to that statement. No one has seen an angel in centuries. Even if they were walking around with us, they've got to be incredibly difficult to kill. They are immortals after all.

The room started spinning again, and I argued with him. Told him it couldn't have been an angel. As I was trying my hardest to focus on the facts, Fem said quietly that Chaosta had tried to tell him this months ago.

So many truths I've clung to were being ripped apart in front of us. Fem shared that at the time she'd said it, he'd thought it was the pain meds from her leg injury. That he thought she was seeing things. She'd been upset by receiving care from, what she claimed was, an angel healer. I hadn't heard about that specific incident, but the other guys had told me about how she'd hallucinated when she was on pain meds.

Malam shared that there are angels walking among

us and only demons can see them, well, demons and Chaosta. He said demons are also able to disguise them-selves, but he has no need to with us because we knew that we were summoning a demon.

He also confirmed that angels are extremely hard to kill, but they can be killed more easily with a Demon-forged blade. He told us that angels and demons have an uneasy truce and haven't killed each other outright in centuries, but that wasn't always the case.

I'm not proud, but I lost it again. I was suddenly screaming at him about how he'd gotten us into this mess with how he spoils her. I'd finally put everything together and realized that by "create," he must have meant that he taught her how to wield a sword. I screamed at him about how I couldn't believe how irre-sponsible it was that he allowed this "unstable weapon" to live with us. I was upset about him allowing her to continue to carry a sword when he knew she had hurt or killed someone previously. All I could think of was the risk he's taken with her. She's clearly not in any place to be carrying a sword around. It's not a surprise that she ended up in trouble.

I can still picture all their faces. In the end, I put my fist through a wall before I left the mansion to get some air. When I got back, Fem needed to stitch me up. Not like he didn't already have enough on his mind.

I need to get control of my shit.

Even now, a day later, my hands are shaking, and I

haven't been able to concentrate. Fem is being surprisingly kind to me, even though I can tell he thinks I'm out of control. The others are treading carefully like I'm a bomb that's about to go off.

Damn it, I'm going boxing again, stitches and Fem's advice be damned.

DIO'S JOURNAL - ENTRY 211

Annum:5614

Entry 211 - torpeō

Fuck, I really messed up my hand, so this is a few days late, and it's going to be a short entry. If I ever decide to punch a wall again, I need to remember to use my non-dominant hand. I did end up going boxing, which felt like a good idea at the time. In retrospect, I've had better. Not that I've had many winners recently.

I Need To Stop Spiraling

When I got back to the mansion, I could tell by the others' expressions that I may have overdone it. I thought Fem was going to punch me when he got me into the office and finally got a chance to see my injuries. Joke's on him, I already had two black eyes. I'd also torn the stitches open on my hand, and there were others, but that's not important. I thought I'd taped my hand up well enough, but I guess not.

I didn't even complain as he got me patched up. I thought he'd be rough because of his frustration at me, but he was surprisingly gentle. I almost asked him not to be, but even I'm not that much of a masochist.

I still can't quite believe she's not been dealing with addiction this whole time. I know what Malam said, but her behavior is just so familiar to me.

I don't know what to do. The nightmares are getting worse, so I'm getting far too little sleep. With her out of the house and locked in a government cell, there is plenty of fuel for my imagination. I need to contact the government again to see if there are any updates on the case. All I can hope is that maybe, if Malam is wrong, she's getting the help she needs while she's locked up.

DIO'S JOURNAL - ENTRY 271

Annum:5614

Entry 271 - finem mortuorum

Whatever my feelings are about what happened and why Chaosta is incarcerated, it's been over a month, and we haven't heard anything. We've tried communicating with the city office, and it's a dead end. At this point, we've exhausted every other option. When I mentioned this as a last-ditch option to the others a month ago, I meant it. There is nothing I'd like less than needing to reach out to my brother, but none of us know what else to do about Chaosta.

I can now admit she was leading the research that was helping us make progress, since, with her gone, we've stalled out completely. In our current circumstances, as things continue to get more and more grim, I can't overlook how helpful it would be to have her back with us.

Of course, there is also the fact that the night-mares and my imagination continue to be unkind. I've known people who were incarcerated, and they were fine. Some of them came out of it more healed than they went in. Still, it feels like my imagination won't stop making up awful scenarios about what might be happening to her.

I mentioned my lawyer brother, Alexander, shortly after Chaosta was arrested. The others have been pressuring me to reach out to him for a while now. I just couldn't make myself do so until I knew we'd tried working with the city office directly. Dragging up the past isn't something to do lightly. Since it was clear this morning that we have no other options, I've attempted to make contact. Because he's such an ass, and I guess I can acknowledge he's busy, it may take a little while.

I think what finally convinced me was learning that another of my old contacts is sick from the poison in the air. He has always struggled with his health, but still, it feels too close to home. I think the other guys are also feeling pressure to make progress on our magic again because of the state of the world. It's as though this distasteful task we've given ourselves, with the cause, is becoming lighter as things continue to grow more grim. We desperately need to get back on track with that work.

DIO'S JOURNAL - ENTRY 290

Annum:5614
Entry 290 - causidicus

I finally got a meeting scheduled with my brother. I'd rather slam my fingers in a door than see him, but if anyone can get Chaosta out of there, it's him. The meeting is a fortnight out, but at least it's scheduled.

I've had plenty of time to reflect recently. The more I think about it, the more I realize I need to trust what Malam says. If he says she's not dealing with addiction, I guess I need to believe that. Maybe my own experience has just blinded me. Or maybe I've just been trying to avoid the other emotions I feel when I'm around her.

I still can't believe the government officials have her. I hope she's not actually being held by angels, or even Alexander might not be able to get her out. We should have been able to keep her safe, and the fact that she may not be is tearing at my self-control. The intensity of these feelings reminds me far too much of how I felt back when I was in treatment, and I'm white knuckling every day right now.

Finally, though, at least the meeting with Alexander means I'm making some progress toward getting her out and just in time for our concert tomorrow. I have no idea how we're going to pull this off with how distracted we've all been, but at least this meeting is something else to focus on.

EXISTENCE IS PERSISTENT

The days all blend together here. I'm not sure how much time has passed, but it's significant, more like several months than several weeks.

For a while at the beginning of my incarceration, I kept track, but it got depressing, so now I just exist.

My ribs itch, and I rub at them, but it doesn't stop. If past experience is anything to go by, and it's a large enough collection of knowledge that I suspect it is, the itching won't stop until they take the stitches out. At least since the wounds are still fresh, I likely have a fortnight until they question me again.

I miss the drugs from the center. At least there I was numb.

I wonder if the boys even remember me.

I can't stop thinking about Dio.

I don't dare try to summon Malam here; the risk is too great. That's if he would even show up, and I wouldn't blame him for not. It was my actions alone that led to my arrest, and I can't help but think there is a purpose to all of this. I guess I'll continue existing until I figure it out or someone decides to make that decision for me.

At least my chest finally stopped aching.

DIO'S JOURNAL - ENTRY 291

Annum:5615
Entry 291 - turbatio

The less we speak about that concert, the better.
We packed the space with fans. I think most of them
had a pretty good time. We got through the full set, and
I guess no one got hurt.

I, however, feel like a failure. I was a mess. I kept
screwing up the keys, couldn't remember all of the lyrics,
and I nearly dropped the entire last chorus of one of our
new songs. I don't know what was going on with me. I
couldn't concentrate. I tried to push through, but I still
failed and giving the performance I wanted to. I could
tell that the other guys were disappointed.

I might as well start using again at this point. My
feelings about what might be going on with Chaosta are
really messing me up. I'm probably in worse shape than

if I would be if I started injecting again. I'm kidding, of course. I know I shouldn't be even joking about it, but that is what this journal started as, right? A way to get my feelings out that's healthier than my previous coping mechanism.

What a fantastic way to be feeling before the upcoming meeting with my judgmental, asshole of a brother.

DIO'S JOURNAL - ENTRY 302

Annum: 5615

Entry 302 - pēnem

It's no fucking wonder I struggled as a kid. Being in the same room as that jerk for a few hours, even after all this time, made me want to strangle him or bash my head into a wall. His office is a piece of work, all set up to make him feel powerful. He was truly created by my parents to be just like them. Being the black sheep of the family makes more and more sense to me.

I refused to let the others accompany me to the meeting. This needed to be navigated carefully. Alexander is aligned with the other side after all, aligned with the very scum who have Chaosta locked up. Of course, that positions him well for this, but only if I could convince him to help me rather than them.

It's not like I haven't had time to prepare. Perhaps

the main factor on my side is that my brain works like his now that I'm not high. A fact I don't think he realized. I believe it gave me the advantage in our meeting. I was able to carefully navigate the line of truth and fiction and paint a fairly compelling fucking picture. Or at least I must have been able to because he's agreed to help us.

Like any good lawyer, he didn't make any guarantees. He also said that it might take a while, but he is willing to help. Thank all the dark gods for the name The Boys made for themselves, or I don't think he'd have been willing.

I can't even be thankful that my brother is a famous lawyer right now, not after the old wounds are so freshly opened from that interaction. At least I was hopefully able to contribute in some way to getting Chaosta released.

When I got back to the mansion after the meeting and told the others he'd promised to help, Lent fucking hugged me. The others looked a little less hopeless, and Fem even awkwardly patted me on the back. It's the first time he's acknowledged me since Chasota was arrested, other than to doctor my injuries. Not like I need his approval, but I'll admit it's been hard to see how angry he's been with me. If I'm honest, it's been hard to see how angry all three of them have been at me since I screamed at Malam in front of them. They've still been treating me like a bomb about to go off. I know my temper can be bad, but fuck, it feels extreme how careful they're being to avoid me.

I know they don't know my brother. Until they see what he can do with their own eyes, they likely won't believe getting her out is possible, but I know my blood. I may despise him, but he's nearly as stubborn as I am. He'll get this done.

A WEAPON HONED

As I count through this set of push-ups, I wonder numbly how many I've done in this room.

The space I'm being held in is small, with a single foam pad on the floor, one blanket, and a toilet. Food is delivered through a slit in the door on a completely random pattern. Nothing like being kept guessing when your next meal will be delivered for some much-needed variety.

There's not much room, but along with push-ups, jumping jacks, and sit-ups, I've been able to practice some of the sword-fighting footwork. It's all probably an exercise in futility since, at this rate, I'll never get out of here. At least it gives me something useful to do. I could probably also do burpees, but I'd frankly rather die. Especially with the pain I'm in right now.

Earlier today, I made it through the worst session of torture yet. In addition to the standard, freshly stitched knife wounds on my torso, upper legs, and upper arms, I have two black eyes from a broken nose and two broken fingers. I thought this angel, who was different than my normal torturer, was going to break my arm, but someone stopped her before she could go that far.

When I was initially incarcerated and the angels began to torture me, they asked questions about the demons. Questions I knew better than to answer. That strange intelligence told me they already knew the answers to the questions they were asking. I suspect they were trying to see if I did too.

Then they began to ask questions about Piquory Center and how I got out. Questions that made my gut churn as I remembered Malam's plea in the carriage to not say anything about Lily.

More recently, they have been asking questions about the boys. How I ended up living with them and why. They are clearly also trying to gather more information about each of them.

At first, I remained quiet and didn't respond to their questions. After a while, I began to make up seemingly valid, but fake, answers. Now I just give the most random answers I can think of, and it is clearly beginning to get to them.

They're quick to remind me that this will stop as soon as I promise to join their "side." They also like to remind me I'm lucky they're providing me with "top of the line medical care," and "breaks between sessions."

Today, their questions centered around the boys, and when they asked about Dio, I felt rage surging through me and struggled to maintain my usual impassivity. When I had an opportunity, I reminded them that "top of the line care includes pain management." They really didn't like that response, and it earned me the broken nose.

Seeing the anger on their angelic faces almost makes the pain worth it. Almost.

I only make it through the first half of my second set of pushups before I need to lie down. I can tell if I don't, I will pass out, and I would rather not wake in a pool of my own vomit again.

Twice was enough, thank you very much.

As I attempt to reduce the pain and get the room to stop spinning, I close my eyes and lie on my back on the foam pad, trying to take steady breaths through my mouth. The healers set and taped my nose, but I can't breathe through it yet, and bigger breaths pull at the freshly stitched knife wounds across my ribs.

My whole body is covered in scars and knife wounds at various stages of healing at this point. However, until now, they have avoided marking areas that aren't typically covered by clothing. Honestly, if it weren't for the "top of the line medical care," I would probably have died from infection multiple times over at this point.

I am just beginning to fade into sweet, blessed unconsciousness with a memory playing behind my eyelids. A memory that, for some reason, I've been focusing on to keep myself sane. Behind my eyelids, I replay those images of Dio rescuing me at the concert.

I'm once again questioning *why this memory*, when there's a knock on my door. Now that is unusual.

"Come to apologize?" I yell through the closed door.

It opens and roll myself up as quickly as my damaged body will allow as I catch sight of a guard rushing at me. Before I can do anything to defend myself, someone behind him reaches out, catching the front of his throat and effectively clotheslining him.

The guard falls, choking to the ground, clutching his neck.

As I look up at my would-be savior, I'm irritated to see Bonum standing in the door.

They are staring through me, their head tilted slightly. "It's your lucky day, little bird," they rasp. "You get to spread your wings again." They seem to either not notice or not care about the guard, coughing and choking on the ground.

I push myself up against the wall to stand, wobbling on my feet.

Without another word, a second guard emerges from behind

Bonum, drags the guard on the floor back into the hallway by the arm, and then enters the room again, walking towards me. I prepare to defend myself, which is laughable in my current state, even to me.

Before I can do anything, I hear Bonum rasp almost joyfully, "Oh, by all means, give us a reason to keep you here."

I look up and see them standing, unmoving in the doorway, still staring through me with a blank grin on their face.

I feel myself shudder slightly, and it's just enough to push the instincts down. I submit to having my hands bound and allow the guard to direct me toward the door.

"Good choice," Bonum rasps as we move past, and I hear them turn and move after us. The coughing and whimpering guard on the floor clearly still doesn't draw their attention.

The hair pricks along the back of my neck with them behind me, and my heart pounds. Every instinct pushes me to try to fight and break loose before we arrive at whatever fate I'm due.

My mind, however, is as clear as it's been. With the intelligence given to me by the little boy, I run probabilities on my ability to escape and don't like my odds. Instead, I stay quiet to wait and watch. If they mean to break me, they have not yet accomplished that goal. What they have, so far, failed to realize is that the actions they're taking are simply honing a blade, and at this point, it's sharp as hell.

DIO'S JOURNAL - ENTRY 336

Annum: 5615

Entry 336 - solamen

He's done it.

He's fucking done it. I don't pretend to understand
all the lawyer language Alexander just spewed at me, but
he's serving some sort of papers to some important
person, and then in a day or more, Chaosta will be free.
I don't even know how to feel right now, relieved?
Scared? Hopeful?

As I write this, Reem is organizing transportation
for her. After a firm warning not to say anything or
ask questions other than those pertaining to her travel
arrangements, I gave him Alexander's assistant's
contact information. That shit is much more his area of
expertise than mine.

While I wasn't exactly incarcerated, my time in

treatment centers wasn't a walk in the park. I also know plenty of people who have been incarcerated. I've seen the scars it can leave mentally. I'm terrified of what that might mean for her. At least with her back here, where I can keep an eye on her, I hope my emotions will settle.

Still, I need to be careful to keep my distance. Even if she's not dealing with an addiction, I won't allow myself to get close. I'm a liability to those around me, and I don't want to cause her any more pain.

A few days ago, I finally brought Fem into my confidence. I recognized that I hadn't been able to pull myself out of the spiral, and somehow he seemed like the right person to tell. At first, I thought I'd made a mistake when his response was to glare at me and tell me about how Chaosta had been right again. Then he softened, and he's been damnably gentle and kind to me, hovering even and making sure I remember to eat.

I'm not sure if this is better or worse, but it was a necessary evil, I think, to share with him. I need to not keep trying to do this alone, at least not in my current state. I made him promise not to tell anyone else, and he agreed to keep it to himself. If this gets out, I don't know what I'll do. I'm not good at letting people in.

Back when I was early in my recovery, I allowed myself to be too casual and spend time around others who were still addicted. I nearly lost myself again, and if I hadn't been taken under the wing of a talented magic user and introduced to this world, I'm sure I would have started back down that destructive road. Instead, I lost him, my dearest friend, just over a year ago now. After he passed, I began looking for a cause that I could believe in. It feels tenuous to have found that here, but to still feel as though there are factors trying to pull me back to that addiction. I'll handle it, of course. I have ever since, and I won't allow his sacrifice to be in vain.

HABEAS CORPUS

This hallway feels as though it might continue forever. Part of me doesn't want it to end, and part of me, the small bit of me that still has some hope, wants to get to our destination. Maybe, that part of me says, it will mean freedom from this place. Realistically, I know it is unlikely, but hope is a funny thing.

Eventually, the hallway we're in joins another, and the guard, who is still holding my arm, directs me down a different hallway that branches off. Soon, we arrive at a door and he knocks.

The door is opened by a pretty young woman in a fitted red dress. Her eyes widen, and she pauses momentarily when she sees me. Then she steps back into the room and says politely, "Come in, please, sir," to the guard.

I look behind me and see Bonum standing a short distance back in the hallway. They're leaning against the wall in a way that would be casual for anyone else. Somehow, they make it look predatory.

I turn back to the room as the guard pushes me through the

door and notice that, along with the young woman, there is a man in the room. He's sitting behind a table, but when he sees us, he stands.

He is focused on me, and his eyes narrow slightly as he takes in my appearance. He doesn't speak until the guard finishes removing the bindings from my hands and leaves. The young woman closes the door after him, but remains in the room with us.

I hear the man say my name and turn back to him. "My name is Alexander Magnus. Please sit," he says as he gestures at a chair.

I sit down as instructed, careful to school my expression against the increased pain as I do so.

He looks familiar, but in a way I can't place.

He also sits and begins shuffling some paperwork on the desk, his attention still on me. "Do you know why you're here?" he asks.

His voice is firm and has a musical quality that doesn't disguise the sense of power and control that seems to exude from him. I'm confident that he is a very important person. It is also immediately clear, though, that he is not an angel, and neither is the young woman.

I simply respond, "No," as I meet his eyes.

"Hmm," he says, and his attention goes to the paperwork for a moment that feels like it stretches on interminably. Finally, he says, "You are being released today. We have some paperwork for you to complete. Documents saying you won't sue or press charges against anyone."

I suddenly feel as though I can breathe for the first time in months.

He pauses for a moment and looks searchingly at me again. "What happened to your face?" While he asks the question casually, I can see that his expression is calculating.

"I got into a fight with another prisoner," I say.

"Hmm," he says, "and your hand?"

"Same."

"How did they make out?" he asks.

"Look at me, I'm tiny, how do you think they made out?" I grit out, my jaw tight at the discomfort of the lie.

His eyes narrow, but he doesn't ask any additional questions.

It is not as though I would have told him anything else if he did. I got myself incarcerated here by siding with the demons. Nothing the angels have done to me, despite all the pain, has yet caused me to regret that decision. This is my fight, not this man's.

Instead, he pushes one neat pile of paperwork towards me across the table. "Will you be able to sign?" he asks, looking at my right hand and the broken fingers.

I nod and hold out my left for the pen, and he hands it to me with a slight narrowing of his eyes.

This stack of paperwork is all about how the city officials bear no responsibility for any physical or psychological harm I've suffered, and I will be unable to receive "damages." The shadow of a sneer crosses my face as I sign. It's not "damages" I want from them.

As I continue through the stack of paperwork, I ask Alexander, "Why am I being freed?"

"We were able to get you out based on a lack of evidence and holes in the investigative process," he says firmly. "When I dug into your case and started asking questions, they were not able to produce a body. Even if they had followed the correct procedure, if you had ever been called in front of a court, without a massive amount of evidence on their side, I would have been able to get the charges dismissed. You clearly don't look as though you could kill a city enforcer," he says, and I feel him looking at my pink hair and small stature.

Underestimation makes everything easier, so I let him believe that.

As I work through the piles of paperwork, signing away my right to damages, we sit in relative silence. Eventually, I finish, pushing the last stack of paperwork back across the table toward him.

He looks through the last set of signatures, then says in an authoritative voice, "That concludes my role here." He stacks the paperwork and puts it into a leather bag that is hanging from the back of his chair. Without looking up, he says, "Roxana will help get you on your way."

Then he says, "It has been nice to meet you, Chaosta, but hopefully we don't have a need to meet again."

"Thank you for your help," I say, my voice sharing the sincerity I feel.

He nods back and then makes his way out of the room.

Meanwhile, Roxana walks to the end of the table and sets down a familiar-looking linen bag. "Here are some of your things," she says, "I'll step out so you can get dressed. Once you're ready to go, we have transportation arranged to bring you home."

I thank her. As she leaves, I rise shakily. I am glad I'm alone and have no need to mask my reactions anymore.

Before I do anything else, I give myself a moment, leaning against the table with my eyes closed. I breathe slowly through my mouth and attempt to settle my pounding heart and calm the pain in my body. After a few moments pass, I begin to rifle through the linen bag.

As I review the options, though, it is clear I don't want to wear any of it. Whoever packed it thoughtfully sent some of my favorite things from before I was arrested. However, the short skirts, long stockings, puffed sleeves, and frills everywhere seem far too foreign for me to be willing to wear them now.

Instead, I open the door to the hallway. As I hoped, Roxana is standing just outside.

"I don't want to wear any of that," I say to her and hear the note of annoyance in my voice.

"I wondered," she says conspiratorially. "Whenever men pack for us, it's a disaster. I have some other things here you could try." She pulls a thin pile of folded clothing out of her leather bag and hands it to me.

"Thank you," I say, meeting her eyes and meaning it.

She smiles brilliantly at me, and her face goes from rather plain to intoxicating in a moment.

I can't help but smile back. Then I go back into the room and sort through this clothing. It all feels better than my old clothes, but it's not mine, so I choose one dress. The dress is dark green, long-sleeved, and cowled. The material it is made out of is stretchy. It is fitted through the upper body to my hips, but then falls more loosely to mid calf. There are two slits along the fronts of my legs that go to my mid-thigh, conveniently ending just below where the evidence of my torture begins.

I pull it on along with a pair of my boots that someone, my guess is Lent, sent with. I leave the uniform piled on the floor, collect the linen bag with my clothes, and carry the remaining pile of clothes back to Roxana.

She looks me up and down, her expression appraising. "It suits you," she says with a smile.

I follow her out of a maze of hallways to a desk with a city official sitting behind it. They watch me closely. The bright wings behind their shoulders make me flinch involuntarily. Thankfully, Roxana talks with them, and I don't need to speak. They hand over a paper-wrapped package with "her things," which she hands to me. I manage to stuff it into the linen bag on my shoulder.

With that done, she walks me out to a waiting carriage at the front of the building. I feel my shoulders relax as we get outside.

As I approach it, I wonder if the boys will be waiting for me inside. I don't feel quite ready to face them. When I peer into the door of the carriage, though it is blessedly empty. As I sit, I see her waiting just outside the door.

"Be safe?" she says.

I nod without looking at her. It's a lie, safety is the furthest thing from my mind.

SOMETHING UNSAID

Despite the fact that I've been on this route a couple of times now, I guess I hadn't understood how far the angel stronghold is from the mansion. As time passes, I somehow manage some fitful sleep, and of course, the dreams won't leave me alone, even now.

* * *

In this dream, I am in manacles in a small stone space. The dream moves back instead of forward. Even knowing this is just a dream, I feel dizzy with the odd movement. I see myself, surrounded by blackness, carving a twisting shape onto the underside of my wrist with the point of a small knife. It burns, and then the skin there is covered with flame. As I scream and thrash, I am suddenly jolted into wakefulness.

* * *

*A*s I wake with my heart pounding, I register that the carriage driver just knocked on the roof. Finding the carriage stopped, before I can be dragged out by the driver, I remove myself and stand on shaking legs outside the mansion.

Home.

There is nothing else to do at the moment, so I square my shoulders, firm up my legs the best I can, and walk to the front door. When I get there, I pause, unsure what to do.

Do I knock? Just walk in? Is anyone even there?

Before I can decide, the door opens and I see Lent standing there, staring at me, his hand still on the doorknob. I'm frozen for a moment, but while I'm trying to decide what is appropriate, he steps forward and wraps his arms around me. He is gentle, but I still have to exert every bit of control to keep myself from crying out as he presses against my battered body.

As he embraces me, I hear someone call out from behind him, but it's muffled with my ear pressed against Lent's chest.

The rumble as he responds, "Just a minute," makes me wince slightly, and with that, he pulls back. Concern is clear on his face.

"It's so good to see you, Lent," I say quietly.

He swallows, his jaw slack as though he wants to say something. Instead, he simply nods at me, his face uncharacteristically serious. Then he steps aside to allow me through the door.

As I walk into the entry hall, I see the other boys at various points in the room. They look mostly as I remember them, although their faces are clearly horrified by the injuries they can see.

Well, that is, except Dio. He's leaning slightly against the back wall, facing me, his hands shoved into his pockets. His shirt is wrinkled, and his hair is longer than I've seen it and messy. I watch him clench his jaw, his face a mask of emotions, most of which I can't read. His cheeks are more hollow than I remember, and his shirt is looser; he has clearly lost weight. He's staring at my face, and then his gaze tracks down to my broken fingers. His hands clench into fists.

Before I can begin to wonder what's going on, I sense the feeling of shadow at my periphery and turn to see Malam.

His gaze quickly scans over me, and I see rage briefly cross his face before he composes himself.

He opens his mouth to speak, but before he can utter a word, I say, "I need to speak with you privately."

He gestures at someone behind my back and says, "Fem," in a clear order for Fem to come with us.

I shake my head at him as I move to the office door and say, "Just you."

He bows his head and follows me into the room.

Once in the office, I place myself behind the chair facing the door, holding the back of it to give me some support. I am unwilling to sit for this conversation.

Malam closes the door and then turns to me and strides closer. As he gets near, I move to keep the chair between us, and he stops.

His face is a mask of anger as he glares at me. "I can smell the blood on you," he says with a snarl.

"I can handle it," I say, still meeting his eyes.

For better or worse, I'm not the person I was before. There is no reason to share what I went through with him. I am sure he has some conjecture, but there is no need to confirm it. This isn't his battle. He created me with a purpose, and I will fulfill it.

Almost as though he can read those thoughts on my face, I see his posture relax slightly, and he takes a step back to sit in a chair facing me. "At least tell me what happened to your face and hand," he says.

"I got into a fight with another prisoner," I say, meeting his eyes while I carefully mask my face against the lie.

From the expression on his face, he doesn't believe me, but

instead of asking more questions about my injuries, he growls, "What did you want to talk about then?"

"Was it you who got me out?" I ask.

"No," he says, and I see pain on his face at that statement. "You know my position in this. Action begets action, and in this, my hands were tied. I won't be the one to break the unspoken truce."

"Then how?" I ask.

"The band worked it out," he says.

I nod silently.

I don't need the details at this moment; I just had my suspicions that it was all part of a plot by the angels. If they had chosen to release me of their own accord, I was aware that it was likely part of a trap. That might have changed the landscape on the map in my head, potentially forcing a specific path. I take a breath, relaxing slightly as I process the information that it was instead the boys who got me released.

Malam is clearly appraising whatever expression is showing on my face.

"Bonum was there," I finally say, breaking the silence.

"Based on the description Reem gave me of the officials who arrested you, I gathered that," he says.

"I don't think Bonum agreed with what happened to me," I say, knowing I risk more questions about my condition. It still needs to be said.

Malam closes his eyes and scrubs his hand across his face. When he looks at me again, I briefly see the weight of ancient power he carries reflected in them. Then he blinks, and it's gone. "And yet their actions don't speak to that," he says grimly.

I can't say I entirely disagree, so I remain quiet. I never intended to defend an angel's actions to myself or to the leader of the demons. My instincts tell me I have done what I need for the time being.

"I took the sword so it wouldn't fall into the wrong hands," he finally says into the silence. "I will return one to you soon."

"Thank you, Malam," I say quietly, hoping he didn't look at anything else under my bed when he took the sword.

We are both silent for a long moment, and then he asks, "Can I do anything else for you, Chaosta?"

I simply shake my head.

He stands and says, "Tell the coven I'll see them soon." Then he vanishes in a swirling cloud of shadow and wingbeats.

I sit on the chair I was just standing behind and rest my head on one hand. I take a moment, steeling myself for the flood of emotions I know will hit me when I leave the room.

Eventually, when I can put it off no longer, I rise and walk through the door. The boys are waiting still, at the edges of this open space. They begin to move toward me as I walk into the room. Other than Dio, who's still leaning against the wall as though it's the only thing keeping him on his feet. I momentarily feel the familiar sting of glass shards on my skin, but when I glance at him, he quickly looks at the ground, avoiding my eyes.

Lent is standing close to Reem. They were clearly having a conversation before I left the office.

Fem is standing a little way away, and in particular, he is appraising me, clearly noting my injuries. His face is full of concern.

Fem opens his mouth as though to say something, but before he can, I say to no one in particular, "Malam said he'll see you soon." I pause for a moment and then finish, "I'm going to go to my room to get some rest. It's been a long day." With that, I turn and walk out of the entry hall.

As I step into my room, another wave of emotion hits, and once the door is fully closed, the sob I've been restraining escapes from my chest. I carefully lower myself to the floor, my legs wobbling badly enough that I'm not sure if they'll be able to carry me to the bed. I rest, leaning back against the door, carefully controlling my breathing and letting the pain recede.

After several minutes, I close my eyes, but all I can see in the blackness is Dio's, his cheekbones more hollow than I remember. With a curse, I open my eyes again.

Feeling stronger for the brief rest and also annoyed with myself and needing a distraction, I carefully and slowly push myself to my feet and move to the bed. I take a book from a pile under the edge my bed and disturb a stack of papers. They fall across the floor. A mess which I carefully ignore.

Swearing at myself, emotions still crashing into me, I clamber slowly and painfully into bed. After settling myself against some pillows, I open the book and begin to try to focus on words that, despite my best efforts, begin to blur with tears.

DIO'S JOURNAL - ENTRY 337

Annum:5615
Entry 337 - obsequium

I was so wrong to think I'd be able to get control of my emotions once Chaosta got back. I need to figure this out and address it soon. My control is too imperative.

I think we were all anxious this morning as we waited for her arrival. I know I was. Alexander contacted me midday to let me know everything was running later than expected because the officials had been dragging their feet. Nothing unexpected, but waiting for the additional time was agonizing.

He also told me he suspected they'd beaten her after they got the paperwork to release her. He said that when he asked her what had happened, she'd told him she'd been in a fight. When I asked how bad it was, all he'd say was, "Bad enough." My emotions really tried to take over when he said that. I felt so much anger. Of course, my control always needs to be iron-clad. Emotions like this just chip away at it, and things get more volatile than they should. In retrospect, perhaps I understand why the guys have been treading so carefully around me recently.

Fuck. I really should talk to them about it. My control is better than they might assume.

I don't know why she'd lie about getting in a fight like that, but at the time, I couldn't exactly picture her surviving a scuffle with another inmate. However, I knew I'd spent enough time underestimating or not believing her. I had promised myself I'd do better, so I told him I was sure if she said she was in a fight, that's what happened.

The conversation with him actually wasn't that bad. Maybe he's maturing, or maybe I was just distracted enough about her return that I ignored his typical behavior. No matter, he's fulfilled his role and now I won't ever need to talk to him again.

It was about an hour later when Lent, who'd taken it upon himself to serve as a lookout, called out that there was a carriage stopped outside. We all joined him in the entry hall. If I ever wanted the familiar feeling of a high to dull my emotions, it was then.

After another agonizing wait, he opened the door, and I watched as he wrapped his arms around her. I was hit with a wave of envy when I saw her in his arms. I'm sure if I'm envious, it's because there isn't a history of arguments and distrust hanging over Lent's head. Now that she's back, I'm sure he'll continue to court her. Though I know I should be happy for him, for some reason, it just makes me want to punch him.

When he FINALLY let her go, and I could see her, I suddenly couldn't breathe. Her nose was broken with the accompanying black eyes, and the way the fingers on her right hand were taped, they're clearly broken as well.

While I'm not surprised Alexander thought she might have been beaten, the placement of her injuries screams hand-to-hand combat. I've walked away from boxing matches looking not dissimilar on multiple occasions. Also, I'm beginning to wonder if she won the fight because other than those injuries, she looked surprisingly well. She looked really good, actually.

She walked into the room with more confidence than I remember. Maybe it was the dress, so different from the frilly, ruffly things she used to wear. She looked like a queen. Then Malam came out of somewhere. I'm not sure if the others knew he was here, but I didn't until that moment. I was momentarily distracted from my surprise at his appearance as she looked at me. I so badly wanted to say something to her, but the weight of the disagreements between us was too much. I couldn't find the words.

Instead, I was silent, just wishing I could breathe as she glanced around and then fucking ordered Malam to the office. I felt myself readying for a fight since there's no way a demon follows a human's orders. However, not only did he obey when he told Fem to go with them, a decision I frankly still side with him on, and she denied him, he fucking bowed his head to her. Then he just meekly followed her into the room without another word.

Even if I hadn't been distracted by trying to retain control, even if I'd been feeling my best, I don't think I'd have known what to do with that.

After a quarter hour or more had passed, she emerged from the office by herself. Somehow, she must have un-summoned Malam because he was gone. She told us that he'd see us soon. Again, I wanted so badly to say something to her, but even as I write this, I don't have the words. Instead, she told us she was going to her room to rest and then left us all standing there.

After she left, Reem went over to Lent, put his arm around his shoulders, and led him into the dining room, telling him he needed to eat something. I realized I must not be the only one who's seen how smitten he is. I'm glad Reem is supporting him. Fuck if I'd be able to talk to him about how broken he must feel after seeing her like that.

Fem came over to me and, gods, the amount of concern on his face was hard to see. I still almost wish I hadn't said anything to him about my past. When he asked if I was ok, I responded that I was fine. Glad she was out. He told me I needed to eat something, and I told him I would after I got some sleep. I haven't really slept in days now. I haven't been eating well either, but I knew I wouldn't be able to keep any food down. I must have been convincing enough because Fem just awkwardly patted me on the shoulder and then followed the other two into the dining room.

I'm supposed to be sleeping now, but I needed to write this down first. Maybe if I get some of the feelings out on paper, I'll be able to breathe again. I need to get my focus back so my control isn't so threatened. Sometimes I wish I were just another person, coddled by our government, unaware of how bad things are getting. I lost that innocence so long ago. The day I did, I got my first tattoo, and since then, I've been working to hone my craft. Despite the level of skill I've built, though, without help, it's not like I'd be able to do much, certainly not enough. Moments like this make me wonder if I'm strong enough to put that skill to use.

Despite the conviction I feel, I continue to wish that this massive impact we're planning wasn't needed. I'm a monster for being willing to do this, and I know it. If being a monster is what it takes to save this world, though, I'll embrace that darkness with a smile on my face.

I'm honestly surprised the food shortages aren't already worse, with what I know about where our food comes from. Information that the population at large isn't aware of, since it doesn't suit the narrative of our government. We need to return the wild spaces to this world to allow for more food to be grown, and that means clearing some land. It also means reducing the population. It is that part of the plan which often keeps me up at night. We've all tried to find other options, and I just don't see another way.

The weight of the work and the darkness of it make all these other emotions about a girl particularly unwelcome. Besides, even if she were interested, what could I give her, violence and a blackened heart?

EXCERPTS FROM MALAM

The following passage is one I have written based on a summary of notes provided to me by Malam. Please indulge me for any inaccuracies, and know they are an artist's liberties. Malam would want this to be as factual as possible. I would have avoided sharing this entirely, but it provides important context to the story, which I wanted you, dear reader, to have.

The hour is late, and it is dark as I materialize in a small alcove outside the mansion that the band owns. As I regain my footing, I momentarily struggle to maintain my composure. I can feel her pain from here, I'm dizzy with it.

Being around her the day prior was agony. The pain alone would have been bad enough, but I could smell blood and antiseptic so strongly that I'm confident she's covered in wounds. Of course, the fucking angels believe themselves to be "civilized" and abstained from marking her extremities to avoid visible scarring. Currently, it means she can attempt to hide her injuries from the others. That is an action I am trying not to have an opinion about.

It doesn't even surprise me that the angels beat her on top of whatever other wounds she has. I could taste the lie on her when she said she had been in a fight. The broken nose and fingers were courtesy of the angels. My only comfort is that she was giving them hell if they varied from their tenets, since, with angels, those are the strength of granite.

I rest my forehead against the front door before I enter, taking a moment to breathe and try to compose myself. I need to be at my best for this, or rather, my people need me to be at my best for this.

I finally enter and make my way to the lower level, where the coven is getting set up. They are preparing for my instruction in the practice of group magic. It has been more than a fortnight since we last met, and we need to get back on track.

Reem glances at me as I enter the room and gives me a single nod before going back to his work. He is preparing the magic circle in the middle of the stone floor that is needed for coven work.

Lent is here as well, paging through a book. I suspect he's looking for the passages we've been working through. Now that Chaosta is back, hopefully we will begin to make more progress again. Growling to myself, I think again about how much more progress we could be making if Dio hadn't sent her away to that treatment center all those months ago.

I wish the answer to all this strife were as easy as my people fighting the angels directly, but because of the unspoken truce, my hands are tied. Of course, as hard as I try to forget it, there's also the pesky fact that they outnumber us by a significant margin. An extremely significant margin.

As part of my solution to that imbalance, these four men are being forged into a weapon I will point not at the angels directly but at their hideous city. This is my first move to end this subversive war of inaction that is killing our planet. A silent, slow war that, without action on my part, will also mean the end of my people. Hopefully, the actions I have set in motion will be enough to save us. I need these men to develop their skill in magic enough and learn ancient, nearly forgotten magic. That esoteric weather magic is the key to the action I have planned.

Chaosta's creation wasn't about giving me another weapon to wield. Instead, I created her with the elements I thought necessary to gain a powerful ally. One who will do what is needed to begin to even the balance between demons and angels, dark and light. At first, I wondered if I had made some mistake; she seemed so meek and unassuming. Now, though, I see how her actions, or maybe even just her existence, have already caused the beginning of an avalanche. One, I don't think any of us truly know the scope of.

Unfortunately, I have also begun to care for her. Likely a side effect of giving her some of my life force. As a demon, it's not in my nature to care for any but my own kind.

I remain in the shadows as Fem and Dio arrive in this large space.

I watch Dio closely. Where the others have been holding up well as we make progress toward our goal, Dio is rapidly crumbling. I can't have weak steel in my weapon, especially Dio. His emotions are his weak point, and his control needs work if he is going to survive this.

After seeing his tattoos and discovering what he is capable of as a solo, magic practitioner, he is the card up my sleeve. However, since I still haven't forgiven him for what he did to Chaosta, or that he has believed me to be a liar, I must admit my feelings on his usefulness are now clouded.

As I observe Dio, I note that Fem is approaching me. I

mentally prepare for whatever conversation we are about to have.

Sharing as much information about Chaosta as I have with Fem has been a necessary evil. After I got her out of Piquory Center, someone needed to keep an eye on her to ensure she didn't harm herself again. Fem was the obvious choice with his training in healing.

When I saw how seriously he was taking his role as Chaosta's protector, I encouraged him to attempt to get closer to Dio, hoping that his support might help. I am not sure if it is working, but that's neither here nor there.

Before Fem has a chance to begin the conversation the way he wants, I ask him quietly, "Has she allowed you to examine her yet?" My chest tightens as he shakes his head. "But she hasn't harmed herself, right?" I ask.

"That's actually what I wanted to talk to you about," he says, and I feel my muscles tense.

I'm on a razor's edge already, with her pain echoing through me, so it takes a massive amount of strength to pull myself back from the edge and compose myself. "What's that?" I ask. My voice sounds harsh even to my ears. I see him flinch.

"I've been thinking about it, and I started to wonder how she would've had access to a knife or blade at the center," he says.

I relax slightly. I have the answer to this. "The notes in her medical record said she got violent, broke a table, and stabbed herself with the broken table leg," I say, careful to keep my voice low.

"That wound wasn't made by a jagged piece of wood; that was made by a blade," he says.

There is a loud ringing in my ears. The room ceases to exist as rage causes me to dematerialize without intent and reform in the alley behind Lily's building.

Fuck, that hasn't happened since I was merely a few centuries old.

Thankfully, with the sudden cessation of pain now that I'm

further from Chaosta, I am able to get control of myself fairly quickly.

Momentarily, I wonder if creating her and giving her as much of my strength as I did was a good idea, but I shake off that thought. The map is spread out ahead of both of us at this point, and while there are still large gaps, this is the only viable path.

Rage continues to course through me, and I begin to plan. I will find answers, and if it is as I suspect, based on what Fem just said, people will pay. Direct action on this problem will be a refreshing change of pace.

THUSLY ARMED

It is late evening, almost night, of my second day back at the mansion, and I'm lying in bed trying to focus on reading. I am sure the boys must be downstairs working on their magic with Malam. I wish I could be practicing with my sword. I consider briefly how long it might take for Malam to bring me another blade.

Eventually, unable to ignore the need any longer, I rise and go to the restroom. With the movement, additional pain hits me, and I'm glad when I can return to my bed. As I get back to the side of the bed, almost able to lie down again, I hear paper tear as I step on the pile I disturbed the day before. Emotions pulse through me. Emotions that are stronger than I feel they should be. Tears prick at my eyes.

Without looking, I bend down and gather up the pages. Looking at the wall, I stand beside the bed holding them. My fingers clench into fists, crumpling the edges, and I feel a tear slide down my cheek.

I thought about these nearly the entire time I was being held by the angels. I thought of tearing them up or burning them. I also thought of framing them and hanging them on my wall.

I relax my fingers and, without looking, smooth the wrinkles I created. Then I finally look down at the paper in my hands and the sketch on it, a sketch of Dio.

They're almost all sketches of Dio.

When I was drawing them, I thought it was my anger that led me to sketch him. Or maybe there were interesting lines there in his forearm, or his jaw, things that my eye caught on.

However, while I was incarcerated and had nothing else to focus on, too often it was Dio whom my thoughts turned to. Eventually, I couldn't ignore it anymore. Despite many months to think about it, I still don't know how to untangle this knot of emotions. His action in sending me to the treatment center still feels unforgivable. Yet somehow I'm here, holding a stack of sketches with him as the subject, unable to stop thinking about him.

Not wanting to think about any of it at the moment, I crouch and tuck the papers between two books in the pile under my bed. Then I lay down, propping myself back up on my pillows and covering myself with a blanket.

I'm just done wiping the remaining tears from my eyes when I hear something. The sound of wings fills the space, and shadow materializes, quickly forming into Malam.

He grimaces as he stabilizes himself, and I wonder if he is injured. He has his eyes tightly shut and, without opening them, asks, "Are you fully clothed?"

"Yes, or at least I'm covered," I say, and he opens his eyes.

I note the sheathed sword in his hand as he moves to the end of my bed and places it there. At a brief glance, I can tell it isn't the sword he lent me before, and my curiosity piques, momentarily distracting me from the emotions and pain. Before I can move to examine it, he speaks again.

"I won't be around much for at least the next fortnight," he says gently, "but I'm always here if you need me."

I look up at him and briefly see rage on his face before he masks it. "Are you alright?" I ask.

"I'm fine," he says flatly.

"It's just, I saw you wince when you arrived," I say as he glares daggers at the wall behind my head.

"I'm not injured," he says, his tone still flat.

"Everything else ok?" I ask, thinking of Lily and hoping nothing has happened to her.

"It will be," he says, and there is a dark and dangerous tone to his voice that I don't miss.

Since it's clear I am not going to get any information out of him, instead, I thank him for the sword. He nods briefly, still not looking at me, and then, without another word, dissolves into shadow again.

With him gone, I move gingerly to the end of my bed and pick up the sword to look at it more closely. Like the last sword, it's a saber, but that is where the similarity ends. The handle of this sword is wrapped in black leather instead of brown, and there's delicate red detailing set into it. The metal handguard is silver rather than gold, and there is a floral pattern engraved on it.

When I bare a couple of inches of blade, I pause, struck by the beauty of it. The blade is made from a black metal, and it continues the floral engraving, only this stands out more starkly because it's silver set against the black. I unsheathe it fully and see that the entire blade looks like this. I hold it out in front of me and comprehend immediately how immaculate the balance is. I also notice it's shorter, a better length for my diminutive height.

It is clear to me as I look down at the blade in my hand that it was made specifically for me. Whether by Malam's hands directly or not, he was the force behind it. I suddenly wish I could call him back to thank him profusely for such a wonderful gift. I remember him telling me he wouldn't make the journey often, however, and decided to wait until I see him next. Besides, the best way to thank him is to put the sword to the use it was created to fulfill.

With that thought in mind, I pull on clothes I can practice in. I'm in pain, but at this point, I will take any opportunity to distract myself from the emotions I am feeling. So I sneak to the empty room and spend some time gingerly practicing with *my* sword.

DIO'S JOURNAL - ENTRY 338

Annum:5615
Entry 338 - lateo

It's late in the evening, the day after Chaosta got back, and yet the reprieve I was hoping for has not yet materialized.

I'll admit I was looking forward to working with the other guys on our magic tonight. It seemed like a positive thing to focus on in the midst of everything. I always find practicing magic to be centering for me.

At the start of my recovery, those who supported me helped me find a passion for boxing. It was at the first boxing gym that I met the man, my now departed friend, who eventually recruited me into a group that practiced dark magic. They supported the demons and took action to support the darkness. Being part of that group and having something to focus on eventually became an even more integral part of my recovery than boxing. After I lost him, I was glad to find this band and coven. I believe it is the right thing for me to put my energy into. I just wish we had more time to figure out this difficult magic. I also wish we had fewer issues distracting us from it.

Anyway, tonight when I arrived in the ballroom, I watched as Fem had a brief, tense conversation with Malam in the corner while I gathered our blood magic instruments. Out of nowhere, Malam just turned into fucking shadow or smoke or something and disappeared.

Poor Fem. He was pale and needed to sit down. He was standing so close and said it actually hurt physically when Malam did that. I don't typically encourage it, but I got him to drink some brandy to try to settle his nerves. None of us even realized demons could do that. I suppose it's how he gets to Chaosta when she summons him? If so, she clearly has a steel constitution to deal with whatever that is.

It took a few hours to get everyone settled, but in the end, we decided to forge on and try to get some work done on our own. We weren't even able to produce a single raindrop. I blame the fact that we were all still unsettled from what just happened.

We did try to ask Fem what caused Malam to disappear like that, but he refused to tell us. I think we're all tired of secrets, but none of us were going to push him after that.

EXCERPTS FROM MALAM

I am careful to be quiet when I get back to Lily's home after delivering the sword. I don't want to wake her. My poor love has been dealing with my volatile emotions recently, and she certainly deserves the sleep.

I should be in bed with her, but this task can't wait. Instead, I pull on the clothing I stole from the center. My disguise from when I was there to remove Chaosta all those months ago. It is a happy accident that I still have it, one less thing to deal with on this mission.

I get ready to leave, but can't help myself; I need to check on Lily. As I stand beside the bed and see her sleeping, I feel my emotions stabilize. I don't know what I'd do without her.

I lean down and gently kiss her forehead. She mumbles and smiles in her sleep, and it takes all of my inner strength to pull away from the bed I've begun to think of as my own. I make myself leave the bedroom and transport myself to a dark alley outside the treatment center.

I shake off thoughts of her as I walk through the front door. She doesn't belong anywhere near the upcoming violence.

I move confidently past the front desk and into the hallway

that leads to the rest of the treatment center. The guard at the front desk just nods to me, recognizing my outfit if not me. My lack of hesitation makes him feel comfortable. Humans are stupid.

It doesn't take me long to find an empty terminal, and I hack past the security screen and locate Chaosta's records. I may not be a talented hacker, like some of our people. However, I am capable of simple hacking with small things like this.

When I was here last, I only scanned for one thing. Back then, I needed to know what medications they were giving her so I knew what care she would need as she recovered. At the time, I was distracted by the sheer volume of antipsychotics and other mind medications they had been giving her. I was careful to avoid looking at everything else since that seemed like an intrusion of her privacy.

Now that I believe portions of this record are a lie, it doesn't feel as much like an intrusion as it did, so I read the entirety.

*I*t takes nearly an hour, and while there are some inconsistencies, nothing here tells me what actually happened. I lock down the terminal, choking back the growl that wants to emerge from my throat. This is going to take more time than I had hoped.

I walk back out through the front door, still not raising suspicion. Once I'm out on the street, I light a cigarette and walk for a bit. The air is already poisonous, adding a little more to my lungs can't hurt. Besides, I am immortal and not plagued by human conditions.

Smoking is a new thing for me, a way of coping with the increased stress I'm under in the race to try to save my people. As unhealthy as it is, there are many worse things I need help coping with.

FRANKLY, A SURPRISING
REQUEST FOR ASSISTANCE

I have been able to sneak away to practice with my new sword twice. The first, on the night Malam gave it to me, went well. I enjoyed practicing with a blade so beautifully balanced and perfect for me. I took it easy, though, moving slowly through the patterns and stopping after a short while.

The second time, this afternoon, however...

I wince as I watch myself in the mirror. I'm pressing a piece of fabric I tore from one of my old skirts to my side. I'm trying to stop the bleeding where I pulled open a couple of the previously healing, knife wounds.

"Fuck abdomens and their fucking inability to stay stitched," I growl quietly to myself.

Of course, someone chooses this moment to knock on my door.

"Just a minute," I yell.

I bend over gingerly and pick up one of the long stockings that is lying in a scattered mess across the floor of my room. I haven't worn these since I got back, so I use them now as a bandage. I wrap it tightly around the folded-up piece of fabric, fastening it snugly over the still bleeding wound.

I find one of my loosest shirts and pull it on, then quickly add a pair of leggings. I go to the door and open it to see Fem standing in the doorway looking concerned.

Behind him, of all the boys I would have liked to see, is Dio. Thanks to the sword practice and increased pain, I've actually managed not to think about him for a bit, but now here he is.

"Is everything ok in there?" Fem asks.

As he begins to look around my disaster of a room, I quickly step out into the hallway and pull the door mostly shut behind me. There are plenty of things I'd rather he not see in there right now.

"Everything's fine," I say as brightly as I can manage, carefully hiding a wince.

He looks suspicious, who wouldn't be, but instead of asking more questions, he says, "We haven't seen Malam in a while. We tried summoning him today, but he never arrived, and that has never happened before. Have you heard from him?"

"He stopped by yesterday and told me he was going to be unavailable for a fortnight."

Fem looks surprised at my quick response. He briefly glances back at Dio, whom I continue to avoid, before turning back to me. "Dio thought you might know."

Before I can figure out how to respond, Fem says, "We were talking, and we're getting worried about our lack of progress. We still can't consistently produce weather effects with our magic. We thought you might be able to help in some way?" His voice becomes quiet at the end as though it is an uncomfortable question.

Unsure what "we" means, I carefully focus on Fem and say, "Sure, I have some ideas, but it might take a little while."

Fem again looks surprised by my answer.

He looks back at Dio again, and we all stand in silence for a moment before Dio says quietly, "Thank you."

I finally risk a glance at him. He's standing nearly against the wall, about as far away from me as he can get in the hallway. He's looking at me with a focused intensity that feels dangerous.

I'm just about to flee, back into my room, when he swallows, his throat bobbing, and then says, "Are you sure you're alright?"

Channeling Malam, I direct my focus to the wall behind him and manage to choke out, "I'm fine."

At the edge of my vision, I see Fem's eyes narrow. He glances at Dio and then back at me.

I risk another glance at Dio and wish I hadn't. Concern has joined the utter focus on his face. Feeling tears beginning to prick at my eyes and knowing I'm quickly losing the battle to control my emotions, I step back through the door of my room.

In my haste to escape before I lose control entirely, the door slams shut harder than I intended. Feeling even less like I know what to do about any of this, I take a few steps back into my room. I press my hand to my mouth, holding in a sob that I'm barely containing.

As a way to focus on anything except that man who is outside my room, I consider the request for help. When I was spending my existence in that small cell, I had ample time to think. While Dio certainly featured in those thoughts, I also had other realizations, such as the importance of the magic work the boys are doing and what I believe they hope to accomplish with the cause. It aligns with my designed purpose in a way I hadn't recognized or at least fully understood before all my time in that tiny cell.

Now that I am aware of the importance of their work, a portion of the map in my mind has filled in. It shows a path I feel compelled to follow.

After calming down and realizing no one is going to knock again, I spend time getting the bleeding stopped. Then I apply what's left of the remaining ointment to several of my other injuries. I manage a better, if still makeshift, bandage for the now partially torn-open gashes on my side. Finally, I pull together enough items from my wardrobe to manage an outfit that doesn't reveal or press against my wounds.

I look at myself in the mirror before I leave and barely recognize the person staring back. I'm dressed in multiple layers of black with my hair tied as well as I can manage with two broken fingers. My eyes still have dark circles under them from my broken nose. They also seem darker than before, despite the familiar mismatched colors.

Before I leave, I strap the sword to my back and pull the cowl hood over my head, obscuring as much of my face as possible. Then I leave the mansion. It is late and everything is dark. The boys are likely in bed, or at least not in the common spaces, and the house employees are not around, so no one sees me leave.

When I get to the street, I move along it until I see what I'm looking for. An off-duty carriage horse, a stallion, stands tied to the side of a carriage, his head low and foot resting in sleep.

When the horse sees me, though, I am surprised by his reaction. He lifts his head, the whites of his eyes showing, and pins his ears flat, a clear warning to stay away. I hesitate a moment; horses have never reacted to me like this before.

I reach for some understanding, consulting my instincts. The realization that I am not who I was before hits me. When it does, as though the horse appreciates the honesty, he relaxes. He is still restless but less so. I offer him my breath, blowing gently into his nostrils. To my relief, he calms further and blows a gentle breath at me.

Carefully so I don't alert the, hopefully sleeping, carriage master, I untie the horse. He honors me by lowering himself onto his knees so I can clamber, still with much difficulty and pain, onto his back. As soon as I am settled, the horse leaps forward down the street as I grip tightly to his harness.

The speed of a carriage horse is like nothing else. Without the protection of the carriage around me, the wind beats and batters at me. Instead of fear, though, I feel laughter emerging from my throat as I urge him on.

We soon arrive at the familiar building. This time, I am directed to its location in some part by both the horse and my memory. As the pain pounds through me, I dismount as carefully as I can. Then I wrap my arms briefly around the horse's head, thanking him for the gift he just gave me. When I release the large head, the horse turns and leaps back down the street, and I silently wish him safe travels to whatever destination.

I look up at the large building ahead of me and take a steadying breath. The massive black facade is nothing if not intimidating. I almost wish for the dreamlike haze I was in last time I was here. Squaring my shoulders, I take a breath and push through the front door. The lit candles and smoke are familiar, but what I need is a way to the top floors. After a few moments of searching, I locate a lift at the far side of the massive entry hall.

I enter the open lift and press the button for the top floor. Nothing happens. I growl at it, but that obviously doesn't do anything. I let out a sigh and rest my head against the panel, reaching for some idea, anything that might help with this. I can't hit a dead end here, I feel that clearly.

I also know full well that my body isn't even capable of climbing several flights of stairs. Certainly not the hundreds of flights it would take to get to the top of this building. At least not without a demon's aid.

As my forehead touches the panel, the memory of the place I'm seeking comes to mind. Unbidden, the tall trees and that clearing play in my memory. In this vision, Malam says simply, "What do you need, Chaosta?"

"Entrance," I think back, and I am suddenly brought back to the lift, which is now moving upward, chiming at each floor.

As I wait, I lift my shirt and inspect my wounds. I note that I have bled completely through my makeshift bandage and torn a couple of other stitches besides. Since there is nothing I can do about it at the moment, I lower my shirt and hope that one of the demons might be convinced to aid me with this as well.

I am beginning to feel dizzy as the lift continues to rise, so I lock my knees to keep standing and rest my head back against the wall. Even with the pain, this is progress toward a goal that has been compelling me for a long time. I couldn't see it clearly for a while, but now that I can, the forward motion is fulfilling some need in me. It is soothing in some way to be on this path.

With one final ding, the upward motion stops. The doors slide open, and I see the thick, familiar smoke that fills the stronghold beginning to creep into the lift. Pulling at the dregs of my remaining strength, I stiffen my legs and proceed. I am disoriented by the smoke and the pain. The drug-induced haze I was in last time I was here also isn't conducive to recognizing where to go now.

As I walk forward, the smoke suddenly clears a bit, and I find myself standing in front of two demons. Their hands are on the swords strapped to their backs. One unsheathes his blade as he looks at me. The other says something in their guttural language. I recognize the word Malam. Then he asks me something in that same language.

Instead of trying to understand the question, I just say, "Chiron?" and he nods and leaves through the smoke.

The other demon, his sword in hand, remains where he is. He glares at me, clearly doubting my intent regardless of whatever the other said. I wobble as I wait, focusing on not allowing my knees to buckle. Somehow, I must still look dangerous because he doesn't sheath the sword and seems poised to strike.

Luckily, it doesn't take long for the other to come back with a demon I recognize as Chiron.

As he gets close, Chiron wrinkles his nose and says to me in strongly accented words, "You're bleeding."

It's not a question, but I nod.

"You need healing?" he asks abruptly.

I nod again.

Without another word, he walks away. I glance at the guards, silently asking permission of the one with the drawn sword. He sheaths it in response, so I follow Chiron.

He leads me to a small room and begins to gather things from a large cabinet. "Strip," he says, the accent still rough but his meaning clear.

I remove my clothing, leaning one hand against the wall for balance as needed.

When he turns around, his eyes start slowly at my face and trail down to my thighs, his face blank. "What..." he says, gesturing as though he wants to ask more but can't think of the words. "How did this happen to you?" he asks without looking away from the makeshift bandage at my side.

I shake my head briefly without responding.

"Not going to tell me?" he asks. His accent makes it more difficult to understand the tone, but he sounds irritated.

I shake my head in agreement.

He seems to consider for a moment, but without pushing me further for an answer, he begins to tend to my injuries. Occasionally, he steadies me, and I gladly accept the support. After a bit, I let my mind wander, going somewhere else, away from the pain.

Eventually, he finishes, and I look down to see a neat bandage wrapped around my entire torso, along with bandages wrapped around the top of each of my arms and each of my legs. He's cleaning up at a basin at the back of the room.

"Stitches don't hold well there," he grumbles.

"I noticed," I say quietly.

When he finishes washing up, he hands me a small tin. "Leave the bandages on for three days. When you remove them, apply that daily for the next three days," he says. He looks at me as though to check my understanding and then gestures to my clothes on the floor, silently telling me to get dressed.

I stay where I am and say, "I need something else."

He says something in the guttural language that doesn't sound kind.

I persevere.

"Malam is indisposed, but some work he began, which is important to me, remains unfinished," I say to him evenly. I can tell that I have his attention.

"What work?" he asks.

"I have a few acquaintances who are attempting to learn weather magic in order to strike back against the angels. Malam has been guiding them."

I watch as Chiron's eyes narrow slightly. "Humans?" he growls.

"Yes."

"How well do they speak our language?" he asks, and the unkindness is clear in his voice this time.

"I don't believe they do."

"Well then, there is nothing I can do. Those who might help them don't speak their language, so we are at an impasse," he says as he begins to turn away.

Some memory, likely one of Malam's, pulls at me, and I respond to his back as he walks away, "But you speak the language and I suspect you know weather magic." I modulate my tone carefully.

He freezes, and I see his body tense. A laugh that is certainly not kind bursts from his throat. "You are a crazy one if you think I will get involved with humans."

I ignore the attempt at an insult and say, "Perhaps that's how your people got to this point."

He reels back like I slapped him, and glares at me.

I maintain eye contact, silently begging whatever deity is available at the moment for help with this. Suddenly, as though someone literally speaks to him from above, he closes his eyes as a shudder runs through his body. When he opens them, most of the anger and disgust are gone. "You make a valid point," he says more quietly.

He remains quiet for a few moments as he seems to consider. "I will help, but I will not have them summoning me at all hours. If they are committed to doing this, it will be on a regular schedule. I will arrive promptly at ten each evening and stay for as long as I like. You will inform them of this."

I nod, silently thanking the deity.

"Get dressed," he says roughly.

I carefully and slowly pull on my clothes. Once I'm dressed, he walks out of the room and I follow. I hesitate when he continues past the path I remember, which leads to the lift.

Seeming to sense my hesitation, he says, "I'll take you."

I nod and continue after him.

As we walk into a small clearing, he stops and turns toward me while holding out his hand. I step forward and take it without pause. "Show me," he says.

Without needing further instruction, I close my eyes and picture the street in front of the boys' mansion. A moment later, I open my eyes to shadows and the sound of wings in flight wrapping around us, and then, just as suddenly, it fades and reveals the side of the boys' mansion.

Chiron releases my hand and takes a step back. I look at him, and he meets my eyes. "Ten sharp, tomorrow evening," he says and then disappears in a slithering cloud of shadow that is both like and unlike Malam's.

With that, I turn and head into the mansion to my bed. It is well past time for me to get some rest.

DIO'S JOURNAL - ENTRY 339

Annum:5615
Entry 339 - tueor

So much has happened that it feels like it's been a year when actually it's only been a busy few days. I didn't sleep well last night after Malam disappeared like that. The inability to achieve even the same level of magic we have been just served to unsettle me further. My dreams were horrifying, death and destruction featured strongly.

After that night, I knew we needed to make some real progress today. We started the summoning ritual a little early to give us plenty of time with Malam. I think we were all anxious to learn more about what happened.

Other than Reem, who was fussing and fretting about our upcoming record release, I don't know what the others did to pass the time during the day. I went for a run that ended at the boxing gym. Nothing better than fresh bruises to distract me from my emotions.

When I got back from boxing, I actually took a shower and ate some food. Thanks to the run and the resolution of the prison situation with Chaosta, I had some appetite. I actually felt a little better after eating.

Then the time arrived, and we went to the ballroom to prepare the magic circle and instruments for his instruction. Time stretched on, though, and Malam didn't show. We checked our ritual and couldn't find anything wrong. We were all starting to spiral, but because my mind was clearer again, I was able to be the voice of reason. I brought up asking Chaosta for help. After all, she is close with him.

Fem elected himself to speak with her despite Lent wanting to be the one to do it. I could tell Fem wanted an excuse to check on her. I guess I hadn't registered just how close he's been watching her since she got out of the treatment center until that moment.

I'm a little surprised that Lent isn't trying harder to see her and that she hasn't seemed to seek him out since she's been back. Maybe I misread the relationship between the two of them. Maybe it's actually Fem who's more interested in her.

When Fem asked me to go with him, I tried to refuse. Her anger wasn't going to be appeased by my wanting to ask her for help. The fact that I haven't made any progress in figuring out how to mend what happened between us isn't something I'm capable of dwelling on at the moment. Instead, I'm avoiding it. My favorite way of coping, or I guess my second favorite.

Despite my reservations, I found myself following Fem to Chaosta's room. Torn between seeing her and not wanting to make her feel uncomfortable, I stayed back. Fem tried to get me to knock on the door and talk with her, but again, I refused. I knew enough to understand she wouldn't handle that well. Instead, Fem knocked on the door. When I heard how annoyed she sounded, I almost left, but I still wanted to see her myself and make sure she looked all right. I know intimately how painful a broken nose and broken fingers can be.

It took her far too long to come to the door for my comfort, and when she did, I didn't feel at all reassured. Something about her body language screamed at my instincts. I don't know why. Her nose and the bruising from it didn't look any worse, and her fingers were still well taped. I actually felt a little better when she glared at me because it was so normal. Then I immediately got more concerned when she stepped into Fem's space and pulled the door closed behind her so he couldn't see what was in the room. That rang alarm bells for sure. She's clearly hiding something.

I'm starting to know Fem well enough that I could see it concerned him as well. He still followed through with our plan and asked her about Malam and if she could help us. I just wanted to push past her and check her room, but I controlled myself, letting him lead in this.

I guess I wasn't too surprised when she told us she had heard from Malam. However, hearing that he will be gone for a fortnight distracted me from my worry about her for a minute. Honestly, we can't wait a fortnight. We're already fucked enough. Before I recognized what was happening, Fem was pulling me into the conversation, just like I told him not to. She looked at me, and suddenly I couldn't help myself. I asked if she was alright. She said she was fine, but for some reason I don't believe she is. Then, before either of us could say anything else, she shut herself back in her room.

After the door slammed in his face, I could tell by the set of his shoulders that Fem was pissed. He looked ready to march through the door and scold her for being rude. Honestly, that was the last thing on my mind.

He turned to me, and I could tell he was expecting my anger and support for his desire to scold her. I was still staring at the door, trying to keep myself from battering it down, but for a much different reason. At that moment, I wanted to ask if he'd seen her flinch or how pale she was.

I have this feeling now that she's more hurt than we realize, and suddenly the distance from her is killing me.

Instead, I asked if he wanted to go boxing with me.

He didn't respond for a moment. Then he looked me over as though he thought I might need his medical experience, but he said yes. I came back to my room to get ready and couldn't help but get this written down. I should go, though. I'm sure he's waiting on me to head to the boxing gym. Twice in a day can't hurt, right?

DIO'S JOURNAL - ENTRY 340

Annum:5615

Entry 340 - fractura ossis

I guess boxing twice in one day can hurt. I'm in a lot of pain, actually.

I busted up my knuckles, have yet another black eye, and I'm fairly sure at least one of my ribs is broken. Fem needed to pull me out of the ring. That smug asshole I fought at the end just wouldn't quit, and the pain was helping me concentrate on something other than Chaosta. Without Fem, I'd be in much worse shape.

Fem gave me a lecture on the walk, or in my case limp, back about taking better care of myself but I wasn't really listening. Not like I haven't heard it all before. I just need something to care about again, and this will all get better. The cause and our weather magic worked for a while, but it feels brittle right now, especially with Malam deserting us.

I slept restlessly that night because of the pain and unease about what we're up against. I had an appetite for breakfast, though, so at least the physical exertion did help a bit. Chaosta didn't come to breakfast, but she hasn't since she got back, so I wasn't overly concerned. I know Reem has asked the staff to bring food to her room, so she's not going hungry. I can't complain about the lack of awkwardness and tension.

After breakfast, we had a "band meeting" that Reem pulled together. He's hired us an assistant who's going to be working double time to help pull together everything we need to get this record released on time. He pleaded with us to help out where we can. I've been trying to remember the high from the last concert and get my mind back in the game for our music. I just can't concentrate on anything right now. Well, that's not quite right. There is someone I can't stop thinking about.

Fuck.

The meeting finished quickly enough that we had some time before lunch, so we actually managed to find some time to rehearse. Gods, we need to do that more. Our next concert is looming, and if we play like we did today, I wouldn't blame our entire fan base if they all deserted us. I thought Reem was going to lose it. The band is just so important to him. He was white faced

after we finished. He left while we were still getting
cleaned up.

When we went to lunch after, licking our wounds, I
think we were all surprised when Chaosta joined us. Fem
opened his mouth, and I could tell he was going to scold
her for slamming the door on us the day before. I may
have "accidentally" tripped him. By the time we cleaned
the food up and got reorganized, he must have forgotten.
Clumsy me, I guess. Ha!

When everything settled and we were eating lunch,
Chaosta shared that she had "enlisted the help of a
different demon" and said, "he'll be here tonight." She
said he's less patient than Malam, and we need to be
ready right at ten each night. No summoning this one, I
guess.

I don't think any of us quite knew what to think.
It's odd to think of working with a different demon. I'm
sure for the others in particular, since they've known
Malam for far longer than I have.

Despite those misgivings, I could have thrown her a
parade. Especially when she announced she's going to get
back to researching weather magic and wanted Fem and
Lent to join her when they can. Fuck, we might actually
have a chance to get this figured out in time thanks
to her.

EXCERPTS FROM MALAM

I slam the knife into the human's throat, stepping to the side carefully to avoid the spray. Of course, I am already covered in his blood, but I may as well avoid the amount an arterial puncture would add.

This wasn't a kind death. He's been bleeding for me for nearly a day now, but it was worth it. I finally have the last piece of the puzzle.

I'm in a small basement space, a sort of bunker, which has fully stone walls, a stone floor, and a stone ceiling. It makes cleanup easier.

I walk to the edge of the room where I've set up a small changing station. I strip and clean myself as well as I can. I will still need a shower later, but I want to avoid bringing this much blood back to the stronghold or Lily's home.

I chuckle to myself at still thinking of the apartment as Lily's home. I spend so much time at the stronghold or on tasks such as this that it is not as though I'm fully living there. I do spend more nights there than anywhere else.

Once I have removed all traces of the human's blood and changed into fresh clothing, I walk into the hallway. Pointing through the open door at the magic circle, I drew on the floor of the bunker, I send my energy to it, and the fire begins. The magic will cause the fire to quickly consume everything in the room without needing more air. It will burn hot enough that nothing will remain other than a little ash.

I press the door shut quickly and trace a rune on its surface to lock it. Despite my general ambivalence regarding their kind, I wouldn't want a human to mistakenly open it while the fire burns. They must be guarded against their own stupidity.

With that done, I dematerialize, transporting myself to our stronghold to gather the last pieces of information I need before I speak with Chaosta.

I stumble as I materialize and nearly fall. That isn't like me. Resisting the band's summons just over a fortnight ago was agony, physically and mentally, and it clearly depleted my energy. I have continued to struggle with transporting myself ever since, though it does seem to be improving with time.

I hope they don't try to summon me again. If they do, someone is going to end up dead, and it is less likely to be me.

DIO'S JOURNAL - ENTRY 341

Annum: 5615

Entry 341 - ~~praecanto~~ praecantatio

It's been almost a fortnight since I wrote in this journal. This time it's because we've been making so much progress.

As I write this entry, I can say confidently that we've mastered the basics of weather magic. Chiron isn't nearly as skilled a teacher as Malam was. However, between the passages and runes Chaosta has found for us and the consistent help we have finally figured it out. Despite that, I have to admit I'll be glad when Malam returns and replaces this new demon. This one is even more irritable and is quite prone to rudeness. I didn't think I'd ever say it, but I think I prefer Malam.

There is so much more magic to learn, but this was our first real step. To have achieved this is a significant relief. Of course, it also means it is time to pick up the magical item we need for our end goal. The guys and I talked about it last night after Chiron left. This magical item was part of Malam's plan, and I'm not sure if we should include the new demon or not. Since we aren't sure of his relationship with Malam, to be cautious, we decided to keep it to ourselves.

The plan is to pick the stone up on the way to our next concert. The shop that has the stone is near our concert venue, so we decided it made the most sense to add a stop rather than taking the time to go separately. It feels to me as though we are combining two worlds we have attempted to keep apart. That seems like asking for bad luck, but I'm probably just being grim.

We have also made time to focus on our music again. Since we're on a strict schedule with Chiron, we've moved band rehearsal to earlier in the day. Reem is coming apart at the seams with the stress of the upcoming concert, and Fem, Lent, and I agreed to daytime rehearsals mainly to try to calm him. That man sure cares about the band. Earlier rehearsals have meant that most of the time, Chaosta is researching by herself. However, I'm not at all surprised at this point that she seems to be doing as well on her own as the three did together.

Also, thanks mostly to Reem and our new assistant, who has the strange name of Pepper, our record was released without a hitch. While I despised dedicating time to posing for photographs and being asked nearly an infinite number of times to review wording and layouts, it is good to have it in physical form, finally. We're planning to do a signing at the upcoming concert as well as another independent signing a few weeks later. I can't even begrudge the time for band shit now with how we've improved with our weather magic. Also, anything to settle Reem.

WELL, THAT CHANGES
EVERYTHING

I flinch as I remove this final stitch from the wound at the bottom edge of my ribs. I'm glad I am nearly done with this now. Just one more wound to go.

I take a minute to compose myself. Looking in the mirror, I see a tendril of my pink hair stuck to my forehead by perspiration. There are still dark circles under my mismatched eyes, but my nose is mostly healed. A mix of scars and still-healing wounds covers my entire torso. Because of the fortnight that has passed, even the freshest wounds have healed considerably. I've had to re-tape my fingers as they aren't healed yet, but they are feeling better. Time and demon healing magic have done wonders, and I've been feeling more and more physically capable again.

Taking another breath, I steel myself and begin on the last wound. As a distraction from this unpleasant task, I focus on how well things have been going with the boys. The atmosphere of the house changed completely once they successfully released their album. They have also been telling me how much progress they've made with their magic work.

I am honestly not seeing much of them at this point. Since

they have nightly commitments with Chiron, they've been rehearsing their music during the day. It means I've been on my own for research, which is lonely. It also feels slower, but based on what they have told me, it sounds as though the information I've been giving them has still been helping.

Interactions between Dio and me are still strained, but because I barely see him, things between us haven't felt as tense. Other than the incident where he showed up with a black eye and bloody knuckles, he seems to be recovering from whatever was bothering him before. His clothes aren't hanging on him like they were, and the dark circles under his eyes are mostly gone.

Knowing now what addiction means, when I got released and saw Dio looking so unkempt, I thought perhaps my gut reaction was right. Perhaps he thought he was seeing something in me that had plagued him and had begun to struggle again. Now, though, as he has begun to look better, it seems unlikely.

With research, sword practice, and the pain I am still in, I've had plenty of distractions, and yet there is still far too much time available for me to obsess. I have made, and then promptly not acted on, so many plans regarding my relationship with Dio. Finally, deciding the intense swirl of emotions was too much to deal with all at once, I made a different plan. I am going to talk with him and see if we can manage an easy relationship. I would like to at least feel as though I can consider him a friend.

I wish I could have that with Reem as well, but I have been a thorn in his side for too long. I know how much I have distracted from the band. Also, I don't have much motivation to deal with that relationship until I have things figured out with Dio.

Suddenly, I am hit by the sound of wings in flight. I know what I'm going to see before I look up to the mirror, but I do so anyway. Malam is standing behind me, as I suspected, only this time his eyes are wide and fixed on me.

I had been trying to keep the evidence of my torture from him. Malam seeing what the angels did to his creation isn't something I felt would help anyone. I have known he was aware there were wounds he couldn't see, but I had hoped to keep the significance of them from him.

Nothing else for it now, I look down and focus on removing the next stitch as I say, "Hello Malam, what brings you here?" Silence hangs over the room as I continue with my task.

Just as I am about to ask again, he chokes out some sound, syllables that don't make sense.

Without looking at him, I say, "Are you going to answer my question or are you going to make me kick you out of my room?"

Silence again fills the space. By the time he responds, I'm removing the last stitch, carefully controlling my breathing in an attempt not to further upset him.

"I came to share some information I've gathered," he finally says. His guttural voice is so tight that I have to think for a minute to understand the words.

I stand and move to my wardrobe, still not looking at him, and pull on a shirt and leggings. I finish dressing and turn to face him again as I ask, "What did you find?"

Yet again, he's staring at the wall behind me. I can tell he's exerting a significant amount of control to stand there even this calmly. He eventually responds, "Rex was behind your time at the center."

I blink at him, my world spinning. I turn the chair I was just sitting on and drop myself onto it. "What do you mean?" I ask.

"There's a data trail which shows that the angels became aware of *Dio* committing you to the center," he says.

His voice sounds particularly dark on Dio's name, and I trap an unwelcome snarl in my throat before it can emerge.

"Even as you were in the carriage on the way to the treatment center, there were drugs ordered for you. A significant number and high dose of psychiatric medication were in your medical record before you even arrived. Most of those drugs would never be used to treat addiction."

"They never intended to help me recover," I say as I realize the impact of what he's telling me.

"No," says Malam. "In fact, I think you might still be there if I hadn't removed you."

"So my time at the angel stronghold was them remedying their loss of me from Piquory Center."

"Likely yes," Malam says. "If they had actually wanted to prosecute you for the death of one of their own, they could have more easily done that closer to when it occurred."

"Thank you, Malam," I say. My mind is spinning, and I want some time to think.

"There's more," he says. I note that his hands tighten into fists.

"You never harmed yourself."

These words, along with so many others, hang over me, and something shifts. Some part of the map in my head is being redrawn.

Even as I think of it, I hear Malam speaking. "An angel showed up at the treatment center, likely to confirm your status for the others. Even though you were nearly catatonic, you recognized what he was and attacked him, knocking him down and breaking a table in the process. Then he stabbed you with a knife. Thankfully, a steel knife and not an Angelforged blade, or I'm sure you wouldn't have survived."

The room closes in further, and there is a ringing in my ears. A blurry memory of a blade being pulled from my abdomen and bright green eyes looking into mine plays in my mind's eye.

"In the video, I saw him hide the blade quickly on his person. He then made it look as though he had been trying to restrain you as you stabbed at yourself with a shard from the table. The humans weren't even to blame for that. I think they really did believe you harmed yourself."

So did I, I think to myself, but don't say it.

"If they reacted so quickly to me being sent there, they must be watching me closely," I say after a moment.

I see surprise pass quickly over Malam's face before he says, "Whatever the angels are doing, or did, if *Dio* had not sent you to treatment without your consent, none of this would have happened."

Again, the tone of his voice as he says Dio's name makes rage swirl in me, and I carefully school my expression. "Do you think I'm endangering the boys by being here?"

"I think you are all in danger either way, and since you're capable of defending yourself and others, they are lucky to have you," he snarls.

I nod, still considering. "The boys will be happy to have you back," I say.

His whole body tenses as he looks away. "I'm not coming back," he growls.

"What do you mean?"

"I refuse to spend any more time in the same house as *that man*," he spits.

Unbidden, my fingers clench into fists, and rage pushes at me. I swallow it down, shoving it away. Whatever else I'm feeling, this isn't my fight. After another quiet, tense moment where I consider asking Malam to reconsider, I decide to drop it. Something tells me this isn't the time. Instead, I ask, "Do you have anything else for me?"

He blinks as though he is surprised at the question and then stares at me and says, "No."

Just as I'm thinking I may have to ask him to leave, he takes a step forward and holds his hand out, his mouth slightly open as though he wants to say something.

As I watch, he drops his hand to his side as he says, "No matter how I feel about the other people living here, I will always show up when you need me."

As the shadow begins to coalesce in the room, I say quietly, "Thank you, Malam."

Then he is gone. For a moment, I stay where I'm sitting, again trying to unpick the knot of emotions in my chest. Before I can get far, I'm filled with annoyance at myself. I have a plan, and it's only cowardice that is keeping me from following it. With that thought, I rise and go to find Dio.

EXCERPTS FROM MALAM

I am digging in the dirt back at the demon stronghold and trying to numb my emotions. I have decided to try to recreate a specific type of vine, and having something else to concentrate on is helping the ever-present tension in my shoulders to finally unwind.

I was supposed to be leading the conclave, but the other elders took one look at me when I arrived after my conversation with Chaosta and told me they could handle it without me.

I don't know what I was expecting when I went to speak to her, but it was not that. My intent was to share the information I had gathered. I was so focused on what I planned to say to her that I was distracted and didn't ensure her privacy as I should have. It was a mistake on my part not to have my eyes closed. Even I can admit that. I have been so careful to respect her privacy, and then I had to go and mess up in such a spectacular fashion.

When I saw the scars covering nearly her entire torso, I was overwhelmed by rage. However, as she casually sat there, ignoring me and removing her own stitches, a realization came to me. She's different. She seems to be even stronger somehow.

Whatever happened to her in the angel stronghold rasped away the casual, childlike innocence she possessed and left a much more predatory strength in its wake. Whether that is good or bad will remain to be seen, but some of the protectiveness I have felt for her has faded. In its place, a quiet respect is growing.

I must say, what they did to her felt especially evil set against the backdrop of bright wings rising from her shoulders. It makes me wonder who they made torture her and why they were willing to ignore their tenets like that. Even if it is technically a grey area, since she isn't an angel. They must consider her a significant threat to themselves and their wards in order to have been willing to hurt her like that. The angels protect the human race with a single-mindedness that would be admirable if humans were worth it.

I still have my doubts that she'll be strong enough to accomplish what I created her for. When I dwell, I try to remind myself that she has already killed an angel. I wish I could have seen it with my own eyes, then maybe I'd be able to believe it.

Either way, at this point, I am confident that the best thing I can do is stay out of her way.

DIO'S JOURNAL - ENTRY 342

Annum: 5615
Entry 342 - esuritio

Gods, it feels like the ground is going to crumble from beneath me. I don't know if I've ever been more disappointed in myself.

Chaosta tracked me down several moments ago and said she wanted to talk. I couldn't even speak. I was in so much turmoil, I think I must have just kind of stared at her. Fuck, I hope she didn't think I was glaring at her. Maybe that's why she seemed so irritated.

She said she wanted a fresh start. She said we'd both said things and done things that were inexcusable. At that moment, I was annoyed with her for telling me I'd done something wrong. Now I just wish I'd taken the peace offering she was trying to extend to me. Instead, I fucking stood there with my hands in my fucking pockets trying to control my emotions. I just didn't want to cause her pain.

I've been having so much trouble not staring at her recently, and this was no exception. Her nose is mostly healed, and the bruising around her eyes has almost completely faded. She looked good. Fuck, she looked like water in the desert.

I was trying to remind myself that I can't have this. She's not for me. I'll destroy her. I'll darken her innocence with the shadows in my black heart. It took everything in me to respond to her simply that I was willing to try a fresh start. Then she nodded at me and stomped out of the room.

I don't know what that means. I don't know what to do.

PART V

VIOLENCE IN THE STREETS

Dim light filters through the windows in the flower room where I am currently sitting. I'm surrounded by books as I continue to research weather magic for the boys. I have been distracted and struggling to focus on reading, though. A few days have passed, and I am still unsure what to think about the interaction I had with Dio. He agreed to a fresh start, but he didn't say much. I didn't know what to do with the intensity of his stare.

Gods, I'm bad at this.

Since then, things between us have still been awkward but not openly hostile. I guess that is some improvement, at least.

Suddenly, I feel a familiar tightness in my chest that I haven't felt in a while. The map flashes suddenly and violently in my mind, and without pausing, I stride to my bedroom.

Reaching under the bed without the need to look, I grasp the hilt of my sword. As I stand without slowing, I give it a quick twist, which removes the sheath. It falls to the floor as I stride back out through my bedroom and towards the front door.

With instincts screaming at me, I control my breathing, walking quickly but not running. I stride through the door with bare feet, ignoring shoes. My instincts pull me to the left towards the alley along our building, and I follow that pull, moving forward into the increasing darkness.

What I see both surprises me and doesn't, as the path on the map has somehow already acknowledged this. In the shadows, against our building, two angels are attempting to subdue someone. As I get closer, I realize it is Dio.

Rage pours through me, and without pause, using their distraction against them, I slam the point of the sword through the spine, between the wings of light, of the angel closer to me. As he falls, I pull the sword free with a twisting motion.

Dio looks at me, one eye wide, one swollen shut with blood running over it. I tear my eyes from him and look toward the other angel. The element of surprise is gone as he, realizing I'm a threat, takes a step back. As he takes a second step back, he pulls a sword from the sheath at his hip.

Dio makes a desperate sound and attempts to move between us, presumably to defend me. However, my instincts tell me he'll be unable to rise. I see the instincts are correct as he struggles and fails to get up. I'm relieved that I won't need to try to stop him. He is in no shape to fight and will just be a liability. Fear regarding the severity of his injuries tears at me.

Dragging my attention back to the fight at hand, I stalk toward the other angel who, momentarily caught off guard, is stepping back to give himself space.

I am happy to put him on the defensive.

I take two running steps and launch myself forward at him. He slams his sword up roughly, but he clearly didn't expect it. He barely deflects my blade in time, and I feel his arms shake as he counteracts my strike. I land neatly, counterbalanced against his defensive movement, and immediately twist the swords up. Pressing my momentary advantage, I manage to draw blood with the tip of my sword.

As though the pain cuts through whatever was holding him

back, he finally comes at me. I neatly meet his blows with my sword and allow him to press me back a few steps. My feet moving in the familiar pattern, my blood singing with the familiar feeling of this dance.

He presses, I press, we both defend, but in the end, I'm better. As I pull my sword from his gut and he slumps to the ground, I see open surprise on his beautiful face before it goes blank at the end.

Even as he drops to the ground, the intelligence in me is running through options. Settling quickly on an answer, I step back, away from the body, and say Malam's name quietly. He arrives in the familiar cloud of shadow and whispering sound, and for a moment, I see him prepare to save me.

Then he looks around the alley behind me. When he focuses back on me, his eyes are wide, and his normally olive complexion is paler than normal.

Before he can do or say anything, I say, "I think maybe it's best their bodies aren't found here so close to the mansion. Can you help with that?"

He doesn't say anything for a breath, and then he wordlessly gestures to where I know Dio is sitting.

"He'll be fine, I will take care of him," I say. As I wait for his response, I register belatedly that I am ready to defend Dio from Malam should I need to.

Malam finally shakes himself out of whatever muteness had hold of him and says, "I will take care of this, get him inside."

"Thank you, Malam," I say quietly, meaning it deeply.

Dio watches me as I approach, only one eye able to open. As I get closer, he coughs weakly, clutching his abdomen, and then turns and spits blood onto the ground beside him.

"Can you walk if I help?" I ask.

He nods, and I reach out to him. He hesitates a moment, looking at my hand. I see him looking at my fingers, which are still taped. I'll be damned if I'll set the sword down, though, until we get someplace safe.

"Come on, Dio," I say.

"I don't want to hurt you," he slurs past a swollen lip.

"And I want to get you medical attention," I manage to say past the tightness in my throat.

As though that snaps him out of it, he takes my hand carefully and leans heavily on me as I help him up.

He groans and winces, but with his arm over my shoulders and me taking as much of his weight as I can, we manage. Leaving the alley, we make it slowly up the steps and through the door of the mansion. As we arrive in the entry hall, I call for help.

After I shout, he mutters into the resounding silence that he's really fine.

I scoff and must make a sound because I hear him growl something about not needing help. I ignore him.

Reem comes striding into the room, clearly concerned. When he sees Dio's injuries, Reem's face goes white. Then he sees the sword in my hand and the blood on my clothing, and he freezes.

"Dio's been hurt, where's Fem?" I ask quickly.

That seems to snap him out of it, and without saying anything else, he leaves, presumably to find Fem.

I support Dio into the office and get him sitting, slumped over on the couch despite his weak, mumbled protests. As we wait, I check my sword again, ensuring that no angel blood remains on the blade.

I can't help but glance at Dio. His injuries are significant, and I want desperately to help him. Despite that, I'm not trained in first aid. I also know that if I try to help, I won't be able to control the emotions I've been hiding from him. I don't feel ready yet to share them.

Then Fem strides through the doorway, his face white.

As he walks toward me, I say, "Dio's hurt, I'm fine."

He hesitates, looking doubtful, but then Dio coughs again. Fem redirects his attention to him. He quickly moves to the couch and begins triaging. While he's occupied, I bring him his medical kit. As I set the medical kit down beside Fem, I glance at Dio again.

He meets my eyes for a moment.

We both freeze, and everything else seems to fade into the background. Dio opens his mouth as though he wants to say something. Then Fem does something that makes him gasp and shut his eyes.

Feeling suddenly nauseous, I drag my eyes away from him. Then I force myself to leave the office. I know I can't stay and see him in pain. Especially not right now with this much adrenaline still flowing through me.

Reem meets me in the entry hall, his face white. He's staring at the dark blood on my skirt, and I say, "It's not mine."

He looks briefly at the sword in my hand, and if possible, he goes even whiter. "Please tell me you didn't kill someone again."

"Would you believe me this time if I said I had?"

Some color returns to his cheeks, and I can tell that anger is beginning to push past his initial shock. "Tell me plainly, Chaosta," he says, his voice grating, "did you just kill someone?"

"It's better if I don't tell you," I say as I move toward my room, heading past him.

He steps in front of me as I get close, his body blocking mine.

I feel the fingers of my left hand wrap more tightly around my sword, and I breathe slowly, pulling my instincts back from the brink.

"If you put us, our work, or our name at risk with your actions again, I will have no choice but to remove you from this house and our support," he hisses at me.

I remain where I am, meeting his eyes without saying anything.

"Do you even understand that you can't just go around hurting people?" he nearly yells.

After a moment, perhaps when he recognizes that I'm not going to respond, he moves aside and I stride to my room. I want to make sure Dio is alright, but I am not willing to wait in the entry hall with Reem in this mood.

As I close the door behind me, I lean back against it for a moment. After I catch my breath, I fully clean and re-sheath my sword. The aftershock of those instincts leaving me makes my body shake. With too much adrenaline still pulsing through me for me to rest, I pace instead. As I move, caged in the room, all I can picture is the moment with Dio in the office where he looked at me, and everything else ceased to exist.

DIO'S JOURNAL - ENTRY 345

Annum: 5615

Entry 345 - demiror

Yet another diary entry where I need to apologize if my handwriting isn't as neat as normal. It's been a few days since the incident in the alley, and I'm still struggling to hold a pen. The men who attacked me did a lot of damage.

I should be embarrassed, not only that two men were able to subdue and beat me this badly, but that I was ultimately saved by a girl. Of course, the old me from several months ago would find who saved me particularly distasteful.

Chaosta, who I think might kind of despise me, killed my attackers with a fucking sword.

She has another Demonforged blade. I don't know

where she got it, but that's immaterial at the moment. I'm just glad she showed up when she did. I'm not sure if it was because of the blow to the head, but I tried to subdue them with magic, and it didn't work as it should have.

Not only did she kill them, she did it with brutal efficiency. She looked like some sort of beautifully unholy predator as she took them out without flinching. After she killed the second one, she summoned Malam as though it was normal, spoke with him for a few moments, and then helped me. I wasn't quite sure what to do. She offered me her hand. She fucking held out her right hand with the fucking broken fingers and, without a sound, helped me to my feet. All the while holding the sword as though she was ready for some additional threat. Then she supported and half-carried me into the house.

The less we say about the following few days, the better. Fem says I have internal bruising, likely a few broken ribs, a broken cheekbone, busted up hands, and my shoulder was dislocated, along with other sundry bruising. He wanted to get me a healer, but I refused. I've had my share of injuries, and I was fairly certain I could cope. Plus, I didn't want to have the conversation about not taking pain medication with anyone other than him. Besides, I know how skilled Fem is as a healer with his background.

As he was seeing to my injuries, I tried to thank

her. Then Fem did something that distracted me, and when I looked for her again, she was gone.

When the other guys asked what had happened, I asked what Chaosta said, and they seemed surprised. Well, Reem seemed irritated. I wasn't sure if it was my ears ringing, but I thought I might have heard him yelling at her while Fem tended to me. Why he would do that, I don't quite know. If he did, we're going to have words at some point.

When Reem told me she wouldn't tell him anything, I decided not to share what actually happened. I still don't know if it was the right call or not, but it certainly didn't seem like it was my secret to share. Instead, I simply told them she'd "fought off my attackers," and it seemed to appease them.

Now that we've had time to talk about it, we're pretty sure they were stalkers we occasionally hear from. Based on their behavior, I think they were trying to kidnap me. I still don't know why they weren't impacted as they should have been by magic. The other thing I can't explain is why a stalker would be so capable with a sword. That seems odd.

Reem has been closely watching the news, worried officials will be here to claim that Chaosta assaulted someone. For a while, he wanted me to report that I'd been assaulted, but I adamantly refused. Of course, he couldn't know that bringing attention to the murder of two people outside of our building would be a likely side effect.

I can only hope the reason Chaosta summoned Malam that day was for him to dispose of the bodies. I'm just worried it seems too easy, especially since, as I mentioned in my last entry, Malam isn't willing to work with us anymore.

IF NOT FANS, WHY FAN SHAPED?

A couple of weeks have passed since I fought the angels in the street, and things have been relatively quiet. Partially as a distraction for myself, a few days ago, I finally convinced Lent to bring me shopping so I could buy some of my own clothes. I have been wanting things I could feel more comfortable in.

Fem and Reem went back and forth about whether one of them should join us, and I could tell the subtext was that they were worried there would be trouble. I don't think Reem trusted Lent to be up to the task of accompanying me alone. Especially in light of the incident in the alley with Dio, however, in the end, it was just Lent and I who went.

I won't bore you with all the details. I love shopping for books, but this was not that. We went to three different shops and I found several new outfits. I despised trying things on, but at least Lent was joking around and entertaining me. Each time I walked out of the dressing room to show him something, he paid me a compliment or had a goofy expression on his face. I'm not quite sure why he acts like such an idiot sometimes, but it's nice to be able to relax and have fun with him.

My priority in getting new clothes was to ensure I'd be able to wield a sword and move freely. I also couldn't stand the frills and ruffles on the other things I was wearing. It was nice to be able to replace them.

After we got back to the mansion, I thanked Lent, Fem, and Reem for their willingness to indulge me and pay for these things. They seemed surprised by the comment, and Lent said that with all the research I'd been doing, I'm practically an honorary coven member. Still, though, it was kind of them.

They also all seemed relieved that the trip passed without incident. I am not quite sure what they must think of me. Of course I've been plagued with violence from the angels. I suppose to them it must seem strangely random.

Reem has continued to act irritated with me, and we are barely on speaking terms at the moment. I am hoping it's just the stress from the upcoming concert and that once it is done, we will be able to mend things.

*T*he days since the shopping trip have passed mostly as normal. I have continued to research by myself and sneak away as often as I can to practice with my sword.

The boys asked Chiron to skip magic practice for the past few evenings because of the concert tomorrow. This is their largest yet, and I know they are all feeling the stress of it.

We were all worried that, because of his injuries, Dio might not be capable of performing. However, he has been recovering well. I know they are still planning to have a chair for him on stage despite his protests. Honestly, I would rather he stay here and rest, but I don't get a say, and "the show must go on," as Reem keeps saying.

It has been painful worrying about him from a distance. At first, he stayed in his room, and I carefully avoided thinking about going to check on him. I wanted to badly, but I knew if I did, I wouldn't be able to continue hiding my emotions from him. I'm still not ready to share those. It just feels far too vulnerable.

The past few days, though, he's been showing up at meals. It has been a new kind of pain watching him limp or seeing him wince. Even at meals, we don't speak to each other. I carefully avoid looking at him. Often I feel his eyes on me.

* * *

*T*he night before the concert, I dream vividly. In the dream, Dio is singing one of The Boy's songs, but the words are different from what I remember. His head is thrown back, his dark brown hair hanging in sweaty tendrils that brush his eyelashes.

He is absorbed completely in the music, and the familiarity of it pangs through my chest even as the different words send chills down my spine.

> "They've come to kill, they've come to maim
> We'll find ourselves too easily slain"

Fear hits me as I hear the unexpected words, but I take comfort in the familiar sight of The Boys performing. Droplets of sweat decorate their cheeks and hair like glittering beads. They seem unaware of the unfamiliar lyrics.

> "The angels come, they'll no longer wait
> So fast they move, their numbers great"

Then Dio looks straight at me, and I watch as blood begins to drip from his eyes and nose. He is focused on me as though he's trying to tell me something as he continues to sing.

"We have magic, we have strength
We've worked hard and trained at length"

In the dream, I reach for my sword as I begin to walk towards Dio. Something is wrong, and I need to protect him. My fingers close on nothing, and I feel a scream building in my throat as Dio's bloody face continues to stare at me.

"And yet my hands shake, my blood runs cold
My strength will fail, and then I'll fold"

* * *

I wake with a cry, soaked with sweat. I glance around for danger, but instead I see my familiar room, the sky outside the window a bit too light for early morning. Realizing I might have overslept, I push myself out of bed and get ready quickly.

As I dress, my instincts pull at me, but there is nothing clear enough yet to give me a path.

The weather has been colder recently, so I dress in multiple layers with a cowl I can use as a hood. I also strap the sword to my back. I was going to leave it behind to avoid any argument, but after that dream, fuck if I'm going anywhere unarmed for a while.

As usual, by the time I get myself dressed and head for the front door, I am later than the rest. I pull my boots on quickly and then run to the carriages stopped out front. Apparently, everything and everyone we need for this won't fit in just one.

The moment I enter the carriage, Reem says, "You can't bring the sword. First—"

Before he can get any further, Dio, who apparently I'm sitting beside, says, "Come on, Reem, clearly we have a few fans out there who are taking their obsession to a dangerous level. It's probably a good thing for one of us to be able to do something about it."

I'm surprised to hear Dio defending me, and in my momentary shock, I miss Reem's response. Because of that, I'm not sure what exactly prompts Dio to say, "Well, I've seen her and she's skilled with that sword."

That seems to cut off any further argument. Reem looks angry, but he remains silent.

The carriage ride is mostly silent and certainly awkward, with Reem avoiding Dio and occasionally glaring at me.

It is also awkward since there are three of us sitting on this seat, and I can't move far enough away to not press against Dio. My heart pounds and I feel like I can barely breathe. His body is tense against mine as though he is trying to stay as far away as he can as well.

My hip and arm, where they rest against him, feel unusually warm, a fact I carefully avoid thinking about.

I can also feel him flinching anytime we go over a bump.

After a couple of hours pass, and yet again his breath catches as the carriage bounces slightly, I take a chance and ask quietly, "Are you sure you're up to this?" My voice is barely above a whisper.

For a few moments, he doesn't respond, and I'm wondering if he's going to avoid answering or if he even heard me. Then, finally, he says quietly, "I won't let the others down. I've dealt with worse."

I grit my teeth and my hands clench into fists, crumpling the cloth of my skirt.

My heart threatens to stop as Dio's hand appears in my field of vision and he gently wraps his fingers briefly over one of my clenched fists.

"It'll be fine," he says so quietly that I wonder if he even meant to say it. He sets his hand back in his lap, and I fight to return my breath to normal.

It's not fine, though. It's torture feeling the evidence of his pain for the remaining hours it takes for us to get to our destination.

Eventually, the carriage stops, and I jump out as quickly as I can to put some space between us. As I move away from the carriages, though, I realize I don't know where we are going. I pause, turning back to the group.

I wait, emotions swirling, until Lent walks up to me and wraps his arm around my shoulders. He is in high spirits even for him. "This is when the real adventure begins, Shorty," he says and pulls me along toward an alley.

I tense slightly as we move into the darker, more enclosed space, but Lent confidently leads me to a staircase and down through a small door that is painted red. In my periphery, I see the others following. Reem is almost directly behind us, and Dio is moving more slowly behind him with Fem walking at his side.

As we move through the door, a bell chimes, and I look around in wonder. I have never seen anything like this. Various small bundles of dried reeds and the stalks of some plants hang from the ceiling. There are small glass bottles containing different colored liquids on nearly every surface. Stacks of cards, leather-bound books, and small wooden boxes with neat labels are everywhere.

As I'm looking around, Lent releases my shoulders and walks over to one of the shelves to look through the various glass bottles. Behind the counter stands a gnarled little old man with only one eye, the empty socket horribly scarred. Behind him, hanging on the wall, are various small knives. There are many different sizes and shapes. A sign that hangs over them says, *Blood Magic Instruments*. As I look at them, one stands out, somehow seeming familiar. I note it, but stay back, curious why the boys are here.

My question is answered quickly as Reem walks through the door behind me and moves to the counter. To the small man, he says, "I'm the one who called earlier, I'm here to pick up the stone we talked about."

"Sure, of course," the little man grumbles, as he begins to dig in his pockets for something. "I did tell you it's unlikely the stone is genuine, right?" he asks, squinting his one eye and leaning towards Reem.

"Yes, you mentioned that," Reem says dryly.

As I watch the interaction, Dio, whom I suddenly realize is standing near me, says, "Several times, in fact, if what Reem told us is true."

His voice is pitched low, his words quiet and clearly just for me. The familiarity of the action makes my chest ache. I press the emotions down again as I struggle to breathe with the sudden tightness in my chest. I run the thumb of my hand over the place where he laid his hand on mine in the carriage. It still feels warm, as though I can feel the ghost of his touch.

As I try to focus on anything other than Dio, the little man produces a key from his pocket. Bending slowly, he leans over and opens a locked compartment. When he rises, he puts a small object wrapped in some type of fabric on the counter and looks expectantly at Reem.

Reem steps forward and carefully unwraps what turns out to be a small, normal-looking black stone with a hole in it.

I can't help myself and step closer. As I look at the stone, I feel another piece of the map fill in, and while I'm blind to where that path leads, the message is clear. This stone is important to the overall journey.

Reeling slightly at the sheer weight of this message, I watch as Fem steps forward, looks at the stone, and scoffs. "No way that's genuine," he says.

I take a step back and watch the interaction silently, unsure if I should say anything about the feeling I just had. There is such a lengthy history of them not believing me, and this seems like a stretch.

What would I say? *In my head, there's a map that says this rock is of great importance.*

"Bargaining isn't going to work for you, gentlemen," the little man says. "Like I said, it may not be genuine. I've been upfront, and the price is the price. Take it or leave it."

Fem looks at Reem, who seems to be considering, and makes an exasperated sound.

I realize, as I watch their interaction, just how close to Dio I'm standing. I glance sideways at his profile before returning my attention to the boys' interaction with the shopkeeper.

At the corner of my vision I see Dio look at me. I hear him swallow. "Thank you for saving me in the alley," he says quietly.

I bite my lip. When I risk a glance at him he looks at my lips and swallows as he quickly looks away.

Just then, Lent emerges from one of the aisles and, in a voice too loud for the space, says, "This place is incredible!"

I jump at the sudden noise and then choke out a nervous laugh. I focus on getting my breathing under control as Lent steps forward, crowding the space where Reem and Fem are standing. Barely looking at the stone, he says, "We'll take it!"

Reem begins to open his mouth, but before he can say anything, the little man says, "That will be one hundred and twenty pounds."

I feel my jaw drop at the amount and expect Lent to be put off. Even as Reem opens his mouth to try again, Lent pulls out the money and sets it on the counter. Then he wraps the small stone up and tucks it into his pocket.

Turning to Reem and Fem, he says, "Let me show you something over here. This place is incredible!"

Reem and Fem turn from the shopkeeper, who looks smug,

to Lent and follow him. I can vaguely hear them grumbling about group decisions and listening to each other.

As they disappear, following Lent, Dio steps up to the counter. "How much for the knives?" he asks.

I continue to gnaw on my lip as I watch his back, the knot of emotions seeming to stretch and threaten to tear in my chest.

"One caught your eye, sonny?" the shopkeeper asks. When Dio doesn't respond, he says, "Those vary, anywhere from five pounds to twenty, but because you've been good customers, I'll give you a deal. Pick any one for ten pounds."

Dio reaches out to point at one, and I quickly step forward and say, "No, that one," and point at the knife I remember from a dream. I still can't remember when, but something tells me it is important.

Dio glances at me sideways and then says, "Ok, I'll take that knife," indicating the knife I'm pointing to.

"Good choice," the little man says brightly. He removes the small, sharply pointed knife from the wall, adds a small sheath, and wraps it in a thin piece of leather while Dio pays.

As he does so, the others emerge from the shelves. I grit my teeth at the interruption. I can feel Dio's eyes on the side of my face.

Reem is still grumbling at Lent, who doesn't look at all repentant. As they get back to us, we all turn to leave.

When we get near the door, though, tension fills me, and I throw my arm out to stop the others. However, before I can do anything more to stop him, Lent barges past me and bursts through the door. I rush after him and manage to make it to the edge of the alley and the street before him.

My hand goes to my sword as I see a host of angels arranged on the street in front of us.

Reem presses in front of me and says in a confident and friendly voice, "What's happening here, fellows?"

Damn their inability to see these as angels.

The crowd is eerily silent, every eye on me.

I draw my sword.

"*Chaosta,*" Reem hisses quietly. He looks out at the angels and says with a forced chuckle, "Ignore our guard dog, everyone. She takes our security *very* seriously."

The angels still don't move, don't speak, their eyes remain focused on me.

Behind me, Lent pipes up and says, "I'm pretty sure we have some extra records in the carriage we'd be happy to sign for our amazing fans."

Then I hear Dio's voice directly behind me say, "What's going on?"

Without turning to him, I say quietly, "They're angels."

"Fuck," he says harshly. "Hey guys, those aren't fans."

There's a sound like the snarl of a steel beast as at least twenty blades are drawn nearly simultaneously.

Behind me, I hear Lent, of all people, say in a quiet but confident tone, "We'll distract them with some weather work, then you can do your thing, Dio."

The angels begin to move forward toward me.

Dio's voice behind me chokes out, "Be careful, please."

I tense and then quickly grasp at the calm, focused instincts that I know I'm going to need to survive this. As I do so, I move into the first form.

Deja vu hits me hard, pulling me briefly into a past dream as I hear Dio's voice say, "You didn't need to cut that deep, fuck that hurt."

Then my instincts fully kick in, and I can't hear anything but the blood pounding in my ears. I meet the charge of the first few angels and quickly kill two who moved before thinking and were caught off balance. Another I pin to the ground with her own sword.

Sweat begins to bead on my brow as I work to maintain the

ground I've won so far. The only benefit I have in being so outnumbered is that such a large group is unable to attack at once.

Suddenly, the ground at the back of the group of angels erupts, and I see a couple of angels fall. There is a strange feeling to the air that seems to pull at my hair, making it stand on end. Then, another eruption occurs to the right of the initial blast. Moments later, heavy rain begins to fall around us, obscuring everything outside of the space where the three angels are attacking me.

I hear another loud crack, the sound cutting through the silence in my head. I briefly feel my arms aching, and my chest heaving, before I pull the numbness of focus back around me.

These angels are clever, trying to place themselves between me and the boys and cut me off. Thanks to all the practice with my footwork, however, I manage to avoid that fate. That innate intelligence strategizes, and each attempted blow is blocked; each attempt to isolate me is counteracted.

Eventually, I manage to incapacitate one with a hard enough blow of my hilt to her face, and she falls to the ground, her nose gushing blood. As she drops, and I note that the other two are retreating, I sense something at the edge of my awareness.

My gut churns, instincts screaming, and I run and throw myself into Dio, knocking him to the ground as a dagger flies past my ear.

Everything is suddenly loud, my focus gone as rain pours down around me, where I sit straddling Dio.

He blinks up at me, looking upset. "I was going to help you," he says breathlessly.

Then I see the pain in his face and push myself off him, only to see Reem, Lent, and Fem glaring at me, their chests heaving. Before I can do or say anything, Fem walks past me, presumably to check on Dio.

Reem rounds on me. There's some blood staining his shirt,

vivid against the white, and his jacket is rumpled. "Everywhere we go, everything we do, you're causing some sort of disruption," he snarls.

"Not only am I confident this whole thing started because of you, but then you fucking knock Dio off his feet as he's about to cast something. He could have killed you both when all we were trying to do was help."

Every bit of breath leaves my lungs, and I take a step back.

"You are no longer welcome," Reem says. "Not to live with us. You're risking everything we built and putting all of us in danger. We can no longer do you the favor of housing you." He's shaking as he looks at the sky as though he's asking a deity for help.

I can hear Dio saying something. His voice is harsh, but I can't understand the words with the blood pounding in my ears.

Unable to think of anything to say for myself, I call for my own help. As I say Malam's name, he's suddenly standing here, between me and Reem.

As he looks at me, I know it's lucky for the boys that he is facing me and not them. Behind Malam, I see that Lent has moved toward Reem and seems to be trying to reason with him. I don't have it in me to fight for myself, though. Reem is right, I am causing them danger and disrupting their work.

Glancing at Dio, my chest aching, all I can do is step closer to Malam and say as quietly as I can, "Please take me somewhere else."

Malam is looking over my shoulder, and I know he is seeing the rubble from the explosions and the wet pavement from the rain in the street behind me. I know there are bodies scattered across the street still, although it seems the angels must have already removed some.

If he is aware of the boys behind him, he doesn't show it. "Where?" he asks, holding out his hand.

I take it, and without having to put much thought into it, I picture Lily's apartment. Even as I do so, the shadow wraps around us and the alley, street, and the boys fade.

The last thing I see is Fem facing Dio with his hand pressed to Dio's chest as Dio stares at me. There is something in his expression I cannot name.

DIO'S JOURNAL - ENTRY 346

Annum:5615
Entry 346 - tempesta

It's been a couple of weeks since I last wrote. Not much has been happening, and I've been listening to Fem's orders and getting some rest. Of course, the pain from my ribs and other internal injuries has given me good reason to. It was tough to concentrate on writing in this journal when I was in that much pain.

Despite my injuries, we had managed to practice a few times for the scheduled concert. This would have been our biggest yet. It was a massive number of tickets because we had an outdoor space booked for this. The others had booked it before I even joined the band because it needed to be scheduled so far in advance.

The timing was perfect with our recent record release. Not so perfect with my injuries. I wasn't going to let the others down, though, and I was ready to push through the pain. On the carriage ride to the shop, Chaosta seemed worried about me. I wanted to tell her that it was the least I deserved. Instead, I just tried to comfort her. Fuck, I wanted so badly to keep hold of her hand.

At any rate, in the end, the concert didn't happen.

Remember how I mentioned I thought there might be some bad energy with our plan to pick up the magical item we needed on the way to the concert? Well fuck was that ever an understatement. We arrived at the shop and picked up the magical stone Malam told us about. Not sure what we'll do with it if we can't get Malam to work with us again, but for now, in the absence of anything else to do, we're following the plan.

Honestly, I'm not convinced it's anything other than a rock with a hole in it. We might not have even purchased it once we saw the damn thing, but Lent, ever the force of chaos, paid for it before we could stop him. He's in some hot water now with the other guys, which is honestly kind of refreshing. I was distracted from the whole interaction because she was standing so close. I did finally get a chance to thank her for saving me. She didn't respond but I think she heard me. She was biting her fucking lip and I had to look away. If I hadn't I don't know what I would have done. I need to get control of these feelings.

Back on topic, though. We finished up at the shop and left, but as we approached the street, there was a whole crowd of people. The others seemed to think they were fans who were following us. However, I noticed that Chaosta was acting oddly and had drawn her sword, so I knew something was up. As the other guys were trying to be diplomatic, I asked her what was going on, and she told me they were angels.

I'm still not sure which of them were angels. There were at least thirty people standing there. No way were they all angels. I have no idea how she can see them when we can't, but no wonder no one has seen an angel in centuries. They look just like normal people.

She was standing there, poised for violence, holding her sword, and they were all staring at her. I told the guys what she'd said, and we were all in shock for a second. Then, surprisingly, Lent pulled us together and made a plan. As we were calling rain as a distraction, she was suddenly at the center of a sword fight in the middle of the street. Thank the dark gods she handled them while we tried to get ourselves figured out.

There is coven protocol for something like this, so I tossed Reem the knife I'd just bought, and he started working on his blood runes. Everything was going so fast that I let him cut my arm, and he cut too deep. I ended up needing stitches. I can hardly blame him, though. We were all thrown off in the moment. Something, I guess, we need to practice as a group, although it's not as though weather magic is meant for combat. We do need to be able to keep our heads about us, though. Who knows what might happen after we trigger the storm. If the government decides to send guards after us, being able to use weather magic in combat might be needed.

I would have started off using the combat magic I'm more familiar with, but as I said, there's coven protocol. Also, while they technically know what I'm capable of, they've never seen me use magic in combat. I initially wasn't sure if this was the time to do so. Also, like I said, Lent had a plan.

Speaking of that, once we got the rain started, we couldn't see that far. I could barely see her silhouette fighting through the downpour. The others were calling lightning. I finally made a decision to use combat magic because I couldn't leave her out there alone to fight. Then she incapacitated one, and the others began to flee.

I went to release the spell to mop things up, and suddenly I was on the ground and she was on top of me. I still don't know why. Thankfully, I was able to pull the spell back in time. This is why training for quick instincts is so important.

The rain was still pouring down around us. I should have been angry that she'd just taken the risk when I was ready to cast something. Instead, all I could think of for a moment was brushing the wet tendril of hair off her cheek, and all I could see were the raindrops running over her lips.

Fuck, I can't do this to her. I need to fucking be stronger than this.

I tried to tell her I was looking out for her and wanted to help, but I couldn't find the words. Then she pushed away from me suddenly as though I was burning her, and she walked right into an argument with Reem.

He kicked her out of the mansion. Speaking of team decisions, I'm not sure what gave him the right to do that to her. I had words with him at the moment, but he just glared at me.

We all tried to talk to him while we got cleaned up, and then as we took the carriages back home. At first, he refused to speak with us. Then, when he finally did, none of us could get him to change his mind. He's just too protective of us and the band. I'm not on speaking terms with him at the moment.

Of course, we ended up canceling the concert. We would have arrived too late, and it's not as though we could've made it through a set after that. Especially me with the freshly injured ribs and new wound. It was a blow to all of us, but Reem, in particular, is beside himself about it.

Yet another piece of advice for my future self: getting a deep cut stitched up while in a moving carriage, while everyone glares at each other, isn't ideal. Of course, it's not like I listened to my own damned advice last time.

DIO'S JOURNAL - ENTRY 2

Annum:5615
Entry 2 - remissio

I finally filled up my previous journal, so I started a
new one. Hopefully, these entries will be less exciting.

Physically, I continue to feel better, even though it
has been slower than I'd like. While I've been healing,
I've continued to miss boxing. If ever there was a time
for me to be able to manage my emotions with that
physicality and the pain of some fresh bruises, it would
be now. Especially because boxing is really the only outlet
I have anymore.

I think my feelings for Chaosta run much deeper
than I thought. Of course, that still doesn't mean I can
allow myself to have her. Fuck that hurts. I'm working
on accepting it, though. I've been trying to convince
myself that maybe this space is good. Maybe it's better

this way. Also, just because I can't be with her that way doesn't mean I can't make sure she's safe. I've been spending some time trying to track her down. All of this was easier somehow when she was around, and at least I could keep an eye on her. Now she's gone, my imagination has been unkind. It's been too easy to imagine her getting hurt or killed. Of course, my mind is also torturing me with thoughts of her with someone else.

I've had plenty of time to think about where she might have gone. My guess is that Malam brought her to the demon stronghold. While I realize the danger in locating such a well-guarded secret and trying to break in, I can't help myself. I need to see her so I can convince myself she's safe. I think the only thing that's keeping the nightmares at bay is that she left with Malam.

Somehow, though, knowing why I've been in mental agony makes it easier not to lash out. I've even mended things with Reem. While the relationship is still strained, I can understand caring about something like he cares about the band.

As I've been recovering, we've been getting back to rehearsing. We have also managed to find a large venue where we can hold a rescheduled concert later this year. Although it's not as large as the outdoor space we had booked, at least we will be able to honor many of the tickets our fans had for that concert. We also sent a free record to everyone whose tickets we won't be able to honor. Some people are upset, but not many, so overall, that seems to be resolved and settled. Our rehearsal has been going well, and I'm confident our next concert will go well. In the last few days, we've even started working on some new material. I've been inspired to write some stuff. As our typical lyric writer, Fem has been gracious enough to step aside for me.

Unfortunately, our magic work hasn't been going as well. Being able to produce weather effects like we did when that crowd came after us felt good. However, Chiron has also stopped showing up to teach us, and we have no way to contact him to ask why. My suspicion is that Chaosta told him not to continue helping us. I can hardly blame her for it. We'll just continue to do what we can to practice. It is giving me more time to try to locate the demon stronghold, time that I think will be much needed.

A DIFFERENT TYPE OF
LIGHTNING STRIKES

S pending time with Lily over the last couple of months has been healing in an entirely different way than the last time I was here. Lily has a calm strength that settles my emotions, which is particularly welcome right now.

I have been missing the mansion and the boys. Not seeing Dio all the time is both a relief and complete agony. I've also been able to delay figuring out that knot of emotions because I am under strict orders from Malam not to leave Lily's apartment. The last thing I want to do is put Lily at risk, so I have been willingly staying in the apartment.

During the day, Lily works at a small medical clinic. Remembering how well she cared for me after my time at Piquory Center, I know how lucky they are to have her. She is always tired and a little tense when she gets home in the evening, so after we eat dinner together, I usually sketch while she sculpts with clay.

She's an amazing artist, but unfortunately, there isn't much interest in art or sculpture, so most of her creations remain shelved around the apartment. When I asked why she spends her time creating things no one else will ever see, she had to think for a while. Finally, she said, "It helps me express feelings from the day and gives me something to do to pass the time." I recognize it's what practicing the sword does for me.

After I had been living here for a few days, we cleared out some space in the main room for sword practice. Lily isn't pleased with the idea of me carrying a sword, or maybe, as a healer, the very idea of any weapon is abhorrent. However, she has been supportive of me, and I think she has seen me going a little mad with the house arrest and took pity on me.

When I am not sketching or spending time practicing with my sword, I usually read. Without my own books, I have started reading some selections from Lily's personal library. The content of these books is similar to the books I read at the center. They are all about people falling in love with each other despite circumstances trying to keep them apart.

Lily calls them "mushy love stories," and while at first I wasn't quite sure what she meant, I can now understand.

The emotions I feel when I read these books are different from those I've been familiar with up until now. The word mushy doesn't quite seem to capture the feelings I experience as I read about two people falling in love with each other and fighting to be together.

These feelings are powerful and make me feel like I do when I'm fighting. They also remind me of the way the boys look when they play their music. I also see those feelings expressed when Malam is here with Lily. The way he looks at her and she looks back at him brings back the familiar pang in my abdomen. I try to avoid thoughts about who that feeling reminds me of.

Of course, my time so far hasn't been entirely peaceful and "mushy."

When Malam brought me some of my things, gathered into a variety of linen bags, the day after I arrived at Lily's, it made my chest hurt with the pain of missing the boys. It has been difficult being away from the only people I could consider family.

Those things still sit, mostly packed, other than the few outfits I've dug out to wear. I'm sleeping on a couch since Lily's place is small and contains only one bed, and the pile of bags sits in a corner beside my couch.

I've also spent most of my nights having vivid but unmemorable dreams. I wake most mornings unsure what I've been dreaming, with the sheets soaked in sweat and tangled around me. What I do remember is that some of the dreams have featured Dio.

One nightmare was particularly bad, and I woke Lily with a scream. When she asked what happened, I told her it was just a bad dream. Then I managed to calm her down enough to go back to sleep.

As I sat on the couch after, trying to settle myself enough to sleep, I tried futilely to recall the dream. The only thing I could remember was Dio being held to the ground by a group of men in healer's outfits as he thrashed and screamed. The only reason I was eventually able to return to sleep was that my instincts weren't prodding me toward action.

*W*hen I woke up the following morning, though, the only thing I could think about was making sure Dio was alright. However, I still didn't know what to say to him. After an agonizing morning of pacing as I tried to plan out the conversation with him, I finally decided just seeing him would be enough.

As long as he's healing and doing alright, it would be enough for me to move on, I lied silently to myself.

Since I don't know where Dio goes boxing, I decided attending a concert would be the most favorable option. I was luckily able to access Lily's terminal to figure out their schedule.

With some careful searching, I discovered that The Boys are scheduled to have a small, for them, concert nearby.

The concert is intended for a specific group of long-term fans and wasn't well-advertised, so it took me a while to find the details of the time and location. Thankfully, it turned out that fate is in my favor. The concert is being held in the basement of a building on the block next to Lily's apartment.

I decided the risk of not following Malam's orders was worth it to be able to check on Dio. After all, the angels hadn't begun to follow me immediately when I moved into the mansion, and they never attacked the boys directly. They also never set foot in the mansion.

I feel bad, but I knew if I told Lily she would tell Malam, so instead I have kept it to myself.

*T*hat concert is tonight. I'm especially glad now that I have the extra clothes because I want to look nice for this. I also want to be able to hide in the crowd.

I leave Lily a note with the message that I need to step out for a moment. I let her know I will be careful and will see her soon. Hopefully, she won't worry. I also let her know I will talk with Malam, so she doesn't need to have that conversation for me. This is my own risk I'm taking, and I am ready to accept the consequences.

Dressed in all black with my sword strapped to my back, I make my way out of the apartment before Lily can return. My immediate destination is a small shop nearby where I can spend the time until the concert starts.

As I stride toward the shop, I can't stop brushing my thumb along the side of my fingers. It's become a bit of a habit. Sometimes I almost think I can feel Dio's palm resting there.

DIO'S JOURNAL - ENTRY 15

Annum:5615
Entry 15 - inopinata perficientur

The peace with our fans didn't last long. Someone started some trash about how we were trying to cheat people out of tickets because we got in over our heads. Thank goodness for our assistant Pepper. She not only responded politely to all the concerns but got a quick concert scheduled at an "intimate" venue for those whose tickets we had canceled.

Honestly, there isn't going to be anything intimate about it. That damned outdoor venue was massive, so we had to cancel a lot of tickets. Hopefully, this will be the end of it. However, I will admit, I'm looking forward to performing again. It's been too long.

This concert has been a good thing to focus on because another month has passed, and I don't feel like

I'm any closer to finding the demon stronghold. I thought I had a solid lead, but it was a dead end. Even if it was the correct building, the damned lift was broken or something because the buttons didn't work. I'm still working on locating the godsforsaken place, but it's beginning to feel rather hopeless. I don't know what to do with the emotional agony that accompanies that feeling.

Anyway, I'd better go get ready since the concert is just a few hours away now. Hopefully, these fans aren't too angry about the canceled tickets, so we can all enjoy the concert.

LET'S START A RIOT

Somehow, I've survived the past couple of hours. My emotions are swirling. Trying to pretend to browse at various shops and getting some food from a little deli did nothing to calm them. I picked out a sandwich, but then couldn't make myself eat it.

Finally, I am heading to the concert venue. It is odd to be going there by myself rather than as part of The Boys' entourage.

I have been wondering how I'm going to get in. I am hoping not to need to threaten anyone. That doesn't seem like a good start to the night.

When I'm nearly at the door to the venue, though, fate is on my side. A man is standing near the entrance selling his tickets. The others passing don't seem interested, so by the time I make my way over to him, he still has them. I'm prepared and have a small amount of money that's mine. Luckily, the cost is less than what I have, so I am able to purchase a ticket from him.

I approach the door, hoping the people at the entrance won't try to take my sword. Thankfully, they simply take my ticket, make a mark with ink on the back of my hand, and allow me through.

I move with the crowd until I am standing somewhere in the middle, centered on the stage. I ensure my hood stays up to hide my unusual pink hair. I have no intention of revealing my presence to anyone.

I'm jostled by the crowd as is familiar, but all the practice with footwork from sword fighting, and my experience at past concerts, keep me standing easily this time.

As The Boys finally walk out on stage, the experience is both like and unlike past concerts. This time, I'm a part of the crowd in a way I have not been in the past. However, unlike the crowd, I don't scream and cheer.

If I were to open my mouth at this moment, I think I might vomit.

My heart races.

Dio shows up on stage last. My first thought is how immensely glad I am to see that he seems to be healed and is looking better than he has in a while. However, when he looks out at the crowd and introduces the band, I see the dark circles under his eyes. As I stand quietly in the screaming crowd, I also notice that his suit doesn't have its carefully pressed creases. He looks almost rumpled.

I don't have much time to worry about him, though, because at that moment the band begins to play and I am forced to focus on keeping my feet as the crowd surges. The momentary distraction is helpful, as with the physical effort, I manage to regain some of the internal stillness I had been clinging to.

Just as always, The Boys' performance is glorious to watch. The focus and joy are clear on their faces as they perform songs that I now know by heart.

The band eventually breaks for intermission, and I stay where I am. I keep my spot as the crowd shifts, and other fans leave to get refreshments or try to find a better spot.

When the band appears on stage again, I see that Dio has removed his suit jacket and vest. His sleeves are slightly rolled, his collar open, displaying the familiar hint of tattoos. My heart pounds in my chest. My palm sweats as I run my thumb along my finger in the familiar movement.

I glance at the others and see that they have also stripped off layers. I can hardly blame them. It is hot in here with all the bodies, and they're working harder than the crowd, even though we are constantly trying to maintain our feet.

The Boys start the next set, and again I'm pulled along by the music as they perform one of their most popular songs. The crowd is screaming out the words with Dio, and I am completely surrounded by the sound. Suddenly, I'm pulled from the moment as I realize Dio is looking directly at me. I meet his eyes and watch as he stills, losing a few words in the song before starting back up again.

He doesn't look away from me.

I can't read his expression, emotions seeming to riot across his face as he stares at me openly while singing.

He manages to sing a few more lines but seems distracted, the words stilted, and his voice tight. Then, suddenly, without warning, he stops singing, lets go of the microphone, and jumps off the stage into the crowd.

The crowd in front, nearest to him, is screaming at a fever pitch. Back where I am standing, people are beginning to grumble as slowly the rest of the band stops playing and the music fades out. I watch as Reem, Lent, and Fem move to the edge of the stage, looking out at the crowd as they try to determine what happened to their lead singer.

I tip my face down, not wanting to be seen by them. I attempt to force myself to turn and leave, but freeze as I have a flash of memory of Dio telling me to be careful as I stepped forward to fight the angels in the street.

As I hesitate, the louder, feverish screams from the crowd

move closer to me in a wave. Then Dio emerges in front of me. His chest is heaving, and his shirt is untucked and slightly torn along one sleeve.

We're standing in a small break in the crowd. As I see Dio, somehow the sound of it fades out of my awareness. He blinks at me as though he's surprised that I'm still standing here.

My heart pounds in my chest.

He steps forward, closing the distance between us slightly. He reaches out and gently pushes the hood off my head.

I blink at him, still frozen in place and hardly daring to breathe.

He takes another step and brushes a tendril of hair behind my ear. His jaw ticks as he searches my face. "I've been looking for you," he finally says. His voice is only just loud enough for me to hear him over the noise of the crowd.

I take a step toward him, standing so close that I can see the specks of gold in his eyes.

He cups my cheek in his palm before slowly pulling his hand away and clenching his fingers into a fist. As he does so, he heaves in a breath. "I'm just glad to see you're alright," he says tightly. He drops his hand to his side, still clenched in a fist. His shoulders slump slightly, and it looks as though he's going to turn and walk away.

"Wait," I say, and he stops moving.

He stares at me briefly before blinking and looking away. His throat bobs.

"I can't stop thinking about you," I mumble, and his eyes flash to mine. How he heard that over the crowd, I don't know, but the intense focus on his face tells me that somehow he did.

"I can't—you deserve better," he grits out as he continues to stare intensely at me.

"Don't I get a say?" I growl.

He bites the inside of his cheek, seeming to consider.

Then, before he can say anything, I take a chance and step

forward, closing the last bit of distance between us. Standing on my toes, I tangle my hands in his hair and pull him into a kiss. For a second, I feel him tense, and then he returns it, sighing into my mouth. I feel one of his arms curl around me, and then he's pulling me against him.

All sound fades away, other than the sound of my heart and a hungry-sounding moan from Dio. The kiss has a frantic feeling to it. Our teeth bruise lips, our tongues steal breath from each other. It feels as though I am being created all over again in this moment. The knot of emotions feels as though it might leave a burning hole in my chest. Where our bodies touch, it feels like falling stars burning out, universes colliding.

Soon, my lungs are aching from the lack of oxygen. After another moment, we both break for air. His eyes search mine, and whatever he sees there seems to make some decision for him.

I hear Reem saying, "Sorry, everyone, it seems something is going on with our illustrious singer. We'll look into this and get him back up on stage so we can finish our set for you all."

I don't think anyone is appeased. In fact, as Dio and I stand there in the crowd, still staring openly at each other, the people around us seem to be getting angrier and angrier. The female voices in particular seem to be rising in volume and pitch.

Suddenly, we are in the middle of a riot.

It is at this moment that I realize I might not have been the only one who has wanted to kiss Dio.

Before it can get worse, Dio pushes carefully past me toward the back of the venue, pulling me after him. This time, instead of dragging, he carefully supports me, and we both use our elbows to free ourselves from the rioting fans.

On stage, the remaining members of The Boys continue with what seem to be futile attempts to settle the crowd. However, I'm confident they aren't going to be able to locate Dio as we make our way through the press of humanity and escape out a side door. As we push the door open, a sudden loud sound begins to scream over us, and water begins to spray from the ceiling.

Dio doesn't hesitate; instead, his hand wraps tighter around mine, and he continues to pull me forward. After quickly making our way down a few more hallways, we emerge into an alleyway along the side of the building.

As the door closes behind us, he pulls me around and presses my back against the stone wall. Then he kisses me again hungrily, his hand pushing my now soaked hood back and tangling in my wet hair.

This time it's me who moans into his mouth as his hand runs down my side until he grips my hip, his fingers pressing into the skin there firmly enough that I'm sure I'll bruise. The heat from the knot of emotions in my chest feels as though it might consume me. Every part of my body, every inch of skin, feels oversensitive. My back arches, pressing my head against the wall behind me as Dio deepens the kiss.

I suddenly pull away, gasping, my instincts telling me something. He steps back, allowing me to move away from the wall and around a tall pile of detritus that's stacked against the building.

I freeze as I see the cherry from a lit cigarette and a dark figure smoking. As I try to figure out what my instincts are telling me, the figure looks at me, and I recognize it to be Malam.

Out of everyone who could be here, of course, it's Malam.

I attempt to both compose myself and prepare for this next conversation. A conversation that is clearly going to happen so much quicker than I had hoped.

Malam tenses as he notices me. "Chaosta, why are you outside of the apartment?" His tone sounds dangerous.

"I just stepped out for a minute," I say. "I've been careful, and

I promise I won't leave again. There was just something I needed to do."

He steps forward and, with a snarl, says, "You are putting the only other person in this world I care about at risk with your thoughtless actions."

I flinch, unable to help myself when hit with the venom in his voice.

He scrubs his hand across his eyes. Then a look of panic flashes across his face. "I need to go make sure she is safe. Don't think we won't discuss this later," he growls at me. Even as he finishes the sentence, he disappears in the familiar swirl of shadow and wingbeats.

I hear Dio walk out from behind the pile of trash and approach me. Standing close, he sets his hands gently on my shoulders. I reach up and wrap my fingers around his, carefully pulling my emotions back under control.

He says quietly, "Are you ok?"

I look up at his face and realize there's stubble along his jaw. He has always been so neatly shaven that it is a surprise to see it there. "I'm good," I say unexpectedly.

"Well, I don't think we can go back in there to the venue at this point."

"What about the others?" I ask.

"They'll have to figure it out," he says as he stares at me, and I see hunger in his expression.

I wonder if perhaps he might not be fully grasping the trouble they're in, but honestly, I don't want him to go back. I want him here with me. "We need to talk, and I don't think I can bring you to where I'm staying right now," I say, looking back briefly over my shoulder at where Malam was just standing.

A look of worry crosses Dio's face. Then, clearly coming to some decision, he says, "Want to go back to the mansion with me?"

"What about Reem?" I ask.

"I think he'll be busy for a while. I'll talk with him when he gets back," Dio says quietly, still staring at me as though he's trying to solve a puzzle.

I nod, and he takes my hand and turns to leave the alley.

Silence falls as we walk side by side back to the mansion. I feel him occasionally glancing at me as though I might disappear, and I can't wipe the smile off my face. He doesn't let go of my hand.

DIO'S JOURNAL - ENTRY 16

Annum:5615

Entry 16 - destituo

It's been a few days and gods.

Fuck.

I don't know how to write this.

That concert didn't go to plan, that's for sure. We really need to get our concerts back on track at this point. It all started normally enough, and thankfully, the crowd seemed to have forgiven us. Pepper's idea seemed to be paying off, and it was honestly great to get to perform again. I was still feeling surprisingly unfocused but luckily the rehearsal paid off and I didn't mess up. Not for the first set anyway.

Sometime in the second set, in the middle of one of our most popular songs, I looked out in the crowd and she was just standing there staring at me. Chaosta, I mean. She wasn't moving, wasn't singing along. She was just staring at me. Not the others, at me. I forgot what I was singing for a moment, but then got back on track. I couldn't stop looking at her, though. Then I lost the words again.

I don't know why I did it, but I couldn't even try to fake it anymore. I jumped down off the stage and went to her. I just wanted to talk with her, see if she was alright. I thought maybe I could figure out where she was staying so I could check on her occasionally.

I thought the crowd was going to tear my clothes off before I got there. That would have been awkward. Apparently, more of our fans have a thing for me than I realized. At that moment, all I could think of was getting to her. Thanks to my physical ability, I made it there in one piece.

I broke through the last line of people between us, and she was there in front of me. I've never seen anything so beautiful. I didn't know what to do or what to say, but I couldn't help myself. She was wearing a hood, and I pushed it off her head. I needed to really see her, make sure she was alright. Then I couldn't help myself, and I brushed a piece of her hair behind her ear. I was just starting to get control of myself and make myself leave when she said that she couldn't stop thinking of me. I was in agony. Then suddenly she was kissing me. I think we were both surprised. I knew I shouldn't kiss her back, but even I only have so much control.

Gods, that kiss. Her mouth. Fuck.

I could hear one of the other guys trying to settle everyone down and saying they needed to look for me so I could go back and finish the set. Fuck that.

Suddenly, I realized that perhaps the crowd was still kind of angry, rioting even, because everything was starting to feel pretty violent, so I got us out of there. She kept her hand in mine and was right there with me.

I saw a side exit and went for it, but there must have been a fire alarm on the door because sprinklers started to spray water everywhere. Luckily, I know now that our instruments weren't ruined. At the time, that was the furthest thing from my mind.

We got out into the alley, and I couldn't help myself, I kissed her, and she kissed me back. Ok, that doesn't even begin to describe what she did. Fuck.

Suddenly, she was pulling away, and I waited for everything to implode, but she just walked around a stack of trash. Then I saw Malam, standing there smoking. Of all times for him to show up, it just had to be then, didn't it? They had some words. I was getting ready to fucking punch a demon as he spoke rudely to her. Then he was just gone.

I went to check on her and make sure she was alright. I was trying to get my equilibrium back. All those reasons I can't have her were buried so deep at that moment. I tried to find them and talk some sense into myself, but then she looked at me again, and everything else just faded out. I still wanted to keep her away from me, but gods, I couldn't stop staring at her. Couldn't stop thinking about that kiss.

I realized belatedly that she was asking me about the other guys, and I don't even remember what I said. Then she said we needed to talk, but she couldn't bring me back to where she's staying. I guess I get that. I'm sure I wouldn't be welcome in the demon stronghold. I offered that she could come back to the mansion with me, and I really thought she might decline, but she agreed.

That walk felt like it took a fucking year. My thoughts were spiraling so badly. I can't even tell you how I got us back to the mansion on foot. Luck probably.

When we got there, I took her to my room. I kissed her again before I could stop myself. After the kiss, I realized she'd never been in this room as she walked around looking at my things. It was more of a mess than I would have liked. I've been distracted lately, well, with her, and haven't kept up on cleaning.

I just stood there staring at her as I tried to talk some sense into myself. I finally managed to regain enough internal strength to decide to apologize to her, but to tell her the kiss was a mistake. To tell her that we couldn't be together. I just couldn't actually say the words. She was standing there watching me. I couldn't tell what she was thinking. I wouldn't have been surprised if she told me I could go fuck myself.

I was beginning to spiral badly. Then she looked me dead in the eye and said she was sorry she'd been rude, sorry she'd made it personal. I don't know what my face looked like. I was so surprised by her apology. I had never expected it. Sure, what she'd said had hurt, but she wasn't wrong, and I know I pushed her to that point. I didn't deserve an apology.

She's far too good for me.

That decided me, and I was just beginning to open my mouth to apologize, but also to tell her I couldn't have her. Words I knew were going to hurt both of us. Then I don't know what happened, or why, but suddenly she was in my arms, her legs wrapped around my waist, kissing me, and I was fucking kissing her back. I couldn't help myself.

Thank goodness my instincts were more capable than my thoughts at that point because I caught her. I've never felt anything better than having her in my arms like that. Then she was biting my neck, and licking the edge of my jaw, and fuck, I was hard.

I wanted some space so I could think. I went to set her down so my damn cock didn't make things awkward. She ended up standing on my bed. She was taller than me there, and she was looking down at me, her hand on my jaw, just staring at me.

She stood there for a moment looking like a fucking godsdamned siren. I was wavering, wondering if it would be so bad to let myself love this girl, and then she started to remove her clothing.

Fuck. I can't do this right now.

DIO'S JOURNAL - ENTRY 17

Annum:5615

Entry 17 - quis tibi hoc fecit

I needed some time before I could write this. That day when Chaosta was in my room, she began to slowly strip out of her hood and then some other layer of clothing. She was standing there on my bed in just a thin shirt. It was stretched over her body. It showed everything. I could see the peaks of her nipples through the fabric. I was completely frozen.

I'm such a bastard, I knew I needed to tell her to stop, to leave, to find someone else, but I couldn't. I was far too weak to do that with her standing there so close.

I never wanted to take advantage of her, I just couldn't figure out my shit. I took a step toward her and put my hand on her hip to get her to sit down, slow down a little so we could talk. When I touched her there, I felt them through the fabric. She flinched before I could look away, and I had to ask. Instead of telling me, she pulled the side of her shirt up, and I saw them.

Fuck I want to tear this page into tiny pieces. As though that will help.

Be. Factual. Dio. Come on.

Chaosta's entire side is covered in fresh scars. They're all about the same size, same length, same angle. Other than one, larger, puckered scar that's just below her ribs, which looks like an old stab wound. I can't emphasize enough how many of them there are. It looked like there were more that were still covered by her shirt.

I have no doubt they're from torture. I may not have Fem's experience with healing, but I haven't had an easy life despite my parents' early attempts to coddle me, and, while I've never experienced torture, I'm certain those scars didn't come from anything else.

I couldn't stop staring. I didn't know what to do. Rage like I've never felt before filled me. I don't know when she was tortured, but I'm fairly certain it was while she was imprisoned. The timeline makes sense. My instincts were trying to tell me she was more hurt than she let on when she got back from the angel stronghold.

If I had acted quicker in getting Alexander involved, I likely could have saved her at least some pain, and the

fact that I could have saved her any amount and didn't.
FUCK.

Then, after she did get out, I was too childish and
just avoided her because I didn't want her mad at me. I
didn't ask her if she was ok. I didn't push for her to let
Fem help her. Instead, I know now that she suffered in
silence. Here I've been trying to keep her safe from me,
and she ended up being hurt by my stubborn refusal to
get closer to her.

If I'd listened, if I'd gotten to know her, I wouldn't
have let anything stop me from getting her out of there.
I'd have wiped out the whole fucking lot of them in the
process. I'll never forgive myself.

Worse, as I stood there staring at her, she eventually froze. Then she yelled at me. She was clearly angry,
and I don't blame her. She said something about me
thinking she was ugly, and then she left my room, slamming the door in her wake. When I came back to myself,
I put my fist through the wall again. I should've gone
after her, but by the time I came out of whatever state
I was in, she was too long gone, and I knew I wouldn't
be able to find her.

Not like it's ever a good idea to put one's hand
through the wall. You'd have thought I'd have figured
this out after the last time. Worse, it took a while for
the others to get back to the mansion after the carnage
of that concert, so I had to messily tend to it myself
until Fem could look at it. I broke bones this time, but I

think the pain was the only thing that helped me keep it together after.

PART VI

LOVE IS A PHOENIX

I'm moving through the sword fighting forms in Lily's apartment, a week after I last saw Dio. Suddenly, I miss a step and my legs tangle. Thankfully, I catch myself before I can fall face-first on my sword. Limbs shaking, I push my sword to the side and then drop and lie on my back on the floor. Looking at the ceiling, I feel tears begin to trail down my temples.

It's not like me to let distractions in during sword practice.

My chest is so tight it's painful, and after a few more moments of trying to breathe, a sob breaks free. I haven't been able to stop thinking about what happened the last time I saw Dio. That concert did not go at all how I expected. I couldn't believe he left the stage and came to me. I can't believe I kissed him. Goddess, I feel stupid.

At the concert and in the alley, it seemed as though he had feelings for me as well. Then we arrived at his room, and it was glorious at first. Kissing him, my legs around his waist, the knot of emotions finally untying itself.

Thinking about it frees another sob. As it comes scraping out of my throat, I turn onto my side and curl in on myself.

At the time, I thought maybe I had a chance, but somehow I must have fucked up. I was standing on his bed and he reached out and touched my side. When he did, his expression went from heated to flames of anger in an instant. The feeling of being pierced by shards of glass was back, only it was worse this time, much more painful. Then he asked if I was wounded. I realized that he could feel my scars and I didn't know what to do so I showed them to him. The pain from his glare intensified and he didn't say anything for several long moments. I was hurt and angry at his reaction, and I didn't know what else to do, so I left.

When I got back to Lily's apartment, she was gone. I was scared she had been hurt and was just about to leave to search for her when Malam showed up. He was so angry.

In the state I was in, I just let him yell at me. I didn't have much to say for myself. I left the apartment against his wishes despite his explicit order, and by doing so, I put Lily in danger. I understand his protectiveness of her. I guess I can relate. When he asked me why, I just said I had made a mistake.

I was crying at that point, and I think when he saw my tears, he must have felt bad about his tirade because he didn't push. There was no way I was going to tell him about Dio and what happened. I felt so stupid. No, I feel so stupid.

Another sob crawls its way out of my throat at the memory.

Malam shared that when he got to the apartment and found Lily safe, he had moved her immediately to another location. He told me I could continue to stay at Lily's place for now, but he wouldn't be responding to my summons anymore. When he said that, there was a sudden pain, like a tearing in my head. He left soon after, and I made it to the bathroom just in time to vomit. I haven't seen him or Lily since. I haven't seen anyone I know for a week now.

I still don't know what to think about Dio's reaction. Based on his actions before that day, I'm sure he had feelings for me.

He didn't stop me when I left, but I didn't give him a chance to say much before I ran. Goddess, I'm so bad at this.

I know I should probably try to find him and talk to him, but I haven't been able to make myself. If I was wrong and he doesn't have feelings for me, I'll just be tearing open this wound again.

*M*ore time passes in a haze. I don't feel up to reading, at least not the books Lily has in her apartment. I've continued to practice with my sword because it is the only thing I can do, but it feels hollow, and it's a monumental task to focus. I've even tried sculpting with some of Lily's clay, but all I make is a mess.

Now, because there is no reason for me not to go out, I do. Every evening, once it gets dark, I leave the apartment. I dress in all black with a hood to hide my hair and strap my sword to my back and just walk, following my feet wherever they take me.

On one of my walks, I accidentally find work. As I am walking down the street, I notice a carriage driver feeding and caring for four carriage horses. The carriage is larger than those we typically rent, and the man appears to have his hands full.

He is older, and I notice him struggling to get water to the horses, so I help. After a moment of surprise when he sees my appearance, he thanks me genuinely. As I turn to leave, he asks if I might be interested in joining him as an Assistant Whip. When I ask what that is, he explains the duties to me, most of which include assisting him with navigating the city, sometimes driving, and helping care for the horses. I immediately agree.

I knew I would need to find work at some point, but hadn't explicitly sought it out because I wasn't sure how. This fortuitous exchange solves that issue, and working with carriage horses is something I never dreamed I would be able to do.

After I start my job, I spend most of my time, when I'm not

sleeping, working on the carriage. The man wasn't wrong when he said he needed help. This carriage is one of the few in this area that seats more than six, and it is constantly booked with one journey or another.

The work is hard, tiring, and constant, but at night, or sometimes during the day, when I get a break, I fall into bed exhausted and sleep well. Thankfully, because of the exhaustion, I barely dream.

I find time here and there to continue my sword practice, but at this point, the purpose is to maintain skills. The work on the carriage has other benefits, including building my strength.

Staying so busy has other benefits, of course, and I manage to distract myself enough that I barely have time to think of Dio. A month has flown by before I realize. When I do finally notice how much time has passed, I decide I should probably try to talk with him. However, the work just keeps coming, and it is too easy to avoid that particular wound, so I do. Then suddenly I can't ignore it anymore.

The carriage has been particularly busy, and we have been working for over 24 hours when one of the carriage horses is injured by some creature. I manage to get to it and stab the beast before it can kill that horse or hurt the others, but the damage is done.

My boss is impressed and incredibly grateful. Until now, he didn't have any reason to believe that I could be effective with the sword he is used to seeing me wear. At any rate, he seems surprised but pleased I was able to wound and chase off the beast.

As a thank you, he gives me a few days off, which will also allow him some time to get the horse seen by a healer and either replace it or borrow another for a time.

. . .

$\mathcal{I}$t is late in the evening, the day after the incident with the horse, and for the first time in a while, I find myself in Lily's apartment with nothing to do. I try to fill some time reading, but the books Lily has just reminded me of my broken heart. I try to sketch, but sketching my typical subject certainly doesn't help distract me.

Instead, I'm pacing and doing my best to grapple with my feelings when someone knocks. I grab my sword, remove the sheath, and walk to the door. I look through the peephole and see Dio standing in the hallway.

My world suddenly narrows down to just a pinprick of focus, all of it consumed by the man standing outside the door.

I let out a breath, resting my forehead against the cool door for a minute as I'm flooded with emotions. I look out the peephole again just as he glances at the door, his body tense. I can see him trying to decide if he should knock again or leave. Before he can make the decision, I make it for him and open the door.

His eyes widen slightly as he sees the sword. He takes a step back and presses his hands into his pockets, glancing somewhere along the doorframe. His shoulders hunch as though he's preparing for a blow.

"Are you going to come in or just stand out there?" I ask, somehow managing the words past the utter agony of emotion that is tightening my chest.

He looks at me finally, and I think I see hope in his eyes. He doesn't respond, but he does take a step forward, and I move to the side, allowing him through the door.

He glances around the space, and his eyes widen as he takes in the cozy apartment. "It's not mine," I say.

"You're staying here, though?" he asks.

"It belongs to a friend."

"Until recently, I thought you were staying at the demon stronghold."

"You thought about where I was staying?" I ask quietly.

I watch his shoulders tense, but he nods. "I've been trying to find you so I could apologize."

"For what?"

"For everything. Sending you to treatment when you didn't need it, not getting you out of prison quicker, not having the words to tell you what I was thinking when I saw your scars." He is speaking quickly as though if he doesn't say the words now, he won't be able to.

"Well?" I ask.

"When I saw them, I felt the weight of how awfully I'd treated you. If I'd tried harder to listen to you, to understand sooner, nothing would have stopped me from saving you." He's avoiding my eyes and runs one hand shakily through his hair.

It feels as though everything that makes me who I am has been ambushed by too much emotion. I look at his face, seeing again the dark circles under his eyes and the hint of a beard along his jaw. I can't help myself, and I look at his lips, remembering our kiss.

"Chaosta?" he asks, a pleading note in his voice. "What are you thinking?"

I swallow. "You look like shit," I say.

I flinch, quickly looking away from him. *That certainly wasn't what I intended to say. I'm making a mess of this already.*

Instead of looking angry, though, when I glance back at him, I see that a corner of his mouth is quirked up. "I've been feeling like shit about how I treated you, so I guess that's appropriate."

I swallow, trying to figure out how to respond. However, all I can think about at this moment are the muscles under his fitted, button-up shirt. The line of his forearm to his hand is artistic, or maybe that's just because I have sketched it so many times.

Glancing up, I see him searching my face. "Chaosta?" he asks, his voice quiet.

I quickly look back up, meeting his eyes. "Mmhmm?" I mutter to him.

"Give me the sword," he says, a crooked smile spread across his face.

I bite my lip and hand him the sword.

He takes it, and I hear him set it somewhere. Then he closes the space between us and takes my chin, tipping it up so I meet his eyes. He gently frees my lip from between my teeth as he says, "I want to warn you to run, but I am not a strong enough man to deal with the loss."

I wobble, and my chest is so tight that I feel as though I can't take another breath.

"Despite my feelings about this, you need to tell me what you want. If you want me to leave, I will walk out that door and never haunt you again."

As his eyes search mine, I feel myself looking at him as though I've already lost him.

"I want you to stay, please," I somehow manage to say.

I feel his breath brush against the skin of my cheek, and then his lips are pressed to mine, and he kisses me until I'm breathless. His tongue tangles with mine, claiming some part of me as his fingers trace a blazing trail down my spine.

Finally ending the kiss, he presses his forehead to mine for a moment. Then he takes a step away, and I hear myself whimper quietly.

"Hush, I'm right here," he says with a self-satisfied smirk. "I saw your scars, now I'll show you mine."

He begins to slowly and carefully unbutton his shirt, neatly rolling down each sleeve. I take a step forward, but without glancing up, he says, "Don't. You are going to watch while I do this."

I stop moving with a groan, and he chuckles darkly.

Then he's sliding his arms out of his sleeves. Because he's Dio, he can't just allow the shirt to fall to the floor. Instead, he folds it carefully before setting it neatly over the back of a chair. As he does, I watch his muscles bunch under all the tattoos.

When he faces me again, I can't help myself and step forward, closing the distance. I feel him looking at my face as I stare at the tattoos and scars that cover his abdomen. Then I reach out and trace the tattooed rune I watched Malam trace all those months ago.

As I do so, he wraps his fingers around my wrist, his hand dwarfing mine. His hold is firm but not overly tight. As he holds my hand immobile, I look up at his face. His expression is now shielded as he says, "You saw that when you were spying, didn't you?" I can't read the tone, and I tense slightly, unsure where this is going. "Chaosta?" he asks. There's a quiet warning in his tone I don't understand.

"Yes, I saw Malam trace it through the crack in the door," I say, my voice quiet.

"Do you know what that rune means?" he asks gruffly.

I shake my head, suddenly worried I've done something I shouldn't.

"We'll need to talk about that later," he says quietly. Then he looks down at my hand, caught in his still, and closes his eyes for a moment. An expression of pain flashes across his face.

"Fuck," he says, "if I were a stronger man…" Then he releases my wrist and steps back away from me. His eyes are still closed, and I feel as though I'm losing him again.

Cursing myself internally and near tears, I take a step forward and put my hand in his, intertwining our fingers. "Dio?" I ask quietly.

"Hmm?" he mumbles, eyes still closed.

"Where did you go?" I ask quietly.

His eyes open, and they are dark as he stares at me. Finally, just as I'm sure he is going to turn and leave, he seems to make a decision. With a tight voice, he says, "The monster in me is hungry for you, and it is glorious and unbearable. I have been trying to save you from the shadows of it, but I'm clearly not virtuous enough."

It is clear to me that he is referring to more than just his treatment of me. I feel a chill pebble my skin at his words, and yet I am also not a virtuous being. I wasn't created to be anything other than a tool, a weapon against the power of the angels. My very existence threatens not only them but their human wards. Dio may not be aware of it yet, but I am the villain of this story.

My voice still shakes slightly as I say, "I've seen what a prick you can be and yet, for some reason, I can't stop thinking of you."

His mouth quirks in a crooked grin again.

"I haven't been able to stop thinking about you since the record signing where you helped me. I don't need some divine being, I want you."

The smile is gone from his face, destroyed by an expression of complete intensity as he stares at me. "You would willingly accept my darkness?"

I draw in a shaky breath before saying, "If you accept mine?"

I see an expression cross his face, *acceptance maybe*? He continues to look at me as though nothing else exists. Then he cups my jaw as he says, "I'm not a patient man, but I'll be patient with this. We'll go slow, hmm? I'd never forgive myself if I pushed you too far."

I nod, unable to pull my gaze from his.

He focuses on my lips, and I feel his thumb against them. I part them, and he takes the invitation. When I open my mouth for him, he presses the pad of his thumb against my tongue, tipping my head down. I bite gently, and he groans and closes his eyes.

My teeth still gently holding his thumb, I reach out and unbutton his pants.

"Chaosta," he warns. "We're going slow, remember?"

"Mhmm," I mumble around his thumb as I press my hand into his pants.

I moan as I feel how hard he is, the size of him, the heat. As I wrap my hand around his cock and run my fingers over the smooth, taut skin, he wobbles slightly, and I open my mouth, releasing his thumb.

He grabs the back of the nearby leather chair and leans against the support of it as he groans again.

I have a moment to wonder what he looks like under the pants he's still wearing before he gasps, "I should really leave now."

"Do you want me to stop?" I ask.

He closes his eyes and groans again as his fingers tighten against the back of the chair. "No, I don't want you to stop, but I mean it," he says roughly, "I should leave."

I continue my exploration, and he groans again, "Unless you want me to stay?"

"Yes, stay."

"Fuck," he growls. Then he's reaching for me. He slides his fingers under the edge of my shirt and pulls it up. I need to let go of him to allow it. Somehow, I force the compliance of my fingers and release him as he pulls it over my head.

"If it's ever too much, just tell me to stop," he says. His voice is quiet, entreating as he meets my eyes.

"Ok, I'll tell you," I say breathlessly.

This time, I have no doubt as he looks at me whether he finds me, including my scars, ugly or not. The expression on his face would have already told me how he felt, even if he didn't immediately take a step to close the space between us and kiss the side of my neck. His body is pressed against mine, and I reach out and explore the hard plane of his chest. My fingers find the raised ridges of muscle and the fainter feeling of scars.

He works his way to my collarbone, the heat of his breath

scraping over already sensitive nerve endings. When he nips the skin there lightly, I gasp, my back arching. My knees wobble.

I'm thankful for the support as he wraps an arm around me, his hand against my lower back, further pressing me against him.

His lips and tongue work their way down past my collarbone to my breast. His tongue plays with my nipple, and I gasp again with a quiet, high sound escaping me on the exhalation. As he continues to play with the now hard bud, my skin pebbles, and I wobble again.

He lifts me up against him just as my legs give out. "Already?" he chuckles darkly, "Gods, you're sensitive."

I wrap my legs around his waist and realize he's carrying me to the bedroom. I manage to gasp, "Not there."

"Fuck," he grumbles as he hesitates for just a moment. Then he turns us slightly, and I feel my back pressed against the wall outside Lily's room, his hands holding my hips.

It's my turn to kiss my way along the side of his neck. I scrape my teeth over the skin there, tasting the slight saltiness. Then I can't help myself, and I bite gently. As my teeth pinch his skin, he moans.

His chest heaving, he gasps, "Fuck, it's like you're my darkest godsdamned desires come to life."

I feel myself grin even as I move lower and nip his collarbone lightly. He grinds against me, and I wrap my legs more tightly around him, further increasing the contact. Heat pools between my thighs as I feel how hard he is. The back of my hips are pressed firmly enough against the wall that I'm sure I'll be bruised.

I feel his fingers toying with the band of my leggings. Reluctantly, I unwrap my legs from his waist.

He slowly and hesitantly allows me to slide down and stand on my own, still pinned between him and the wall. His eyes are on mine, and his expression is full of heat.

The energy is charged as I lay my hands over his, where they still rest on my hips.

His fingers tighten slightly, possessively, as though he is suddenly worried I'm going to push him away. Then I feel his thumbs rub against my skin as he presses them into the waistband. He takes one step back, and then another, guiding me gently with him. Despite the possessiveness, his eyes searching my face, as though watching for any hesitation. Once we're in the center of the room again, he presses my leggings off my hips. He kneels in front of me as he carefully removes them from each ankle. I rest a hand on his shoulder to help keep my balance.

My skin pebbles further as I stand, fully exposed, in front of him. I watch as his eyes scan over my entire body, ending as he meets my gaze.

"Dark gods, you're gorgeous," he says. His voice is tight and full of heat. His expression makes the ragged edges of my breath catch in my throat.

Still watching me, looking through his eyelashes, he kisses one hip bone and then the other.

This might be new to me, but some part of me, some instinct, understands pleasure and knows what I desire. Where that knowledge comes from doesn't matter now, so I give it no more than a brief moment of awareness. Then I tangle my hands in his hair and guide him where I want.

All thought leaves me as his tongue touches my clit. My knees go weak, and he chuckles as I wobble yet again, and then they fully give out, and he guides me gently down to the floor. Kneeling between my drawn-up legs, he leans over me, a hand resting on the floor on either side of me. The image of being trapped in the cage of his arms at the concert flashes across my memory yet again.

He leans down and kisses my temple, then he leans down

further, his face along the side of mine, and whispers, "Tell me you're mine."

"Just yours," I manage to gasp as he pulls back to stare at me.

His pupils are blown. He lets out a similarly ragged breath and then kisses his way down my body. Then his tongue is on my clit again, and my hips buck against his face. I feel pressure on my abdomen as his hand presses firmly against my stomach, pinning my hips against the floor.

He pulls his head back, and I whimper as his voice rumbles, "You're going to come so beautifully for me, but I need you not to move so much."

Then he presses his tongue against me again, and this time I feel him sucking slightly. I see stars, and my hips grind against the firm pressure of his hand. He continues, licking and sucking, and the pressure builds in my body until I feel like there has to be some sort of release. Then I cry out as I feel exactly that crest over me.

I'm blinking the stars from my eyes, my body a limp pool as he kneels between my legs, one hand on each to keep me from closing them. When my eyes finally focus, I see him licking my release from his lips.

He reaches up as I watch and wipes his chin with the back of his hand. Then he's propped over me again, his eyes running over my face and down my body. "Gods, you're gorgeous when you do that," he says. "As though I needed any more encouragement."

He leans onto his elbows and runs his thumb over my bottom lip. I feel a sting and realize I must have broken the skin earlier when I bit them. He's staring at my lips. "Fuck. You're going to kill me," he grumbles. Then he leans down and kisses me.

By the time he pulls his lips from mine, his tongue lingering against my cupid's bow, I'm seeing stars. Need is just beginning to build in me again from the kiss. The way my body is craving him, craving everything about him, feels dangerous.

The breath crashes out of me as I stare at him. "Please?" I somehow manage.

"Oh no, we're not being greedy tonight, remember?" Dio says huskily. "We have plenty of time for all the things I want to do to you."

Then he rises and lifts me, holding me against his chest.

He carries me to the bathroom and begins to fill the tub. Once it is sufficiently filled, he lowers me gently into the warm water. I hiss as it wraps around me, finding every aching muscle. It begins to soak in, and my body goes languid with the heat. I rest my head back against the tub, feeling utterly at peace.

Then he washes me, his hands gentle. As he does so, I can't help the moan that escapes with my breath.

"Fuck I love it when you make that sound," he groans.

I'm beginning to fall asleep by the time he lifts me out of the water. He dries me and wraps me gently in a large towel. Then he carries me out to one of the soft armchairs. "Stay right here while I clean up," he says.

I close my eyes, cuddling back against the chair, my feet drawn up, tucked into a ball. He's back soon with a towel wrapped low around his waist, his hair hanging in damp tendrils on his forehead. I stare at him, feeling as though I might lose my mind at the feeling in my heart.

"Stop looking at me like that," he rumbles at me with a smirk. "I just got you cleaned up."

He holds out a hand. I take it, and as he guides me back to the thick rug, he says, "This will have to do for tonight."

As I sit, he goes to the couch, my normal bed, and takes a blanket and sheet from the pile beside it before joining me. As he wraps himself around me and pulls the covers over us, sleep is already claiming me.

. . .

J wake, not immediately remembering where I am. The couch feels particularly firm beneath me, and then I hear his breathing and remember.

Dio's sleeping form is tangled with mine, and we're partially covered in one of Lily's clean white sheets. His face is turned toward me, and it is relaxed with sleep. I don't think I have ever seen him look this peaceful.

I have never experienced love before, but I know now, as I look at him, that's what this feeling is. It is so much more than what the books made it sound like, so much more than what I feel in Malam's memories. I feel as though a wildfire blazed through my chest, consumed my heart, and in its place left a phoenix, risen from the ashes. As I continue to look at Dio, it feels as though the phoenix spreads its wings in my chest. I'm filled with beautiful, burning agony as I take a breath, the utter intensity of the love I feel for this man.

I notice a shock of hair that rests over one of his eyes. I reach out to brush it aside. Before I can do so, suddenly my whole body tenses as my instincts scream so loudly at me it is as though I can't breathe, can't see.

Somehow, I untangle myself without waking him, dress, strap my sword to my back, and rush as quickly as I can from the building.

There happens to be a carriage outside the building, and I press too many pounds, which I don't remember grabbing, into the carriage driver's palm. I give him an address that I don't know or recognize, even as I say it out loud. Climbing quickly into the carriage, it takes off, the driver taking my request for speed seriously.

The trip passes in a blur, and I leap from the carriage even as it stops. I rush into the building that I find myself in front of. I run through the door and up several flights of stairs. My feet follow a path I have no conscious awareness of. I move from the stairs down a hallway to a door that stands partially open.

I hear a screaming in my head.

I push through the door. Even in this focused state, I freeze for a moment as I see the scene in front of me.

Two angels crowd a table with Lily behind it, a kitchen knife in her hand. I register belatedly that the screaming wasn't in my head.

I don't remember drawing my sword, but suddenly I am between Lily and the angels, pushing her back through a doorway. I have no care for the knife she holds. Somehow, I manage to avoid being stabbed.

I face down the angels, the sword held casually in my hand as I study them. For some reason, my vision chooses this moment to partially blur, and when it clears, one of the angels is too close. I barely block him in time, and it is clumsy. His sword leaves a mark on my arm that feels like acid.

I press forward into his space, and he parries my blows, his eyes on mine, reading my face and my next move. My wings, where they meet my shoulders, pulse slightly with pain. Instincts scream at me. This is different, be careful.

The awful dance continues, and I mark him, but this time, so does he mark me. There is a hazy feeling in my head, and my body feels sluggish. I am so focused on the angel in front of me that I don't recognize I have made an error until there is a sudden ache in my chest, but not that of a blade.

Even as I try to understand the reason for the ache, I see a knife leave the hand of the other angel, the one who has been watching us fight. I brace myself for the impact, but it goes past me.

I wasn't the intended target.

I turn around to see the knife bury itself in the middle of Lily's forehead. She dies so quickly that she doesn't even cry out, but I do. Even as I hear the scream leave my lips, I feel an impact against my back, and looking down, I see a sword protruding from my abdomen.

I suddenly have no breath.

My body jerks as the sword is pulled free, and I slump to the ground. I feel or hear footsteps leaving and the door closing behind them.

The room spins. I think my instincts are screaming at me, but all I can see is the knife hitting Lily playing on repeat in my mind.

My instincts finally manage to take over, and I drag myself into another room, some sort of living space. Everything is going dark; the speed with which the room is spinning is increasing. Pain continues to explode through me.

A trail of black blood trails out behind me, marking my path.

My body, as though it is listening to some other master, takes a clay sculpture from a short table beside me and throws it through a nearby window with nearly all the remaining strength I possess. Unsure why I even made the effort, I roll over onto my back and close my eyes.

However, as I close my eyes, black wings seem to cross my vision, and I scrape my eyelids back open and tilt my head to see that there is a single, familiar crow perched on a railing outside the window.

"Get Malam," I choke out, feeling blood on my lips, only just able to make out the crow as it takes flight.

With my strength then fully gone, I close my eyes and let the darkness pull me away.

DIO'S JOURNAL - ENTRY 37

Annum:5615
Entry 37 - diligo

When I woke this morning on the floor of a strange apartment, I slowly remembered what had happened. Then I had a moment of panic when I realized I was alone. As consciousness fully returned to me, I remembered that Chaosta works on a carriage and I was able to relax a little and ready myself before leaving the apartment and returning here. Of course, she needed to go to work. She's clearly been working hard, too hard for my comfort.

Actually, it was her work on the carriage that helped me figure out where she was staying. After many dead ends, I suddenly saw pink hair and a form I recognized clinging to the back of a carriage as it flew past me. After some additional investigation, I managed to locate where she was staying, which led to me showing up, unannounced, last night.

She answered the door with a sword in her hand. I had already been sure she'd turn me away. For a moment, I worried she might not stop there. Not like it was the first time I wondered what she might do to me when I saw a sword in her hand. At least this time I wasn't bleeding internally, Ha! Then she surprised me by letting me in. I'm still kind of shocked by the space she was living in. She said it wasn't hers, but it made me wonder to whom it does belong. It was homey and sweet, completely at odds with Chaosta's steel and spice.

I was trying to go slow and just talk. I tried to warn her about me. I was trying to be careful, trying to give her the respect she's always deserved from me. I wanted her to take time to think.

I finally got the words out I wanted to say. I think I did all right and shared how I feel. Things were getting hot, and I was still trying to go slow. I figured it would be only fair to show her my scars. Then she traced the rune on my chest, and I nearly decided, yet again, that she deserves better than me. I almost had myself convinced to leave, but she wouldn't let me go. She asked if I'd accept her darkness too, and I finally understood.

I couldn't breathe for a moment. I've been so blind to it, but she's not some innocent soul either. Fuck, she's killed angels, even killed to protect me, and did so without a second thought. I wish I had put that together before last night. I also wish I had realized sooner that my heart belongs to her, has belonged to her for a long time.

I have to confess that this morning, before I left, I saw one of her sketches sticking out of a notebook, and I took it. I just needed something of her as I left that place. Her absence this morning, especially waking up without her, is nearly a physical pain.

When I got home, I couldn't help myself. I went right to Reem and told him that either he needs to allow Chaosta to return or I'll be moving out. He wasn't happy about it, but of course, I got my way. I think he realized he had acted rashly that day after the fight in the street. I get it, emotions were high, and he'd been particularly stressed about things with the band. He's still upset and stomped out of the room after we talked, so I'm going to have some work to do to mend things.

Lent went with him to try to settle him. Thank the gods for him being the peacekeeper. I have to admit I'm also glad Lent left because with how smitten he seems to be with Chaosta, I'm not sure how I'm going to tell him she's mine. I already feel so fucking possessive. I need to get a handle on this, or having her living here with three other guys is going to get messy. I just can't believe I deserve her, and the other guys are certainly better options. It's going to be difficult to trust that she won't decide to move on and date one of them instead.

Maybe I should reconsider moving us to our own place. At least maybe if we aren't living with a bunch of other attractive, successful guys, it will be easier to convince myself that she'll stay with me.

Anyway, let me get back on track. Fem stuck around after Reem and Lent left and asked me what had happened. I think for a minute he might have worried I was using again. I'm sure I looked high as fuck, I mean, I was, but not on drugs.

When I told him the brief, appropriate version of what happened, though the smug bastard just grinned and basically said it had taken me long enough. Have I been that transparent?

Now I'm just waiting for time to pass so I can track her down again and tell her she doesn't need to work anymore. I'm trying to convince myself I'll respect her decision if she wants to keep working. I'm not sure I will be able to, though. I have nearly unlimited resources at my disposal, and I think it's going to break me if she's out working such a dangerous job. I want her here with me now, and I'm not a patient man.

I don't know how I'm going to get through the rest of the day

EXCERPTS FROM MALAM

I am in a conclave when a familiar crow shows up. I hold out my hand for him as a perch. I'm curious what he might have to tell me, but when his claws hit my arm, I am consumed by sudden pain.

A weak vision, more of a feeling really, of Lily and Chaosta in mortal danger hits me.

I barely manage the magic to transport myself, and when I materialize in the safe house, the scene from a nightmare greets me.

This is literally the scene from one of my repeated nightmares.

Stupid of me to think I might have been able to avoid it. However, perhaps it is that familiarity which allows me the ability to move quickly enough to try to save Chaosta. I make myself leave Lily, I knew she was dead even as I materialized, and get to Chaosta while she's still clinging to life. There is no time for weakness. She doesn't have any. I scoop her as gently as I can into my arms and transport us back to the demon stronghold.

As we reform in our sanctuary, I am already screaming for

help. Chiron and others arrive quickly. When they see Chaosta hanging limply in my arms and whatever expression is on my face, they take her without a word. I watch as Chiron carries her quickly to one of our medical rooms. As I remain where I am, covered in black blood, I send out a prayer to any deity that will listen to at least spare her.

Then I return for Lily.

I treat Lily, not her, I guess, her body in the way I know she would have wanted. I remove the knife, clean the blood from her carefully, and then transport her to a space in the central city mausoleum. The entire time, tears run down my face.

As a demon, I'm not meant to be plagued with emotions; that is a human weakness. Unfortunately, when I allowed Lily into my heart, I left space for those emotions. Emotions that are both good and bad.

I am just placing the stone on her final resting space, ready to come apart entirely when the summoning cracks through my head.

Apparently, I had the one free pass on ignoring a summons. Or perhaps it is my current mental state because, before I can resist, I'm pulled to a familiar alcove to the side of the band's apartment.

I'm not sure if it's the overwhelming emotions or the part of me that is looking for a fight, but instead of leaving, I turn and walk through the front door.

The band is all here.

They are standing in the entry hall, clearly waiting for me. I walk into the center of the space and somehow choke out, "What do you need?"

Their eyes are all wide as they stare at me. They must see the blood covering my front and hands. Reem steps forward, as always, the leader of the group. I sneer at him as he gets closer to me.

"Look," he says quietly, finally tearing his eyes from the

blood to my face. "I'm extremely sorry if we interrupted anything, but—"

"Yes, Reem, you interrupted. You interrupted me carrying Chaosta, who was near death and may be dead even now, back to the healers. You interrupted me as I was burying the love of my life. Both were once again the victims of angels. The force in this world that I have been supporting your little group in fighting against. Yet, instead of learning the magic needed, you've been fucking around with your music!"

There's a gasp and a thud behind Reem as I speak, and I vaguely note that Dio has fallen to his knees. His face is completely white, and his eyes are wide and staring at me.

Fem goes quickly to Dio. I can almost hear Lent asking me questions past the buzzing in my ears.

Then Reem interrupts, drawing my attention. "We only summoned you because there was a city official asking for you. They said their name is Bonum." His voice is choked, and he sounds afraid. Whether of me, or for Chaosta's life, I don't know and I don't care.

As he says it, rage spikes through my chest, and I can't breathe. I don't know what happens to my face, but whatever it is makes Reem gasp and take a step back, away from me. "Where. Is. Bonum." I grit out.

"Actually, they showed up again a few minutes ago to be ready for you to get here. I think they're waiting in the alley across the street."

Even as he finishes the sentence, I turn and stride out the door. I cross the street without looking, yet somehow I'm not run down by a carriage. My hands are in fists as I proceed into the narrow space between buildings, stalking my prey. As I walk further into the relative darkness, I see Bonum, who was leaning against the wall toward the end of the alley, push away and stalk toward me.

Their eyes look through me, and as I watch, they roll their shoulders in their familiar, demented way.

We meet somewhere in the middle, the tall buildings overlooking us at either side, our only audience. As we collide, we are already striking with bare fists. We don't need swords for this fight. We don't want to kill each other. This is about pain, giving, and receiving, and we don't need swords for that. Barehanded, we already have plenty of brutality to share.

I strike their face, and satisfaction fills me as I feel their nose break and my knuckles split. They strike my abdomen, and the breath rushes from me. I stumble back two steps and then strike at their side. I get a blow in, ribs snapping under my hand, the knuckles on my other hand split, a matched set.

That blow knocks them off balance, and they collide with the wall behind them. I hear them cough. They use the wall to their advantage, though, and get a kick in with both feet against my chest. I hit the ground, the friction tearing through my shirt and the skin beneath.

There is a moment of immobility as we both get our lungs filled with air again, and then we are back up, going at each other. I try to sweep their legs, but they get them out of the way quickly enough, and when they land again, they kick me, this time in the leg, and the breath grunts out of me as my knee nearly dislocates.

I trip forward, but this time it's my turn to use the momentum against them. I grab them as I fall and pull them to the ground beneath me. We wrestle there for a while, both trying to gain some advantage.

We punch, kick, break bones, and try to steal the breath from each other.

Finally pressing apart, we each sit, hunched over.

We are both gasping for breath, bleeding with broken bones, our clothes torn.

"Enough," Bonum rasps quietly between gasped breaths.

Moments pass with just the sound of heaving breaths filling the silence.

"They killed Lily," I finally say. Again, I feel the mental pain crash through me. It is so much worse than this physical pain, and I feel tears pricking at my eyes again.

"I know," Bonum rasps. "I was going to warn you, but they moved up the timeline. By the time I found out, it was too late for me to do anything about it."

I feel myself reeling at the fact that Bonum was going to warn me. They certainly have many reasons not to. Their story isn't one for this moment, but while we have an uneasy and unspoken truce with the angels as a whole, I would consider most of them enemies. Somehow, Bonum is either less or more than that to me. Still, in all this time, I have never known them to take any action against their own kind.

"Is Chaosta yet alive?" they rasp quietly.

"I'm not sure," I say, and there is silence for a few moments. We have each nearly caught our breath, and I know the remainder of this conversation will determine if we leave or return to the fight.

"It was her imprisonment that changed things for me," they rasp.

I find myself looking at them in shock. Their blind eyes look through me. I'm yet again struck by how well they navigate the world with whatever sensory adaptations they have developed.

"I avoided seeing her tortured at first. I don't approve of those methods as you might expect," they rasp quietly. They roll their shoulders again, silent for a moment.

"After a while, I decided I shouldn't stay away. I felt having someone there who did not approve would be a good safeguard."

"The first session I watched, she refused to say anything despite the immense pain she must have been in," they say with a wince. "I attended every session after."

"The torture was one thing. It is a barbarity that I know we can agree has a place. However, it is simply excessive over that much time." I see pain cross their features as they remember whatever it is that occurred.

"However, as I watched session after session, I saw her get stronger, not weaker. I saw how the *High Leader* turned that which could have been a boon for us into a weapon. One that now has an excessively good reason to point itself at us. All because she challenged him when he made me drag her in front of him all those months ago."

As I watch, they droop slightly, upper arms resting over their knees, and then lean forward and spit past the blood running down their face.

"I will not continue to sit silently in the shadows as *Rex* takes inadvisable actions," they rasp. "Instead, if there is information I think might help your work, I will deliver it to you."

I close my eyes for a moment, taking in a deep breath and considering. A clear new path is showing in my head, and yet speaking the words I know I must gives it a solidity that terrifies me. That terror makes me take some time to consider.

Finally, I say, "It is a kind offer you make, and I understand some of what it took to say it. However, this is not only on your shoulders. We don't change things by continuing the actions that resulted in this outcome."

I pause, and when I look up, I see Bonum's face aimed at me. The disconcerting feeling of their eyes looking through me draws me back in my memory. Somehow, that memory solidifies my resolve.

"Whatever it is you decide to do or not do. After what has just occurred, my people and I can no longer remain on the sidelines. There is no room for neutrality. The demons will begin to prepare to fight."

With that, I rise slowly to my feet and take a step back.

I watch as Bonum does the same. The air, or is it the energy, suddenly uneasy between us.

Then Bonum turns and walks with a slight limp out of the alley, their back to me.

"Bonum," I call.

They stop walking and turn their head slightly.

"Don't mistake this as a real truce. You are not my ally."

"And you are not mine," Bonum rasps. Then, without moving, they say, "I hope Chaosta survives."

With that, they leave the alley. I take a moment to quiet my emotions before transporting myself back to the demon stronghold.

I know I need to check on Chaosta, but I am terrified that when I get there, I will just receive the news that she's dead. As long as I remain away, she somehow continues to live. Yet, especially after this conversation with Bonum, I fully comprehend how important she is to this. If there is anything I can do to help save her, it must be done. It is becoming clear that because of her actions, we are moving ever quicker toward balance.

I also have an army to rouse, like a dragon from a great slumber, and after all these years, it will not wake easily.

WHAT HAPPENED TO DIO?

The following record is written by me regarding what happened next with Dio. For reasons you will soon understand, there is no diary entry for this next span of time. However, it was important to me that you should know some of what happened. Please forgive any artistic liberties I take with this part of the tale. I have heard the story enough times from Dio that I am fairly certain I will do it justice. I am confident Dio would forgive me for this indulgence.

W hen I wake, it is clearly late. The darkness coming through the window feels the way my heart does. All three of the others are in this room. Reem is pacing, and Lent seems to be trying to read but is looking at me worriedly from the table in the corner.

Fem is sitting on the couch across from me with pain in his expression. "I told them," he says quietly.

I immediately understand that he means he shared the feelings I have for Chaosta.

Pausing in his pacing, Reem says quietly, "I'm so sorry, Dio."

I press myself up quickly and ask "How long have I been out?"

"Several hours," Fem says quietly.

"Has there been any word?" I ask. I can hear the pain and desperation in my voice.

Fem's eyes immediately tell me there hasn't been any good news, even as he responds, "Nothing yet."

A sob leaves my throat as I lean forward, catching my head in my hands.

Time passes in a haze as I let the guys get me to my room. I accept another sedative from Fem, willingly this time. I make them promise to wake me when they hear something and then swallow the sedative and fall back into familiar blackness.

*W*hen I wake next, light filters through the window of my room, marking it as day. I stumble out of my bed and to the small, attached bathroom to relieve myself. I don't even look in the mirror, not wanting to see myself in this state, as I know it will bring back too many old memories.

There is a knock on my door, and I hear Fem calling my name. Not even pausing to consider how awful my appearance is, I leave the bathroom and go to the door. He cracks it open as I get there, and I can tell something is wrong by the look on his face.

I hear myself say, "Please no." The room begins to spin.

"It's not that," Fem says quickly, his expression tightening as he reaches out a hand to steady me. "We still haven't heard anything about Chaosta."

I feel momentarily relieved, but the look of fear is still there on Fem's face. His eyes search mine for a long moment. Finally, he says, "There are some people here for you. They have paperwork..." he pauses as though he doesn't quite know how to continue.

"What paperwork?" I ask.

"Commitment paperwork," he says finally, his voice breaking. "It seems your brother may have signed it."

I wobble, and Fem firms up his hand, working hard to help me keep my feet.

"The paperwork says that you've been using again. They believe you are likely to cause harm to yourself or others if allowed to continue without intervention."

For some reason, the spinning stops, and in its wake is complete numbness. There is a ringing in my ears. "I need to see it. The paperwork."

"Ok," Fem says, but he doesn't move for a minute. I'm looking at the door and not at him, but I hear him say, "We'll get this figured out. Just please don't do anything stupid."

I don't remember nodding or agreeing, but he must have taken my silence as assent because he opens the door and steps through with me in his wake.

As we arrive in the entry hall, I both see and don't see the two men wearing healers' uniforms standing just inside the front door. One has a stack of paperwork in his hand.

"Ah, there he is," that healer says, and his voice has a note of kindness to it.

Fem walks over to them with me and asks for the paperwork. The healer hands it to Fem, who then hands it to me. I numbly page through, the words blurring in front of my eyes until I get to the signature page. Alexander's signature is there as clear as anything.

The room proceeds to spin again, adding to the din in my head as my ears ring. My eyes are still unable to focus as I hand the paperwork back to him and feel the healers close in around me. They grasp each of my arms firmly and begin to direct me out the front door of the mansion. I can hear the guys saying something, but I don't know what it is. I'm unable to clearly hear past the ringing and, honestly, don't really care to try.

Using all my strength, I grasp for control. I know I'm at the edge of a precipice, and a loss of control right now would be catastrophic, at the very least to those around me.

As I concentrate on my control, I am not aware of much beyond the healer's hands on my arms during the walk to the carriage and the following carriage ride. Even in my numb state, I recognize that, while Alexander is even more of an asshole than I realized, if Chaosta doesn't survive, I may have ended up here anyway.

As we leave the carriage, the healers' hands still grasping my arms, I look up, and my eyes choose that moment to focus. I feel rage burst through me as I see a familiar building. I remember it from the promotional material. It's the place where I sent Chaosta.

In that moment of anger, I lose a modicum of control and feel myself lashing out at the guards. Momentarily intent on causing harm to those who harmed the woman I love. Especially now. What I know for sure is that I take down at least two men before I get control again. I'm concentrating so fully on regaining power over the swirling emotions that I barely notice additional healers flooding from the front door of the building. Then they are on me, restraining me.

I feel a sharp stab against the side of my neck, and everything goes black.

CONTENT INFORMATION

Potential triggers include, but may not be limited to, the following:
Implication and discussion of self harm
Incorrect/overuse of psychiatric medications with ill intent
Psychiatric hospitalization
Psychiatric "treatment" without consent
Hallucination
Implication of attempted suicide
Discussion of addiction
Implication/memories of addiction (drugs, injected)
Violence
Gore
Medical procedures (not explicit)
Torture
Imprisonment and incarceration

ABOUT THE AUTHOR

Charli Nile is an indie author of fantasy romance novels that feature pining men and strong women. She's also queer, polyamorous, and lives with her amazing wife and a tiny dog. She has been writing since she was a teenager, but only recently thought of publishing any of her work. Her younger self would be proud.

She is passionate about storytelling and loves easter eggs and foreshadowing.

She has been a voracious reader for her entire life and has been inspired by more books than she could ever possibly list here.

When she's not writing, it's likely she's spending time running or riding her horse. On quiet evenings, you will certainly find her reading.